Love Finds You

in

Bridal Veil
Oregon

Love Finds You
in Bridal Veil Oregon

BY MIRALEE FERRELL

summerside
PRESS

Summerside Press™
Minneapolis, MN 55438
www.summersidepress.com
Love Finds You in Bridal Veil, Oregon
© 2010 by Miralee Ferrell

ISBN 978-1-935416-63-0

All rights reserved. No part of this book may be reproduced
in any form, except for brief quotations in printed reviews,
without permission in writing from the publisher.

Scripture references are from the following sources:
The Holy Bible, King James Version (KJV).

The town depicted in this book is a real place, but the story is
entirely fictional. Any resemblances to actual people or events are
purely coincidental, or else used by permission (see author's note).

Cover and interior design by Müllerhaus Publishing Group
www.mullerhaus.net

Back cover photo of Bridal Veil Falls taken by Miralee Ferrell.
Interior photos of Bridal Veil taken from The Cowling Collection,
© Tom Cowling.

*Summerside Press™ is an inspirational publisher offering fresh,
irresistible books to uplift the heart and engage the mind.*

Printed in USA.

BRIDAL VEIL
1902
ORE.

Dedication

....

This book is gratefully dedicated to Stephen Bly, whose
three-sentence brainstorming suggestion over two years
ago led to the storyline for *Bridal Veil*. Thank you,
Stephen, for your willingness to help another writer.

Acknowledgments

．．．．．．．．．．．．．．．．．．．．

There are so many people who've blessed and supported me while writing this book. First, my husband, Allen, who patiently listened to my brainstorming, my rejoicing, the times I complained when nothing seemed to be coming together, and the hours I spent just wanting to talk about my writing in general. You're a saint! The rest of my extended family has cheered me on through each book I've written and enthusiastically waited for news on the next one, as have so many of my friends and church family members. A special thanks to Debbie Fluit, who committed to praying for me through the writing of the entire manuscript.

My heartfelt thanks go to Tom Cowling, historian extraordinaire. Tom grew up in Bridal Veil, and his interest in and love for his community continued on into his later years. His book, *Stories of Bridal Veil: A Company Mill Town (1886–1960)*, comprises a wealth of first-hand accounts gathered from residents living there all the way back into the eighteen nineties, along with marvelous historical facts about Bridal Veil Lumbering Company and the town of Palmer, also depicted in this book.

Summerside Press and each member of their team deserve special mention. I've so appreciated their support and belief in me and willingness to publish a second book. Thank you, Carlton, Jason, Rachel, and Ramona; you're the best!

I couldn't have gotten through this book without the members of my critique group and editor friends who supported and worked with me at different points along the way. Thank you, Kimberly Johnson, Teresa Morgan, Sherri Sand, Barbara Warren, and Susan Lohrer. Also, I so appreciate three very special ladies who take their time to act as advance readers and offer their impressions—Tammy, Kristy, and Amanda!

I pray this book will bless my reading audience. My primary goal is to reveal the Lord and show ways He can impact an average life if we allow Him to. And second, to entertain and encourage through the stories I weave. I'd love to hear from you if this story ministered to you. Meeting my readers' needs and bringing glory to the Lord are my main objectives.

A special thanks to everyone who's taken the time to read the words that God has placed on my heart!

Bridal Veil, Oregon, 1900

THE TOWN OF BRIDAL VEIL, OREGON, WAS FOUNDED IN 1886 in the heart of the beautiful Columbia River Gorge. The town began as a paper mill and soon evolved into a lumber and planing mill. Its sister sawmill lay in nearby Palmer, where the timber was broken down into lumber and transported by flume to the lower mill. A thriving community grew up in both Bridal Veil and nearby Palmer, with the two towns' commerce and social lives intertwined. For over fifty years the towns worked together—until 1936, when fire consumed some of the planer buildings in Bridal Veil. The timber supply was almost depleted, and the company moved out of Palmer. The Kraft Company purchased the existing buildings and equipment and produced moldings and boxes. World War II brought yet more change when women were hired to work at the mill, which produced ammunition boxes. After the war, Kraft expanded its operation, and by 1955 the company and town were booming. The end of the nineteen fifties saw a huge downturn in sales, and in 1960, Kraft made the decision to shut down. Homes and buildings were slowly abandoned, and the mill was never reopened.

Miralee Ferrell

Prologue

....

Bridal Veil, Oregon
July 1898

Yes.

The simple word staring up at Jacob Garvey from the piece of white paper hit him so hard it nearly knocked him to his knees. He'd been afraid of something like this for weeks. The note tucked in the wooden box lying under the tree confirmed his fears.

Maybe this wasn't what it seemed. Jacob turned the piece of paper over, hoping to find an explanation. His hand trembled as his gaze slid over the words printed in the bold handwriting.

Margaret. I'm leaving town this evening and not coming back. I want to marry you. I'll come for your answer after work. If I find the word Yes, then I'll meet you here after dark. Only bring what you need. I love you and can't wait to make you my wife.
—Nathaniel

P.S. If I don't find your reply, I'll know you can't go through with it.

A soft groan passed Jacob's lips, and he rocked on his heels. His eyes returned to the answer written in his daughter's clear script—willing it to change, willing it to disappear. *Yes.* Margaret was everything to him and had filled the awful void after his dear wife died. His sweet girl deserved so much better. There had to be a way to protect her from her own immaturity.

Why did Margaret persist in seeing Nathaniel Cooper? To Jacob's way of thinking, the man had no prospects and even less ambition. The Garvey family might not have much in the way of money, but they had history—their roots extended back to some of the hardy pioneers who helped settle this land.

What did that young man have? Hopeless dreams and no family—at least, none that Jacob knew of. A drifter with no prospects whom Margaret had met only a scant six months ago. From what he'd heard, Cooper jumped from one job to the next, with no thought for the future. He'd lasted less than a year here and was already moving on. Margaret could end up destitute if that ne'er-do-well wasn't careful. Besides, she was only sixteen.

Jacob placed the paper back in the box and stood. He'd hide the box with the note inside until he was sure Margaret's future was safe. When Nathaniel came back, he'd think she didn't want to marry him and leave town. Jacob snapped the lid shut and hurried back down the trail, anxious to get home.

The gate hinges squealed when he pushed through into his yard. He paused with a glance at the house, praying Margaret hadn't heard. Now, where to dump this box? Starting a fire might raise questions, with the forest so dry this time of year. His gaze lit on his shovel lying next to an unplanted rosebush bound in burlap. He'd prepared the hole but hadn't unwrapped the roots or set the bush. He glanced at the box in his hand, then back at the hole.

Hurrying over to the small rosebed, he peered over his shoulder, praying Margaret wouldn't offer to help. When no movement showed through the windows on the south side of the house, he bent to his task.

He withdrew a sharp knife from his pocket and cut away the burlap from the roots of the rose, then wrapped a strip around the box and laid it aside. Quickly he enlarged the hole, creating a side pocket at the base, then slipped the box and its message into the cool grave. The rose took its place in the hole, then he tamped in the soil and watered the rose. Another glance at the house assured him of success. Margaret would never know. His daughter's future was safe.

Chapter One
....

Four years later
Late May 1902

Margaret hurried to the two-story house set against the base of the tree-clad hill, anxiety dogging her steps. Papa had been tired when he'd left the house early this morning, but he'd been working at the mill long hours of late. Nothing to worry about, he'd assured her— he just needed the Sabbath to catch up on his rest, and he'd be right as rain. But she didn't believe it. He looked peaked and moved as though weights were attached to his limbs. Best to keep an eye on him, in case he was coming down with the grippe.

"Papa? You home yet?" She flung off her sweater and dumped her books on a nearby table. She'd not meant to stay so long at the school, but little Mark James had thrown one of his temper tantrums and needed a talking to. Then the chores had to be done— the floor swept, the board erased, her desk straightened—all things that didn't normally take much time, but Gertrude Graham had stopped by on her way home from the Company store and slowed Margaret down further. Gertrude was a sweetie, but everyone in town knew her propensity for gossip ran as deep as the nearby Columbia River.

Margaret had at last made her excuses and headed home. Part of her hoped Papa had kept his promise to leave work early and rest, while the other part wanted to light the stove and get supper going before he arrived.

Dusk wouldn't settle in for another hour or so, but she lit one lamp just the same, wanting a cheerful glow to penetrate the gloom when he made his way down the trail.

An hour later she glanced out the window again, hoping to see his familiar figure trudging up the path. Nothing. She dusted the flour from her hands and finished mixing the dough for the chicken and dumplings, then dropped globs of dough onto the steaming mixture in the pan and covered the large cast-iron skillet with a domed lid. At least the house was warm. In a few minutes the dumplings would rise, filling the room with their fragrance. Her mouth watered at the thought, and her lips tipped up at the happiness that would light Papa's eyes when he stepped through the door.

Just then the front door rattled, and her hand flew to her throat. Papa wouldn't shake the door handle or knock; he'd stride in with his booming greeting and big smile. Margaret stood in the middle of the kitchen frozen by uncertainty—but only for a moment. Could it be a neighbor in need of help or one of the unsavory characters riding the railroad cars of late? Hobos had been increasing in number, and her father had warned her not to open the door to a stranger if he wasn't home.

She reached for the heavy wooden rolling pin resting on the painted countertop Papa had built and gripped it tight. "Who's there?" She took a step toward the door in the nearby living room.

No reply. The knob moved again but this time with less energy. What in the world? She gripped her makeshift weapon tighter and crept to the door.

A quick twist of the round metal knob and a jerk of the door brought her face-to-face with Papa slumped against the doorjamb, his head lolled to the side. Margaret dropped the pin, and it clattered to the floor. She grasped his shoulders and gave him a small shake. "Papa? Are you sick? Papa!" She ran her gaze over his body, trying to find any sign of what might be wrong.

A low groan escaped his pale mouth, and his head rolled like a broken-necked doll. His eyes opened, and he raised a shaking hand. "Not. Feeling well. Help me. Inside."

She slipped her arm around his waist and tried to support his sagging weight, stumbling as his feet barely cleared the threshold. Somehow she managed to half carry, half drag him to the worn couch against a nearby wall. He settled down with a groan and started to shake. Beads of sweat popped out on his forehead, and his breath came in shallow gasps.

"What's wrong, Papa? Where does it hurt? Should I go for Doc Albert?"

Margaret leaned over her prone father and clutched his hand, willing her own to stop trembling.

His eyes fluttered open, and the stark pain in them revealed the effort it took to speak. "Chest. Hurts. Shoulder. Jaw. It's bad. No time."

"Hush, Papa. You've been working too hard, that's all. Let me go for the doc."

He gripped her hand with a sense of urgency and persisted. "No time. You need…to listen."

"No. Don't talk, just rest. You'll be fine." She bit her lip, wanting to race down the path to the doctor's home a quarter mile away but was terrified to leave him alone. Instead she lifted the knitted afghan off the back of the couch, spread it over his shaking form, and smoothed back his hair.

A movement outside the window caught her attention, and she squeezed his hand. "Hold on, Papa. I'll be right back."

She flew to the door and jerked it open in time to see eight-year-old Harry Waters swinging up the path with a fishing pole over his shoulder. "Harry?"

The boy halted midstride and turned toward her. "Yes, Miss Garvey? You need somethin'?"

"Yes. Run as fast as you can and get Doc Albert. Tell him my father is ill, and we need him to come. Hurry!"

The black hair flopped on his forehead as he nodded in assent. "Yes, ma'am." A flick of his wrist tossed the pole into the nearby brush and the boy was off, racing along the path on the shortcut back toward town.

Margaret rushed inside and sank to her knees next to her father. She drew in a deep breath, suddenly frightened by his face drained of color and his tightly closed eyes. "Papa? Are you awake?"

There was a slight movement of his head. Then something resembling a frown crossed his face, but it could have been a spasm of pain. "Sorry, Beth." His pet name for her slipped out as his eyes struggled to open. "Forgive me."

"Shh, it's all right, Papa. There's nothing to forgive. Rest now."

"No. Shouldn't have done it," he panted. "Tried. To fix it. Forgive me." The words trailed off, but his imploring eyes didn't leave her face.

"Of course I forgive you. Hang on, Papa. Doc Albert will be here any minute."

A deep sigh escaped, and his eyes closed again. Margaret grasped his hand tighter and prayed. God couldn't let her father die. She wouldn't allow it. Mama had died twelve years ago, and her grandfather just last year. Between that and losing Nathaniel… That was enough for one person to bear. Papa had the grippe. He'd be back on his feet soon, laughing and teasing about her temper matching her auburn hair and living up to Mama's Irish heritage.

That moment her father's body convulsed. The muscles around his mouth tightened, then suddenly relaxed, and the already weak fingers grew limp in her hand.

"Papa?" She gently disengaged her grip and stroked his forehead. "Papa, can you hear me?"

He lay still with not even a twitch of his eyelids.

Panic sucked the breath from Margaret's lungs, leaving her dizzy and faint. She shook her head, drew a deep breath, and forced the reaction away. No time for foolishness. Papa needed her strong.

She drew close to his face, praying for movement, hoping for another breath. "Papa. You can't leave me alone." A sob tore at her throat and slipped out in spite of her effort to quell it. "I need you, Papa. Please, please stay with me." She lifted a shaking hand and patted his cheek, hoping and praying he'd respond.

All of a sudden, realization struck her with its deadly truth, and she moaned. Frantically she searched for some sign of life—breathing—a flicker of his eyelids. But there was nothing. Papa was gone. He'd never smile or tease her again. Never enjoy the meal she'd prepared or sit in a church pew beside her on Sunday mornings.

How could she stand it? What would she do now? Oh, why had God seen fit to take him when he was still young and she had no one else in her life? She dropped her head on his shoulder and sobs welled up from a place so deep, a place terrified of the pain and loneliness she knew would come. Just like it had with Mother. Just like it had with Grandpa. And just like it had with Nathaniel. No. She'd not wallow in that now.

A knock sounded at the door, and the knob turned. She only vaguely felt gentle hands stroking her hair and a strong arm wrapping around her shoulders, drawing her away from the still figure on the couch.

Chapter Two
....

Early July 1902

Margaret still hadn't figured out what her father had needed her to forgive. She wracked her memory but couldn't imagine what had plagued him so close to his death.

She tapped the nails into the wooden crate, then brushed the drooping lock of hair from her eyes and dusted off her hands. That was the last box, and just in time, too. The wagon would arrive in an hour. One more walk through the house, and she'd be ready to go.

Everything had happened so fast. One day her father was here, the next he was gone. His sudden death had ripped a hole in her life. So many losses these past years. Her battered emotions had begun to heal after Mama passed, and then Nathaniel disappeared. Now this. Grief swamped her again, and she choked back the need to cry. All she'd done this past five weeks was mourn. No more tears today. She must concentrate on the gift the Lord had given her by allowing her time to tell Papa good-bye.

Margaret shook her head and continued her inspection. The past three years she'd stayed here to help take care of Papa, even though the town fathers preferred she live next to the school. The house belonged to the owners of the Bridal Veil Lumbering Company and would be leased to another tenant now that Papa was gone, leaving her free to occupy the teacher's cabin.

Margaret wandered from the kitchen and headed toward the stairs. Just one more peek at her bedroom to be sure nothing still hid in a corner. She smiled, thinking about the games she'd played in that room with friends growing up and the times they'd hidden under the covers, certain that monsters hid under the bed.

She trailed her fingers along the fir banister on the way up the stairs and patted the newel post at the top one last time. Regret at parting with her old home hit her again, but she pushed it away. Regret didn't belong in her life, and she'd not let it get a stranglehold over her emotions again. Life should be lived *forward*, and constant time spent looking back only brought pain. She'd learned that these past four years.

The schoolmarm's cabin was small, so she'd given some of her furniture to a needy mill family with six children. But she kept the treasured pieces she could never part with—her bed, which her father had fashioned himself, and also the solid pine table and chairs he'd built for her mother.

The creaking of wagon wheels and a jingling harness drew her thoughts back to the present. She looked at the gold watch hanging on a chain around her neck and smiled. Julius was right on time.

"Hello, the house," a ringing masculine voice called.

Margaret swung open the front door and stepped onto the small covered porch, shading her eyes from the summer sun's reflection off the nearby Columbia River. "Afternoon, Julius. Your mules are looking good today." She nodded at the matched pair of dark bay mules that were his pride and joy and was rewarded by a beaming grin.

Julius Winston's mouth sported a gap where a tooth used to re-side, rumored to have been dislodged by a kick from a disgruntled mule. But that hadn't changed his near worship of the creatures. No one who saw Julius's contagious smile thought long about the missing tooth, as the man's entire face was transformed by his grin. A happier teamster she'd never met, and that was saying a lot in this bustling, growing mill town.

He jumped off the wagon seat and dusted his hands against his pant legs. "Yep—they shore do, don't they, Miss Margaret? Why, just t'other day I was tellin' Grant down at the Company store—'Grant,' I said—'don't ya just think Molly and Verna is looking spry and sassy this summer? Why, their coats is shining so bright sometimes, they like to hurt m'eyes.'" He chuckled and slapped his leg.

Margaret's spirits lifted a bit at the happy chatter from the older man. With Julius warmed up to his favorite subject she doubted she'd need say more than yes, no, or smile the rest of the time it took to load the wagon.

* * *

Julius drew the mules to a halt in front of the cabin, and Margaret sat on the hard seat of the wagon, taking in the features of her new home. She and some ladies from church had readied the cabin, giving it a sound cleaning earlier in the week and leaving the doors and windows ajar to air it out for a day. By the time they'd finished scrubbing the floors and windows, it opened its welcoming arms with a freshness and sparkle that brought joy to Margaret's weary heart.

Papa would be happy she'd made the decision to move. He'd always worried about her staying to care for him instead of taking up official residence in the schoolteacher's cabin. The teacher for the upper grades was married and didn't need the little house, so it had stood empty the past two years.

A sense of loss swept over her. Her father, both protective and proud, had loved her with a fierce paternal love that had helped fill the chasm created by the death of her mother when Margaret was young. But now she needed to draw her thoughts away from the past and try to absorb herself in the future.

The cabin sat back from the Columbia River, close to the base of the hill. She wished it were within view of the magnificent Bridal Veil Falls. The awesome pounding of the water and the mist dancing like prisms in the sun were a constant source of pleasure whenever she found time to walk the mile or so to its base.

It was only a one-minute walk from her new home to the two-story schoolhouse, recently built to accommodate the growing number of students. Who'd have believed this small town would ever boast nearly forty students, ranging from the first reader to the seventh? Margaret loved teaching, even with the challenges some of the more trying students often presented.

Julius jumped down from the seat and scurried around to reach for her hand. "Help you down, Teacher?"

"I think I'd like to sit for a few moments, if you don't mind. Would you tie the mules, and then I'll join you?"

His expression softened as he glanced from her to the cabin and back, seeming to understand her need for some time alone. She welcomed this move, but sadness also pervaded her heart. Change so often resulted from some type of difficulty. Yes, it could be mixed with joy, but she appreciated the time to make the adjustment.

She loved this two-room cabin in the clearing, built of lumber sawed at their local mill and lovingly crafted by several of the towns-people. Glass windows, brought by train from Portland, flanked both sides of the sturdy door. The cabin could easily withstand the heavy winds that often blew rain and snow through the Columbia River Gorge, keeping its occupant snug and dry.

Margaret loved the cheerful, multicolored patch of flowers along the front, planted by her students early this spring and tended by a different family each week. A mix of towering fir and maple trees created a welcome spot of shade during the heat of the summer months. And possibly best of all, the cabin boasted a small vegetable garden in the back lot. Her father had been an avid gardener, and Margaret had hated the thought of giving up the summer vegetables. Now she'd simply grow her own.

Julius hitched the mules to a nearby tree and turned back toward the wagon but halted at the sound of a man's hail a few yards up the path. A young man in his early twenties strode into sight. Sunlight danced on his uncovered, curly brown hair, and his rugged face lit in appreciation when he saw Margaret. "I see I made it in time to help you unload." He stopped several feet from the wagon and grinned.

Margaret's pulse skipped a beat, and her breath quickened. Andrew Browning had started coming around a few weeks before her father's death, and she knew that he'd developed an interest in her, but she hadn't quite decided how she felt about him. Right now her heart felt too sore to think about courting so soon after Papa's passing. Thank-fully, Andrew hadn't pushed his suit and seemed content to remain friends. But his appearance today and offer of help warmed her, and she gave him what she hoped was a pleasing smile. "Thank you,

Andrew. There isn't much to unload, and Julius assures me he can handle it without much bother."

Julius's chest puffed out at her words, and his whiskered cheeks turned pink. "Yes, ma'am. No bother a'tall."

Andrew's expression lost some of its excitement, so Margaret hastened to his rescue. "Julius?"

"Yes, Miss Margaret?" He swept off his hat and looked up.

"I know you don't really need any help, but do you suppose Andrew might stay and offer a hand?" She rose from the buckboard seat and grasped the rail, but Julius stepped to the side of the wagon and helped her down.

"Guess it wouldn't hurt, if'n he stays and helps." The wide smile again lit the older man's countenance. "Nothin' here I can't do myself, but it might go faster with another set of hands." He cast a sly glance at the once again grinning Andrew. "Although it do appear he's cleaned up some after workin' at the planer mill—might be a shame to get them nice duds dirty packing in boxes and furniture." Julius winked.

Andrew hurried to the back of the wagon and hoisted a wooden crate onto his muscular shoulder. "Don't you worry about my clothes, Julius. They're not my Sunday best. I didn't want to get planer shavings on Miss Margaret's nice things, so I changed before I came."

Julius patted his mule on the rump as he headed toward the back of the wagon. "Ah-huh. Well, let's get to work, so Miss Margaret is feelin' to home before the sun goes down." He nodded at Margaret. "How 'bout you stand inside and direct where you want these things? No sense you gettin' dirty or hurtin' yourself packin' in heavy boxes."

The next half hour flew by as the two men toted boxes inside. The furniture she'd brought quickly found a place in her new home, and within a short time she stood at the door and surveyed her small domain. The kitchen was just inside the door, with her pine table and chairs a few feet from the sink that boasted a water pump. The far side of the room contained her comfortable old sofa, a round pine table next to it, and two wing-backed stuffed chairs.

Her bedroom lay beyond the cozy living area. The men had set up her bed, matching dresser, and nightstand. It was now a warm, friendly place with colorful braided rugs, polished pine furniture, and a woodstove for the cold winter months.

Julius stepped up beside her. "Looks like that about does it. Want I should stay and pry the lids off those crates?"

Andrew picked up a hammer and strode to the nearest box. "I can get these, Julius."

"Ah-huh." Julius plucked his hat off the table. "Well, then, I guess I'll go split a little kindlin' before I head home. Wouldn't want the neighbors' tongues waggin', the two of you bein' alone in the house without a chaperone." He grinned on his way out the door.

Margaret leaned against a post on the edge of the porch. "Thank you again, Julius. You're a blessing."

The red crept up his neck and washed across his cheeks, and his infectious grin erupted. "Aw, it were nothin'." He moved past the wagon where the patient mules dozed and headed toward the chopping block.

The screeching of nails reluctantly parting from a crate drew Margaret back inside. "Andrew? I appreciate your help."

"Happy to." His warm smile gave her heart a jolt. He reached for another box and applied the claw of the hammer to a stubborn nail. "Everything out of your house, or do you need more help?"

She sank down onto the nearby sofa and shook her head. "It's all here, and the ladies at church offered to help me clean the old place for the new tenant. I hear he's arriving next week."

Andrew raised sparkling brown eyes that smiled into hers. "Good. I'd hate to see you do that alone." He sat back on his haunches. "Looks like that's the last box. Want me to stay and help you unpack?"

"No, you've done enough. Besides, I'm not sure where I want things to go just yet. I think I'll sit for a while—maybe rest my feet and decide what I want to put where."

"Sounds like a fine idea." He rose and brushed back the hank of curly hair that insisted on draping over his forehead, then set his hat on his head.

Margaret glanced with appreciation at his well-built frame. He wasn't tall but had broad shoulders and muscular arms from off-bearing boards at the planer mill. When he grinned two dimples peeked out at the corners of his mouth, giving him a decidedly roguish look.

Her thoughts drifted to another pair of dark, intense eyes and a tall, slender man. Nothing about Andrew reminded her of that other man, but just thinking about Nathaniel now caused a thrill of excitement to course through her body. After four years she still remembered how she'd felt any time she'd heard Nathaniel's voice or looked into his eyes.

When Andrew cleared his throat, Margaret pulled her thoughts back with a reluctance that surprised her. She'd left the past behind long ago and had worked hard to put the anger and hurt away as well. It wasn't fair to compare Andrew to Nathaniel. Besides, Andrew seemed too kind and honest to disappear from the life of a girl he'd sworn to love.

"If you're sure you don't need any more help, I'll get to my supper, such as it is." Mischief lit his brown eyes. "Sure would be nice to have someone around who loved cooking."

Margaret's mouth twitched in a smile. "Gertrude was just telling me that Sally Mae Kent is looking for a beau. I hear she's a fine cook."

Andrew's face fell. "Oh. I don't think. I mean, I don't want...." He took off his hat and slapped it against his leg.

Margaret stifled a giggle.

Andrew stared at her with a straight face. "Blast it, Margaret, that's not funny."

She shook her head as she tried to contain the first bit of real humor that had sliced through her heart since Papa's passing. Sally Mae was a nice girl, even if she did chatter like a magpie. She latched onto any young man who glanced her way, and Papa used to say she'd marry anything wearing trousers.

"I'm sorry, Andrew. And don't worry, I won't let on to Sally Mae that you're looking for a good cook." She covered her mouth with her hand in hopes of hiding the smirk that wouldn't be stilled. Poor Andrew, he was such fun to tease.

He jammed his hat back on his head and grimaced. "You'd best not." His lips quirked, but for a moment it didn't appear that a smile would win the tug-of-war.

Margaret couldn't hold the laughter back any longer—it spilled out of her mouth. Andrew sat for a full minute, then threw back his head and guffawed, his twin dimples breaking out. "Guess you got me that time," he choked as he tried to catch his breath. Swiping a hand across his eyes, he took a step toward the door. "Well, good night, Margaret. And please let me know if you need anything more. I'll let Julius know he can head on home."

Margaret sensed Andrew's reluctance to leave, but she wasn't in a position to ask him to dinner and wasn't sure she'd want to, even if her kitchen was in order. Her heart had mended after Nathaniel's betrayal, but could she really know that Andrew was different? Besides, hadn't God assured her while seeing Nathaniel that He was in control and her future was secure? Hadn't that meant she had a future with Nathaniel? She shook her head. Trust didn't come easy nowadays—not in her own ability to hear God's voice, nor in a man's ability to keep his word.

She enjoyed Andrew's company but felt in no hurry to be courted. Her married friends didn't understand her hesitation, as many women at the age of twenty-one were married and had a child by now.

Andrew was the first man who'd tempted her to forget Nathaniel. Silly, she knew. It had been four years. For months she'd swung between anger and grief—first furious that he hadn't come to take her away when he'd sworn he loved her, then crushed that he hadn't returned to explain.

"Margaret, did you hear me?" Andrew tentatively touched her shoulder, and she jumped. "I'm sorry. I didn't mean to startle you."

She shook her head and smiled. "No. I was gathering wool for a moment. What were you saying?"

He bent his head and drew a deep breath, then raised his eyes to meet hers. "There's an ice-cream social at the church in two weeks. Would you care to come with me?" His expression was both hopeful and full of doubt.

Margaret's thoughts stilled. She hated to encourage him, but staying trapped in the gloom that had surrounded her for so long didn't set well. "Yes. I'd like that."

His face went from blank amazement to joy in two swift seconds. "You would? Wonderful! Maybe I'll see you at church tomorrow, as well?"

"That would be nice, Andrew." She walked him to the door and watched as he strode down the path. Maybe life would settle down and bring some positive changes. After four years, it was time to move on.

* * *

Andrew walked down the path away from Margaret's cabin, a lightness in his step that he hadn't expected. He'd come to her house to help in an effort to keep the promise he'd made to her father a couple of weeks prior to his death. He hadn't expected to find his heart pounding and his palms sweaty when he'd asked Margaret to accompany him to the ice-cream social. Sure, he'd been interested in Margaret since he first saw her. What man wouldn't be? She was a beautiful woman with a generous heart and a quick intellect, although she could also be a bit stubborn and independent when the mood hit her.

He glanced over at the quiet mill as he walked past the first large building to his right. With no trains running and the planer mill shut down, one could actually hear the birds singing in the fir trees that lined the path.

He hadn't thought too much of Mr. Garvey's request to watch out for Margaret in the event anything happened—after all, Jacob

Garvey was only in his late forties and had appeared to be in good health. But something about the urgency of the request had made Andrew wonder if Jacob knew something he'd not shared, and it seemed that *had* been the case. Now Andrew found himself in a quandary—the woman he'd been somewhat interested in had been placed in his care by her deceased father, and without her knowledge. From what he knew of Margaret, he guessed that she'd be none too happy if she discovered the truth. Of course, with her father gone there'd be no way for her to know, and Andrew would certainly never willingly share what had passed between Jacob and himself. There was no point in upsetting her or making her doubt that his interest in her was genuine.

If his reaction to her nearness back at the cabin was any indication of the turn his heart had taken, his interest was even stronger than he'd realized when he'd given his word to Margaret's father. He smiled as he recalled the flush on her cheeks when she'd laughed at his discomfort. Yes, indeed. He was going to enjoy keeping his word to Mr. Garvey.

Chapter Three

....

Salem, Oregon

"I declare, Samantha! You are the clumsiest girl. You'd think at thirteen years old you'd be more careful. Why I took you and your no-account brother in, I'll never know." Hands on her hips, Mrs. Stedman stood over the skinny girl, then leaned to pick up the soiled linen that had slipped to the ground under the sagging clothesline.

Samantha McGavin narrowed her eyes and shook her head, sending the dark blond braids into a mad dance around her shoulders. The heavyset woman wouldn't hesitate to dole out punishment if sassed, but Samantha couldn't tolerate the words she'd just heard. "I thought I pinned it on tight. But I wish you wouldn't talk so about my brother. It's not his fault he's a little slow."

Mrs. Stedman's loud snort sounded like the grunt of one of the hogs. "Joel's not slow, he's dim-witted. If I'd a'known he didn't have a brain in his head when I took you in, I'd a'sent you packin', even if that orphanage woman said you was good workers." She raised a finger. "You get it through that boy's head that he don't break no eggs or scare the hens, or I'll ship him back. Alone."

Samantha willed her legs not to shake and her feet to hold steady in their place. The hot anger of the coarse woman had lashed out many times in the past, but so far Samantha had taken the brunt of her wrath. Joel had been punished before, but the worst beatings had

33

been reserved for Samantha, probably due to the boy's almost un-natural growth. At fourteen her older brother was almost the size of a man. However, the woman's rage had been building toward Joel for days, and one more mistake on his part would push the woman over the edge, regardless of his size.

Samantha pushed down the hot retort that fairly screamed to be let out and nodded instead. "Yes'm. I'll see that he does things right."

Mrs. Stedman drew her hand away. It hovered in the air, seemingly unsure whether it should settle on her hip. "I don't want you sneakin' around doin' his chores, neither. He'd best learn to do 'em right." She swiveled her stocky hip away and took a step, then turned back. "I've given you kids a'plenty. I expect obedience from both of you, ya hear me, Samantha?" She leaned close to the girl's face, her brows scrunched over the hard hazel eyes.

This time Samantha did take a step back. Those pale, washed-out eyes that seemed to change from hazel to an almost sickly yellow had always unnerved her. "Yes, Mrs. Stedman. We'll try harder. I promise."

"See that you do." She frowned, turned as fast as her bulk would allow, and waddled toward the house.

"Sammie?" A tug at her hand drew Samantha's attention around to the oversized boy who'd slipped quietly into place beside her.

She patted his arm. "Did you finish your chores?"

A scared shadow chased itself across the wide face looking down into hers. "I think so." His voice dropped to a whisper. "I broke another egg." He held up the basket of eggs and pointed at the gooey mess smeared across the layer of intact shells.

"Oh no," Samantha breathed.

"Mrs. Stedman's gonna be mad." Joel stated the fact so low that Samantha barely heard. His eyes grew wide and his voice rose. "She's gonna smack me when she sees. Please don't let her hit me, Sammie."

"Shh." She gave his shaking shoulders a squeeze. "Come on, let's head to the barn and see if we can fix this mess."

The boy's quivering lip grew still, and he raised a hopeful gaze. "You can fix it?"

"Yeah. Come on."

She took him by the hand and hefted the basket on her opposite hip. The animals' water trough lay on the backside of the barn, out of sight of the watchful eyes. When they rounded the corner of the building, Sammie let out a sigh. Safe for now, as long as no one came looking. She reached under the hem of her skirt and drew up the corner of her frayed cotton petticoat. Giving it a yank, she ripped off a strip of cloth. The trough was lined with slime, and she hesitated a moment before dipping the rag into the water.

"Sit down, Joel, and hold still." She waited till the boy obeyed, then picked up an egg and carefully wiped it down. Each oval treasure was placed in his lap, end to end from his knees down the length of his tightly pressed legs. "There, all clean." Sammie rinsed the wire basket in the trough, wrinkling her nose in distaste.

"Will Mrs. Stedman be mad that you washed the eggs in the trough?" Joel touched one of the eggs closest to him, and Samantha gently pushed aside his hand.

"Don't touch them, Joel. We don't want any more broken." She patted his fingers and smiled. "We're not going to tell her about washing them, all right?"

Joel frowned, and troubled eyes gazed into hers. "Isn't that lying? You always tell me not to lie, Sammie."

She bit her lip, unsure how to explain. "If she asks if we washed them, we'll say yes. But we don't need to mention we washed them because one broke. We can't put the broken egg back together again, and there's no sense in upsetting her. Do you understand?"

He twisted his mouth to the side and squinted, then nodded. "Ah-huh, I understand. Don't say nothin' about broken eggs; just say we washed 'em if she asks. Right, Sammie?"

"Right." All she could do was pray that God would somehow keep her brother safe from Mrs. Stedman's wrath.

* * *

Samantha lay in bed later that night, bone weary and heart sore. She'd kept Mrs. Stedman from finding out about the eggs, but it wouldn't be the last time Joel would teeter on the edge of a thrashing. The woman's tongue had harmed her brother enough, and Sammie was determined that no physical abuse be heaped on his body. She'd pondered the problem for weeks. Only one thing scared her about taking Joel and running away, and that was Mrs. Stedman's no-account son who stopped in from time to time.

Wallace Stedman was a lazy man who got surly when he drank. Mrs. Stedman never put the same demands on him as she did Sammie and Joel. He'd been by just three days ago, and they didn't see him but every fortnight—unless he'd already drunk up all the money his mother had parceled out. Drink changed Wallace from a whining nuisance to something worse.

Sammie never quite figured out why his stare bothered her when he'd been drinking. Mrs. Stedman would send him after them if they ran, unless they could put enough time and space between this farm and themselves before Wallace came around again.

She rolled over on the hard cot and shifted her weight, trying to find a more comfortable spot for her hip. The thin blanket barely reached from side-to-side and offered little in the way of warmth. A mission barrel at the church they attended on the outskirts of Salem, Oregon, had produced some clothing and coats that almost fit, along with a pair of sturdy shoes, or they'd still be wearing last year's cast-offs.

Could they slip out without being seen, and would Mrs. Stedman send Wallace when she discovered they'd gone? How would they travel without food or blankets? Joel would never keep up for long. He didn't have much stamina.

Why did her parents have to die and leave them alone? Didn't they know how much she and Joel needed them? Didn't God care that they'd been whisked up by neighbors and dumped in an orphanage just minutes after the horse-drawn carriage had taken her unconscious mother and deathly still father to the hospital? The woman in charge told her that both their parents had died. No hugs, no sorrow, just that ugly, hurtful word. *Dead.* Eleven-year-old Samantha had cried most of the night while clinging to her twelve-year-old brother, lying on the pallet in the corner of the upstairs room.

Now Samantha knew that somehow they must get away, no matter the risk. Staying here would only get them separated, and she couldn't take that chance. She sighed and snuggled deeper into the narrow cot. More than anything in the world she wanted a real home.

One that cared about children and didn't scream or stike them. One that had love to share—and smiles and hugs instead of frowns and curses.

Just then the lonely wail of the train whistle cut through the troubled silence. Samantha rarely noticed it anymore, although it had kept her awake when she first arrived at Mrs. Stedman's. A rush of excitement jolted her wide awake, and she barely restrained the urge to jump from the bed and dance a jig. *The train.* Why hadn't she thought of it before? It stopped for water just a half mile or so up the road every night. If she and Joel were careful, they could sneak onto a freight car in the dark. Many a time she'd seen the train stop at the water tank in the daytime, and several cars always stood empty with doors gaping wide. She'd never understood why they weren't locked, but now the thought brought hope. They'd only have to endure one more day. Tomorrow night they'd sneak off and ride the train to freedom.

Chapter Four

....

The Columbia River, just past Bridal Veil, Oregon

Nathaniel Cooper stood at the rail of the steamboat as the large paddle drove it up the Columbia River past the small town of Bridal Veil. Too bad Sand Island sat so close to the bank and prohibited large boats from docking. His gaze lit on the magnificent, floating mist that hovered over the two-step fall, giving it the look of a bride's veil—hence the name. It had been four years since he'd seen that sight. The memory of a pair of blue eyes lingered right alongside the one of the falls.

He'd tried to push the memory of those eyes and the sweetness of that face out of his mind but had never completely succeeded. Why hadn't Margaret left him a note, instead of taking the box? Would it have been so difficult to let him know she'd changed her mind?

His gaze traveled out across the swelling Columbia River, and he grabbed his hat just as a gust of wind whipped it off his head. He'd forgotten how fierce the wind howled through this stretch. When an eastern wind blew in the winter, the temperature could drop several degrees in a matter of minutes.

As he turned away and headed inside, his thoughts returned to Margaret. If she'd shown up that night, would he have a son that he could take fishing? She knew his plans and could have found him. Or maybe she was just too young at the time.

More than likely she'd married some man who provided a good living, making her doting father happy that she'd escaped the likes of him. He shook his head. No need to harbor ill thoughts. It had been hard to accept the position at the upper mill in the small community of Palmer just two miles above Bridal Veil. If she and her husband lived here, he'd do the honorable thing and treat her as though their paths had never crossed.

It was time to put the past behind him and be thankful for his new position. It still wasn't clear why he'd been chosen, but he wouldn't question such a stroke of good fortune—however mixed it might be.

"Stand clear!" The booming voice of the boat's bosun rang out just before ropes lowered the large gangplank. Nathaniel's musing had taken them on past the town site and two miles upriver to the docking point, not far from Multnomah Falls.

Slinging his bag over his shoulder, he swung down the plank and onto the grassy shore. He pushed through the knot of people waiting in the docking area and headed toward the team of horses hitched to a nearby wagon.

A voice at his elbow drew him up short. "Nate Cooper. Well, I'll swan. What brings you back to our neck o' the woods?"

Nathaniel stood close to six-foot tall, but his eyes had to travel up to meet the man at his side. He recognized the voice before he saw Dan Meadows' broad, heavily whiskered face, split by a grin. His massive hand reached out and gripped Nathaniel's.

"It's good to see you again, Dan." Nathaniel returned the handshake with as much strength as he could muster. "You still the bull whacker up at the logging camp outside Palmer?"

Dan nodded his shaggy head. "Yep, sure am. Got me eight new oxen comin' in on the train tomorrow and a new man comin' in with a horse team, as well."

"Horses? Since when did you hire a horse team to skid logs?"

Dan grunted. "The boss tells me this young man—Art Gibbs is his name—comes with the best six-horse team in the state and wants to give him a chance. I'll believe it when I see it: that horses can do a good job without spookin' and causin' trouble."

Nathaniel set his bedroll down next to his bag and leaned against a post at the end of the wharf. "The mill staying busy? How much timber are you hauling out, up at the Palmer site?"

"The boss is expandin' the operation, and with this second team pullin', we plan on gettin' out twenty-four thousand feet of timber each trip the train makes back to the Palmer mill."

Nathaniel whistled. "Not bad. You're still pulling them on the greased skid trail to the railroad landing?"

"Best way to get them to the tracks. Not much has changed since you left. Still plenty of timber to feed the upper sawmill. Martin Jenkins is the new skidder boss now, and he made one change I'm not happy about—we got two donkey engines up in the hills. He thought my teams weren't doin' a good job on the steeper pulls." He shook his head and scowled. "I hate seein' newfangled machinery come in. Nothing will ever take the place of a good team of oxen."

Nathaniel wasn't so sure, but he kept his thoughts to himself. The big man loved his team and was known to wager bets about the amount of weight the beasts could pull from the forest in one haul. The idea of new technology didn't set well with many of these old-timers, so Nathaniel had found it best to simply nod and agree. Too many times even a mild disagreement could be taken as an insult and land a man in a ditch with a busted jaw, or worse. "Yeah, I'm sure you're right."

Dan crossed his arms across his massive chest. "What brings you back to town? Heard you lit a shuck out of here and never planned on comin' back." He cast a shrewd glance at the bag and bedroll Nathaniel carried. "Or are you just visitin' our berg?"

Nathaniel shook his head. "Nope. I'm here to stay. I put in an application, and Mr. Palmer hired me as the assistant supervisor for the upper mill."

Dan's eyebrows shot up till they disappeared under his bushy hair, smashed down by the brim of his hat. "Assistant supervisor, huh?" He gave a slow wag of his head and glowered. "Always thought I might have that job someday." One shoulder hunched and his features smoothed out. "No matter. Wouldn't want to give up my team. How'd you land that job?"

"Not sure, to tell the truth. Guess someone's watching out for me." Nathaniel smiled. "Although God and I aren't on close speaking terms, so I'm not sure why He'd bother."

"Huh. Doubtful God had much to do with it." Dan's dark brown eyes narrowed. He hefted his bedroll over his shoulder. "Best be goin'. Got to make sure everythin's ready for that team comin' in tomorrow."

"See you around." Nathaniel slung his gear onto his back. Time to find a ride and get settled into whatever house the Company provided. With his elevated status, he assumed it would be better than the shack he'd shared with three other mill hands the last time he'd worked there.

Dan's question returned to his mind. He'd not been entirely truth-ful with the man. The memory of a young woman and what might have been had drawn him back to this town, almost against his will. The new job was an added bonus, but not one he'd keep for long if things didn't turn out as he hoped.

Chapter Five

. . . .

Bridal Veil, Oregon

Margaret shut the wooden door behind her, then looked around her new home with satisfaction. Yesterday had been spent unpacking her belongings and placing her personal items on the kitchen table and in nearby cupboards. The cabin boasted only one tiny closet, but her clothing needs were simple, and the limited space didn't pose a problem. The mattress of soft feather ticking the schoolboard supplied was a luxury compared to the harder one she'd left behind in her old house, and she'd slept more soundly than she'd expected. Now all she needed was some foodstuffs to stock her cupboards.

The walk to the Company-owned store wasn't far, but the thought of carrying the heavy wooden crate full of food tins, flour bags, and fresh meat made her arms ache. She'd ask Grant Cowling, the manager, if he'd send over an employee with her goods.

The day shone with warmth that seemed determined to spill over into her sore heart. She had so much to be thankful for: a classroom of children she loved, a new home close to her work, a young man seemingly intent on courting her, a town she'd grown up in that loved her—but her heart still protested. A gaping spot remained, left there by the loss of her father. Over five weeks had passed, but it felt like yesterday that she'd knelt beside him as he drew his last breath.

She knew she'd feel his loss for a long time to come, but a small part of her heart felt a sense of wonder at being on her own. No longer would she be bound by others' dictates and expectations. She could discover who she was and revel in the freedom to choose her own destiny. Papa had loved her—that she knew. But she'd always imagined that she didn't quite measure up. Not that he scolded too often, but his displeasure was often apparent when her choices clashed with his own. The lack of being accepted for who she was, rather than what she did, sometimes left her feeling hollow inside.

She walked around the trunk of a giant gnarly pine, inhaling the sharp fragrance. Thankfully these old pine trees weren't sought after by the mill, or they wouldn't have many in town. A flash of color showed through the trees ahead, and she spied her friend Clara White coming her way. "Clara!" Margaret drew to a halt and waited for the girl in the commonsense gingham dress and sturdy leather shoes.

Clara's broad smile lightened Margaret's heart, and the inner beauty of the young woman's spirit shone through. "Hi, Margaret. You heading to the store?"

"I am. I was hoping for some company."

Clara fell into step beside her. "I haven't seen you since before you moved to the teacher's cabin. I wish I could have helped you move."

"Your mother was sick, and I understood."

Clara picked up the hem of her skirt as she stepped around a small bush. "How've you been doing?"

Margaret shrugged. "I was just thinking about something you said the last time we spoke."

"About time easing your hurt?"

"Yes, but I can't see it. I still ache to hear Mama's voice after all these years. Then I lost Grandpa, and now Papa. I'm not so sure time will dampen my longing."

A pair of chickadees swooped low overhead, chasing a crow away from their nest. Clara shaded her eyes to peer up at the pursuing birds. "See those birds protecting their family?"

"Yes." Margaret wrinkled her brow. "So?"

Clara caught Margaret's hand, pulled her over to a fallen tree, and patted the rough bark beside her. "I don't need to tell you that God cares about the sparrows. But I'm guessing that includes the chickadees, as well. What makes you think He doesn't care about all you're dealing with right now?"

Margaret lifted a shoulder and grimaced. "I know He cares, but that doesn't change the hurt and loneliness."

Clara squeezed her hand. "But knowing it with your head and letting it find its way to your heart are two different things. You have to turn all the pain over to Him, and ask Him to heal your hurt."

"It's hard." Margaret sighed. "I've got to work at trusting Him more. You headed home?"

"Yes." Clara lifted the basket from the pine-needle-carpeted ground and stood. "Mother needs these things for supper, so I'd best be going. Come over and have a cup of tea soon?"

Margaret embraced her friend. "I'd love that. Give your mother my best. If she's fixing supper she must be over her cold."

"She is, and back to her feisty self." Clara's laugh was gentle. "I'll see you later, and remember: Keep trusting your heavenly Father. He'll never fail you." She turned away, the wicker basket swinging beside her skirt. A song drifted back on the still air.

Margaret drew a deep breath and picked up her pace. Thank the

Lord for Clara and her wisdom. She'd store those words in her heart and spend time praying soon. God made the daytime for taking care of chores and responsibilities, and she'd best tend to her business. Papa always said, "We mustn't slack on what we put our hand to," and she intended to keep that at the fore of her thinking.

The fragrant fir trees thinned, and she moved out from under the last row of boughs and onto the path leading past the planer yard. Her heart quickened a bit at the possibility of seeing Andrew among the workers outside. His job off-bearing for the planer and doing some of the maintenance kept him inside most of his working hours, but that didn't stop her from taking a peek.

More than one man gave a nod or smiled as she met their eyes. A number of them had children in her school, and she'd grown up with some of the younger ones who'd found work at the planer mill. The sprawling buildings covered a large portion of the long, narrow space of level ground between the far ends of Bridal Veil, backed up against the bluffs of the towering Cascade Range. Rough-cut lumber coming down the mountain flume from the Palmer sawmill two miles above them fed the lower mill's insatiable appetite.

As the tangy fragrance of fresh-cut lumber rose on the waves of warm air gusting through the mill yard, Margaret drew in a deep breath. She'd been raised around the noise of the chugging steam engines that ran the massive planer as it turned out the finished lumber sought after by so many builders.

The blast of a train whistle cut through the air, and the wheels of the nearby engine began to churn. Freight trains ran through Bridal Veil nearly every day, and Margaret rarely noticed them anymore unless she was walking by the mill yard at unloading time.

A young man leading a fine team of draft horses came into sight, and she swerved out of their path. The man slowed his pace and tugged at the lead horse's reins. "Whoa there, Stormy. Easy, Samson. We don't want to trample the lady." The large black gelding snorted and tossed his head but drew to a stop at the man's firm touch. "Sorry, miss. Didn't mean to run over you with these beasts of mine."

Margaret stroked the horse's neck. "What a nice team. Are you new in town?"

"Yes, ma'am. Name's Arthur Gibbs, Art for short. Come to Bridal Veil to work for Mr. Palmer skiddin' logs at the upper mill." He seemed to grow another inch, and his slender frame expanded with his intake of breath. "Got me six of the best skiddin' horses in the state. I hear the bull whacker don't think my horses can keep up, but I aim to show him they can."

"I'm Margaret Garvey, one of the teachers. Do you have any little ones?"

"No, ma'am." A touch of red stained his cheeks. "But I'm gettin' married next spring, and Glenna, my intended, will be along after we marry."

"That's lovely! Be sure to bring her by the schoolhouse and introduce her. It's always nice to have another young woman in town."

He nodded, then clucked to the horses. "I'll surely do that, and I thank you for the invite."

A shout swung them both around, and Art placed his arm in front of Margaret. "Watch yerself, ma'am."

A team of oxen surged around the corner with a perspiring man at their heels. He dragged on the long lines and drew the beasts to a halt. "Sorry, Miss Garvey."

"Not to worry, Mr. Meadows. But I haven't seen your team this close to town in some time."

"My new brace of oxen came in on the train." He frowned at the young man standing silent beside Margaret. "This fella bothering you, Miss Garvey?"

"Not at all."

Meadows narrowed his eyes. "If you're sure." He turned his attention back to Art. "Don't you got anything better to do than block the road? Move them horses outta the way."

Art crossed his arms over his chest. "Who might you be?"

"Dan Meadows. I'm the boss of the teamsters at the upper mill."

"Ah-huh. Guess that means I'll be reporting to you, then."

Meadows grunted. "You the new man they brought in that's supposed to have a team of wonder horses?" He barked a short laugh, then spit and wiped his sleeve across his mouth. "They don't look like any great shakes to me."

Art squared his shoulders. "They'll do."

Meadows snapped the lines on the oxen's shoulders. "They'd better, or you'll be looking for another job." He gripped the lines in one hand and tipped his hat at Margaret. "Have a fine day, Miss Garvey."

Margaret glanced from one man to the other. "Same to you, Mr. Meadows."

One of the oxen bellowed and the team lumbered away. Silence settled around them until Art Gibbs stirred. "Best be gettin' home. It was nice to make your acquaintance. Good day, ma'am."

The horses' massive hooves kicked pebbles in their wake as they ambled after the man.

Margaret walked the last few yards to the whitewashed Company store, not for the first time wishing they had more stores than this small one. It carried much of what they needed for day-to-day survival, but there were so many womanly things she'd sorely love to buy. That was one of the drawbacks to the Company owning the entire mill site, homes, and store. They offered what they felt the mill workers needed, and nothing more. Families had to travel by rail or steamboat to nearby Portland for anything more, or send off an order to the Montgomery Ward catalog.

Margaret walked up the three steps to the covered porch and pushed through the door into the one-story building. "Afternoon, Grant." As she held on to the doorhandle to let her eyes adjust to the dimmer light inside the building, a gust of wind nearly jerked the handle out of her grasp. After pulling the door shut behind her, she inhaled slowly. The store smelled of cinnamon and peppermint sticks, with a mingling of new leather and tangy dill pickles. Her mouth watered and her stomach rumbled, reminding her it was almost dinnertime.

Grant Cowling turned toward her, a smile creasing his ruddy face, and his white, bushy eyebrows rose to touch the wisp of hair on his forehead. "Afternoon, Missy. Haven't seen you for a while." He pushed the straggling hair aside. "It's a mite windy today. I haven't had time to poke my noggin outside, what with the train bringin' in freight this mornin'. What might you be needin'?"

Quiet warmth flowed through Margaret at the childhood name a few of the old-timers still used. Grant reminded her of Papa—the same rugged build and amiable demeanor. Calm poured like oil from his voice.

She handed him a list. "A ten-pound bag of flour, a sack of sugar, walnuts, raisins, a small bucket of lard, and a slab of beef if you've got it. Oh, and do you have any fresh milk and eggs from the dairy?"

"I sure do. You goin' to make your raisin cookies? Makes my mouth water just thinkin' about it."

She chuckled and patted his arm. "I'll bring you a plate the next time I come."

"I'm beholden to you, Missy. That's one of the worst things about being an old curmudgeon of a bachelor. I got to eat my own cookin'." He wiped his hands down the front of his lightly soiled apron and turned his head. "Donnie! Get yourself up here, will you? Crate these things for Miss Margaret and tote them over to her house."

A young man in his early twenties swung up the aisle. Although his stubby legs were dwarfed by his powerful body and muscular arms, he covered the distance in a surprisingly brief time. "Howdy, Miss Margaret." He grinned. "I'd be more'n happy to help you."

Margaret allowed herself a flicker of a smile. Donnie had come to Bridal Veil a couple of years before, but no one knew much about him. He'd always been friendly the times she'd stopped by the store, but something about him set her teeth on edge. The young man turned back to his boss. "What all you needin' me to fetch, Mr. Cowling?"

The proprietor lined Donnie out and Margaret wandered off, drawn by the table displaying sewing notions. She picked up a spool of bright blue thread and shook her head. Pretty, but there wasn't a stitch of material that it matched. Too bad. The more common browns, dark green, black, and white thread nestled together nearby. She'd used her last spool of thread—might be a good idea to stock up while she had the chance.

Footsteps sounded on the wood floor, and Margaret turned to see Donnie standing with a wooden crate in his arms, his face split by a sappy grin. "Ready to go?"

"I'll just be another minute." She headed to the short, low counter and placed two spools of thread in front of Grant. "Would you mind putting these on my account as well?"

"Surely will, Missy. Have yourself a good day—and don't forget those cookies." He rubbed his hands together and winked.

Donnie trotted along beside her, matching his short-legged stride to her longer one, while balancing the crate in his arms. They traveled past the mill and headed into the trees in silence, with only an occasional grunt from Donnie. The wind gusts seemed to have died down as quickly as they'd come.

When they reached Margaret's cabin, Donnie swung easily onto the porch. "Where do you want these put, Miss Margaret?"

Stepping past him, she pushed open the door and nodded inside. "On the table, if you please." She gave him a bright smile as he carefully deposited the box onto the smooth surface. "Thank you for your help, Donnie, it's much appreciated."

The young man beamed and took a step toward her. "I like you, Miss Margaret." He reached out an eager hand and grasped her fingers, leaning in close to her face and stroking her hand. "Would you let me take you to the ice-cream social?"

She tried to pull her hand from his clammy grip, but Donnie's hold tightened. A hard yank and a quick step took her out of his reach. "I'm sure you mean well, Donnie, but please don't take those liberties again."

His visage clouded and the grin disappeared, turning instead to a harsh line darkening his face. "But you've been smilin' at me whenever you come to the store. I figured you liked me and wanted to court."

The intensity of his voice started a quiver deep inside Margaret's stomach, and she backed up another step. "I'm sorry if you misunderstood. I'm going to the social with Andrew—Mr. Browning. I appreciate you bringing my order, but I think it's best if you return to the store."

Donnie jerked the cap from his head and slapped it against his leg. A low growl started somewhere in the depths of his chest. He swung on his heel and stormed out the door, then stopped and peered back in. "I'm a better man than that Browning feller. You'll see if I'm not."

He stomped across the porch and strode across the clearing. As he disappeared into the trees, the sound of an oath floated back to the cabin.

Chapter Six

. . . .

Onboard a freight train in Portland, Oregon

The swaying train car slowed to a crawl and finally jerked to a stop. Samantha drew a dank-smelling blanket over Joel's sleeping form and burrowed next to him in the shadowy corner. They'd found an empty car with bales of hay littering the floor and had crawled behind one, tossing remnants of loose hay over and around themselves.

Outside, a voice shouted something she couldn't understand, and footsteps drew near. A cold sweat broke out on her forehead, and her fingers fumbled at the edge of the blanket. What seemed like an eternity passed as a man with a lantern poked his head into the car. "Don't see nothin' in here." He withdrew the lantern and started to turn.

At a whiffling snore from Joel, the dim light returned, barely penetrating the blanket. She wanted to slip her hand over her sleeping brother's mouth but knew he'd probably awake at the touch. *Please, God, don't let them find us and send us back.* The prayer screamed from her mind and almost tore from her mouth, but she clamped her lips shut.

"Hey, Bob, you might want to come check over here. Thought I heard something." The crunch of gravel under heavy boots sounded clearly inside the now quiet car.

"Meooww!" A hiss and a sharp cry broke from under the edge of the open door and one of the men scrambled back.

"Ha! That's just an old tomcat wanting a free ride. Nothin' to worry about." The man slapped his hand against the open door and swung the lantern away. "Best get a move on. This train's going to be late if we don't hustle. The boss down at the Bridal Veil mill ordered a car load of supplies for the Company store and wants it before first light."

Two sets of feet moved away, and Samantha drew in an unsteady breath. Her heart slammed against her chest, and she placed her shaking hand over it, willing it to calm down. God had kept Joel from waking and sent the cat to save them. She stretched out beside her brother's still form and closed her eyes again. *Bridal Veil.* What a pretty name. The man said the train would be unloading supplies for a store. Best get off there before it got light and someone decided to search each car.

Sometime later, the short staccato burst of the train whistle followed by the long screech of brakes jerked Samantha from her uneasy sleep. She glanced at Joel, still curled in the pile of dirty hay. A quick shake of his shoulder and the boy came awake.

"What's wrong, Sammie? Is it time to get up and do chores?" He rubbed his eyes and yawned. "I want to sleep longer."

"Shh." She placed her fingertip against his mouth. "We're on an adventure, remember? We're going to find a new home."

He sat up and pushed back the blanket. "Can I have a dog when we get there?"

Samantha smoothed his hair and plucked pieces of hay from the brown curls. "We'll have to wait and see. Now I need you to listen. We mustn't make any noise when we get off the train. Can you do that?"

"Ah-huh. But how we gonna see to get off the train?" He pushed to his knees and peered outside. "I'm hungry, Sammie."

"We'll find something to eat soon. It's starting to get light, so we'll need to hustle after we jump off." She tugged at his hand and pulled him back onto the hay. "We have to stay away from the door until the train stops. Men will be unloading the cars. We'll jump down, and we'll have to run and find a place to hide."

The boy trembled as he leaned against her shoulder. "I'm scared, Sammie. And I'm hungry. Let's go back to Mrs. Stedman's house and have some breakfast, all right?"

She placed her arm across his broad shoulders and squeezed. "We're never going back there again. We're going to find food and a new home, don't you worry."

He gave a loud sigh and leaned his head against hers. "All right. I won't worry no more."

* * *

An hour later Samantha and Joel crawled out from under a dense rhododendron bush as the rising sun stretched its tentative fingers over the gently rolling Columbia River. No breeze stirred the tree boughs, and only the crash of the waterfall hitting the rocks a distance away broke the morning calm.

Joel stretched his long arms over his tousled head and yawned, then patted his stomach. "I'm starving. How far is it to our new home, Sammie?"

Samantha grimaced, then tried to smile. "I'm not sure, but I think we're getting close." She sucked in a breath and patted his arm as her own stomach rumbled in protest. "We'll get some food first, then try to find somewhere to stay."

The boy reached for the burlap bag at his feet. "I'll tote the bag of clothes. Nothin' in here I can break." A smile spread across his freckled face. "Good thing we don't have no eggs with us, huh, Sammie?"

She chuckled, then took a step forward and glanced around, suddenly unsure of their surroundings and praying they'd not been heard. It looked like they'd ventured a ways from the railroad tracks, but huge piles of lumber and sawdust loomed not far to the east and down the slope. The whining of machinery and the shouting voices of men above the din floated across what appeared to be a huge lumberyard dotted with buildings. They'd climbed up a hill and into a stand of dense trees a little west of town. Now she heard water tumbling not far away, making her realize how dry her mouth had become the past couple of hours. She lifted the small earthenware jug she'd tucked into her bag and shook it. Nearly empty, and no doubt stale.

"Come on, Joel, let's find some fresh water. Maybe we can wash our faces and get a drink." She grasped his hand and headed up a narrow path in the direction of the falling water, growing louder with each step. They rounded a clump of trees and both gasped at the same time. A cascade of water dropped from what seemed to be the top of the earth, then a second shelf of water appeared and fell from the base of the first. It tumbled into a pool among several large, moss-covered boulders, one rising at least fifty feet in the air. The churning water spread its soothing waves out across a sparkling pool that narrowed into a rushing stream, headed straight for the Columbia River.

Joel stood drinking in the sight, then clapped his hands and whooped. "Can I go swimming, Sammie?" He unbuttoned the top button of his shirt, then bent over and unlaced his boots.

Samantha gripped his arm. "Wait. We don't know how deep it is or if it's safe. You can roll your pants legs up, sit on the edge of the stream, and put your feet in the water, but that's all. We'll get cleaned up as best we can and fill our water jug, but we can't swim in the water yet."

Joel's face drooped, and he heaved a sigh. "But the sun's been hot, and I'm all sticky." A wise look crossed his face, and his eyes twinkled. "You don't smell so good either, Sammie."

She wrinkled her nose and laughed, then swatted his arm. "Thanks a lot, Joel. Guess we'll do the best we can, but I sure wish I'd thought to bring soap." Samantha looked around, but this area didn't seem to be occupied. She'd watched the ground as they'd approached the stream and seen no tracks other than those of deer. The next several minutes passed in silence as they peeled off shoes, socks, and outer clothing, and scrubbed as much of themselves as possible.

After slipping her dress back on over her petticoat and tugging on her socks and shoes over still-damp feet, she stood and shook out her calf-length skirt. While she waited for Joel to finish, she took a small notebook and pencil from her pocket and began to write.

O Lord, thank You for bringing us to this nice place. Please keep us safe and help us find a real home.

She slipped the book back into her pocket, feeling better now that she'd taken time to write down her prayer.

Joel plunked down beside her and laced his boots. Sammie held out her hand and helped him rise. "We're going to head back through the trees and up this hill a ways. I want to look over the area and find a place to stay."

They tramped through the brush, ducking under low-hanging limbs of mixed fir, larch, and other leafy trees that she didn't recognize. How pretty it would have been a couple of months ago when the sprinkling of rhododendron bushes that dotted the hillside were in bloom. They'd been her mother's favorite flower, and the sight of the bushes, with blooms already spent, brought a sadness she found hard to push away.

Joel tugged at her hand and drew her to a stop. "You're awful quiet, Sammie. Somethin' wrong?"

It never failed to amaze her how sensitive her brother was to her moods. He might not be smart when it came to book learning, figures, or commonsense things, but he understood people and animals more than most people she'd met. "Just thinking about Mama and how much I miss her."

He nodded, a faraway look on his face. "Me too. I think she's still out there somewhere, Sammie. God wouldn't a'took her to heaven when we needed her so bad. I just know He wouldn't a'done that."

Samantha hugged his arm. "God didn't mean nothing bad when He took her home to heaven, Joel. I think maybe it was her time, that's all."

"Can we go see their graves after we find a new home? I want to tell them good-bye."

She shook her head and tried to smile, not wanting to upset her brother any more than he already was. "We're too far away from the town where they're buried, but we can remember them in our hearts."

Memories from the day they'd been put on the train to Mrs. Stedman's rushed back. It hadn't felt right, leaving without saying good-bye to her parents, even if only at their graveside. They'd been told she and Joel were too young to see bodies laid out for burial after their parents' wagon had wrecked, but Samantha had also known Mrs. Stedman was anxious for her new charges to arrive.

Samantha reached for Joel's hand. "Come on, we need to find a place to sleep and hide for a while." She led the way on a narrow trail that wove up the side of the hill, panting as she neared the top. A vista opened up before her that took her breath away.

Down below, a long, winding, wooden snake-like apparatus rose above the ground, held up on tall stilts. Water gushed down the trough, carrying what looked like long sticks—no, it must be lumber—all the way down near the mill yard. The entire flat area appeared covered by large buildings, lumber piles, and scurrying men. The railroad tracks lay beyond, between the buildings and the river. Up the hill from the mill buildings a number of houses were scattered through the trees.

What a strange town. She didn't see any stores or businesses and not even a city street winding through the area. It was nothing at all like Salem. This looked more like someone built the huge sawmill first, then decided to tuck homes and maybe a school and a store wherever they'd fit. She could see horses pulling wagons through the lumberyard down below, but no sign of buggies, women, or children.

"We need to be quiet for a while, Joel. Let's pretend everyone else is sleeping, and we have to be little mice, slipping around trying to find our cheese."

Joel clapped his hands and grinned. "Goodie! And we don't want no cats to come gobble us up, huh?"

Samantha nodded, glad the boy didn't realize how close he'd described their situation. "That's right. Now come on. Follow me close, and don't say a word."

They spent the next ten minutes slipping through the woods, skirting away from the braces holding up the flume. The last thing Samantha wanted was some passerby noticing two children sneaking from tree to tree and turning them in. Of course, with it being summertime, most people would suspect they were locals out playing in the woods, but she couldn't take the chance that word of their disappearance had made it this far.

A sound up ahead brought her to a halt, and she held her arm out in front of Joel's belly. "Shh. There's a house up ahead. Remember, we don't want that hungry cat to find the little mice."

Joel put his finger to his lips and mimicked her action. "I'm very quiet." His whispered words barely reached ahead of him.

Samantha turned and gripped his arm. "I want you to stay there." She pointed to a large hemlock tree about twenty feet away, its drooping limbs hanging down nearly to the ground. "I'll be back soon with some food. Do you promise to stay put and not make any noise?"

Joel allowed her to lead him under the canopy of branches and settled down with his back to the trunk without protest. "I promise. No noise. Stay put. Don't let the cat know we're here."

"Good boy. I'll hurry."

Samantha peered out between the fir needles for a moment, then slipped through and walked toward the small, weathered gray house in the distance. The fact that no smoke rose from the chimney and no sound emanated from an open window convinced her that no one was home. But when she reached the door, she hesitated as a chill crept over her body and set her arms and legs to shaking. What if she were caught? What would happen to Joel? Surely the law would put her in jail and send her brother back to Mrs. Stedman. She almost turned and fled back to Joel's hiding place, but her stomach's loud protest and the aroma of fresh bread stayed her retreat. Her mouth watered and her fingers trembled as she gently turned the knob. The people in this town must not be as fearful as the city dwellers in Salem.

The small kitchen at the back of the house appeared deserted, but a cloth-covered lump sat in plain sight on the rough wooden table several feet away. In two strides she reached the source of the fragrance and slipped off the cloth. Three loaves of fresh bread lay gleaming in a row, their tops freshly basted with butter, the rivulets now cooled on the sides. Nearby a chunk of yellow cheese snuggled under a glass-domed dish and a sharp knife rested beside it, as though someone planned a picnic but got called away before they could satisfy their hunger.

Samantha reached for the food, then stopped. Stealing was wrong. Her mother had taught her that as a very young child. Even when they were hungry and Joel was crying, Mama had told her they must trust God. So even now, when her fingers itched to grab the food and run—her brother was hungry—she couldn't disappoint Mama, even if she was dead. A low groan slipped out of Samantha's mouth and she quickly stifled it with her fingers. *Please help me, God. We're hungry.*

Then a thought flashed through her mind: *Leave them a note.* She slipped her hand into her apron pocket and pulled out the small notebook and pencil. She ripped out a piece of paper and placed it on the table, then leaned over it, biting her lower lip and concentrating on the words.

I'm sorry to take your food. We're hungry. I'll pay for it as soon as I can.

She tucked the note under the edge of a bowl and reached for the knife, the bread, and the cheese. Money would be better, but since she didn't have any, she'd keep track of what she took. Someday she'd come back and pay the people whose food they'd eaten. Surely they'd understand.

Minutes later she pushed back the limbs of the tree and found Joel leaning against the coarse trunk, head canted to the side and eyes closed. She tiptoed over and knelt beside him. "Joel?"

"Huh?" His eyes flew open, and he looked wildly around, something he'd done when awakened since arriving at Mrs. Stedman's house. "I didn't do nothin' wrong, I promise."

Samantha placed the bag on the ground, then reached to stroke his hair. "Shh. I know, Joel. It's all right. You were good to stay quiet and not move. I brought food."

A smile lit his face, chasing away the cloud of confusion. "No cats came, Sammie. I did just what you said and didn't make a peep." He looked at the loaf of bread she drew out of the bag, and his eyes grew round. "Hmm—that smells good. You're a nice sister, Sammie. Thank you for taking care of me."

A lump formed in her throat that threatened to choke her, but she swallowed it. *Please, God, may I always be here to care for my brother.*

Chapter Seven

....

Martin Jenkins swung his lunch pail in his hand and whistled. The sun shone, the wind wasn't blowing, and work was over for the week. Time for a hearty dinner, and then he'd sit on the porch and smoke his pipe for an hour. Maybe he'd even swing over to his friend Joe's house and have a pint in celebration of the coming weekend.

A gray squirrel raced across the path a few feet ahead and then stopped, sat up on his haunches, and commenced to chatter as though his life depended on it. Well, maybe it did. The little fellow scampered up a nearby tree and disappeared into a hole, probably bent on protecting his winter store from the marauding stranger tramping through his kingdom.

Martin slowed his pace and frowned, then spit into the bushes, irritation swelling in his breast. Life would be so much better if it weren't for that good-for-nothing scoundrel—the gall of the man, thinking he could destroy another person's life and get away with it. Martin kicked at a pinecone, sending it flying across the clearing and pinging off a nearby tree.

His thoughts shifted as he neared home. No warm food on the table tonight, not with his Jenny in Portland these past few days. What a good girl his Jenny was. No man could ask for a better daughter. She didn't deserve to be hounded by someone like—No! He'd not even think the man's name. He'd expose him soon enough—the nerve of the man, pretending to care about the town. He needed to be tarred and feathered and run out on a rail. Then his Jenny wouldn't have to worry anymore, and the town would be safe. Not to mention the money.

* * *

Two hours later Martin woke with a start, his pipe dangling from his hand, ash scattered across the porch floor. He grunted and lifted it, peering into the bowl. *Dead.* Just as well. He stood and stretched, glad for his dinner and nap but ready for something more. Not too late to head over to Joe's for a quick game of cards and a nip or two. He hitched up his pants and adjusted the suspenders, then scratched a spot on his side.

Hmm. Guess I should a'taken a bath, but a clean shirt'll take care of the problem. 'Sides, Joe won't smell much better.

Just then hair prickled on the back of Martin's neck. He swung away from the door he'd pulled ajar and stared out into the gathering gloom. An owl hooted, but nothing else stirred that warranted his attention. Must be not having Jenny home that made him so touchy. If only his wife hadn't died when his girl was just a toddler…

Life would get back to normal when Jenny returned.

Martin sauntered into the house and gave a sharp pull to the door. It bounced against the frame but didn't latch. No matter. He'd be gone again in a matter of minutes. *Gettin' dark in here.* He grabbed the tin of matches lying next to the lantern on a shelf near the kitchen door. Lifting the glass chimney, he lit the wick and then settled the chimney securely in place.

His journal perched on the mantel caught his attention, and he grasped it as he passed by. He'd been writing down the things he'd discovered lately, lest he forget. Not that he would, but having these things in writing could help, if push came to shove. Now where had he put his fancy pen? He spotted it on the seat of a chair drawn out from the wood table parked in a corner, not far from his bedroom door. *Good.* He'd hate to lose that gift from Jenny.

He tossed the book on the table, and it slid almost to the edge, tottering and holding its balance right at the last. What was he doing? He scratched his head. *Oh yes, a clean shirt.* He trooped into his bedroom, grabbed a blue-checked shirt, and tossed his dirty one onto the floor by his bed.

A board creaked in the kitchen. Or was that the wind scraping a branch across the tin roof? No. The day had been still without a breath of wind. *Should a'lit a lantern in the front room, instead of just dependin' on the light from the kitchen.*

"Someone in there?" He stepped into the side room and waited, listening for another sound. Nothing. Must be his imagination working overtime, or the sleep hadn't cleared from his brain. He grinned. Jenny always teased him about talking in his sleep, loud enough for her to hear him through the bedroom door. Maybe he was dreaming now and didn't know it.

Another board creaked, and the hair rose again on the back of his neck.

He peered into the dark but couldn't see so much as the outline of a man. Blast it all, he needed light. "Who goes there?"

An indistinct form moved away from the light cast from the kitchen and deeper into the shadows.

"Who are you?" A shiver passed up Jenkins' spine, and he straightened his shoulders. "What do you want?"

The man didn't move, and the air in the room crackled with unanswered questions.

"Get out of my house."

The shadowy figure moved two steps closer, and the dim light fell across his face.

Martin curled his hands into fists. "You." His breathing quickened, and he took a step forward.

The intruder dropped his voice and hissed through clenched teeth, "I don't want to hurt you, but you got to keep quiet."

"I don't think so. Now get out."

The man's head jerked up. "Not going to happen." He raised a fist and took a step closer. "Maybe we ought to settle this right now."

Martin crossed his arms over his chest and raised his voice. "No sir. I ain't fightin' you. But I'm warning you: I know what you did not long ago."

"Ah-huh." The man paused and the moment seemed suspended somewhere between reality and nightmare. He took another step forward and slightly to one side, stepping into full view. "You got to keep quiet."

"I'm tellin' the sheriff. You can't get away with what you've been pullin'." Martin crossed his arms over his chest, satisfied at the flicker of fear he'd seen in the intruder's eyes.

The man jumped forward and swept up his arm. Too late Martin saw the cast-iron skillet grasped in the man's fist that he'd held behind his back. He tried to duck, but the heavy pan bounced hard off the side of his skull. He felt himself falling into the table—heard a chair smash into the wall and objects hitting the floor.

Jenny. He couldn't let Jenny find him here. Not like this. That man mustn't win; he couldn't allow it. His journal. Had to get his journal. He groaned and struggled to rise, but sharp pain drove him back to the floor, and merciful darkness covered his mind.

* * *

Margaret folded the letter she'd picked up from their post office earlier that afternoon and slipped it back into its envelope. Poor Jenny. Her friend's homesickness poured out between the lines, even though she'd tried to disguise it with lighthearted accounts of her cousin's escapades in the big city of Portland. Jenny thought she might return home in another fortnight, but she was worried her father might not be eating properly.

An idea flickered through Margaret's mind. Mr. Jenkins must be the reason she'd made such a large pot of venison stew earlier this morning. The father of one of her students had brought a roast as a thank-you for tutoring his son during the school year, and she'd used part of it for the stew. She'd eaten it for dinner and again for supper, and had wondered what she'd do with all that was left.

Humming, she dipped a generous portion into a bowl, covered it with a cloth, and headed out of her cabin. It was well past suppertime, but maybe Mr. Jenkins would appreciate a bite, just the same.

When she reached the Jenkins' cabin, she placed the bowl on a porch chair and rapped on the door. A soft light shone from the kitchen window, but no footsteps sounded inside. She knocked again and waited. Nothing. What to do now? Leave the bowl on the chair and hope Mr. Jenkins found it when he came home? But what if it lured a skunk or raccoon, and the animal tipped the bowl and made a mess?

She pondered for a moment, then picked up the bowl and turned to go. A sudden *crack* in the woods not far from the porch stilled her movement and she waited. The muscles of her stomach clenched, and her breathing quickened. "Is someone there?" She peered into the darkness and lifted her lantern, wishing for more light than what the half moon cast.

Something stirred close to the porch rail. Prickles ran down her arms and she clutched the covered dish, torn between bolting off the porch and beating on the front door.

"Is anyone out there?"

An owl hooted. The rushing of its wings lifting from a nearby tree filled the air.

Margaret relaxed and tried to laugh. Only an owl. Nothing to worry about. She'd been thinking about the walking travelers who followed the tracks from town to town, looking for work, and had allowed her imagination to run wild. Time to get home and into the security of her cabin.

She stepped off the porch and walked quickly down the path but couldn't quite keep from looking over her shoulder and back into the woods.

Chapter Eight

....

Andrew Browning rapped on Martin Jenkins' door for the third time, then stepped to the edge of the porch, frustration tugging at his nerves. Jenkins was known for sipping a pint on a Friday night, and more than likely he was sleeping it off at this time on a Saturday morning. Andrew would need to find someone else to help at the mill today. It wasn't often they pulled men in on their day off, but this rush order had them scrambling to find extra hands.

The color of sunshine flashed through the brush a hundred feet from the house, and Margaret Garvey stepped into view, wearing a bright yellow dress. The thought of spending time in Margaret's company on this fine day brought a surge of pleasure to Andrew's heart. Then, just as quickly, it plummeted. If only he didn't have to move on to the next mill worker's house, then hurry back to work. "Margaret, what brings you out this early?"

"Andrew." She drew to a halt a couple yards away. "I thought I'd bring Mr. Jenkins a dish of stew, since Jenny's still gone, then I'm off to help Mrs. Hearn for a bit."

Andrew leaned an arm against the wood post on the edge of the porch. "You do so much for people in this town. You'd best be careful, or you'll take sick."

"Nonsense. I'm strong and healthy and perfectly able to help where I'm needed. Besides, I don't see you taking much time away from work."

He straightened and felt a flush rise up the back of his neck. "That's different. I'm a man and I'm supposed to work. You're a woman and, well…"

She cocked her head and her smile faded. "And I'm in need of a man to take care of me, is that it?"

Now he felt his face flame in earnest. "No. I'm sorry. I didn't mean…" He swiped at his hot forehead with the back of his sleeve. "I just meant, it's nice for women to get to stay home and not have to work—aw shucks, I'd better quit while I'm ahead."

"I'm not so sure you are ahead, Andrew." She took a step forward. "And I'd better get moving. Mrs. Hearn's husband's been feeling poorly for several days."

"Ho there, Andrew Browning." A young man with a stocky body and short legs emerged from the trees into the light. Donnie Williams stopped at the edge of the hard-packed dirt yard and glared at Andrew, then over at Margaret. "What're you two doin' here?"

Andrew stepped off the porch and strode over to the younger man. "Looking for extra help at the mill. You working at the store today?"

Donnie's eyes narrowed. "Nope. Not workin', but don't care to work for you, either." He shot a glance at Margaret. "Guess you came over here to meet up with him, huh?"

Margaret's head shot up, and she crossed her arms over her chest. "Not that it's any of your business, Donnie, but no, I didn't." She nodded at Andrew and turned her back on Donnie. "Good day, Mr. Browning. I hope you're able to find help soon."

Andrew's eyebrows shot up, and he frowned. He'd been trying to watch out for Margaret's welfare the way her father had asked, but it appeared she didn't care for the effort. The last thing he wanted was to drive Margaret away, since his interest increased whenever he spent time in her presence. Was that hasty exit directed at him, or at Donnie? The young man's suspicious tone hadn't set well with him, and he wondered what could be behind it. He turned to the silent man standing close by. "You know anyone else who wants to work?"

Donnie hunched his shoulder and smirked. "No idea. I'm going fishin'. Guess you'd best figure it out yourself."

Andrew watched him saunter away, then glanced at his watch and groaned. The yard boss would bawl him out for sure if he didn't get back with help soon.

* * *

Irritated at the exchange with Andrew, Margaret picked up her pace across the clearing. As much as she'd loved her father, that same attitude cropping up in Andrew bothered her. Her father always thought he knew better than she. She'd often wondered if Nathaniel had disappeared due to her Papa's overprotectiveness. What man would want his father-in-law peering over his shoulder all the time, making sure his little girl was being properly cared for? She wanted to choose the man she'd marry and the life she'd live for herself, not have someone trying to do it for her. If Andrew tried bossing her, she'd give him a talking-to.

The walk between Mr. Jenkins' cabin and Mrs. Hearn's home took only a couple of minutes, but it gave her time to gather her thoughts. She lifted her hand to knock and drew in a deep breath. No time to worry over men or her future right now. Someone else needed her help, and her own problems would have to step aside for a time.

BRIDAL VEIL
1902
OREG

Chapter Nine

Samantha's stomach twisted. The last batch of bread and the two apples they'd taken had lasted the entire day and well into Saturday morning, but now it was suppertime. Hunger pangs drove them out of the woods and back toward the homes on the far edge of the town. This wasn't the best time to find food, but she couldn't stand the thought of her brother going hungry all night. They'd been hiding behind a house for the past two hours, watching for any sign of movement behind the gingham curtains, but nothing had stirred. No lanterns lit, even though dusk would soon fall. She wanted to leave Joel behind again but couldn't take the chance that he'd stay hidden. He'd been restless all day, and it had taken all of her persuasive powers to keep him calm as the day drew to a close.

"Come on, Joel. We'll see if we can find some food." She gripped his hand and tugged, willing him to move forward and not make any noise. Joel stopped abruptly. She stumbled on a rock and caught herself. "What's wrong?"

His eyes grew wide. "Is the people in the house going to feed us and let us sleep in a real bed?"

She stopped on the carpet of fir needles and faced her brother. The fragrance of wood smoke carried on the breeze, and the soft melodic chirp of birds gave their hiding place a sense of safety and peace. But she knew how quickly that safety could shatter. Approaching a homeowner and asking for food or shelter wasn't something she was willing to do—at least not yet. "I'm sorry, Joel, but we can't talk to the people in the houses."

"But I want somebody to play with. I'm tired of sleeping on the ground in a smelly barn and washing in the stream. Why can't we live in a real house again, Sammie?" His plaintive cry increased to almost a wail.

Samantha gripped his hands tighter and whispered, "Because we don't want Mrs. Stedman to know we're here. We're playing hide-and-seek right now. You like to play that, don't you?"

His contorted features relaxed, and a smile chased away the pout. "Ah-huh, I do. But isn't it stealing when we take people's food? How come food's all right to take?"

Samantha wanted nothing more than to lay her head down on the cushiony ground and cry. But she'd always tried to be honest with Joel and teach him right from wrong. It's what Mama would have done if she'd lived. "It's not right to steal anything, even food." She looked him straight in his eyes. "I'm writing them a note." She dug in her pocket and took out her notepad. "See?" She flipped a couple pages, showing him the writing he'd struggle to decipher, but wanting to help him understand. "I tell the people that we're hungry, and we'll come back and pay for everything as soon as we can."

"Oh." A soft light shone from the boy's eyes. "Kind of like when the man Papa worked for paid him after he got done working?"

"That's right. Now come on. I want you to come with me, but you have to be very quiet."

Joel put his finger to his pursed lips. "Shh…not a peep."

"Good boy." She patted his arm and drew him forward, praying he'd remember his promise. They tiptoed from tree trunk to brush clumps until they reached the back door, and Samantha peeked in the window. No movement or sounds that she could tell. It looked like the door opened into the kitchen. They slipped inside and she moved swiftly to the cupboard. The quicker they filled their bag, left a note, and got out, the safer they'd be.

* * *

Joel stood, fidgeting, in the middle of the kitchen as Samantha hunted for something edible. "My feet hurt. I want to sit down."

Samantha glanced around and frowned at the filthy table and chairs. "Do you promise not to bother anything if I let you sit in the front room?"

Joel nodded and grinned. "Promise, Sammie. I'll be good." He wandered into the nearby room and stopped, then tiptoed a few more steps, peering into a side room. A man was lying on the floor, and he'd made a mess. Why would the man tip over his chair and throw papers on the floor? Maybe he should get Sammie so she could wake the man and help clean up his house. He shook his head. *No. Sammie said to be quiet and not bother nothing.*

Then he saw a small book under the edge of the tipped-over chair. Maybe he could write things like Sammie did. Ah, a pretty pen rested on the edge of another chair, almost ready to fall. He snatched it up and gripped it tight, then leaned over and plucked the book from the floor and turned its pages. He wished he could read better, but most of the words didn't make sense. The man wrote funny anyway, all curly and twisty, instead of the easy letters his sister was teaching him to write. Maybe Sammie could read stories to him out of this book.

What did she say about leaving a note? He'd best let the man know he'd come back and pay for it. He tore out a small piece of the page with no writing on it, then picked up the pen.

I pay fer buk

There. He laid the note on the chair, then shoved the book and the pen in his pocket and grinned. Too bad that man was still sleeping and didn't want to eat, too. Joel tiptoed back into the kitchen.

Chapter Ten

....

On Sunday morning Nathaniel unpacked the last of his belongings and sank onto the sofa in the tidy, if stark, living room. How ironic that he'd been given the same house where Margaret and her father once lived. He could almost feel her presence. Not that he'd been allowed to visit here much; her father was too protective for that. But he'd been in the house a couple of times and hadn't forgotten.

A rush of memories poured over him, bringing a sadness he found hard to push down. What would this new adventure bring? He'd almost turned down the offer when it came, in spite of the attractive wages. He'd been making four dollars a day at his last job—not bad by any means—but the six dollars a day he'd make managing the upper millpond would allow him to put money away. Maybe someday he'd marry and settle down. Since achieving the age of twenty-four, he'd begun to realize life was speeding by.

He felt a twinge of regret at the thought of the young Margaret who'd been so deeply in love with him—or so he'd thought. Her sweetness and innocence had drawn him from the start. At first he'd tried to ignore her hero worship, knowing that four years separated them. But after repeated encounters at social gatherings in the small town, he'd found her hard to resist. What would she be like now? Would the grown-up Margaret still remain unspoiled, or would she be like so many other selfish, conceited women he'd known, wanting to wring what they could from a man?

He'd nearly married his boss's daughter two years ago but had discovered his bride-to-be socially ambitious and caring more for what he might bring to their union than for himself. When it became apparent that Marie and her father were planning his life, he'd fled the job and the engagement. He doubted Marie had been too broken-hearted. She had a roving eye for handsome men.

He shook his head and pushed the thought away. It didn't matter. His new job must remain his focus, not a woman, no matter how attractive. Margaret probably had a couple of kids clinging to her skirts by now. And if she wasn't married, it would be due to her overprotective father keeping the men at bay.

He'd start work tomorrow at the upper Palmer mill. He could have lived in one of the small cabins above but had been happy they'd offered him this house for the summer. The trail up the mountain was steep, and not something he cared to hike while the early morning fog curled around the base of the cliffs. Good thing he'd brought his horse. Of course, he could always ride on one of the wagons making the trek, but his supervisor job would require him to put in more time than most of the men.

A glance at his pocket watch brought him up short. If he remembered correctly, church service began in just under a half hour. Not that he'd frequented it much in earlier years, but he might give it a try. If nothing else, he could see some familiar faces and secure an invitation to dinner—and possibly find out if Margaret still lived in the area.

He changed quickly and struck out for the church, confident the good people of Bridal Veil were still meeting in the same place. A bird's happy melody put a spring in his step as he strode along.

The town had grown—new homes had cropped up not far from the river's edge, and bright flowers bloomed in front of a number of porches. A strong east wind kicked up, blowing fircones along the path. The wind sighed through the fir and larch trees on the hillside nearby, and the tangy fragrance of fir needles rose on the warm air.

Other stragglers were crossing the threshold of the small wooden church when he entered the needle-strewn dirt yard. A handful of people looked around, but he didn't recognize any faces. He stepped inside the wide-open set of double doors and paused, glancing over the congregation.

"Howdy, stranger. Glad you could join us." The booming voice turned him around at the same time a meaty hand slapped his shoulder. "I'm Tom. Tom Mabry."

Nathaniel shook the extended hand. "Nathaniel Cooper." His arm pumped up and down until he wondered if his shoulder joint would give out.

Tom must have sensed he'd made his welcome apparent and loosened his grip. He jerked a bushy eyebrow toward the grouping of pews ahead. "Don't stand on ceremony, son. Trot on down and grab you a seat."

"Thank you, I'll do that." Nathaniel slipped away just as the man's hand poised for another welcoming slap. He spotted an empty pew not far from the back on the right and slipped in. Talking to strangers didn't appeal to him at the moment, but watching the faces of those around the room did.

His gaze rested on the back of a woman's head, only two rows in front and across the aisle. Her face was turned away as she talked to a young brown-haired man sitting alongside. A wide smile broke the solemnity of the man's face, and his look of genuine relief was palpable. The light red curls tied at the nape of the woman's neck swayed as she turned her head. Nathaniel jumped as though he'd been stung by a dozen bees. Margaret Garvey's wide, beautiful eyes met his.

* * *

Margaret felt the blood drain from her face as she stared into the eyes of the last man she expected to see in this church, or anywhere else in town, for that matter. Nathaniel Cooper sat across the aisle. Alone. She gathered her thoughts, snapped shut her gaping mouth, and jerked her head back toward Andrew.

Just a moment before, she'd felt such a flood of peace as she'd made amends with Andrew for the small disagreement in front of Mr. Jenkins' cabin the day before. Now, peace was the furthest thing from her mind. She gripped the edge of the hard wooden pew until her fingers turned numb. Why was Nathaniel in Bridal Veil? Her heart hammered, but not from fear or excitement. Hot anger filled her veins, and she struggled to stay in her seat. She wanted to fly at the man and vent her frustration over his callous treatment of her four years ago.

A hand touched her arm, and she jerked her attention back to Andrew. "I'm sorry, you said something?"

A worried pucker lined Andrew's forehead. "Are you feeling well, Margaret? You seem…distraught."

She waved her hand and tried to muster a laugh. "It's nothing." She picked up a hymnal and leafed through the pages. "It's just a little warm. I guess I'm still adjusting to the heat."

Andrew settled against the high wooden back and tugged at his collar. "I quite agree. Maybe you'd like to take a walk at the end of the service before heading home?"

The organ struck a chord and Margaret smiled, then bent her head over the hymnal. "That sounds fine, Andrew. Thank you." She would *not* give in to her emotions. She squared her shoulders. Andrew was twice the man that Nathaniel was, as well as handsome and trustworthy. She'd be proud to spend time with him. Nathaniel Cooper would *not* know he'd impacted her life one bit. Not today, or any day in the future.

Chapter Eleven

....

Nathaniel strode from the office at the upper mill toward the bridge spanning the narrow canyon. The ingenuity of the twisting, plummeting flume, precariously balanced on the side of the canyon that transported cut lumber down to the lower planer mill in Bridal Veil, never failed to impress him.

It was his first day on the job, but his mind wouldn't focus. Seeing Margaret at church with a young man—presumably her husband—hadn't made it easy. And he'd not received an invitation to dinner from anyone.

He stepped onto the wooden bridge and crossed over, intent on getting to the millpond where the logs were dumped after the train brought them down the mountain. The loud shriek of a train whistle approaching the bridge raised its voice above the constant whine of the saw in the nearby building as it sliced its way through the massive larch and fir logs. Amazing. The addition of the two large locomotives to the logging operation was staggering. They could haul an incredible load from the landing site miles up the mountain where the teams dragged the logs out of the woods.

"Hey, boss!" A man flagged him from across the bridge and close to the edge of the upper pond.

Nathaniel jogged across the short expanse and drew up in front of the bewhiskered, rough-clad worker. "Everything all right?"

"No, sir. Word just came down that Martin Jenkins didn't show up at the log landing."

Nathaniel removed his hat and scratched his head. "Anyone find out where Jenkins is?"

"Figured we'd best ask you before sending someone down the mountain to his place."

"Fine. Who can you spare?"

"I'll find someone and report back."

Nathaniel spun on his heel and raised a hand in dismissal. "I'll be in the office." He made the rounds from the millpond to the train unloading its cargo and back to the office on the slight rise above the tracks. The paperwork that had built up since the last manager left covered the desk. He'd best get to it.

The next hour passed without incident, but the calm was broken when a man he didn't recognize burst through the door, panting and gasping for breath. "Excuse me. You Mr. Cooper?"

Nathaniel swung around in his office chair. "I am."

"Sampson sent me down to check on Martin Jenkins. I couldn't raise anyone at the door, and the curtains were drawn, so I asked at the general store. No one's seen Martin for at least a couple of days. Went back to the house and pounded, then tried the door. The smell hit me, and I nearly gagged. I walked through the kitchen to the back room. Found Jenkins on the floor. Dead."

Nathaniel stood to his feet, shock slowing down his response. "Dead? You're sure? Did you call for the doc?"

"Yes, sir, I did, although I didn't need to. He's for sure dead and stunk something fierce." The man grimaced. "Looks like he was bashed in the head."

Nathaniel's chin jerked up. "That's terrible. Does Jenkins have a family?"

"His wife's dead, and his daughter has been out of town visiting kin this past couple of weeks.

Nathaniel grabbed his hat and shoved it onto his head. "I'd better ride down and see what I can do. It might take a couple of days before the sheriff can get here from Troutdale. Find someone to notify Jenkins' crew."

The man nodded and left the shack. Nathaniel strode to the door and stepped outside. Trouble on the first day didn't bode well for the future.

* * *

Andrew stood on the fringe of onlookers grouped near Jenkins' porch and shook his head. No good would come of this day. He stared at the blanket-draped body being carried out the front door by two sawmill workers. Both mills had closed early as a result of the unexpected death, and word had spread through the small community.

A tall man with dark brown hair and a small mustache stood on Jenkins' porch and waved his arms. "Could I have everyone's attention?" The voices around him stilled, and the man continued. "My name is Nathaniel Cooper. I started today as assistant supervisor of the Palmer mill, and the supervisor is out of town for the week. Did any of you know Jenkins well?"

"Yes, sir. Lots of us did. Martin worked at the sawmill for years before being promoted to skidding supervisor at the log landing." Vernon Mills, a man wearing grease-stained overalls, wiped his palm on his leg and stared at the man standing next to him. "Laws, Joe, how long you think Martin worked here in Bridal Veil, anyway?"

Joe Kline removed his hat and twisted it in his hands. "Don't rightly recall, but it's been a number of years. Most of us knew him. I played cards with him many a time and counted him a good friend." He wagged his head. "Can't believe he's dead."

"How'd Martin die, anyway?" a voice called out from the back of the gathering.

Nathaniel hunched a shoulder and frowned. "Looked like he hit his head. Might have slipped and fallen. Doc's going to take a look at him as soon as he arrives from another call."

"Sure is goin' to be hard on Jenny. She's always been close to her pa." Joe dusted his hat against his leg, then shoved it back on his head.

Donnie Williams stepped to the fore and raised his voice. "Or someone could a'clubbed him in the head. Any proof he fell?"

A murmur rose from the people nearby, and Andrew glanced around. Frowns marred several faces, and one of the two men who'd spoken earlier turned with a scowl. "Donnie Williams, shut your trap. Ain't nobody in this town who'd want to harm Martin."

Andrew thought back to Saturday morning when he'd stopped at this house. Was it possible Martin had been killed, or could it be a simple accident? The man hadn't answered the door, and no one had seen him since.

Nathaniel raised a hand, and the crowd quieted. "We don't know anything yet. Anyone see Martin the past couple of days?"

Joe Kline rubbed his bald head and squinted. "Martin was supposed to come over Friday night and play a hand of cards, but he didn't show." A quick shrug. "Figured he found somethin' else to occupy himself with and didn't think on it anymore. Wish now I'd come and checked on him."

Donnie took a long stride toward Andrew and pointed his finger at him. "I seen him at Jenkins' house Saturday morning, comin' out of his door. Maybe he's the one what knocked him in the head."

Andrew jerked his head around and stared at Donnie. Was the man mad, or did he really believe he'd seen him exiting Jenkins' door? "I wasn't in Jenkins' cabin! We were shorthanded, and I came to see if he could fill in at the mill. He didn't come to the door."

"No sir. I seen you come out that door." Donnie pushed his short bulk closer to Andrew. "I also seen Miss Garvey knockin' on Martin's door Friday night. Then Saturday morning Miss Garvey came along and flirted with you. For all I know, she's in on it, too."

"Why you—" Andrew grabbed the front of Donnie's shirt and shoved his nose close to Donnie's face. "Miss Garvey was on her way to help Mrs. Hearn. She had nothing to do with it, and neither did I! You didn't come along till I'd turned away from the door and was speaking to Miss Garvey."

Joe pushed through the group of men clustered nearby. "Donnie, you'd best take that back. We don't take kindly to trash-talkin' about one of our decent women."

Donnie shrugged. "I ain't tryin' to, just tellin' the truth as I seen it, no matter what you say." He turned toward Cooper and sneered. "You mark my words." He jerked his head toward Andrew. "Browning here could a'had somethin' to do with Martin's death." He snapped his mouth shut, then shouldered past the men standing nearby and stomped off into the woods.

Andrew met Nathaniel Cooper's gaze. The man's eyebrows drew down, and a quizzical light shone in his eyes. "If you think of anything that might help, you'll let me know, Mr. Browning?"

Andrew nodded and spread his hands. "Sure. But I told you everything—Jenkins didn't answer the door, and I went on to the next house."

"Can you remember who you saw before you got here?"

"No one. I tried two other places and nobody was home." Andrew felt a surge of fear.

Grant Cowling moved forward and clapped Andrew on the shoulder, then raised his voice. "I believe you, son. I don't know what got into Donnie, suggestin' you and Margaret could have anythin' to do with Martin's death. That boy has worked for me nigh onto two years, and I've never seen him so ornery. Sure hope what he said doesn't reflect poorly on Margaret, her bein' our schoolteacher and all."

"Nothing to worry about there." A strong voice off to Andrew's left sliced through the air, and Robert Ludlow, the head of the Bridal Veil schoolboard, moved up beside Grant. "Besides, I didn't hear him offer any proof." Ludlow directed his gaze toward Cooper and stepped onto the bottom step of the porch. "In fact, it might pay to look into Williams a bit, since he could have been hanging around the house when Browning arrived, and possibly on Friday evening, as well."

Cooper shoved his hat back on his head. "I agree. I'm just gathering what information I can, ahead of time." He cast a direct look at Andrew. "We don't know what happened, yet, but if it wasn't an accident, I imagine the sheriff will need to ask questions." He turned and raised his voice. "If no one else saw or heard anything, I guess we'd all best get back to what we were doing. The doc will let us know his findings, and I'm sure we'll get a visit from the county sheriff, when he has time to get here. Too bad we don't have our own law enforcement in Bridal Veil."

"Good thinking, Cooper." Robert Ludlow extended his hand. "There's been hobos walking and riding the rails of late. I saw at least one person, maybe two, sneak off the train and slip into the woods a week or so back. Be sure to let me know if there's any way I can help."

Ludlow turned to go, and Andrew tapped his shoulder. "Thanks for sticking up for Miss Garvey the way you did. Much appreciated."

"Certainly. She's a lovely lady." He nodded. "I need to go. Good day."

Andrew watched him walk away, thanking the good Lord both Ludlow and Grant had intervened. What was Donnie Williams thinking, claiming he'd been in Jenkins' cabin? And hobos riding the rails? He hadn't noticed any strangers in town who weren't associated with the mill, but it might pay to be careful. He'd have to keep a closer eye on Margaret, her living alone and all. The last thing he wanted was something happening to the woman he'd promised to protect, who was burrowing ever deeper into his heart.

* * *

Nathaniel went back into the cabin after the crowd dispersed and walked from the living area to where they'd found Martin's body. He covered his mouth and nose with a clean cloth, but even so the smell almost overpowered him.

While the man could have slipped and struck his head on the corner of the table, he doubted that was the case. Papers littered the floor, and an empty oil lamp lay shattered on the hearth. Good thing the base had been dry and the wick not lit, or they might have had a worse tragedy on their hands than one dead body. Fire in the woods was a sawmill worker's biggest fear, and prevention was taken seriously.

He headed toward the kitchen and stopped in the doorway. The gingham curtains at the windows showed the evidence of a woman's touch, and he remembered one of the men mentioning a daughter. Poor girl, she'd be returning to Bridal Veil for a funeral instead of to her father's welcome.

He guessed, by the looks of things, that the daughter had been gone for a while. The plank floor was in sore need of a good scrubbing, and unwashed dishes sat on the food-littered table. His gaze traveled to the table where flies buzzed over the remains of what must have been Martin's last meal, then paused on a scrap of paper fluttering across the floor. He strode over and planted his boot on the missive before the breeze could drive it into hiding. Probably something from the desk. He bent over and plucked it from the corner and held it up to the light. Painfully neat letters covered the lined paper in what appeared to be an almost childish hand.

We'll pay you back for the food as soon as we're able. Please forgive us for not asking. We're hungry.

Nathaniel frowned and read it again. No way would Andrew Browning have written something like this if he'd come into the house when Donnie Williams saw him. His thoughts returned to the man who'd stood accused in front of the cabin just minutes before. Browning had been sitting beside Margaret at church, and they'd been smiling and chatting when he'd first spotted them. After hearing the men refer to Margaret as Miss Garvey, he knew that she wasn't married, but could Browning be Margaret's beau? He didn't appear to be the type of man who'd murder someone, but you couldn't always tell. He could have a temper. Or maybe Martin was interested in Margaret as well, and Browning flew into a jealous rage and attacked him. Then there was Donnie. His claims seemed a bit exaggerated, and he wondered what drove the man to spout off as he had, dragging Margaret's name into the mix.

He looked again at the paper clutched in his hand. This didn't make sense. Why would someone leave a note that they were hungry, had taken food, and would pay for it later? Why not come forward and ask? Small towns were known for their hospitality, and most anyone here would feed a hungry person without payment. Someone had mentioned hobos riding the rails. Could one of them have snuck into the house, left the note, and panicked when Martin came home? Of course, it was doubtful anyone would apologize for taking food, then kill the person if they arrived home unexpectedly.

Items were scattered around the floor in the small room where Martin's body had lain. He scanned the room, then stepped to the table, righted the chair, and picked up a book lying facedown on the floor. "*Tom Sawyer.*" He shook his head. "I guess you never really know a man till you see what he likes to read."

He kicked aside the fragments of broken glass. Someone should clean up this mess before the daughter came back. If she did. One of the men had mentioned that the rest of Jenkins' family resided in Portland. Chances were they'd hold the funeral service there, and she might never return. Surely some of the local women would offer to pack her things and ship them back on the train.

Another paper the same size as the first caught his eye, and he stooped over and picked it up. He withdrew the first from his pocket and compared the handwriting. Not even close. The second looked as though it were penned by a child with an unsteady hand and nowhere near the grasp of the English language as the first.

I pay fer buk

What in the world?

He shook his head. These notes would be turned over to the sheriff when he arrived. It wasn't his job to figure it out, but he'd keep his eyes open just the same. Jenkins was under his charge, and it was his responsibility to look out for his men. That included keeping watch on Browning, as well. If something in the man had snapped and he'd attacked Jenkins, then anyone could be in danger, including Margaret. She wasn't his responsibility, but he'd not see any woman come to harm if he could help it, even one who'd toyed with his emotions and then turned away.

Chapter Twelve

....

Samantha scrunched down into a pile of hay in the barn loft and stared out the window at the dusky, predawn sky. The moon was just starting to wane as fingers of morning light pushed over the top of the horizon. For the last two weeks she and Joel had lived in a corner of this rundown barn that appeared to be abandoned, huddled under the hay for warmth in the coolest part of the night. As thankful as she'd been for the food they'd eaten, they were tired of hiding. Besides, they needed a real bath in a sore way. Three times now they'd snuck down to the base of the waterfall near dusk and cleaned up the best they could, but a hot tub and a hair wash sounded mighty good.

Maybe Mrs. Stedman had stopped looking. She could always get more children from the orphanage, couldn't she? Of course, she never let them forget how much they cost her, so it might be good to stay put for a while. She sighed. It would be so nice to find a home.

The sun was just tipping the top of the hills to the east when Samantha slipped out of the barn. Joel wouldn't wake for at least another hour. Her brother seemed increasingly tired—whether from poor food or lack of real exercise, she didn't know. Something had to change soon.

She jogged away from the barn, clutching her flour sack to her chest and praying. The care of her brother sat heavy on her shoulders, and she longed to be a little girl again, like she was before Mama and Papa died and all she'd known was taken from them.

The squeal of train brakes coming up the tracks a hundred feet away slowed her steps, and she dodged into the brush. Sleeping close to the tracks at Mrs. Stedman's, she'd grown so used to trains passing that she rarely noticed them anymore—but she couldn't take a chance that someone might notice her lugging a bag and skulking through the bushes.

The conductor jumped from the caboose and walked down the line of freight cars. Nothing else stirred, and silence settled over the length of the tracks. Samantha darted through the brush away from the train.

A stretch of woods and heavy brush lay between the old barn and the edge of Bridal Veil. Prickles ran up Samantha's back, and she shivered. Normally she loved the woods, but this morning something didn't feel right. She stepped onto the path and started through the trees, then stopped, her heart beginning to drum against her chest.

"Get off the path. Hurry." Her head jerked up. Who had spoken? She waited, not moving.

"Run into the woods. Now."

She caught her breath and dashed forward into the trees, somehow knowing the voice could be trusted.

Voices. She could hear men somewhere behind her.

God, help me please. I can't let them find me. Joel would be all alone. She darted off the path, then stopped, panic gripping her body. Which way to run?

The voices increased in volume. A low, guttural growl and a whining, higher-pitched one spoke back and forth. "You sure you seen her come this way?"

"Yeah. When I peeked outta the train door I seen her dart into the brush, then she took to this path. She disappeared around the corner and headed into these woods."

"She's an awful pretty little thing, even if she is dirty." The man snickered. "Maybe we can take her with us when we get back on the train."

"Like you got room to talk, yer dirty yer own self. Now keep your trap shut. Ya don't want someone hearin' ya, do ya? We don't need the law after us." His voice dropped, and Samantha could barely hear him. "But takin' her might be a good idea. Let's start huntin'."

Samantha sank to her knees, her stomach lurching.

"Get up."

She raised her head and looked around.

The voice again. Firm, yet gentle and kind. *"Get up, Samantha. I'll lead you to safety."*

This time she didn't hesitate. She jumped to her feet and moved. But which direction?

"Go to the left. Now."

She swung to the left and picked up her pace, the voices receding just a bit. She still hadn't seen the men, but the panic didn't lift.

"There's a gully to the left. Go over the bank and follow it. Hurry."

The ground sloped, and Samantha scooted over the edge and into a gully not quite deep enough to hide her from view. She scurried along its length, following the winding path and ducking as she ran. After about a hundred feet, the ditch smoothed out and the trees thickened. "Now what?" She whispered the words as she looked back over her shoulder, cold dread wrapping around her stomach.

"Keep going straight."

It was God speaking, she knew that now. The brush slapped her shoulders and tore at her skin, but she pushed through it, intent on keeping a straight path until the Lord told her different. The voices behind her had disappeared, but she didn't trust them to stop looking. Those men sounded hungry for something, and it made her shiver clear down to her knees. She knew evil when she heard it.

"*Stop.*"

Samantha peered through the brush and trees but couldn't understand what might be special about this spot. "What should I do, Jesus?"

"*Crawl. There's a hollow in the hillside. Stay there until I tell you.*"

Samantha scrambled on her hands and knees, peering forward, then back over her shoulder. She was sure she heard a voice in the distance and faint footfalls. Where was the hollow? She stood and ran forward, bent almost double, pushing at the brush near the path and trying not to cry. She couldn't find it! *Please, God, help me.* She wanted to scream the words but didn't dare even whisper. Branches slapped her face as she poked her head into one bush after another, frantic intensity driving her now. The men must be right behind her—she could practically feel their breath on her neck.

Almost she jumped to her feet and started to run when a sense of peace, like the feel of a gentle hand stroking her hair, calmed her fear. She stopped moving and waited, hoping to hear His quiet, soft voice again.

Nothing.

What had He said? *Crawl.* There's a hollow *in the hillside.* She'd been looking through the trees and the brush near the trail, not at the hillside. Samantha dropped to her knees and scooted over to her right, pushing away the dense brush. Ahh, there it was. And it could only be seen if you were on your knees. A grown man standing up would never see this hiding place.

She crawled around the brush, being careful not to break any branches or disturb the ground too much, and settled into the deep pocket, leaning her back against the curve of the dirt. She drew in a breath and let it out slowly, trying to quiet her racing heart. God had done it. He'd brought her to safety and hidden her. Mama used to tell her about God's angels and how they'd cover a child with their wings if you were afraid at night. Were angels standing over her now, spreading their wings over her hiding place so those men couldn't find her?

A branch snapped and Samantha huddled closer to the ground. "God, don't let them find me," she whispered under her breath.

"Anything over there?" The gravelly voice sounded like it came from the gully.

"Naw. She couldn't just disappear. There's no houses back here, just trees. Keep lookin'."

Feet scuffled in the dry maple leaves dropped last fall, and arms thrashed at the brush. Samantha held her breath. *God, please make them leave.* She closed her eyes, feeling foolish, but somehow hoping if she couldn't see them, maybe they wouldn't see her.

"Nothin'." The rough voice spit a string of oaths. "I figured she'd be an easy catch, but she's plumb gone. And with all these leaves and fir needles, there's nary a track."

"We'd best get back to the train, or we'll get left behind. Sure don't need any coppers in the area tryin' to find us."

"No one knows we're runnin' from the law. We could hang out in these woods. Maybe we'd find us another girl skippin' through the trees." A mirthless laugh followed and sent Samantha's heart plummeting.

"Naw. We need to get farther away from Portland; they could have wanted posters here with our faces on 'em. We'll ride the freight train back and head north to Seattle, so's we're not in Oregon no more. Wouldn't hurt to cross the state line into Washington, just to be safe."

"I suppose, but this burg looks like it might be easy pickin'."

"I said no. Now come on, let's get back."

The grumbling and swearing disappeared into the distance, but Samantha didn't budge. The Lord had said to wait.

A sudden thought hit her, and she almost bolted from her hiding place. *Joel!* What if he went hunting for her? What if those men caught him?

"Oh, Jesus," she whispered. "Please keep Joel safe, and keep him asleep."

A gentle peace flowed over her for the second time that day. God would watch over her brother.

Another twenty minutes passed, and Samantha found herself fighting sleep. Now that the danger had lifted, she felt weak and shaky, and so very tired.

"Go to Joel now. You're safe."

* * *

Samantha burst into the barn and raced to the place where she'd left Joel sleeping. No bulge under the hay. No toes sticking out of the holes in his socks. No bleary-eyed brother asking for breakfast. She wrapped her arms around herself and stifled a sob. Didn't God give her a peace about Joel? Where was he?

She spun around and ran back to the door. He must be outside in the back, taking care of personal business. She hated to intrude on his privacy, but knowing he was safe was more important. Keeping a watch over her shoulder and toward the railroad tracks in the distance, she moved with caution toward the trees. "Joel?"

Nothing.

In the distance, the train engine started to huff. "Joel?" It seemed safe to speak a little louder, but still her brother didn't reply.

Could those men have found him and dragged him to the train? She dashed to the place they used in the mornings, calling frantically. She drew to a stop and looked all around. The maple and larch boughs bobbed gently in the breeze, and a blue jay screeched at her from his perch above her head. The train whistle split the air with its shriek, and steam puffed from the stack as it drew the cars slowly along behind.

"Oh, Lord, what should I do? Where's my brother?" She sank to her knees and sobbed, giving in to the rush of fear she'd held at bay that swamped her now. She couldn't lose Joel.

Suddenly her tears stilled, and she jumped to her feet. She was sitting here bawling like a baby, and Joel could be hurt—or captured!

A dog barked in the distance, and suddenly she knew. Joel had commented before, wondering what color the dog might be that barked each morning. She guessed the owner must work at the mill, and the dog started his barking after he was tied outside.

"God, keep Joel safe. Keep him safe. Keep him safe." Her words chanted in cadence with her pounding feet as she dashed in the direction of the small house where the dog must live.

Five minutes later she arrived panting at a home surrounded with a fenced yard. But there was no sign of a dog—or Joel. A moment later, the dog barked again. Behind the house. She followed the fence as it cornered and arrived at the back of the wood-framed home. Her heart leapt into her throat. Joel sat on the ground patting the head of a huge black dog. Samantha grabbed the gate latch and jerked it up. The dog's tail quit wagging and he started to growl, then dashed toward the fence, barking and lunging at the gate.

Samantha released the latch and jumped back, nearly falling over herself in her anxiety to escape the snapping teeth aimed at the bars of the gate.

Joel struggled to his feet and patted his leg. "Come on, boy. Here, boy. That's my sister. She won't hurt you." The dog ignored the boy's command and continued to bark.

Samantha took another step backward. "Joel! You come out of there this minute."

"He's my friend, Sammie. He likes me. See?" He moved toward the growling dog.

"No, Joel, don't!" Samantha nearly shrieked the words, but her brother didn't seem to hear. He continued to walk toward the animal, talking in a low, soft voice. Seconds later his outstretched fingers touched the dog's back and it immediately calmed, then licked his hand. Samantha slumped against a nearby tree and heaved a sigh. "How did you tame him enough to get in the yard?"

Joel shrugged and stroked the big animal's head, rubbing his ears and crooning quietly. "I stood outside the fence and talked to him. He wagged his tail and told me it was all right to come in and pet him, so I did. He's not a mean dog, Sammie, he just don't trust many people."

She crossed her arms over her chest. "And how do you know that?"

He raised his head and looked at her with knowing eyes. "He told me."

"Well, you come on out of there. We need to get back to the barn." She took a step forward and reached for the gate. The transformation in the dog was instant. He sprang forward again, barking and snarling.

"If you open the gate, Sammie, he might run out. I don't think he likes you."

"I'm afraid you could be right." Samantha's heart sank, and she retreated back to the safety of a large maple tree. "Could you just ease out of the gate, real careful-like?"

Joel reached for the latch, and the dog pushed at Joel's hand, then inserted himself between the boy and the gate. He raised a paw and planted it on Joel's belt buckle, pushing him back, then turned to the gate and growled. "He don't want me to leave, Sammie. He wants me to stay and pet him till his owner gets home."

"We can't do that, Joel. No one must see us, not even this dog's owner."

"But the owner's a nice man, or this dog wouldn't stay with him. I know he is." Joel stroked the dog's back and raised pleading eyes toward Samantha. "I'm tired of hiding and running away. Please, let's stay here and meet the nice man who belongs to this dog?"

Samantha shook her head but didn't reply. She felt trapped and helpless. She slid down against the rough bark of the tree and settled on the ground, thankful the dog hadn't hurt her brother, but wishing she could get him out of that yard and back to the barn.

She wanted a home in the worst way, but it was so hard to trust a stranger.

Joel sat down and wrapped his arms around the animal's neck, and Samantha put her head against the tree and closed her eyes. Just a minute or two of rest was all that she needed, then she'd get back up and figure out what to do. Her head nodded and she felt her body relax. It had been so long since she'd been able to just sit.

"Ho there, what's all this?" A strange man's voice yanked Samantha's eyes open, and she looked wildly around, ready to run.

BRIDAL VEIL
1902
OREG

Chapter Thirteen

....

Samantha jumped to her feet and searched for the voice that had woken her from a troubled sleep. Had the men from the train followed her? Where was Joel?

A short, slender man with dark hair and twinkling eyes looked down at her from his position near the fence, then glanced over at Joel, who sat on the grass. The dog lay beside him, head in Joel's lap.

"Buck!" The man spoke and the dog leapt to his feet and bounded over to the fence. A pat on his head and a stern word, and the animal lay down, head between his paws.

Joel struggled to his feet and beamed. "Is that his name, mister?"

"Yes, it is. What's yours?"

"Joel McGavin. Buck's a nice name. What's his last name?"

Samantha slumped in relief. In his excitement her brother had given his real name, not Joel Stedman, tacked on by the orphanage when Mrs. Stedman took over their care. She'd meant to talk to him about which name to give, but somehow he'd instinctively chosen the right one.

The man laughed and reached over the fence to pat the dog's head. "I guess it would have to be Gibbs, seeing as my name is Art Gibbs. So how did you tame Buck, Joel McGavin? I've never seen him let a stranger into the yard before, or allow someone else to pet him."

Samantha sidled closer to the fence, relieved the man didn't seem concerned about their presence in his yard. "He wouldn't let me touch him, and he snapped at me when I tried to open the gate and take Joel home."

Joel pushed to his feet and squinted at Samantha. "I'm hungry. My tummy is rumbling. Did you bring us somethin' to eat?"

Samantha winced and shook her head, hoping Joel would understand he needed to quit talking.

Joel seemed to wilt at the action. "You didn't bring us nothin' to eat? But I'm hungry, Sammie!" His voice started to rise, and his lips drooped in a pout.

Art Gibbs glanced from the upset boy to Samantha and back again. "You haven't had breakfast?"

Joel shook his head and scowled. "No. And I'm tired of bread and cheese every day. That's all Sammie finds for us to eat, most days. I want some eggs and flapjacks and bacon."

Gibbs' serious eyes lingered on Samantha, then turned back to Joel. "How about you come in, and I'll fix you somethin'? I came home early today, since one of my horses threw a shoe and needs tendin' by the smithy."

Samantha hunched her shoulders, unsure what to do. She longed for a hot meal and the man seemed kind, but after the scare with those two men in the woods, she wasn't happy about trusting any strange man. Then she looked at Joel's pinched face and felt her own stomach twist. Her brother had been hungry for days. The scant bread, cheese, and an occasional piece of fruit weren't enough. Maybe this once they would eat since they'd already been seen. They could hightail it out of here as soon as they'd eaten. "Sure. Food sounds good. But what about your dog? He doesn't like me."

Art reached down and gripped the scruff of Buck's neck. "He'll be fine when he knows I'm allowin' you to come in the yard." He turned to Joel. "You never told me how you made friends with him."

"I just talked to him and told him I wouldn't hurt him. He likes me. He said so."

Art raised his eyebrows. "Is that so?" He scratched his head. "He's never talked to anyone but me before. Guess maybe you'll have to come talk to him again. He gets lonesome when I'm at work all day."

Gibbs swung open the gate and stepped through, still maintaining a grip on Buck's collar, and waited for Samantha to precede him. He carefully latched the gate and motioned them to walk with him to the house.

Joel clapped his hands and bounced up and down. "Oh, good! Thank you, Mr. Gibbs. I get lonesome too, when Sammie has to go hunting for our food. I don't like waiting alone in the woods or the barn."

Samantha cleared her throat and took a step back. "I think we'd best go, Joel. We shouldn't keep bothering Mr. Gibbs."

"Nonsense. You agreed to come have breakfast with me, so come along." He held the back door of his house open and beckoned.

A long moment passed with the man's hand clutching the door before Samantha reluctantly walked through. There was no help for it now. They were going to get shipped back to Mrs. Stedman, she knew it.

* * *

Margaret was startled by the rap at her door. Clara hadn't mentioned stopping by, and Andrew was working. Her heart jumped into her throat. Nathaniel. Would he dare come to her home? Surely not. If he did, she'd slam the door in his face. Nothing that man said would alter his past behavior. She proceeded toward the door slowly, laid her hand on the knob, and opened the door a crack.

A glance showed a man with two children in tow. He looked familiar, but she couldn't quite place him. Oh yes, Mr. Gibbs. The man with the team of horses she'd met on the way to the store. She swung open the door and smiled. "Mr. Gibbs. What a pleasant surprise. Are these youngsters relatives of yours?"

He doffed his hat and tucked it under his arm. "No, ma'am. This here is Samantha and Joel McGavin." A few heartbeats passed in silence before he spoke again. "They, ah…don't have anywhere to live. I fed 'em, but they've been sleepin' in a neighbor's barn."

Margaret stepped aside and motioned. "Come in." She smiled at the two disheveled children. "All of you. Please." She reached out a hand and touched the girl's arm, but she winced and pulled away.

Art Gibbs stood in the middle of the small room, seeming unsure of what to do now that he'd arrived. He twisted his hat in his hands and cleared his throat, but no words came.

Margaret drew out a chair at the table snugged near the wall and waited till he was seated, then turned to the children—although the boy didn't seem like a child, more like a nearly grown man. He stood taller than she, with medium bone structure, brown, curly hair badly in need of cutting, holes in his boots, and stained overalls. The girl hadn't fared much better. Her long blond hair was tangled and matted, looking as though no comb or shampoo had touched it for many a day. The dress she wore was a size too big and hung loosely on her slender frame. A scared expression marred the otherwise pretty face.

It appeared that she'd tried to scrub it but had only managed to smear the dirt from one part of her face to another.

"Would you two care for some cookies and milk? There's a dairy farm not far from here, and they bring milk to the store—and I baked sugar cookies this morning."

The big boy nodded eagerly. "I want cookies, yes, sir."

The girl nudged him in the side. "Yes, ma'am, Joel, not sir. She's a lady, can't you tell?"

Joel hung his head and scuffed a toe against the wood floor. "Sorry, Sammie." He raised his clear blue eyes and smiled, and the sight went straight into Margaret's heart. "Joel would like some cookies, ma'am—lady." He turned to the girl Mr. Gibbs had called Samantha and beamed. "Did I do it right this time, Sammie?"

Samantha patted his arm and smiled. "You did fine, Joel." Then she swung a pair of imploring eyes toward Margaret. "He does the best he can, ma'am."

"I agree. Joel did a fine job, and I'd be pleased to give him as many cookies as he'd like. That is, if you've already had your dinner?"

Art Gibbs leaned forward and nodded. "Yes'm. They ate at my house. Cookies would be a right fine way to finish things off."

Margaret bustled around pouring milk, serving cookies, and getting the two youngsters settled on the sofa in the living area. She poured a cup of coffee for Mr. Gibbs, placed a heaping plate of cookies within his reach, and sank onto a chair across the table. "Now, Mr. Gibbs, please tell me what's going on."

He brushed a crumb from the side of his mouth and swallowed. "These are mighty good, ma'am, thank you." He glanced over at the two children hungrily consuming their treat and dropped his voice. "They showed up at my house today. It was the strangest thing. The boy was in my fenced yard with Buck's head lying in his lap, sweet as you please."

Margaret raised her brows, waiting for him to continue, not seeing anything too strange about the picture he'd painted thus far. "Who's Buck?"

"Sorry, ma'am. Buck's my dog, and you see, he don't like strangers. No sir. I mean, no, ma'am." He blushed and dropped his head, then raised it again with a sheepish grin. "He'd as like to bite a strange man as lick his hand. That boy is near as big as a man, even if his mind is more like a child's. I think Buck sensed that, you know? Buck let Joel come through the gate and waller all over him. The girl— Samantha's her name—was restin' against a tree when I come, with her eyes closed and lookin' all tuckered out. She jumped up when she seen me, as spooked as a young colt on prairie grass. But she has backbone, that one. She didn't bolt—stood her ground even though it was plain she was scared all the way to her toes."

"Scared of what, Mr. Gibbs? You or the dog?"

"I'm not rightly sure, ma'am. She wouldn't tell me. Joel said their last name is McGavin, and they've been livin' in a barn. I think they've been sneakin' food from people's kitchens when they're at work. Joel speaks without thinkin' and said more than his sister would like. I took them in and fed them, but scant more information came out. I think they're on the run, but they won't say who, or why. They been in town nigh on to two weeks and they're dirty, tired, and sick of bread and cheese. They need someone to care for 'em."

She'd taken in all he'd shared without blinking, but at those last words she sat back in her chair. "May I ask why you brought them here?"

He shrugged and ducked his head again. "Didn't know where else to bring 'em." A worried look crossed his face. "I don't have a wife to take on the care of two young'uns, although I'll be gettin' married next spring. Not that I wouldn't be willin', but I dasn't—the girl's too old to be livin' with a bachelor. I figured you bein' a woman, and a teacher and all…"

Margaret leaned forward. "I can't keep two children, especially a big boy like Joel. People wouldn't understand, me being single and all."

"I'm not suggestin' you keep 'em permanent, Miss Garvey. Maybe just for a couple of days, until we can find out where they belong? I'm thinkin' the girl might warm up to a woman and tell you what they're runnin' from. Or you might be able to find a family to take them in."

Margaret sat back hard in her chair. Her eyes took in the two huddled in the corner. They'd finished the cookies and milk, and the big boy was hunkered down with his head on his sister's shoulder. Suddenly the girl raised her eyes, and the hopelessness and fear Margaret saw felt like a knife shoved into her rib cage. How could a child carry that kind of pain?

"All right." She pushed back her chair, suddenly certain of what she must do. She'd felt abandoned more than once in her life. First, when her mother died, then by Nathaniel, and she couldn't tolerate the thought of being the cause of yet another rejection foisted on these helpless youngsters. "They can stay for now, and I'll see what I can do."

Mr. Gibbs' face lit up and he started to rise, but Margaret held up her hand and waved him back down. "Please. I'm not finished." She waited until he sank back into his chair. "I'll need your help. I know nothing about the needs of a boy this age, especially one who's—" she hesitated and dropped her voice—"special. Would you agree to come get him every day or two, to see to his…personal needs?" She dropped her gaze to her hands and rushed on. "And talk to him about anything you deem fitting?"

"Yes, ma'am. I can do that. I promised Joel he could come play with my dog, so I'm guessin' he'll be happy to oblige. Not sure the sister's goin' to let him go off with me willingly, though. She seems pretty protective."

Margaret nodded. "You may be right, but we'll deal with that when the time comes." She rose and stepped toward the door. "I won't keep you. Have a good day, Mr. Gibbs."

Mr. Gibbs rose and reached for the hat he'd laid on the floor. "Guess I should be gettin' along. Thank you, ma'am." He nodded at the two silent youngsters. "I'll be back to visit, and you can come see Buck soon." Mr. Gibbs smiled reassuringly and clomped out the door.

Margaret sank into her chair, draped her arm along its back, and stared at her two young charges. What had she gotten herself into?

* * *

Margaret wiped the flour from her hands and slid the deep-dish apple pie into the oven. Samantha and Joel were outside exploring the area around the cabin while she finished supper preparations. She'd been longing to unpack a box of Papa's papers and get his desk in order but hadn't had sufficient time to give it proper attention. It would take almost an hour for the pie to bake. She leaned over the sink and looked out the window. It appeared that Samantha and Joel were occupied building a stick-and-cone fort under the branches of a drooping hemlock tree, so this might be the perfect time.

She'd been dismayed that the ladies from church had packed the things from Papa's desk before she'd had a chance to go through it, but then realized they may have wanted to save her the heartache right on the heels of his passing. In fact, she'd not been able to bring herself to look too closely in the box since arriving at her new home, but the deep grief had started to lift, and she felt able to face his personal notes without flinching.

His heavy oak desk stood in a corner of her bedroom and the box lay alongside. She removed the blanket she'd draped over the top and sat down on the braid rug, tucking her skirt around her ankles. Account ledgers and three leather-bound journals were on top, and she moved those to the side. Somehow she didn't think she wanted to read his journals right now—maybe some evening after Samantha and Joel were in bed she'd take the time to absorb what he'd recorded. A stack of letters and opened envelopes came next, and she scooped those to the side, then paused. It might be good to make sure that nothing had gone unanswered.

The first stack brought a smile to her face—they were tied with a faded blue ribbon and looked as though they'd been handled more than the rest. Her mother's letters that Papa had saved, written prior to their marriage. She placed those in her lap—they'd go into her chest of drawers. She flipped through the remaining stack until she reached the bottom. What was this? Her hand stilled over the clean envelope bearing her name. Papa left something for her? Her breathing quickened, and her fingers trembled. She should have gone through this box weeks ago.

She tore off the end and shook out the folded paper inside. Her eyes scanned the date—just two weeks prior to his death. Why hadn't he given it to her, and why write instead of speaking to her personally?

My darling girl—if you've found this letter, then what I feared has come to pass. I've been feeling poorly for a while now but didn't want to worry you. On my last trip to Portland I took time to see a doctor, and he informed me I may have a bad heart. I've been having some chest pain, but he doesn't think it's serious yet. I have an uneasy feeling that I may not be around to see you married and have been concerned about your future.

I'm so pleased that Andrew Browning has been coming to visit and am hoping you might be pleased, as well. I've asked Andrew to look out for you, in the event something happens to me. I know he's interested in you on his own behalf, or I'd not have asked him, so please don't be angry. He's a good man, Margaret, and he'd make a fine husband. I know you've been upset about Nathaniel Cooper leaving town years ago, and I'm praying you've finally put it behind you. He wasn't a good match—not being a believer, and a drifter, to boot. I don't believe he'd ever have settled down in one place for long, and he'd hardened his heart where the gospel was concerned.

Please give Andrew a chance? I'm begging you as a father who cares about his little girl—yes, I know you're a woman now, but you'll always be my baby. Don't let an old memory from your childhood come between you and what could be

God's best for your life. Know that I love you, and I'm sorry
for any pain that I may have caused you where Cooper was
concerned, but I did what I thought best for you at the time.
    Your loving Papa

Margaret felt tears slipping down her cheeks and blinked, not realizing she'd been crying. Papa had asked Andrew to look out for her? What—had he come right out and said Andrew should marry her, the way it implied? Her numb fingers refused to hold the single sheet of paper any longer, and it drifted to the floor and slid a few inches away. Had Andrew been coming around because Papa convinced him it was the right thing to do? And what did Papa mean— he'd done what he thought best at the time? She shook her head, barely able to take in the concept. Papa had gone too far this time. How could he interfere in such a way? It was bad enough that he'd stood against her when she'd been in love with Nathaniel, but to try and orchestrate her entire future? That was too much.

She jumped to her feet and bent over to snatch up the letter. The pie must be close to browning, and Samantha and Joel needed checking on. This would have to wait for a quiet time when she could ponder it alone, without interruption. But one thing she knew for sure—she'd no longer take Andrew's interest or seeming desire to court her at face value. He'd have to prove himself before she'd trust that his desire came from his own heart and not just out of a sense of duty to her dead father.

Chapter Fourteen

....

It was the long-awaited Friday. Andrew Browning had hurried home from work, scrubbed himself clean, and dressed in his best. Now he tucked in his shirttail and then tried to smooth down his hair. Why God saw fit to give him dimples and let him inherit his mother's curls, he'd never understand. He'd shave his hair short if Margaret hadn't said one time how lucky he was to have such a fine head of curls. Fine head of curls, indeed. But if she liked it, that was all that mattered. He couldn't believe his good fortune that a girl like her would look at him twice, much less attend the ice-cream social with him this evening. He pulled out his pocket watch, took a look, and stuffed it back into his trousers. Time to get a move on or he'd be late.

No need for a wagon today with the sun still shining and fluffy clouds dancing their way across a bright blue sky. That's exactly what he felt like doing—dancing. He'd been intrigued by Margaret since moving to Bridal Veil two years ago but never had the nerve to approach her until he'd started working with her father. Mr. Garvey hadn't seemed to mind him stopping by occasionally. Besides, they both loved to play chess, and the older man had invited him over the first time with an eagerness that implied a bit of loneliness. Their friendship had just started to form when Mr. Garvey had passed away close to two months ago. Andrew felt blessed that he'd gotten a chance to know Margaret's father, and that the man hadn't seemed averse to him courting his daughter.

He ran down the three steps leading to his porch and bounded across the small front yard. A light breeze blew through the maple and cottonwood trees lining the path, casting a welcome shade. Rain had been scanty this summer, and the brush was beginning to get dry. Thank the Lord for the nearby Columbia River.

His footsteps slowed as he came within sight of Margaret's cabin, and he glanced down at his clothes. Dark plaid, long-sleeved cotton shirt and corduroy trousers were neat and clean even if he wasn't the best hand with an iron. At least he wouldn't embarrass her. Hopefully she'd be pleased that he'd dressed up a bit, as she was used to seeing him in his everyday working garb. He prayed he had a chance to win Margaret's heart. She was everything he'd dreamed of in a woman—intelligent, beautiful, a sparkling sense of humor, and giving to a fault.

A quick rap brought footsteps hurrying to the other side of her door. It swung partway open and Margaret stood there, worried eyes peering out of a flushed face. "Andrew. It's good to see you, but I'm not certain I can come." She didn't step out of the way or invite him inside. Instead, she shot a glance over her shoulder, then closed the door several more inches.

Andrew raised his brows. "What's wrong? Are you ill?"

She shook her head. "No. I'm fine. It's just…" A boy's loud cry behind her made her jump and turn away. "Joel. Are you all right?" She hurried inside, leaving the door ajar.

Andrew stood on the porch, uncertain how to proceed. Soft voices drifted out from the small house, but Margaret didn't return. He gripped the edge of the half open door and opened it another foot, then stepped across the threshold. A young man nearly his size sat on the floor gripping his knee and rocking back and forth. Margaret and a slender wisp of a girl with dark blond hair gathered back in a neat braid leaned over the boy, patting his back.

Andrew closed the door and took a step toward the trio. "Margaret? Is something wrong?"

Margaret's head came up with a start. A blush flooded her cheeks, and her eyes darted from Andrew to the young man she'd called Joel, and back again. Just as quickly her expression cleared, and she stood and smiled. "Andrew I'd like you to meet Joel McGavin and his sister, Samantha. They're staying with me for now."

Andrew leaned over and extended his hand to the boy sitting on the floor. "Nice to meet you."

Joel simply stared at his hand and smiled but didn't move or reply.

The young girl patted Joel's head and met Andrew's inquiring eyes. "He's not used to shaking hands. I don't think anyone's ever offered to do that before." She turned to Joel and gripped his hand. "Come on, stand up. Your knee is fine. You're a big boy, Joel."

He allowed her to pull him to his feet and grinned at Andrew. "I'm not hurt anymore. I banged my knee, but I didn't cry."

Andrew smiled at the boy held captive in a man-sized body. "I'll bet your sister is proud of you."

Joel's eyes sparkled, and he nodded eagerly. "Yep. Sammie loves me. Huh, Sammie?" He swiveled to the girl standing beside him.

She let out a long breath as though she'd been holding it for Andrew's answer. The girl looked young, barely in her teens. Her face glowed as though it had been recently scrubbed, and she wore a dress that was a little too big, but neat and clean. "Yes, I do. I love you just the way you are." The grateful look she cast Andrew revealed the worry she must carry on an ongoing basis for her oversized but gentle brother. She held out her hand. "I'm Samantha, and I'm pleased to meet you, sir."

Andrew met the hand, keeping his face carefully serious. "I'm Andrew Browning. Are you related to Miss Garvey?"

Samantha shook her head and withdrew her hand after a quick squeeze. "No. We're just passing through, trying to find our kin."

Margaret patted Samantha's shoulder and motioned to Andrew. "Would you mind stepping outside for a minute?" She led him back out the door and drew it gently closed behind her. They stepped off the porch and down the path to a fallen log lying in a small clearing, braced with one end still sitting on the broken stump. White daisies with yellow centers grew near where the top of the tree had hit the ground, and Margaret settled onto a smooth part of the tree trunk near the flowers. "I'd like to explain and ask your advice. Would you sit for a moment?"

"Certainly." Andrew took a seat several feet away. "I've never seen those youngsters in town before. They said they're searching for their family?"

Margaret raised one shoulder. "I'm not sure what to think. Art Gibbs, a new teamster in town, brought them over a couple of days ago when he found them in his yard playing with his dog. They were quite ragged and dirty before I gave them baths and found them some clothing. Joel let slip that they were hungry and had been living in a barn. Nothing was said about trying to find family until I started questioning them. Joel doesn't say a lot, mostly due to Samantha making sure she answers first. But he's said enough for me to get an idea of what's going on."

Andrew nodded. "I'm guessing they're runaways."

"I think they could be. Samantha is only willing to say their parents are dead, and that they're trying to find a relative who might be living in Oregon. She won't say where they've been living or how long since her parents died. I'm hoping to win her trust so she'll open up and I can help."

Andrew's eyebrows rose. "You're planning on keeping them? You don't have much room for two extra bodies in this cabin, and I can only guess what the schoolboard will say."

"I've thought of that as well." Margaret paused and stared back toward her home.

Andrew stroked his chin, unsure what to suggest. Margaret was a grown woman, after all. Joel appeared harmless enough, with a sweet, simple mind—but how many people in town would understand or agree with her taking in a boy who was nearly the size of a man—her being single and all? Of course, there was the sister as chaperone, but she was just a child, and tongues could still wag.

He leaned toward her, not wanting to startle her. "Margaret?"

She turned her head, a bemused expression in her eyes. "Sorry. Just thinking on what's best."

"If there's anything I can do?"

She smiled and stood. "Thank you. It's a help knowing you're not pushing me to send them away. I don't see how I can attend the ice-cream social with two strange children in my home."

"Bring them along." Andrew spoke almost without thinking, but he suddenly knew it was the right thing. "Kids love ice cream, and I'll bet they'd like to come. You can't keep them cooped up in your house forever."

"But what will I tell people?" She appeared to be considering it, but worry still creased her forehead.

"Just say they're visiting from out of town. Right now, that's the truth. You don't know any more than that, and who knows? They may be telling the truth about trying to find a relative. You can question them more after you get home tonight. Taking them for ice cream might be just what you need to gain their trust."

She nodded. "I think I will. You're sure you don't mind them coming with us?"

Andrew drew in a short breath. All this time he'd been trying to help Margaret solve her immediate problem, not stopping to think how it would impact the rest of their evening. He'd so looked forward to some time alone with Margaret, and now they'd have two youngsters with them. "I'm sure." He decided with a rush and knew he'd made a good choice when the last vestiges of worry fell away from her pretty face.

She touched his arm, and her smile reached her eyes. "Thank you. We'd better let them know, and I need to change into something a little nicer than this." She ran her hand down the front of her long cotton skirt. "It's not really suited to a social gathering. I'll just need a minute."

"Of course." He stood and walked her to the cabin, his heart lighter than it had been minutes before. *We*, he thought. She could just as easily have relegated him to the outside of the circle, but she'd included him in the next step. Children or not, he was taking Margaret Garvey to the ice-cream social, and nothing would mar this evening.

* * *

Margaret walked beside Andrew with her heart pounding against her rib cage, and not just due to her attraction to Andrew. Not that she didn't like him—that was part of the problem. She did, and she wasn't sure what to do with her feelings after finding her father's letter. Andrew had been kind and attentive, but no more so than any man who'd made a promise to look after another man's daughter. She'd been hurt by Nathaniel in the past, and she'd have to guard her heart from future injury by Andrew, as well.

Then there was the problem of Nathaniel Cooper. Her emotions had been topsy-turvy since her eyes had met his that Sunday morning in church. He'd probably attend the ice-cream social. She gave herself a hard mental shake. What did it matter if he did, for goodness' sake? He wasn't part of her life anymore. She'd simply treat him as she would any old acquaintance and move on with her life.

She hazarded a peek at Andrew, who'd fallen silent. She couldn't blame him. Her answers had been short and distracted—certainly not what they should be for a young woman being escorted on her first outing with a young man. Then there were the children—another spoke in the wheel of her already complicated life. Not for a minute did she believe they were simply hunting for a relative. They were runaways, frightened of something in their past.

Joel and Samantha lagged behind. Samantha's voice broke the silence. "Can't we stay at your house alone? We won't be no trouble there, I promise."

Margaret expelled a soft sigh. They'd already had this discussion at her cabin, and she thought they'd settled it. She turned to glance over her shoulder. "No, I'm sorry. I don't feel good about doing that. There's nothing to worry about. It's just a small group of townspeople, and you'll have a good time. Joel, Mr. Gibbs said you can visit Buck tomorrow if you'd like."

The boy's face brightened, and he quickened his step. "Is Buck comin' today? Can I play with him there?"

Samantha answered before Margaret had a chance. "No, dogs don't eat ice cream. Or do they, Miss Margaret?"

Margaret tried to hide her delight at the more familiar use of her name. The girl had been standoffish for the past forty-eight hours, but it appeared she was starting to relax. "I don't know. Cats like cream and milk, and I imagine they'd like melted ice cream, so maybe a dog would too. But Mr. Gibbs said Buck isn't friendly with strangers, so I imagine he'll leave him at home."

The boy's face fell, and his feet dragged. "Aw, shucks. He was friendly to me. I could a'kept him happy."

Andrew slowed his pace and allowed the two children to catch up. "I'll bet you could, Joel." He paused a beat. "Did you have a dog at your last home?"

"Naw. Mrs. St…"

Samantha jabbed him in the side with her elbow.

"Ouch." He rubbed the spot on his side and frowned. "What'd you do that for, Sammie? I was just going to tell 'em about where we lived."

Samantha stopped on the trail and grabbed his arm, bringing him to a halt, her loud, sibilant whisper still reaching Margaret's ears. "We're not answering any questions, Joel. I told you that before. Not about where we used to live, or anything."

He scuffed his toe in the dirt and dropped his gaze to the ground. "Aw, golly. I plumb forgot. I'm sorry." He raised hopeful eyes to hers. "Can I tell them we didn't have a dog?"

She rolled her eyes and smiled. "Yes, but that's it. It's nobody else's business where we came from or what we're doing." She stared at Andrew and Margaret, who'd stopped a little ways ahead, and raised her voice. "We're beholden to you for your help and hospitality, but we can't be telling you nothing."

Andrew took a step toward her and reached out his hand, then dropped his arm to his side when Samantha pulled away. "Why not? Miss Margaret is trying to help you. Can't you trust her?"

Samantha stubbornly crossed her arms over her chest. "No sir. Can't trust no one. We dasn't. Sorry, ma'am, no disrespect meant, but we won't go back."

Margaret took a step closer to the pair. "Did you run away from your last home?"

The long braid whipped around her shoulders at the hard shake of her head. "I ain't saying, but I'm not going to let anyone hurt my brother, no matter what."

Andrew's brows rose and he glanced at Margaret, then back at Samantha. "Did someone hurt you or your brother? If so, we might be able to help."

The girl shook her head. "No one can help. I'm not saying another word about it, and I'd be beholden to you if you didn't pry."

Margaret sighed, but nodded. "I'll try to respect your wishes, Samantha, but I can't stand back and do nothing if I find you're in danger."

"We're not. So do we have to go inside at this ice-cream society, or whatever you call it, or can Joel and I sit outside and wait for you?"

Joel dropped the wood knot he'd been examining and snapped to attention. "Aww, Sammie, I want to go! Please, Sammie! I ain't never had ice cream." He clutched her arm and looked down at her with eyes that pleaded.

"All right. I don't think we should, but we'll go this one time." Samantha rounded on Margaret and Andrew and dropped her voice. "But I'll ask you not to be talking about us to folks. Don't want people whispering things, or snooping. If anyone asks, just tell 'em we're on the way to our great-aunt's house."

Margaret cast a look at Andrew. "Remember, it's only normal for people to be curious about strangers who come to our little town."

"Can't you just tell them we're kin? You won't be saying we've run away or anything, will you?" Her dark eyes widened, and moisture gathered in the corners, threatening to spill over.

Margaret hesitated, her heart doing a dance with her honesty, and each trouncing on the other's toes as her eyes continued to stare into the big brown ones of the slender girl looking up at her. What had this child gone through in her short thirteen years of life? All she'd been willing to share was that her parents were dead and that she was seeking some unknown relatives that could live somewhere in Oregon.

She glanced at Joel, who'd gone back to studying the knot he'd found on the trail as soon as Samantha had assured him his ice cream was safe. The boy's appearance belied his sweet nature. Not that he would scare anyone, but standing near five-foot-seven inches tall, he was as big and nearly as husky as some men, and as simpleminded as a six-year-old. How long had his younger sister watched over him and what kind of toll had it taken on the girl's emotions? Sure, some girls were working full-time at thirteen to help support their family, but the responsibility for Joel's care must be just as difficult. She'd have had to grow up pretty fast if her parents had been dead for more than a couple of years. No wonder she seemed wise beyond her years and afraid to trust.

Margaret made a quick decision. "I won't lie about it, but I'll do my best to steer the conversation away from anything that might embarrass you. All I ask is that you try to trust me, Samantha. I want to help you, but it's going to be hard if you can't be honest with me."

Samantha gave a half shrug and dropped her gaze to the path, then raised her eyes and met Margaret's. "I'll try. I can't promise how much I can tell you, but I won't lie to you, either."

"Fair enough. Now let's go have some fun and see how much ice cream we can eat, shall we?" Margaret looped her arm through Samantha's and reached out her hand for Joel. He eagerly placed his large palm over hers and squeezed, then extended his other toward Andrew, who gripped it and grinned at the boy. It was nice to see Joel happy and excited. They'd probably had little opportunity in their short lives for much celebrating.

Samantha pressed close to Margaret's side and gripped her hand. Margaret smiled, pleased she seemed as anxious as her brother to attend, but a glance at the girl caused her heart to plummet. Samantha's pinched, anxious face peered out from under her arm.

BRIDAL VEIL 1902 OREG

Chapter Fifteen
....

Nathaniel stood on the outskirts of the milling people hovering around the tables inside the Methodist church that still doubled as the community gathering place for socials, weddings, and such. He didn't care as much for the ice cream as he did watching and listening. Two things interested him today—seeing if Margaret appeared on the arm of Andrew Browning, and listening for any whispers that might give him clues to Martin Jenkins' demise. The doctor had confirmed that a hard blow to the man's head had caused his death, and it was doubtful it came from his fall.

He'd been instructed by his boss to contact the sheriff of Multno-mah County, and the man was due to stop by any day. That was one of the drawbacks to a mill-owned town—there was no local law enforcement, no mayor, no city council—just the man or company who owned the land that the mill and houses sat on. Oftentimes that man didn't care a whit about what went on in his town, as long as it didn't interfere with his money-making venture. Thankfully, that wasn't the case with Mr. Palmer, or his company. He had a reputation as a caring man who looked out for his business as well as his workers, both at the lower Bridal Veil planer mill and the upper Palmer sawmill, as well.

So Nathaniel would keep his ears tuned for any careless words dropped that might implicate one of the men, and keep an especially sharp eye on Andrew Browning and Donnie Williams, both prime suspects in his estimation. His inclination was to lean toward

Browning, but his innate fairness warned him that could be due to Margaret's apparent interest in the man.

A young, fair-haired woman passed by and glanced at him with a smile, then drew to a stop. "Aren't you Nathaniel Cooper? You used to live here a number of years back?"

Her face looked only vaguely familiar. He searched for a name but came up empty. "Yes, ma'am, that I would be."

"I'm Clara White, a friend of Margaret Garvey's." Dimples touched the corner of her cheeks when she smiled, and her eyes lit with warm mirth.

He gave a small bow and returned her smile. "It's a pleasure to meet you, ma'am. Do you know if Miss Garvey is attending tonight?" As soon as the words escaped, he wished he could yank them back. What a fool he was, still pining over a woman who'd lost interest in him years ago.

"I believe she is." She glanced over his shoulder. "In fact, here she is now." She raised her hand and beckoned. "Margaret, Andrew, come over for a moment?"

Nathaniel stifled a groan and closed his eyes, then squared his shoulders and turned. His heart missed a couple of beats as he caught sight of Margaret gliding across the floor toward them, her dark blue skirt swaying from trim hips. Her red gold hair was drawn back at the nape of her neck and curls lay across her shoulder. She wore a white blouse with pearl buttons up the front, trimmed lavishly with lace at the throat and wrists and down the front on each side of the buttons. She looked even more beautiful than she had the Sunday he'd seen her at church. Then his gaze traveled back to her face, and the expression he saw gave him a start. There was no smile, no light in her eyes, and it seemed as though all the color had drained from her cheeks.

Clara took a quick step forward and hugged Margaret, whispering something in her ear. Margaret shook her head and avoided Nathaniel's gaze, saying something in a low voice to the young woman who linked arms and walked beside her.

Nathaniel suddenly noticed her small entourage. Andrew Browning walked to Margaret's left, and two teenage children were close behind. The girl was slight and still wearing short skirts, with the boy a little taller than Margaret and huskily built, his dark hair nearly covered with a hat. None of the trio smiled, and Nathaniel glimpsed Clara White looking from Margaret to Andrew. He didn't care to be the subject of gossip, whatever the case. He'd get through the next few minutes and head back home.

He extended his hand toward Andrew. "Browning, good to see you again."

Andrew gripped the other man's calloused hand, giving it a firm shake. "Same to you. Have you met Miss Garvey?" Andrew turned toward Margaret and smiled.

Nathaniel forced a smile. "Yes, I've had the pleasure. We knew one another some years ago, when I resided in Bridal Veil." He extended his hand. "How do you do, Miss Garvey? You're looking well."

She allowed him to grip her fingertips for only a second before tucking her hand behind her back. "Thank you, Mr. Cooper. I was surprised you returned to our small town, after such a long absence."

He narrowed his eyes, wondering at the words that seemed to hold a double meaning but were delivered in such a sweet tone.

"I was offered a job here." He turned his attention to the children lagging behind. "Are these friends of yours?"

"They are." She held out her hand to the slender young girl. "This is Samantha McGavin and her brother, Joel. They're visiting Bridal Veil for a while and staying with me." She swung back toward Clara, who'd slipped to the back of the small group, and beckoned her forward. "You've met my friend, Clara White?"

Nathaniel nodded and smiled. "I had the pleasure." He then glanced at the large boy and frowned. "With you? That seems a bit—unconventional." His gaze traveled from her to Andrew and back. "Or at least—forgive me if I assumed…"

Margaret blushed and shook her head. "I'm single, Mr. Cooper. Mr. Browning and I are friends."

Something passed across Andrew Browning's face, then swiftly disappeared, but Nathaniel was sure he'd seen mild disappointment mirrored there for that brief moment.

Margaret slipped her arm through Clara's again. "Can you join us?"

The young woman shook her head and squeezed Margaret's hand. "I'm sorry, but not tonight. I was headed over to get a bowl of ice cream for Mama." She inclined her head toward a wall where a diminutive woman wearing a black dress sat ramrod stiff in a hard-backed chair. "I don't want her to tire. Maybe I'll have a chance to visit with you a bit later."

"I'd like that." Margaret hugged her friend, then turned back toward Nathaniel. She grasped the dark blue fabric of her skirt and lifted it an inch or two from the floor and gave a slight curtsy. "You'll have to excuse us, Mr. Cooper. The children are excited about the ice cream and I hate to make them wait."

"Certainly, have a good evening." He reached up and stroked his mustache as he watched Margaret walk away, then turned his attention to Andrew Browning's rigid back and taut shoulders as he walked beside her. He grunted low in his chest. The man didn't have anything to worry about on his account. Margaret wouldn't give him the time of day.

Chapter Sixteen

. . . .

Andrew couldn't seem to concentrate on anything around him. Nathaniel Cooper and Margaret had known one another years before? What kind of relationship had they enjoyed? He'd seen the interest in the other man's eyes when he spoke to Margaret.

A large woman settled her bulk onto the bench beside Andrew and placed her bowl down with a thunk. "How do, Mr. Browning?"

Andrew tried not to sigh. Mrs. Hearn was a kind soul, but she loved knowing everyone's business. "Doing well, and you?"

"Fair to middlin'." She dipped her spoon into her bowl and took a large bite. "Hope I'm not disturbin' you folks, but my feet are killin' me and I need to sit for a spell." She nodded across the table at Margaret. "Miss Garvey, you're lookin' mighty appealin' this evening."

Margaret's eyes lit with pleasure. "Thank you, Mrs. Hearn. Did Arny or your mother come with you?"

"Nope. I left Mama restin' in bed and Arny sittin' at home on the front porch with his pipe between his teeth and his feet in a pot of hot water—he's been tuckered out the past couple of days. Besides, gettin' Arny someplace with this many people is about as hard as givin' a bath to a bobcat." She chuckled and scooped up a large spoon of ice cream. "Told him to go to bed early. Don't want him comin' down with the grippe."

"No ma'am, that wouldn't be good. I hope he feels better soon."

Mrs. Hearn straightened her spine and swiveled toward Samantha. "Who's this pretty little girl, Margaret? She kin of yours? Don't believe I've seen her in town before."

Samantha shrank in her seat and shot a look at Margaret.

"No, she and her brother, Joel, are friends of mine." Margaret patted the young girl's arm, and Samantha scooted over closer to her. "This is Samantha McGavin. They're staying with me for a while."

"Humph." Mrs. Hearn peered around behind Andrew at Joel and appeared to take the boy's measure with a long, silent stare. "Looks to be a big boy. How old is he?"

Samantha drew away from Margaret and broke her silence. "He's fourteen, and he's a good boy."

Andrew stared at Samantha, then over at Mrs. Hearn. Maybe he'd best step in. It appeared Margaret's young visitor had some prickles popping up. "I don't think…"

Mrs. Hearn took another large bite, swallowed, and nodded. "Didn't say he wasn't, young lady, I simply asked his age." Her mellow voice went up a notch and effectively covered Andrew's comment.

He swung back toward Samantha, wondering how she'd take this light rebuke.

Samantha settled back and dropped her head. "Sorry."

"Now don't get your feelin's hurt, darlin', I didn't mean anythin'. I'm sure your brother's a fine lad, and we're happy to have both of you in our town. How long did you say you were stayin'?"

Joel poked a spoonful of vanilla ice cream into his mouth. "How'd they make this ice cream?" His words pulled everyone's attention from Mrs. Hearn's question.

Andrew set his half-full bowl on the table and released the breath he'd been holding. "They use an ice-cream freezer with a crank, thick fresh cream, ice, and rock salt. It's kind of hard to explain, but it sure tastes good, doesn't it?"

Samantha's spoon scraped the bottom of her bowl. "It's awful good. But where do they get ice in the summertime?"

Margaret leaned across the wooden table. "I can answer that, as I've seen where it comes from. In fact, when I was small, my father used to take me to Sand Island to watch men cut the ice out in the summer."

Mrs. Hearn dropped her spoon into her empty bowl with a clatter and pushed back her chair. "I'm sorry to interrupt, young lady, but I'd best be gettin' on home to my Arny, 'fore he falls asleep on the porch." She nodded to Margaret and Andrew. "Have yourselves a lovely evening."

"Yes, ma'am," both Margaret and Andrew echoed at the same time.

Andrew stood and tipped his head. "Tell Arny hello for me, as well."

She nodded. "I'll do that. Good night."

They watched her plod across the room and place her bowl and spoon on a table, then head toward the door.

Andrew met Margaret's eyes across the table and whispered, "Saved by good old Arny."

Margaret stifled a giggle and glanced to her right at Samantha, who sat with head lowered, staring into her bowl.

Joel licked his spoon. "What's Sand Island, and why does it have ice?"

Margaret jumped in her seat, then smiled. "Oh, Joel, I'd almost forgotten what we'd been talking about. Sand Island lies just down the river from Bridal Veil, a few yards offshore. It's a fine place to play in the summertime, but in the winter, when the snow is deep, we often get a lot of cold wind that blows across the river and turns the snow to ice. The wind does something else—it covers the ice with sand and keeps the ice from melting."

Joel cocked his head to the side and twisted his mouth. "I walked on sand in the summer one time and it burned my feet." He shook his head. "I don't think sand can keep ice cold."

Andrew grinned. "Do you have a winter coat?"

"Yes, but the sleeves are too short and the shoulder is torn."

"Well, maybe before next winter we can find you a better one." He leaned forward and grabbed a napkin and folded it several times. "See this napkin? Pretend it's the snow and the sand. A winter coat is kind of like the sand, only the coat keeps you warm and the sand helps keep the ice cold. Over the winter several layers of sand and ice build on top of each other, and the ice doesn't have a chance to melt."

Samantha's eyes widened. "So you mean if we went out there right now, we could dig through the sand and find ice?"

"Yep, if you dug in the right spots and went deep enough, you might."

"I've never had ice cream before. When we lived with Mrs. Stedman, she never let us…" Her face turned pale, and she jumped to her feet. "Come on, Joel, we need to go."

"But I ain't finished my ice cream yet, Sammie." He waved his spoon in the air and whimpered. "I don't want to go nowhere."

Margaret got up from her place at the table and came around to stand beside the girl, pulling her back down to her seat. "You can trust us, Sammie. You can take Joel and keep running, if that's what you think is best, or you can stay here with me. Andrew and I will help if you decide to stay, but it's up to you."

"I haven't trusted anyone in a long time. Not since Mama died." Samantha swiped at her eyes. "It's so hard."

Margaret gently slipped her arm around the trembling shoulders. "I know, honey, but I care about you, and we can ask God for His help as well."

Samantha's head came up. "You believe God hears you when you talk to Him?"

Margaret nodded. "I do."

"As do I," Andrew agreed.

Samantha raised wet eyes to meet Margaret's. "Do you believe He talks to you?"

"God speaks to us through His Word, the Bible."

Samantha shook her head. "No. I mean, talks to you, but it comes from in here somewhere." She tapped a finger against her chest. "And it's not make-believe, either," she ended on a defiant note. "I've heard Him, and He saved me when we first got here."

Andrew raised his brows and leaned his forearms on the table. "Saved you from what, Sammie?"

She glanced at Joel, who didn't seem aware of their conversation, and lowered her voice. "From some bad men who followed me into the woods when I went looking for food. Joel was asleep at the barn, and some hobos riding the train saw me." A shiver coursed through her body and she trembled. "I was so scared, and I didn't know what to do. God spoke to me. He told me where to go and showed me a place to hide."

Margaret looked at Andrew, and he shrugged.

Sammie's voice raised a notch, and she crossed her arms over her chest. "I ain't lying. I heard Him. Those men were out to get me. Don't know what would a'happened to Joel if they'd taken me with them."

Andrew sat up straight and met her eyes. "What do you mean, took you with them?"

"I heard them talking. One of 'em said the law was after 'em, and they'd have to hightail it out of town when the train left. The other said he wanted to catch me and take me with them. He said I was a pretty little thing, and they might not find another girl for a while."

Andrew banged his fist in his open palm, and Sammie jumped. "I'm sorry." Andrew laid his hands on the table. "You said they were riding the train, and they said the law was after them? Did you hear anything else?"

Sammie thought for a moment and started to shake her head, then paused. "Something about crossing over into Washington to be safe, but I'm not sure. They were going to get back on the train."

"Do you remember what day that happened?" Andrew had a feeling he knew what might be coming, but he hoped Sammie might confirm his belief.

"I'm not sure." She reached into a deep pocket on her dress and took out a small book. "Just a minute." She turned a couple of pages, frowned at the book, and closed it. "I think it was on a Saturday, a week ago today, maybe? I kept track of the food—" her voice faltered, then she raised worried eyes—"that we took from people's kitchens.

BRIDAL VEIL
1902
ORE.

I tried to write down something about their house and what day I thought it was, and what we took. Close as I can figure, it was Friday or Saturday."

Andrew turned to Margaret. "Let's see if there's any more ice cream, shall we?" He took her hand, helped her up, and guided her away from the table. He dropped his voice. "You know what that means, don't you?"

Her eyes widened. "Martin Jenkins."

Andrew started to reply, then noted the intent look on Samantha's face. "Samantha, would you mind taking Joel over to the washbasin by the back door and help him clean up? It looks like he's spilled a little ice cream on his shirt."

She looked at her brother, sticky residue on his cheeks and chin. "All right. Come on, Joel." They pushed back their chairs and walked hand-in-hand away from the table.

Andrew felt a surge of relief. That little girl was too sharp to miss much. He turned back to Margaret. "I'm going to tell Cooper about this, since he'll be talking to the sheriff soon." He took a step, but she reached out and grasped his arm.

"Are you sure you should, Andrew? I mean, we don't have any proof and—" Margaret bit her lip. "It might require that Sammie talk to the sheriff."

"What's wrong with that?"

She shrugged. "Sammie is just beginning to trust us. If you bring over a stranger who starts digging, she might take Joel and run again."

Andrew groaned and rolled his eyes. "Yeah." He sighed and shook his head. "We can't just ignore it, though. Those two men might have killed Jenkins, not to mention scaring a young girl."

"I know, but she said they got back on the train and headed across the state line. They're probably long gone by now. What's it going to accomplish when they've been gone for a week?"

"I don't know, but it doesn't seem right not to say anything. They could be dangerous, and if the law's after them, the sheriff needs to know what direction they took."

Her eyes searched his face. "But we don't even know their names or where they came from. There are probably dozens of men the law is looking for, and many of them could be riding the rails. How will they spot those two?"

His resolve weakened as her eyes continued to plead. Why did she have to be so beautiful, sweet, and persuasive? Not to mention having a tender heart that wanted nothing more than to protect the two innocent children under her care. "All right, we won't say anything tonight." He quickly held up a hand. "But I'm going to think on it, and we should make a decision tomorrow. I'm not convinced we should keep this a secret—but I suppose one more night won't make much difference, seeing how long it's already been."

She squeezed his hand, and this time a real smile broke the solemnity of her features. "Thank you, Andrew. You're a good friend, you know that?"

He groaned inwardly. A good friend. Was that all? He wanted so much more. He sighed and squeezed her hand in return. "I'm glad you think so."

Maybe he should be thankful for that much. At least she didn't seem to have eyes for anyone else. He'd keep trying and pray that someday her heart would return the deep devotion he felt for her.

* * *

Saturday morning Margaret woke to soft beams of sunlight tickling her eyelids and whiffling snores from Joel drifting through her closed door. At least, she assumed it was Joel—surely a little scrap of a girl like Samantha couldn't produce sounds like that. She grabbed the edge of her quilt to toss it back and paused. The children were still sleeping, and she needed time to think. Confusing dreams had troubled her in the wee hours and still trounced through her thoughts.

Nathaniel's appearance at the social yesterday evening must have stirred the unease in her spirit and caused the disturbing images. She snuggled back into her down pillow and sighed. Another minute or two of peace before attending to the children's needs sounded good. It had been too many days since she'd taken quiet time with her Lord at the start of her day. Samantha's question about hearing God's voice rang in her memory. Had she ever really heard God speak the way Samantha described it? She wrinkled her forehead and struggled to remember. Yes, she'd thought she had, but nothing had come of the answer she'd received.

Why did life have to become so complex all of a sudden? First Papa's passing, then Nathaniel coming back to work at the upper Palmer mill, finding Papa's letter, and these two children landing on her doorstep. She'd certainly like to hear God speak to her with some type of explanation about the last few weeks, audible voice or not.

A bird landed on a branch close to her window, and his full-throated song reverberated off the inner walls of her cabin. If only she felt like singing. An image of Nathaniel's face when he first saw her last night floated before her eyes. Surprise, irritation, and something else she couldn't quite define. Longing? Desire? Shivers ran up her arms and down her legs to tickle her toes. Did she want Nathaniel to desire her again or long for her love? What about Andrew?

He'd championed her last night in her desire to protect and care for the children—and his integrity, love for the Lord, and strong work ethic drew her even more. She smiled to herself. His roguish good looks when those dimples appeared and his gorgeous brown eyes didn't hurt her feelings, either. Of course, he'd worried over her working too hard on behalf of some of the women in town, but she understood now that was concern for her well-being, rather than a need to be bossy. Papa had been that way—oftentimes scolding her for overdoing, while genuine worry shone in his eyes. It irked her, feeling Papa had still viewed her as a child, but she had to admit it also felt good to have someone care.

Her heart twisted at the memory of her father's letter. What if Andrew didn't care at all but was concerned out of a sense of obligation? She groaned and buried her face in her pillow. How she longed to be able to place all of this in God's hands and know that He'd take care of her life. But she'd been so sure God had told her Nathaniel was the man for her—or, at least, that the Lord would work it out for her best, and that marrying Nathaniel must be God's will. That hadn't happened, and Nathaniel had nearly broken her heart.

Even if God chose to speak to her again she'd probably miss it altogether. Perhaps she'd wanted a life with Nathaniel so badly that she'd imagined hearing God. It was hard to trust her own hearing, not knowing if her desires were coloring what she heard. She'd ask God for direction, but from now on, she'd trust her common sense to do much of the guiding. The last thing she wanted was for her heart to be broken again.

It was so much easier to do kind things for others and not try to figure out issues like God's love, acceptance, or willingness to hear her prayers. At least helping others with their problems gave her a sense of accomplishment and being valued, something she'd lacked for such a long time now. God put her on this earth to minister to others, of that she was sure. And so many people had needs much greater than her own, it wasn't fair to expect God to single her out and answer all her prayers.

She sat up, pushed back the quilt, and swung her feet to the floor. Enough. Nothing would happen with Nathaniel, and she didn't have a formal relationship with Andrew. For all she knew, he wasn't interested at all, and she could end up an old maid. She almost chuckled at the thought. All this worry over something that hadn't happened yet. She needed to push that aside and get to her tasks for the day.

Then she stopped, and shame rolled over her. All her well-meaning thoughts these past weeks about having quiet time with the Lord had only been that. Thoughts, with no action to back them. She slipped to her knees. Whether God answered her in a way she could hear or not, it was time to lay her troubles at His feet.

Samantha had been so sure of God's voice when she'd been at a point of incredible need. Margaret buried her head in her arms. How she longed for that sense of assurance and knowing she'd been led by the Spirit. It had been so long since she'd felt the Holy Spirit's gentle presence—so long since she'd sensed God's love. When had it started to slip away? And, more importantly, why?

Chapter Seventeen

....

Nathaniel grabbed the shovel from the dirt-floored shed in the backyard of his home and headed for the small bed of roses. He'd spent a restless night after leaving the ice-cream social and woke this morning feeling the need for physical activity. He couldn't leave the house and take off up the mountain on a hike, since the sheriff had indicated he might stop by after church this afternoon. It had been over a week since Jenkins' had died, and he'd be thankful to have the responsibility off his shoulders.

The yard that had been Mr. Garvey's joy had deteriorated since the man's untimely death. While Nathaniel didn't pretend to be any great shakes at gardening, the idea of burning off his frustration appealed right now. He'd noticed a dead rosebush stationed in front of the picket fence in the corner, and it needed to go. He stalked over to the pathetic plant and stared at the dead branches, so similar to the barrenness of his own life. Part of him wanted to hack at it and get it out of his sight, while another part wanted to try to bring it back to life. He shook his head, disgusted. He was a man, for goodness' sake, not a baby or an emotional woman. Dig up the stupid thing and throw it out.

He stuck his spade into the firm earth and planted his foot on the top edge of the blade, thrusting it far down into the ground. He pried upward, bringing up a clump of sod laden with dense grass, and set it aside. Working his way around the rose, he plucked out the reluctant sod until the roots of the bush were exposed. One final plunge of the blade and he'd be done with this chore. The midsummer heat caused beads of sweat to rise on his forehead, and he wiped them with the back of his sleeve. Maybe this return to Bridal Veil hadn't been such a great idea. Living in Margaret's old house with her haunting ghost flitting around didn't help, either.

He shoved in his spade again and paused, propping his hands on the end of the wooden handle. Fishing on the bank of the Columbia River sounded mighty fine right now. It was stupid to start this project on such a warm day, especially with the memories of Margaret strolling outside to cut roses dancing before his vision. He tipped the shovel back and pried, then scraped something at the far edge. It didn't sound like a rock—maybe a root? But no large trees grew nearby. He rammed the blade a little deeper and popped up the rose, then tossed it on the grass and looked into the hole. A rounded wooden surface lay exposed in a pocket to the side.

Nathaniel squatted and reached into the hole, working his fingers around the top of the object until he found the corner and tunneled his hand underneath. Only a few inches deep, and not very big. He tugged and the rectangle budged a bit, then slid out of the hole. He sat back on the ground, crossed his legs, and peeled the rotted piece of burlap off the small, ornate box with the curved top. Curious. Why would someone bury a box under a rose?

He pressed his thumb against the front lip and felt for a hinge. Ah—a small metal catch encrusted with mud. He withdrew a handkerchief from his pocket and scrubbed at the dirt, then gently lifted the lid. A tightly folded paper lay inside. Nothing else. Why would someone bury a box with nothing but a scrap of paper?

Now fully engaged, he plucked the paper out and set the box to the side on the ground. The paper wasn't damp or blotted, so the box must have done its job. Slowly he unfolded the three-inch square missive until a larger paper lay before him.

He stared at his own handwriting. *This can't be.* His gaze ran over it again, and he leaned back, tipping his face to the sky. *Dear God, what does this mean?* This was the note he'd left for Margaret under the tree.

He snatched at the box and wiped off more of the mud. And this was the very box they'd used to house their notes.

What was it doing here? Had Margaret found it and despised him so much she'd buried it in hopes of forgetting? He jumped to his feet and threw the note on the ground, watching it flutter on the light breeze until it landed, message pointing up to the sky. He started to walk away and paused. Maybe it would be best to take the note in the house and destroy it. The winds that blew in the Gorge could easily waft it over his fence and into a neighbor's yard. He winced at the thought of someone else reading his plea to the woman who'd rejected his love.

Just as he bent to pick up the offensive note, a gust of wind plucked it from his hand and tumbled it across the grass. He took a long stride, bent over again—and froze. On the back was one simple word in a script he remembered, even after four years: YES.

Chapter Eighteen

....

Matilda Stedman couldn't believe her eyes. The sun had been up for nigh on to two hours, and her lazy son was still lying abed. She crossed her arms over her bosom and huffed, "Enough lollygaggin'. I need your help. You'd think a son would care more about his mother, but not you."

Wallace swung his legs toward the edge of the bed and simpered, "You know I love you, Ma. Just give me a minute ta get decent, and I'll come out ta the kitchen for a cup of your good coffee and hear what ya got to say. There's no one makes coffee like you." He gave her his best smile.

She frowned. "I'll make coffee, but don't take your time gettin' dressed."

Once in the kitchen, she placed the coffeepot onto the round, steel plate on the top of her wood cookstove. Wallace had inherited his bad habits from his pa, so it wasn't all the boy's fault. Of course, at thirty years old she'd hoped he'd have a decent job and be married by now, but he didn't seem to be in a hurry on either account. Instead, he just had a part-time job loading boxes for Mr. Smith down at the dry goods store. And yesterday he'd gotten fed up and quit. Said the old man was always yelling at him for something that wasn't his fault.

Just then Wallace sauntered into the kitchen and grabbed an earthenware mug from an open shelf near the stove. He poured himself some coffee, took a big gulp, and nearly spit it back into the mug. "This ain't coffee." He raised bleary eyes from his recent all-night binge. "What is this stuff? It tastes like water and dandelions. Ya trying to poison me?"

Matilda planted her fists on her hips and leaned forward. "It's coffee and chicory, and I used a bit of dandelion greens to make it stretch. I don't have no sugar left in the house, so I put a dollop of honey in."

"Pretty stingy with the honey, if ya ask me."

"I didn't ask you." She grabbed the cup from his hands. "But I do want to ask you somethin' else." She leaned close and gripped his shoulder, then dropped her voice and hissed, "It's about them kids."

* * *

Nathaniel stared at the note, not sure he understood the implications of the neatly penned, single word. Yes. Margaret had said yes, and then buried it in the rose garden? He shook his head and lifted the note closer, hoping to gain a deeper understanding from the simple reply. Why hadn't she left it in their trysting place as agreed? They'd be married and probably have a couple of kids by now, if she hadn't gotten cold feet.

He stroked his mustache. Had she gotten frightened, or had something else interfered? Or, more to the point, *someone* else? He glanced back over his shoulder at the hole where the rose had once flourished and grown, remembering Margaret—impetuous but thoughtful, caring almost to a fault of others' feelings and needs, and typically punctual. Strong-minded enough to stand up to her father, if she felt the need, and independent enough to consider running away with him the times they'd whispered about the possibility. Or so he'd thought. Would the Margaret he'd known write Yes, then bury the box in her backyard? He shook his head. No. It didn't fit.

He turned and strode back to the house, all thoughts of working in the rosebed pushed aside. Somehow he had to get to the bottom of this, although in his gut he thought he already knew the answer.

Chapter Nineteen

....

Clean clothes flapped on the line that Julius had strung between two slender trees behind Margaret's small, wood-sided cabin. The fir floor inside glistened from the scrub brush and hot, soapy water she'd used. She dragged a straight-backed chair across her threshold and onto the front porch. The sun beat through the boughs of the fir trees, and a tangy fragrance reached her nostrils. She inhaled deeply, savoring the smell that never grew old.

Who'd have thought a little over a week ago that a man would be found dead, possibly murdered, in Bridal Veil? Then Nathaniel Cooper had returned. Two very different problems, to be sure. She sighed and leaned her head against the high-backed chair and closed her eyes.

A twig snapped several yards from the porch and jerked her upright. A lanky woman carrying a wicker basket trooped up the path toward her.

"Gertrude. You gave me a start." Margaret put her hand over her heart and smiled. "Out for a walk on this fine day?"

The woman drew to a halt, her long gray skirt flapping in the light wind. "Afternoon, Miss Garvey. I came to pick some wild blackcaps up against the hill behind your cabin—if you don't mind my crossing your property?"

Margaret rose to her feet. "It is school property, and you're certainly welcome to whatever you find."

Gertrude nodded but didn't smile. "Seen Mr. Ludlow, the head of the schoolboard, down at the store. Said he planned on stopping to see you today, and he seemed none too happy when he said it. I thought I'd best ask, in case he comes by whilst I'm picking."

"Mr. Ludlow? Did he say why? He's generally quite pleasant to me."

Gertrude set her basket on the edge of the porch and shook her head. "Most times he is, but I declare, the man can be moody. Not sure how Mrs. Ludlow deals with him when he gets into a cranky frame of mind. 'Course, you're a pretty young thing, and not attached. I hear Mr. Ludlow has a liking for the young ladies."

Margaret frowned. "Gertrude Graham! That's gossip, pure and simple. Mrs. Ludlow is a sweet woman, and I'm sure her husband adores her. He's been a model of propriety around me."

Gertrude shrugged and plucked her basket off the rough wood floor and swung it by its handle next to her cotton skirt. "I know what I saw with my own eyes, but that was awhile back, and I suppose he could a'changed. I don't want to speak evil of a man who holds power over the kids at our school, me having a boy in your class, and all." She raised pleading eyes to Margaret's. "Please don't mention I said anything about Mr. Ludlow?"

"Of course not. Good picking to you, Mrs. Graham."

The woman lifted her hand in farewell. "Good day to you, Miss Garvey." Mrs. Graham walked past the cabin and followed the trail toward the hillside beyond.

Margaret sank back into her chair, unsure what to think. She didn't know Mr. or Mrs. Ludlow well, as the woman's poor health didn't allow her to attend church often, but she'd heard Mr. Ludlow doted on his ailing wife. He'd been the head of the schoolboard only this past year, so she hadn't come in contact with him more than a handful of times. What could he want with her on a Saturday, with school not in session? Apparently she'd find out soon enough.

She needed a few items from the store, and Mrs. Graham mentioned speaking to Mr. Ludlow there not long ago. Yes. A walk might suit, and if she met her boss on the way there, she'd learn what he needed. Of course, Mrs. Graham could have misunderstood. She had a reputation for gossip, and the hints she'd made about Mr. Ludlow's character certainly fit into that category.

She stepped into her cabin and peeked in the small looking glass next to the door. If there was a chance of meeting her boss, it might be best to tame her curly hair a bit. She plucked a black silk ribbon from the top drawer of her dressing table and gathered her tresses at the nape of her neck. Her dark blue skirt and white shirtwaist blouse were clean and pressed this morning.

Margaret stepped around the corner of the cabin to the place where Sammie and Joel liked to play, and informed them she'd be back in a few minutes. After checking to make sure her home was tidy and in order, she proceeded down the steps and toward the store.

The high-pitched squeal of the planer mill let the town know that Bridal Veil Lumbering Company was in full swing. Funny how over the years she'd managed to block out most of the noise from the mill—until the path drew close to the big buildings that housed the workers and machinery, that is. She glanced at the lumberyard as she walked along, wondering if Andrew might be outside. She slowed her pace and peered toward the largest building that housed the big planer. No sign of him.

The strong stab of disappointment took her by surprise. Had her feelings of friendship for Andrew moved to something deeper? Margaret shook her head and pushed the thought away. It was too confusing right now, and she'd didn't care to analyze what she felt.

Margaret's heart sank as she came within sight of the store without meeting anyone. Gertrude Graham may have taken a scrap of information and stretched it to whole-cloth proportions, as she had the suggestion that Robert Ludlow could be unfaithful to his wife. Still, something was amiss—Margaret felt it. The thought of Samantha and Joel niggled at her mind and left a lump in her chest. It wasn't a good sign that the head of the schoolboard hadn't seemed pleased—not good at all.

* * *

Andrew pivoted at the sound of his name and waited for his boss to catch up as the man jogged across the lumberyard. "Yes, sir, Mr. Arlington?"

The short, stocky man drew to a halt and sucked in several breaths before he spoke. "Been chasin' you clear across the yard, Browning."

"Sorry, sir. I guess with the planer mill screaming in the building, I didn't hear you call." Andrew withdrew his hat and held it gripped in one fist. Arlington's clouded face didn't bode well for what might be coming.

The man jerked his head to one side. "No matter. You're being moved."

"Moved? What do you mean?"

"To the upper mill at Palmer. More exactly, back up to the woods to help fell timber."

Andrew scratched his head. "But why? I've been at the planer mill for over a year."

Arlington shrugged his brawny shoulders. "Beats me, I'm just the shift boss. I'm not too happy about it either, but someone higher than me made the decision. Guess they're shorthanded, and we're not. I imagine since you were a good faller, you were the sensible choice." He raised a hand and started walking, then stopped and turned. "Report up there tomorrow morning to the new man, Nathaniel Cooper. Guess he'll tell you which crew you'll work on."

"Any idea if this is permanent?"

"Not from what I'm told. Probably just until the snow flies, at most."

Andrew watched his boss walk the rest of the way across the yard until he disappeared into the planer building, then clapped his hat back on his head. It was almost quitting time, and a good thing, too. After that news, he wasn't sure he could keep his mind on his job. Falling timber again? There must be more to it than a simple shortage of workers. In his two years working for this company he'd not seen a man taken from a job where he'd proven himself demoted back to an old one.

He loved his job at the lower mill and hated the thought of returning back up the mountain. Until last year he'd lived in the small community of Palmer, but with the transfer to Bridal Veil he'd moved to the lower town. That's what enabled him to start seeing Margaret. Wait a moment. Nathaniel Cooper would be his boss? Arlington said someone with more pull than him had requested the transfer.

Cooper had stated at the ice-cream social the other night that he and Margaret had known one another years before. Four years, if he remembered correctly. That would have made Margaret way too young to be interested in Cooper...or would it? Let's see, she was what? Almost twenty-one now, so she'd have been close to seventeen. Some girls were married by that age, although he'd never seen the sense in it, himself. Was it possible Cooper was still interested in Margaret and hoped to remove the competition? Surely not. Andrew had promised Margaret's father he'd watch over her and keep her from harm—and something about Cooper put his hackles up. Surely Margaret couldn't be interested in the man?

But what did he know of a woman's heart, her likes or dislikes? Margaret had seemed more distant lately. Not sullen, just quiet, withdrawn. That is, until the children appeared at her door. He tried to think back to the last time Margaret had been laughing and happy. Of course, her father's passing had dampened that joy, but she'd teased and laughed the day he'd helped her move into her cabin. After that? He shook his head and stalked toward the office to fill out his timecard. He couldn't be sure, but his heart told him it must have been around the same time that Nathaniel Cooper showed up in town.

What would Mr. Garvey have thought of Cooper? He'd never mentioned him, and Andrew had only moved to Bridal Veil two years ago. But if Margaret and Nathaniel had been friends, why hadn't Mr. Garvey contacted him, rather than Andrew, to watch over his daughter? He narrowed his eyes and kept walking. *Why indeed?*

Chapter Twenty

Margaret drew the broom across the floor of her small home, whisking the last bits of dirt out the door. She'd decided to quit worrying about Mrs. Graham's suggestion that Robert Ludlow was coming to call. She'd simply take care of the children the best she could and hope that no one objected to them staying awhile.

She glanced around the room, happy the area was tidy once more. The space that had seemed more than adequate when she'd moved in had grown more cramped. Not that she was complaining about Samantha and Joel. The two children had grown dear to her during the time they'd spent under her roof. Sleeping on the extra blankets in the corner of the main cabin hadn't drawn a single complaint from either of them.

They'd done their part to keep things tidy as well. Even Joel, who wasn't adept at small details, had helped scrub the floor and carry out buckets of dirty mop water. She lifted the ornate watch dangling from the chain around her neck and peered at the time. Mr. Gibbs, or Mr. Art as the children called him, would be here any moment to take Joel to his house to play. How the boy looked forward to this visit. Art had stopped by a couple of times in the evening to make sure Joel was doing all right, but Buck had stayed behind.

A rap at the door made her start. She pushed a loose tendril of hair behind her ear and swung open the door. A stranger dressed in dark trousers and a white shirt stood beside Nathaniel Cooper, and neither of them was smiling. Nathaniel swept the hat off his head and gave a small bow. "Margaret. Uh…Miss Garvey." He nodded to the silent man standing a half step behind. "This is Sheriff Bryant from Troutdale. May we come in?"

She stood frozen for a moment, her thoughts adrift in a sea of confusion, then she snapped to attention and gripped the edge of the door. "Why?"

Nathaniel's brows drew down and the sheriff's shot up. "We've been talking to people who knew Martin Jenkins. It's the sheriff's third trip to Bridal Veil, and he's trying to wrap things up."

Still she didn't budge. Where were the children? She'd heard them playing behind the cabin not ten minutes ago when she'd released them from doing chores. Surely Joel would be watching for Art by now and would wonder who these strangers were. Had Samantha taken her brother and hidden him in the woods, or worse yet, decided to flee? She made up her mind and swung wide the door. "Forgive me for being rude. Come in, please. You took me by surprise, as I don't know any details about Mr. Jenkins' death."

Sheriff Bryant removed his hat before crossing the threshold. "I'm not here to accuse you of anything, Miss Garvey. This shouldn't take long."

She ushered them in and pointed to the chairs pushed under her kitchen table. "Please, sit down." The coffeepot sat at the back of the stove and she reached for two mugs. "Coffee?"

The sheriff shook his head. "No need, miss. Mr. Cooper gave me a cup before coming over, and we still have other places to visit. Won't you sit for a minute?"

Margaret drew in a deep breath and let it out ever so slowly, while listening for voices outside and praying Art wouldn't appear. If the sheriff didn't know about the children or have any reason to check on them, all might be well. She sat, folded her hands in her lap, and avoided Nathaniel's eyes. "How can I help you, Sheriff?"

He laid his hat on his knees and smiled. The effect was stunning. Once-serious blue eyes now twinkled under bushy brows, and weathered bronze cheeks creased upward. Margaret immediately relaxed. The man sitting across from her wasn't a bad person.

"Mr. Cooper tells me you stopped by Martin Jenkins' cabin a couple of days prior to—" he glanced at his notes and looked up again—"Mr. Minion finding Jenkins', ah…" He rubbed his face and gave a wry smile. "I apologize. I'm not used to talking to ladies about this type of thing."

"I understand. When Mr. Minion found Mr. Jenkins that dreadful day."

Relief crossed his face. "That's right. You stopped by his house?"

She nodded. "Yes, to drop off a pot of stew, but he wasn't at home."

He leaned his forearms on the table. "And what time was that, do you remember?"

"It was early. I intended to go to Mrs. Hearn's home afterward to help with chores before the day warmed too much. I'd say about seven thirty in the morning, more or less. I spoke to Mr. Browning, who told me that Mr. Jenkins hadn't answered the door."

"Do you know why Mr. Browning was there?"

Margaret straightened in her chair and glanced at Nathaniel. He was keeping his gaze carefully trained on the sheriff, but a small muscle at the side of his mouth jerked. Ah, he was nervous. Was he the one who'd told the sheriff about Andrew visiting the Jenkins' home? She narrowed her eyes, irritation pumping the blood through her body at an alarming rate. She drew in a sharp breath, hoping to still her racing heart. "Trying to find someone to fill in at the mill. Nothing more. Why?" She didn't care that the last word was more of a demand than a question.

The sheriff held up a pacifying hand. "Just trying to get a clear picture of everything that took place that day, miss. Mr. Browning's a good friend of yours, is he?" A pair of astute blue eyes peered out from under the bushy brows.

Her heart seemed to still, and she felt blood rush up her neck. "He's a friend, as are many people in this town." She lifted her chin and met his eyes. "And I'll not see one of my friends accused of something he didn't do."

"We're not making accusations, Miss Garvey. Leastwise, not yet. One more question about Mr. Browning, if I may?"

She nodded and folded her arms across her chest.

"Did you see him come out of Jenkins' door?"

Margaret worked to stay calm. "No. He was knocking when I came around a corner and was just starting to step away as I drew closer."

He leaned forward. "So you can't say for certain that he wasn't in the house prior to your arrival?"

"Why, I—" she all but spluttered, then stopped. What had she seen when she came within sight? Surely Andrew wouldn't have been in the house? She gave herself a mental shake and prayed her sudden thought hadn't shown in her eyes. She dropped her head for a moment, then lifted her chin. "I can't say for sure, but I don't believe so. Besides, if he'd attacked someone, would he be so foolish as to walk out the front door in broad daylight?"

Sheriff Bryant shrugged, glanced at Nathaniel, and looked back at her. "You were still there when Donnie Williams stopped and spoke to Mr. Browning?"

She tried to relax. "I was."

"Did anything untoward happen during that time?"

"He asked what Andrew—Mr. Browning—was doing there. Mr. Browning explained and asked if Donnie cared to work. He said no, and I went on my way. I was already running later than I'd planned."

He nodded and smiled, then pushed to his feet. "Thank you, Miss Garvey. You've been a wonderful help." He tucked his hat under his arm. "We'll be on our way now. Good day."

Nathaniel gazed at Margaret with a question in his eyes, but she turned her face away, irritation building again. "Good day, gentlemen. I hope you'll meet with more success the rest of the day."

The sheriff stepped across the threshold and pushed his hat down over his brow. "I aim to, Miss Garvey. I aim to."

* * *

Ten minutes later Margaret dared to breathe again. She hadn't wanted to venture out too soon for fear the men might have forgotten something and would appear at the door again. She bolted from the house and raced behind it, frantic to find the children. What if Samantha had heard Nathaniel introduce the sheriff and assumed he'd come to take them back to the place they'd run away from? She'd waited far too long. Fear drove her from tree to tree, and she called the children's name in a low voice, ever conscious of the need for quiet.

"Miss Garvey?" A man's voice spoke from a yard or two away, and Margaret whirled around, her hand to her heart. Art Gibbs, Julius Winston, and Art's dog, Buck, stood near the corner of her cabin. The two men watched her with troubled expressions. Art swept his hat off his head. "Is something the matter, ma'am?"

Julius took a long look at her face and frowned. "Miss Margaret, you look like yer about to wilt. Why, a snowball on a hot griddle don't got nothin' on you, no sir. What you so het up about? You lose somethin'?"

Margaret gripped her hands to keep from wringing them. "Yes. The children."

Julius gawked, his mouth hanging open. "Children? School's not in during the summer and you don't got no children, Miss Margaret." He scratched his head. "You watchin' young'uns for one o' the women in town?"

Margaret rushed over to Art and gripped his hand. "Please, can you help me? The sheriff arrived with Mr. Cooper and asked questions about Martin Jenkins. If Sammie heard, then she might have thought he came to get them. I'm so afraid they've run away." Tears pooled in her eyes, and she brushed at the one that dared to spill over her lashes and onto her cheek.

Art patted her hand that gripped his arm. "You've called them, and they haven't answered?"

"Yes, and Joel was so excited about playing with Buck today. I know Sammie would have had to force him to leave the cabin. At first I thought they might be hiding, but now I'm not so sure."

Julius snapped his mouth shut and rocked back on his heels. "Don't reckon I know those two names, but I'll help all I can to find the lost little tykes, if'n you say the word."

She cast him a grateful look and took a step back. "Thank you. I'd appreciate your help."

Art tugged on the rope he'd tied around Buck's neck and drew him close. "You got something that belongs to Joel? A piece of clothing, a shoe, anything?"

Margaret thought for a moment, then dashed to the cabin and back. "Here." She thrust a soft-brimmed, floppy hat into his hand. "He only wears this occasionally. Will it help?"

Art nodded and leaned over, sticking the cap under Buck's nose. "Go find Joel, boy. You remember Joel. Go on, find him."

The dog let out a yip and bounded forward, nose to the ground, with Art clinging to the rope and trotting behind him. "Come on," he called over his shoulder.

Margaret picked up her skirt and dashed forward with Julius on her heels. Hope surged with each strike of her foot against the hard-packed earth. Buck liked Joel, and Joel loved the dog. Somehow God would help the dog to find the boy before they got too far away. She'd not heard any trains pass through the town in the last hour or so. Thank the good Lord for that. There were few buggies that traveled in and out of Bridal Veil, and the children couldn't sneak onto a steamboat, so walking or the train would be their only option. More than likely they'd returned to their old hideout in the barn they'd used, but she'd never found out its location.

Buck barked again, then dropped his nose back to the ground and forged ahead. They jogged past houses and wove through brush and trees, continuing west and away from the river. Margaret could hear Bridal Veil Falls in the distance as it cascaded into the pool and pummeled the rocks. Panic rose in her chest. It had never occurred to her to ask if Samantha or Joel could swim. What if they tried to cross the stream close to the waterfall and were injured? *Please, God... Please don't let anything happen to them.*

Julius drew abreast of her on a wide patch and gripped her elbow. "Miss Margaret," he wheezed. "What's goin' on? Who we tryin' to find?"

She slowed a mite but kept Buck and Art in her sights. "A brother and sister—friends of mine who've been staying with me for a while. They wandered off while I spoke to Mr. Cooper and Sheriff Bryant."

"Is they little tots?"

Margaret shook her head. "No. They're thirteen and fourteen years old, but Joel, the brother, is a bit—slow. He can't care for himself, and Sammie—Samantha—is a tiny mite of a thing. They've been worried someone might come looking for them." She gripped his hand and looked in his eyes. "Can I trust you, Julius? To keep quiet about the children?"

He nodded, a solemn cast to his normally cheerful face. "'Course you can, Miss Margaret—with yer life if need be." He lifted his hand and drew an X on his chest. "Cross my heart and hope to die, as I used to say when I was just a little pup."

"Thank you, Julius." She gestured toward Art, who trotted behind Buck as the dog sniffed the trail ahead of them. "Let's keep up, and I'll tell you what's been happening." Over the next minutes she filled him in on the arrival of the children and the little she'd learned of their past. "I wish I knew more, but I'm guessing Sammie's decided to run again."

Julius wagged his head, his long face growing even longer with sympathy. "Poor tykes. No ma or pa to watch out fer 'em. Tough spot to be in. You said the little boy's a mite slow?"

"Yes, but he's not little by any means. He's taller than I am, but gentle, and worships Sammie."

Julius scratched his chin. "I'll keep my ear to the ground and see if there's anything I can find out about their kin. I talk to a lot of the workers at the mill and other freighters from outside the area. Might be one of them knows somethin'."

"Just be careful that you don't say too much. Sammie is terrified the people they lived with will hunt them down and make them return. Andrew and I think they've been mistreated."

"More'n likely. Happens all the time, I'm afeard. You can trust me to keep my trap shut, yessir."

Just then Art gave a shout and waved his arm. "I think Buck's found something."

Julius and Margaret hurried forward and stopped beside Art and the excited dog snuffling around in the brush to the side of the trail. "Did he find the children?"

"Not sure, but he's plumb happy." He leaned over and patted the dog's head, then stuck Joel's hat under Buck's nose again. "Go on, boy. Find Joel."

The dog dashed forward, barking wildly, and ran down a short gully, then stopped and stared into the brush. When Margaret arrived, she could see nothing in the surrounding area and her heart sank. "There's nothing here."

Buck tugged at the rope and whined. Art leaned over and slipped the rope from his neck. The dog leapt into the brush, yipping and wiggling all over, then disappeared until only his tail protruded.

"Ah, Buck. You found me. What a good dog, Buck." Joel's voice echoed from the base of the hillside, and Margaret heard what sounded like a sob from Samantha. She dropped to her knees and peered through the brush. A cavern was carved into the hill, and the two children, with Buck planted firmly in Joel's lap, were curled up inside.

Art crawled around the brush and poked his head into the area behind. "Come on, kids. It's time to come out. You've had Miss Margaret fit to be tied with worry." He grasped Buck's collar and spoke firmly to the dog, who backed out of the brush.

Samantha and Joel scooted out on their bottoms, a gleeful look on Joel's face and worry drawing lines on Samantha's. They scrambled to their feet and stared at the three adults.

Margaret stepped close and reached out a hand toward Samantha, desperately wanting to hug the girl. "Sammie? Honey, why did you run away?"

Tears spilled over the girl's lower lashes and rolled down her cheeks. "The sheriff is after us. He's gonna send us back!" A wail broke from her throat, and she threw her arms around Margaret's waist, burying her face in her chest. Smothered sobs mingled with tears that soaked through the front of Margaret's cotton blouse.

Julius leaned forward, a snowy white handkerchief clutched in his hand. "Here you go, little girl." He tucked it into Sammie's hand and stepped back, worry creasing his own face.

Samantha lifted her head and looked at Julius, then raised the hanky and mopped her face. "Thank you." She whispered the words.

Margaret kept an arm around the trembling girl's shoulders. "You can quit worrying, Sammie. The sheriff wasn't at my house on your account. He came to ask me some questions about a man who died awhile back."

Sammie drew in a shuddering breath and exhaled. "I'm sorry we ran away and caused you grief." A whimper broke the last word. "I was just so scared."

Art leaned over to stroke Buck's head and beam at Joel, who knelt beside the dog. "Sammie, why did you come to this spot? Is this where you stayed before you came to my house? There's no barn near here."

She shook her head and swiped at her eyes. "No." A hiccup sounded. "This is where God brought me the day I ran away from those bad men. He told me I'd be safe here. I figured it was a good place to come back to." She shrugged and dropped her gaze to where she scuffed a toe in the dirt. "But you found me, so I guess it's not such a good place, after all."

Margaret gave the girl's shoulder a squeeze. "It was when you needed it, honey. But God didn't tell you to come here this time."

A small voice within Margaret whispered to tell Samantha that God could be trusted—that she needed to ask Him for direction in every decision—but she couldn't force the words out. So many things about her own past were unanswered where God was concerned. How could she tell Samantha or anyone else to fully trust Him, when she struggled to do it herself?

Chapter Twenty-one

. . . .

After her scare, Margaret kept Sammie and Joel close to the house and didn't let them venture out of her sight. Family had always been the most important thing in her life, and she wasn't about to let anything happen to these children again. Sammie had sobbed well into the night after they'd returned to the cabin, and nothing Margaret said appeared to comfort the girl. Sammie appeared to understand that she and Joel weren't in danger from the sheriff, but she couldn't seem to find peace after her scare.

The last twenty-four hours had brought a change, with Samantha perking up and Joel clamoring to play with Buck. Margaret had allowed them to walk to Art Gibbs' home to play while Art was at work. They'd agreed that the children could play in the yard unattended, as long as they didn't enter the house when Mr. Gibbs was gone.

A sharp rap sounded at her door. Andrew and Art were both at work, and the children wouldn't knock. Her heart picked up its pace, and she felt the blood thrumming in her neck. The sheriff? Had he heard about the children and come to investigate? A glance in the looking glass showed her appearance to be in order. She drew in a deep breath and swung open the door.

The head of the schoolboard, Robert Ludlow, stood on her porch, hat in hand. "Miss Garvey. I hope I haven't come at an inopportune time?"

She hesitated, then beckoned outside where she'd placed a chair on the porch. "Not at all. Please, have a seat and I'll bring another chair. Would you care for a cup of chilled tea?"

"I would indeed, thank you."

She grasped one of her kitchen chairs and set it outside the door, then returned to pour two glasses full of the cool tea she'd just brought up from the cellar. "I'm sorry I don't have any cookies or pie." She handed him one glass and sat down in the chair nearby.

He waved his hand and smiled. "Not to worry, Miss Garvey, this is wonderful." He took a sip. "Very good. I'm sure you're wondering what brought me here."

She nodded but didn't comment. Her thoughts flashed back to the day Mrs. Graham had stopped by on her way to pick berries. How strange Mr. Ludlow's visit had been delayed this long. Still, maybe it wasn't urgent in nature.

A blue jay swooped past the porch, squawking in protest at the lack of crumbs. The pesky creatures would practically steal food from your hand if given the chance.

Mr. Ludlow took another drink, then set his glass aside and folded his hands in his lap. "Ahem. Now then." He peered at the house for a long moment, then turned his attention back to Margaret. "I'll get right to the point. I understand you've allowed some vagrant children to move into the school's cabin."

She sat up straight and raised her chin. "My cabin, Mr. Ludlow. At least for as long as I'm the teacher here."

He nodded. "Absolutely. You are correct, Miss Garvey. But it was given to you with the assumption you were single."

"I am single."

"Yes, but I mean single, as in living alone. We didn't expect you'd be taking in strays." A muscle at the corner of his mouth twitched.

"They aren't strays. They're simply two children who are… visiting."

He seemed to sense her hesitation and leaned forward, dark eyes pinning her. "Visiting. And for how long are they visiting, Miss Garvey?"

She tried not to squirm in her chair, feeling much the same as she knew her students must feel when she called them to task for some type of misbehavior. "I'm not entirely certain."

"Do you have plans to keep them permanently, or do they have a home to return to?" The hands in his lap started to twitch.

Margaret shrugged and stifled a sigh. "I'm not planning on adopting them, but beyond that, I'm not sure. Andrew—Mr. Browning—is trying to help me find their family. They're orphans, but we're hoping they might have other family we can call upon."

He narrowed his eyes. "Orphans. How did they end up in Bridal Veil? Where did they come from? Why can't they return?" The rapid-fire questions shot from his lips like pebbles from a slingshot.

Margaret winced but kept her gaze steady on his. "I wish I could answer your questions, sir, but I can't. We're still trying to discover the truth. All I can tell you is that I hope to find a place for the children to live in the near future."

He rose and placed his hat on his head. "Please see that you do. I understand the, uh, boy is, uh—rather large and, uh—not right in the head in some ways. We don't want any problems that could reflect back on the schoolboard, you know."

She jumped from her chair, nearly knocking it over. "Joel is big for his age, but he's one of the sweetest boys I've ever met. He struggles to learn and isn't as far along as other young people of fourteen, but he'll not cause any trouble for the school, I assure you."

"Let's hope not." He stepped off the porch. "Because if he does, we'll be looking for a new teacher for the lower grades and you'll be vacating this home. Good day, Miss Garvey."

Chapter Twenty-two
....

In the predawn light of Monday morning, Andrew slung his bedroll and pack into the supply wagon and climbed onto the seat beside Julius. He'd arrived at the store early to help the teamster load the supplies for the daily trip up the mountain to Palmer, in exchange for catching a ride to the upper mill. Timber fallers typically started felling trees at daybreak, but they'd allowed Andrew the first hours of daylight to get settled. He was taking clothing for the week, as they'd placed him in one of the small workers' cabins not far from the logging site. He'd return to his house in Bridal Veil on the weekends, until this job ended.

Julius turned to him with a toothy grin. "Everythin' jake? My team's rarin' to go."

"Yep. Ready as I'll ever be."

The lanky man smacked his mules with the reins. "Haw, haw. Gittup there, old girls." He spit over the side of the wagon and wiped his mouth with the back of his sleeve. "You don't seem too 'cited about yer new job up yonder. Pinin' for Miss Margaret already?"

Andrew smiled and leaned against the hard plank seat. "That plain, is it?" He still struggled with the move, even though he'd been able to say good-bye to Margaret the evening before.

Julius tapped a spot just above his right eye as he gripped the reins in his left. "Yep. Got me a discernin' way o' lookin' at things. Seen it right off the day you helped her move that you had a soft spot in yer heart for that young lady." He gripped the reins in both hands again as the wagon hit the bottom of the slope heading up Larch Mountain. "Hold on. Got us some rough road that ain't been fixed since that last big rainfall."

Andrew gripped the sideboard as they jostled over the rutted road up the mountainside. The early morning fog hung like a shroud another hundred yards or so above, blocking the sunlight from shining on the village below. The sun had risen, but no fingers of light penetrated the dense bank that blanketed the top half of the mountain. The mules strained at their harness as they zigzagged up the winding path, pulling the heavy load. Thirty-seven homes dotted the landscape near the Palmer mill, and additional cabins sat in the outlying area that housed the timber fallers, skidders, de-barkers, and other workers who brought the timber in to the mill. Homes were scattered from Angel's Rest, a bluff a mile or so east and above the town of Bridal Veil, and on past the west side of Palmer.

Julius drew back on the reins and called to his team. "Whoa there, girls. Take it easy now." He turned to Andrew and pointed in front of the mules. "Looky there, Andrew. The fog is so deep my mules are goin' to get swallered in it."

Sure enough. Andrew leaned forward and peered ahead, barely believing what he saw. Many a time he'd seen dense fog, but this was downright spooky. The lead mule disappeared into the thick white bank as surely as if he'd stepped into a deep washtub of tapioca. "You going to be able to keep them on the road, or do we get down and walk?"

Julius shook his head and loosened the reins. "No sir. I trust my mules. No way they're lettin' me go over the edge." He peered over the side of bed and into the canyon beyond, and Andrew could have sworn the man's ruddy complexion whitened a shade. "Never seen it quite this bad, but she'll lift, soon as the sun warms up. Just you hold tight now, and these girls o' mine will take us to the top in fine shape. They know the way, yessir. Make it every day, up and down."

The second set of mules disappeared into the damp swirl, and an unreal sensation swept over Andrew as the wagon and its passengers were swallowed up as well. "Julius. You see anything?"

"No sir. Not much. Kin see my hand if I stick it up afore my face, but that's about all. Tarnation! Don't this beat anything you ever did see?"

"It certainly does. I'll be happy when we reach the top." Faint sounds of rocks tumbling over the edge smote his ears, and the smell of sweat reached his nostrils. No birds sang or squirrels barked in the still morning air. Only the creak of the wagon jostling across ruts in the road and bouncing over small rocks that had tumbled down from the hillside above. The mules continued dragging the wagon ever upward through the silent shroud, continuing the forward movement.

Andrew clutched the side of the wagon seat, suddenly glad he couldn't see to his right and over the edge. Maybe not knowing how close the wheels ran to the precipice was a good thing, after all. Walking along behind the wagon still seemed like a wise idea, but Julius was the best teamster around, and if he trusted the mules to take them safely to the top, who was he to question?

The last mile of the trip seemed to take two hours, although he knew it wasn't even a quarter of that. At long last, the increasingly strong rays of the sun broke through the fog—first in slender fingers of light, biting through the gloom in dazzling fragments, then exploding in its full glory at the same time the wagon topped out on the road and drew abreast of the first building. Andrew shot up a prayer of thanksgiving. He'd never realized how amazing a sight the sun could be until he'd plowed his way through white purgatory behind a team of mules balancing a wagon on the side of a cliff.

He stepped off the wagon and shook Julius's hand. "Bless your mules, and bless you for being the man that you are." He wiped his sleeve across his forehead and grinned. "Glad I don't need to take that ride again anytime soon. I hope you'll have clear skies for your return back down the mountain."

"Oh, p'shaw. Weren't nothin'. All in a day's work, don'tcha know?" Julius beamed, and the gap where a tooth once resided winked, giving him a lopsided grin. "Molly and Verna done a good job, though, I'll give 'em that. Best lead mules in the county."

Andrew slapped his hand on the side of Molly's neck as he walked around the team and toward the office. "No, sir. Best team in the state." He waved at the teamster and stepped onto the wooden stoop of the office, just to the side of the main mill building.

He tapped on the plain plank door and stepped inside. He still had a hard time believing he'd been transferred up the mountain but had decided not to fight the change. Maybe God had a reason for sending him here. He gave a mental shrug. One never knew what one small change in your life could bring to pass, in God's scheme of things. Look how the Lord had brought him closer to Margaret in the past couple of weeks, and their relationship had deepened. Staying open to possibilities right now looked to be his best option, and growing bitter or resentful would only make the rest of the summer drag.

Nathaniel Cooper lifted his head from the stack of papers on his desk and met Andrew's eyes. "Morning, Browning." He glanced at the clock on the desk. "I see you're early." A small frown furrowed his brow as though he wasn't sure if this was an admirable trait. "You can ride Peggy or Jumbo from here up to the log landing. You'll be working about four miles back, so it's too far to walk."

"Peggy or Jumbo." Andrew scratched his head, then grinned. "I'd forgotten they named the locomotives. I've only seen Peggy, as Jumbo hadn't arrived when I worked up here a year ago." He leaned a hip against the doorframe.

"They started calling it Jumbo shortly after it arrived, based on the load it can pull." Cooper rose and dropped the papers back on his desk. "You've been assigned to a cabin up there, although I understand you'll be keeping your place in Bridal Veil. Sure you don't want to give that up and stay on as a lumberjack?"

Andrew shook his head. "No, sir. The amount of time they've asked for will be long enough. I love the woods but have come to appreciate my life down below." *Margaret too,* he longed to say, but kept that bit of information to himself.

Cooper shrugged. "Suit yourself. You know your duties when you get to the job site?"

Andrew straightened. "Sure do. I can't imagine too much has changed in the past year where felling is concerned."

"They're bringing in more loads now that Dan Meadows' team of oxen and Art Gibbs' team of horses are both working the woods. They want to increase the number of trees felled each day, so you'll need to push yourself."

"No problem, as long as the boss cares about safety. I've seen too many accidents when men are pushed to cut more than they should."

Cooper frowned and crossed his arms over his chest. "That'll be your boss's lookout, not yours. Do your job, and you'll be fine."

Andrew clamped his mouth shut. He wouldn't endanger himself or the man on the other end of his crosscut saw no matter what this man said, but he'd not argue, either. There was time enough to see how things were handled. He wouldn't be afraid to speak his piece if he saw a situation that warranted it. "That's all, then?"

"Yes. You'll find all the gear you need at the job site. Jump on the train and head out when you hear the whistle blow." He glanced at the clock on his desk, sat back down, and picked up a paper.

Andrew gave a short nod and headed toward the door. "Thanks."

The sun warmed his skin as he walked from the office to the bridge that crossed the gully where the water ran down from the upper millpond. The whine of the head rig with its big circle saw slicing through the gigantic yellow fir logs filled the air, along with the shouts of men rolling logs from the millpond and others overseeing the flume. He'd often marveled at the ingenuity of the men who'd chosen this spot above Bridal Veil, but yet two to three miles from the forest where the giant trees fell. No one seeing this place in its natural state would believe there'd be room for the building housing the head rig, much less a bridge, railroad tracks, and millpond in the gully below.

Andrew had been thankful when he'd been transferred to the lower Bridal Veil planer operation. As much as he loved the woods, his desire to be close to Margaret was stronger. He thought of her independent spirit and sweet nature. What an amazing combination to find in a woman.

He'd really put his foot in it that day at Jenkins' cabin when he'd been thinking of her father's request and suggested she might need a man to care for her. What he'd meant, but hadn't planned on blurting out, was that he had a hankering to care for her the rest of her life, and he hated seeing her wear herself to a frazzle giving so much of herself to others.

He could only hope that Margaret never discovered her father asked that he take care of her. Judging from the look on her face, she'd not take it too kindly. He kicked a large fircone out of the way and leaned his shoulder against the rough bark of the tree as he waited for the locomotive. Sometimes he thought Margaret was beginning to care, and other times he was convinced she didn't see him at all.

The shriek of the train whistle and the grinding of the steel wheels against the tracks caught his attention. Time for work. He'd best get his mind off Margaret and onto the business at hand. A man couldn't cut through the butt of a giant fir towering hundreds of feet in the air and hope to drop it where it was supposed to land without his mind fully engaged on his task.

* * *

Andrew wiped rivulets of sweat from his forehead and rubbed his shoulder, then took a swig of water from the nearby jug. "Ready for another go, Roger?"

The young man standing on the other side of the yellow fir stuffed his handkerchief back in his hip pocket and grinned. "Prob'ly more'n you are, I 'spect. Looks like you been away from cuttin' for too many months. You got soft."

"Huh. I'll show you soft." Andrew grinned back and picked up his axe. "Let's get these springboards in so we can drop this fellow." Both men went to work on the tree, cutting a slice into the side and driving a plank into the notch. They worked swiftly and silently, standing on the short bottom plank and inserting yet another springboard a few feet on up the side of the tree, thereby avoiding the bulge of the trunk and the accumulated pitch near the butt.

Andrew gripped the handle of the crosscut saw and peered at his partner. "Ready?"

Roger grasped the other end and nodded, and the two men started to work on the front of the giant. An amazing rhythm and flow took the saw teeth deeper and deeper into the tree, first through the bark, then through the outer rings, heading right for the heart, and undercutting the massive trunk. When that chore was finished, Andrew jumped down from his perch and helped lift the saw to the ground. "Looks like this one will need some wedges if we're going to drop it through the opening between those two trees."

Roger nodded and grunted. "I'll get them." He jumped down from his precarious perch and tossed up two wedges to Andrew, then clambered back up with a third tucked under his arm. They repositioned the saw blade on the backside of the tree, cutting another slice out, then proceeded to drive the wedges deep into its flesh. The magnificent giant began to sway, and the majestic top leaned away from the driving force of the wedges penetrating into the heart. As the tree slowly tilted forward, moving inch by inch toward its final resting place, Andrew and Roger tossed the axe off to the side and jumped to the ground, running a distance away. The top slowly canted, and with a tremendous roar, the giant boughs whipped through the air, catching the limbs of nearby trees, slowing its fall only momentarily, then breaking free and landing with an ear-splitting, ground-shaking crash.

No sooner had it landed and grown still than a team of men rushed forward, hacking off the limbs, peeling off the bark down to the golden wood, thus allowing the crosscut sawyers to cut the mighty trunk into lengths that could be towed out of the woods by the waiting oxen and horse teams.

"Ho, Andrew Browning." A huge man holding a bullwhip in his hairy left hand strode across the brushy clearing.

Andrew met the man and extended his hand. "Dan Meadows. It's been a long time since I've seen your team at work." He grinned at the big man and waved a hand toward the waiting brace of oxen. "They're looking fit. Still the best in the woods, I daresay?"

Meadows drew to a halt, and his brows hunkered down over his eyes. "That they be, Browning, that they be." He swiveled and glared over his shoulder, then returned his gaze to Andrew. "'Course, some in these parts beg to differ and think a horse team can pull its weight the same as my boys." A stream of tobacco juice shot from between his teeth and splattered against a rock. "Don't care what that new log skidder says. His team can't touch mine, not by a long shot."

Andrew clapped the big man on the shoulder. "I'm sure it can't. So what else is new in this neck of the woods?"

"You heard about the skidder boss bein' killed? Jenkins' decisions caused me all kinds of grief. I can't say I'm sorry to see him gone."

Andrew drew back a half step and stared at the man. "I hadn't heard the sheriff had made a ruling yet on whether it was murder or an accident."

"Yeah. Well." Meadows scratched his side and shrugged. "Maybe it weren't. Guess I just assumed. Don't pay me no mind." He craned his neck around and bellowed, "Hey there, boy. Don't you be touchin' that team." A curse spilled out and he swung off at a rapid pace toward his patient oxen, standing with lowered heads and half-closed eyes. "Go on now. You've no business here."

Andrew thought back over the man's words. He hadn't realized there'd been any bad blood between Meadows and Jenkins, but then Dan Meadows wasn't known to be the most tolerant man on the mountain. His temper had landed him in some scrapes in the past. He felt sorry for the man who owned the horse team hauling logs on the skid trails.

"Hey, Browning. You going to stand there with your hands in your pockets or get to fellin' another tree while the sun's still shinin'?" A brawny man in suspenders and canvas pants pushed his hat to the back of his head and glared.

Andrew picked up his axe, all thought of Meadows pushed to the side.

BRIDAL VEIL
1902
OREG

Chapter Twenty-three

Andrew climbed up on the wagon for the long descent into Bridal Veil, thankful it was Friday afternoon, and even more grateful they'd gotten the trees dropped early enough to catch a ride back with Julius. Getting off early wouldn't have happened, but they were moving to a new location on Monday. By two o'clock they'd cleaned up everything big enough to fell and headed out of the woods. It was four thirty now, but the upper mill still bustled. Most of the crews would work another hour and a half before heading home for their supper.

He braced his feet against the wagon's footrest and leaned back against the low seat. "Looks like there won't be any fog this trip."

"Nope." Julius craned his neck and looked over the side. "Jist missed that big old doniker. Boulder that size could break my axle. Hope the road crew gets it moved outta the way 'fore I come back up tomorrow."

Andrew peered over his shoulder and whistled. "Must have tumbled down the mountainside last night. Glad this road's wide in spots."

"Yep. Molly and Verna are sure-footed, but I'd not enjoy bustin' an axle or losin' a wheel partway down this hill, no sir." He cast a wide-mouthed grin at Andrew. "You hankerin' to get home, are ya?"

Andrew crossed his arms over his chest and smiled. "Yes. It seems like it's been longer than five days."

Julius wrinkled his nose. "Goin' to take a bath 'fore you head over to Miss Margaret's?"

Andrew tipped back his head and hooted, then turned a huge grin on Julius. "So you think she'd appreciate that, do you?"

"Yep. Sure do. You smell jist a mite ripe to this discernin' nose." Julius pulled back on the brake as the mules started descending a particularly steep part of the road. "Whoa there, girls. Easy now."

Andrew held to the side of the seat as they jostled over some ruts in the road, and Julius turned his attention to driving the treacherous downgrade to the base of the mountain. Andrew had wanted to rush straight to Margaret's house as soon as the wagon stopped in Bridal Veil, but Julius was right. He was definitely in need of a scrubbing first. As anxious as he was to see Margaret, he'd not subject anyone else to sitting near him until he'd had a chance to spiff up a bit.

He'd spent the entire week thinking about Margaret and wondering if she ever thought of him. Were Sammie and Joel still at her home, and had anything more been discovered about Martin Jenkins' death? He remembered the comment Donnie had made, trying to cast aspersions on his and Margaret's names the morning they'd found Jenkins' body. No telling what that young man was trying to prove, but he guessed he might be jealous. Margaret had mentioned the night of the ice-cream social that she'd turned Donnie down when he'd asked if he could escort her. That alone would be reason enough. Hopefully, he'd not bothered her since and wouldn't continue to make trouble.

Sammie and Joel were another quandary. Where had the children come from, and where did they belong? He'd grown to care about them, but it wasn't realistic to ignore the fact that the children had run from something, or someone. They'd stated their parents were dead, but how could he know that for sure? They might have an abusive father or possibly a guardian who had a legal right to expect their return, if not a moral one. He needed to discuss their future with Margaret. As much as she cared about them, she couldn't take them in permanently without finding out the truth. He owed it to her father, as well as to Margaret, to help her make a wise decision.

His thoughts swung toward the possibility of a future with Margaret and hung there. It took not seeing her sweet face to realize how deeply he cared. He wanted to rush to her this evening and declare himself, but something held him back. Margaret had always been charming, but there'd been little to indicate she shared his feelings. They'd reached no agreement, and other than attending church and the ice-cream social with him, there'd been nothing close to courtship. The last thing he wanted was to offer his heart and have her turn him aside because he'd rushed her when she wasn't ready. A little more time might be best.

He settled against the bouncing seat and smiled as a house on the edge of Bridal Veil came into view. First things first. He'd get home, take a bath, grab a quick bite to eat, and walk over to Margaret's. Maybe he could convince her to take a long walk with him tomorrow, or better yet, a picnic. That was just the thing. A quiet picnic in the woods near the stream, with time to talk and laugh. Maybe he'd get a better idea what her feelings might be, if they spent some time together while the children played nearby.

* * *

Friday evening Nathaniel stood in his backyard staring at the dead rosebush. The note still burned a hole in his heart every time he thought about it. What might have happened if he'd come to the meeting place early, before Margaret's father must have discovered their secret? Of course, he didn't know for sure that's what happened, and would never know, unless he spoke to Margaret.

The thought stirred his pulse and he drew in a soft breath. Why not? Why hadn't he done it the day he'd found it? After all, what did he have to lose? He shrugged—just another hit to his pride. But what if there was a chance of him and Margaret getting back together? He shook his head and gave a wry laugh. He thought of an old expression his grandmother had been fond of—about as much chance as a snowball on a hot griddle. He could tell from Margaret's demeanor that she had no use for him. Besides, it appeared she'd found a suitor in that Browning fellow.

Another thought struck him as he tossed the rose on the trash pile and swung to leave the yard. What if Margaret believed he'd abandoned her? His heart sank, and he groaned. Why hadn't that occurred to him before now?

He walked back into the house and roamed from the kitchen to the bedroom and back again, then stalked to the mantel and plucked the box off the polished surface and flipped it open. The simple, almost tragic word stared up at him once again. Yes. So much meaning housed in that word. But he'd moved on. He'd made a life for himself beyond Margaret. He'd decided long ago that it wouldn't have worked. She was too young, too innocent, too idealistic in so many ways.

The only times they'd quarreled were when the subject of her faith arose, and she'd insisted they attend church together. He'd humored her at the time, willing to go occasionally if that's what it took to make her happy. Maybe she'd grown past some of that by now. But then again, probably not. After all, she was with Browning in church the one Sunday he'd attended. Not that he had anything personal against church, it just wasn't a priority in his life, and he'd always felt she made it too big of an issue.

A sudden resolve struck him and he grasped the box, withdrew the note, and strode to the door. Church be hanged. Part of his heart still cared about Margaret, and he'd be hog-tied, as Grandpappy used to say, if he'd walk away without at least trying.

Five minutes later he stepped up on the front porch of the small cabin where Margaret lived and rapped on the door. Light footsteps inside sounded through the nearby open window, and his stomach turned to mush. The door whipped ajar, and he opened his mouth to speak, then snapped it shut again. The young, slender girl he'd seen with Margaret at the ice-cream social stood across the threshold, staring at him. "Is Miss Garvey at home?"

"Nope." She began to swing the door shut.

He placed the flat of his hand against the wood surface. "Hold on, miss. I'm an old friend. Can you tell me when she'll be back?"

"Nope. She didn't say." She wrinkled her nose at him.

Frustration rose in his throat and threatened to choke him. "Do you know where she might have gone?"

The girl stared him full in the eyes and cocked her head to the side, looking as though she were trying to see into his mind, or at the least, into his heart. "For a walk, but I don't know where. She don't tell me her business, and I wouldn't tell you if she did."

The snippy little girl wasn't even trying to be polite. He shook his head and tried again. "I'd just like to know…"

"She went to the waterfall," a young man's voice spoke from behind the door.

"Hush, Joel." Snapping brown eyes glared at Nathaniel, then whipped around to the boy standing somewhere behind her. "We don't tell strangers Miss Margaret's business."

LOVE FINDS YOU IN BRIDAL VEIL, OREGON

"But he said he's her friend."

"Huh. Didn't 'pear to be her friend at the ice-cream social. I saw how she looked at him, all frosty and proud. Don't think she'd want us to go tellin' him anything." She swung back to the door. "My brother doesn't know anything, he's just guessin'. Sorry we can't help." This time she succeeded in shutting the door, and Nathaniel didn't stop her.

Why were those youngsters still at Margaret's house? He thought they were family friends visiting for a day or so when he'd met them at the social. Were they taking advantage of Margaret's generous spirit? That girl certainly hadn't learned any manners in her short life, and the boy didn't seem terribly bright, from all appearances. At least he'd spoken up and given a clue to Margaret's whereabouts.

The waterfall. Why hadn't he thought of that? He'd walked across town to get here, and the waterfall was on the other side, close to her old—his new—house. He'd forgotten that was one of her favorite places. He shoved his hat back onto his head. Time to find Margaret and see if he could put some old ghosts to rest.

* * *

Margaret sat on the bank of the stream a hundred feet below the waterfall, plucking at the grass growing close to the water's edge. It was the first time since the children had come, and certainly the first time since they'd tried to run away, that she'd felt comfortable leaving them for any length of time. Samantha had promised with her hand covering her heart that she and Joel would still be home when she got back. The solemn look in Samantha's eyes convinced her that the girl had spoken the truth, and Margaret left with a sense of peace blanketing her soul. Maybe Sammie

MIRALEE FERRELL

....

was beginning to trust her, and she could get beneath the hard shell the girl used to protect her small family.

Margaret couldn't believe how much the two young people had grown on her since they'd arrived. Sure, she'd always enjoyed children, or she wouldn't have taken up teaching, but Samantha and Joel had struck a deep place in her heart. Not that there was a bevy of occupations a girl could turn to in a small town—which made it even nicer that she enjoyed her job. But Samantha and Joel were different. They weren't just any children. Margaret wrinkled her brow and struggled to understand her feelings. They were hurting, scared, and needed someone to protect them—and they accepted her for who she was, demanding little in return. It had been too long since she'd felt needed in just that way.

The sun streaming through the trees warmed her bare ankles, and the soft breeze dried the last drops of water lingering from cooling her feet in the creek. The water still had a bite to it, as the snow in the high Cascades continued to melt and pour into the swollen creeks. The rush of the waterfall and the distance from town softened the whine of the planer mill to the point where the stream and the squawk of a blue jay were the primary sounds breaking the peace of the late afternoon hour.

She leaned back on the grassy bank and laced her fingers under her head. How wonderful to experience such peace, after so much turmoil and pain. Nothing would mar this hour that God had given her. She closed her eyes and lifted her heart to Him, seeking to understand what He might want to share. It had been far too long since she'd opened her soul to His voice, and even now, fear and doubt tried to creep into her spirit. What made her think God would show her the answers to the myriad of questions that sometimes kept her awake at night?

What if she thought she heard His voice again, and made the wrong decision regarding the children—or Andrew? It wasn't just her life that hung in the balance, the way it had been when she thought God told her He'd take care of her future with Nathaniel. Obviously, it hadn't mattered to Nathaniel, but she'd been so sure. So positive…

A nearby bush rustled and her heart jumped, then galloped like a runaway horse. Squirrels and blue jays wouldn't cause that much movement, and deer wouldn't approach with human scent strong on the breeze. That left a man, or a bear. She stared at the bush as the memory of the hobos who'd chased Sammie through the woods raced through her mind. Nothing moved. Maybe she'd imagined it. Her muscles began to relax, and she let out her pent-up breath.

"Margaret?" A low voice spoke a yard or so behind her.

The forest had grown strangely silent other than the pounding of the falling water just upstream.

She sat upright and whirled around, her hand clutched to her breast, trying to calm the thump of her racing heart. Her lips parted, and for a moment no sound would come. "Nathaniel."

He took a tentative step closer, his hat clutched in his hands. "I'm sorry I startled you." He averted his eyes from her bare ankles. "I'd hoped I might speak to you."

His glance reminded her she'd taken off her shoes and stockings and had hitched her skirt up to her calves. She yanked the hem of her dress down, then turned her burning face away from him. "Speak to me?" Her mind fumbled to grasp his words.

Out of the corner of her eye she saw him take a step backward. "I'll just head on home. I'm sorry I intruded."

She drew up her knees and wrapped her arms around them. "You don't have to leave."

He hesitated and spun the hat in his hands. "You're sure?"

"I'm sure." She nodded at a flat rock not far from the bank of the stream. "Please have a seat. I'm afraid I'll get a crick in my neck staring up at you this way."

"Certainly." He settled himself on the hard surface and looked everywhere except at her. "I'm not sure where to begin."

It was hard enough having Nathaniel back in Bridal Veil, but if he were playing games…. She straightened her shoulders. "Please do not trifle with me, Mr. Cooper. If you've come to say you're sorry after all these years, there's no need. I am no longer the young girl you left behind."

His head snapped around, and his startled eyes met hers. "I beg your pardon, Miss Garvey. I did not come to trifle with your feelings, or to ask your forgiveness."

She narrowed her eyes. "What, then?"

He stood to his feet and shoved his hand into his pocket, drawing out a folded piece of paper. A quick step brought him to her side, and he thrust out his hand. "To show you this."

She stared at the note but didn't move to take it. "What is it?"

He shook the missive and pushed it closer to her face. "You'll understand after you see it. Please."

A flash of curiosity flicked through her mind. What could it hurt? "Fine." She gripped the corner of the paper, being careful that her fingers didn't touch his. "How did you find me?"

He sank back onto the boulder. "I went to your house and spoke to the girl who's staying with you. I must say, she's not very forthcoming with information where you're concerned."

"You saw Sammie?" She grasped her skirt and got up on her knees. "Were she and Joel all right? I should get home. I've been away too long."

He held up his hand. "They were fine and knew where you'd gone." A twinkle sparked in his eyes. "The boy let it slip, much to his sister's dismay. I don't think that girl cares too much for me."

She smoothed out her skirt, one hand still gripping the note. "Sammie hasn't learned to trust people yet." She glanced down at her hand, then back up at him. "What is this?"

He placed his forearms on his knees and leaned forward, earnestness lighting his face. "If you read it, I think you'll understand."

Margaret looked at the paper for a long moment, then slowly unfolded it. She read the single word printed there and turned it over. Then she raised her eyes. "I *don't* understand."

A flood of emotions tore through her breast. *All these years, he'd had this note? He got my reply and left me, just as I thought.*

She pushed to her feet and balled up the paper, throwing it on the ground. "I'd finally put you behind me and moved on. Why come back now and bring proof that you found my note and still decided to leave?" She took a step away from where he sat.

Nathaniel rose and bent to pluck the crumpled note from the grass. Shock passed over his features, followed by understanding. He took a step forward and extended his hand. "Margaret—that's not what happened. Please listen? Your father buried it in the rose garden."

His calm voice hit her hard and she drew to a sudden stop. "I don't believe you." She swiveled around and glared. "My father would never have done something like that."

"I have our box back at the house, crusted with dirt. The company assigned me the house where you and your father lived. I noticed a dead rosebush by the back fence and dug it up. I found the box in the hole with the note inside. If you didn't bury it, then who do you think did?"

Margaret felt the blood drain from her face. She leaned against the rough bark of a small fir, trying to take in Nathaniel's words. Her father wouldn't have hurt her that way. She refused to believe it. He knew how much agony she'd gone through when Nathaniel left Bridal Veil. He couldn't have missed the sadness in her eyes, or the number of times she'd locked herself in her room and cried herself to sleep. "There has to be another explanation." She wrapped her arms around herself and shivered.

"You didn't bury the box?" He stood with legs spread wide, arms down at his sides.

She raised her head and stared at him. "No. I never saw it again after leaving my reply. I assumed you found it and changed your mind." She shook her head slowly, trying to understand. "You found it in our garden?"

"Yes. Under a rosebush."

"Was it close to the corner of the fence?"

"It was."

She moaned softly and covered her face. "Daddy planted that rose the afternoon you and I planned to leave. I didn't notice it until the next day when I came out to sit in the yard hoping you hadn't gone, and you'd find me there." Her shoulders shook, and tears slipped from her closed eyes. "Why? Why would he do that to me?"

Nathaniel took a step toward her. "He didn't like me. I always knew that, but you refused to see it. I think in your heart you must have known, since you tried to keep our relationship a secret."

She raised wet lashes and stared at him. "But if he saw the note, he'd have known how much it would hurt me."

He shrugged and smiled wryly. "If he read the note, he'd have known you were running away without telling him, too."

She shoved away from the tree. "I need to get home."

He reached out his hand but didn't touch her. "Please don't go, Margaret."

She took a step back. "I don't understand. Papa married Mama when she was barely seventeen. Why did he think he had the right to interfere in my life? I turned seventeen a month after you left. I wasn't a child, but if he buried that note, then he didn't trust me."

"Or me."

She shook her head. "No. He didn't trust that I could make a good decision, and once again, he stepped in and made it for me."

"I'm sorry. I wanted you to know that I didn't abandon you, but I didn't think it through."

"No. You did what was right. I need time, that's all—time to try and figure out who my father was." She walked over to where her shoes and stockings lay and plucked them up. "I'm going home." She held up a hand when he took a step forward. "I don't want you to walk me. Please, Nathaniel, if you still care at all, please don't come with me."

He hesitated, and a worried frown settled on his mouth. "All right. It goes against everything in my heart to let you walk away, but I understand. May I call on you tomorrow evening?"

"I don't think so. I need some time to sort things out. This is all so—sudden. Confusing. There's more than just you involved here."

A shadow crossed his face. "Browning."

She picked up the hem of her skirt with her left hand and turned away. "Thank you for coming to see me, Nathaniel." She glanced over her shoulder. "You were right that I needed to know the truth."

Chapter Twenty-four

Margaret walked down the dirt path leading away from the stream for a hundred yards or so, then stopped, perched on a fallen log, and slipped on her stockings and shoes. She looked back the way she'd come, dreading to see Nathaniel following her, but it appeared he'd given her an adequate head start. She shook out her skirt and hurried up the path, suddenly aware of the children waiting at the cabin. If only she could go home and think this through alone.

A memory niggled at the back of her thoughts: Papa lying on the couch in the living room, gasping for air, and begging her to forgive him. She'd thought it strange, as there was nothing she could think of to forgive. Now she knew. Papa had carried the burden of guilt for four long years, and only when dying had he decided to ask her forgiveness. Then he'd died before he could utter an explanation, and even the letter he'd written didn't fully explain.

If he'd been able to tell her what he'd done, would she have forgiven him? Yes, she'd have said the words to allow him to pass in peace. But she also knew that true forgiveness is a choice, and she wasn't sure she could make that choice even now. Her father might have been trying to protect his young daughter, but he'd gone too far, interfered too much. And on top of everything with Nathaniel, he'd tried to coerce Andrew to marry her—assumedly to save her from men like Nathaniel.

Why did all the men in her life think they knew what was best for her? Nathaniel left town assuming she didn't care about him without seeking her out to be sure, Papa interfered to the point of changing her future, and Andrew wanted to court her because Papa had pressed him to care for her in the event of his passing. Margaret couldn't stand it any longer; she needed to know if Andrew had taken her on as a duty, and she wouldn't let up until he told her the truth. Then she'd have to face the facts of what Nathaniel had revealed and try to decide what to do with that knowledge.

The walk from the waterfall to her cabin had flown, and she thanked God she'd not met a single person along the way. It was hard enough facing Sammie and Joel without trying to hide her agitation from an adult. She pushed open the door and stepped inside, then stopped, her hand still gripping the metal knob. Sheriff Bryant sat on a chair near the kitchen table, his large hand gripping a mug of coffee.

* * *

Margaret stepped inside the cabin and shut the door behind her, glancing around for Sammie and Joel. Neither was in sight, so she focused on the man sitting quietly in the chair, sipping his drink. She straightened her shoulders and met his eyes. "Sheriff Bryant. Might I ask how you came to be in my house drinking my coffee?"

He set the mug down and rose. "A girl answered the door. She and her brother were in here just moments ago. Samantha, I believe she called herself, said she needed to escort her brother out to the necessary at the back of your cabin."

"I'll be right back." Margaret hastened to the door and onto the porch, certain the excuse had been a ruse for Sammie and Joel to slip away. The girl was terrified of the law, and she couldn't imagine her sticking around. "Samantha?" She sped toward the small structure a hundred feet behind the cabin. "Joel?"

The door of the little building creaked open and Joel carefully shut it behind him, then turned with a smile. "Howdy. You got back."

She released the breath she'd been holding. "Yes. Is Sammie around?"

He swiveled and peered over his shoulder, then stepped around the corner of the privy. "Sammie? You out there?"

"I'm here." Samantha trotted around the corner, one hand clutching some wildflowers. "Miss Margaret, the sheriff is sitting in your kitchen."

Margaret stepped forward and reached for the girl's shoulders, giving her a hug before she could pull away. "I saw him. How long has he been here?"

Sammie shrugged and handed the flowers to Margaret. "Not long. I'd just put the coffee to perking when he knocked at the door. Figured maybe you had your hands full of something and couldn't open it, so I swung it wide." She kicked a fir cone across the clearing. "He stepped inside, pert as you please. Took his hat off and gave me a big smile, then sniffed the fresh coffee and asked for a cup. After he asked after you, that is."

"You told him I wasn't home?"

"I did, but he said he'd like to wait. He's a lawman, and I didn't want to rile him." She turned worried eyes on Margaret. "Did I do wrong, Miss Margaret? Should I have told him to go away till you got home?"

Margaret patted her arm. "You did just fine, honey." She turned to the quiet boy standing nearby. "Come on, Joel, maybe we can find a cookie for you and our visitor."

His face lit with a warm smile. "Whoopee! I love cookies, don't I, Sammie?"

"Yes, you do, Joel. And Miss Margaret's are the best."

Joel turned to Margaret. "Can Andrew and Mr. Gibbs come have some cookies with us? I want to play with Buck, and Andrew can read me a story."

Sammie frowned and shook her head. "Joel. It's enough that you're getting a cookie—you oughtn't complain that you don't have someone to play with. I'll read you a story later."

Joel hung back. "But when is Andrew comin' back, Sammie? He's been gone forever."

Margaret stepped forward and touched the boy's shoulder. "He'll be here tomorrow, I'm sure. Maybe we can let you stop by to see Mr. Gibbs and Buck, as well. But for now, we need to see about those cookies, all right?"

He nodded and looped his arm through Sammie's, and the children trooped back to the porch.

Margaret trailed behind them, wondering at the girl's calm demeanor. Had the sheriff reassured her he wasn't here to take her back to wherever she ran away from? She shook her head, knowing the man would have no reason to do such a thing. Maybe the reassurance she'd received from Andrew and herself the last time they'd tried to run had worked. Whatever had happened, she was truly thankful the Lord had kept them safe and at home this time.

Samantha and Joel entered the house, and Margaret followed on their heels. "I apologize for taking so long. I wanted to check on the children."

His eyebrows rose and he nodded. "Understandable, what with not knowing for sure about Mr. Jenkins' demise. Best to keep an eye on the youngsters." He cast a quick look toward Joel, who stood washing his hands at the kitchen sick under Sammie's supervision, and lowered his voice. "Although the boy looks big enough to take care of himself, and his sister, if the need arose." He turned inquisitive eyes on Margaret and dropped his voice. "You ever have reason to believe he'd hurt someone?"

Margaret sank into a nearby chair, all thought of offering the man a cookie disappearing. She leaned forward and whispered, "No. Certainly not. Why in the world would you ask such a thing?"

Sheriff Bryant hesitated, then reached into his shirt pocket and drew out a folded paper. "Do you recognize the handwriting, Miss Garvey?" He leaned across the table and held out the square missive. "Go ahead. Open it. Please."

Margaret stared at the paper and felt her heart pounding under her cotton blouse. Foreboding seeped into her mind, and it was all she could do to extend her hand and take the paper. She glanced at Sammie and Joel, who'd moved over to the sofa.

"Sammie?" Margaret tucked the paper in the pocket of her apron and took a step toward them. "Would you be willing to get the cookies and read to Joel for a while, so the sheriff and I can visit?"

"Sure." Sammie jumped up, reached into the jar for two cookies, and plucked the book off the bureau where she'd laid it the last time they'd read aloud. She settled down on the sofa and drew Joel down beside her, their backs toward the kitchen table.

Margaret removed the paper from her apron but let it lay un-opened on the palm of her hand. She raised her eyes to meet Sheriff Bryant's. "What is this?"

"It was discovered in Martin Jenkins' house the morning they found him. Someone left it in the kitchen." He reached into his other breast pocket and withdrew another scrap. "And this second one was found in the room where he died." He pressed it into her open palm. "Tell me what you think."

She knew without looking what the paper would contain. Sammie had told her about the notes she'd left when they'd taken food to survive. What in the world did that have to do with Martin Jenkins' death? Stranger still, why would Sammie have left two notes in the same house? Unless...

She tried to stifle a gasp. Perhaps she'd left one and Jenkins didn't find it, then she came back after he died and left the other? Her hand began to tremble and she willed it to stop. Leaving a note about food didn't implicate the children in anything other than being hungry and taking food without permission. It wasn't something they should have done, and she could see why the sheriff would be upset, but just the same....

She unfolded the first note and read the words she'd expected to see, neatly penned by Sammie. Then she carefully opened the second paper and stared down at it, unable to take in the meaning of the poorly printed words:

I pay fer buk

Chapter Twenty-five
....

Andrew hurried through his bath, shaved, dressed, and slipped on his shoes. His clammy hands fumbled with the laces and his stomach lurched. Not seeing Margaret for five days shouldn't cause this type of re-action, but a sudden urgency to get to her cabin drove him forward. He'd probably look like a fool rushing over tonight, but it couldn't be helped. He wanted to see her. When had his feelings for her changed from inter-est into the devotion a man has for a woman he'd like to marry?

The smell of wood smoke and some type of meat roasting made his mouth water as he jogged past the Lambert cabin, reminding him he'd skipped dinner. It would wait, and he doubted his stomach would tolerate food at the moment, regardless.

* * *

A knock sounded at Margaret's door and she rose, but Sheriff Bryant held up his hand. "If you don't mind, miss? The hour is getting a bit late, and maybe I should get it?" He didn't wait for a reply but grasped the doorknob and drew open the door.

A quick look over the sheriff's shoulder showed Andrew Brown-ing standing with narrowed eyes and furrowed brows. "What's going on here? Margaret, are you all right?" He took a step forward and the sheriff moved out of his way, allowing Andrew to pass. Andrew held out his hand toward her, an anxious look in his eyes.

Relief lifted Margaret's heart but she tried to push it away, remembering her father's letter. But her common sense warred with her emotions, reminding her that Andrew cared about Sammie and Joel. She'd have to ignore her personal feelings and deal with what was most important right now. She reached out and squeezed his fingers, then withdrew her hand. "I am now. I'm glad you've come, Andrew." She turned toward the sheriff. "Have you met Mr. Browning?"

"I have, and you were on my list to visit tomorrow, so I'm happy to see you this evening." Bryant leaned his hip against a kitchen cupboard and crossed his arms over his chest. "I hope you won't mind my asking you a few questions?"

Andrew continued to grip Margaret's hand, looking from her to the sheriff. "What's this about? Questions about what?"

"Andrew!" Joel jumped to his feet, Sammie dropped the book she'd been reading, and they both raced to his side. "You came home!"

Andrew grinned at the two as they halted beside him, and he returned Joel's exuberant hug. Sammie stood back a pace and smiled but didn't move closer. "I just got down off the mountain and came right over after I cleaned up." He wrinkled his nose. "You can be glad I didn't come first."

Sammie giggled, and Joel scratched his head. "Why not?"

Sammie elbowed him gently in the side. "He didn't smell good, so he had to scrub himself before comin' to see Miss Margaret."

Joel's brow puckered. "Sammie said I stunk real bad when we came, but Miss Margaret let me in before she made us take a bath."

Andrew patted the boy's arm. "That's because she's a nice lady, but I don't want to take advantage." He turned his attention to Sammie. "Were you reading a book?"

"Yes, sir. I've been reading *Adventures in Wonderland*, and Joel loves the rabbit."

Joel nodded. "Alice falls down a hole."

The sheriff cleared his throat and raised his brows, directing his attention at Margaret and glancing pointedly at the children.

Margaret picked up the book they'd dropped on the floor and handed it to Sammie. "Would you mind reading just a bit longer? You can both have another cookie if you like."

"Goodie! Thank you!" Joel bounced over to the cookie tin and pulled out two sugar cookies, handing one to Sammie and taking a big bite of his own. "Read to me some more, Sammie."

The younger girl took his hand and led him back to the far wall, where they sat down on the sofa. The two heads came close together over the book spread open in Sammie's lap, and the soft sound of her voice drifted across the quiet room.

The sheriff waved a hand at the two chairs next to the small pine table. "Would the two of you mind taking a seat?"

Andrew drew out a chair for Margaret and seated her, then took the other. The sheriff stayed standing but leaned forward and placed the open notes in front of Andrew. "This is what brought me here this evening. I'm still investigating Martin Jenkins' death and trying to find out who his enemies might be, or who could've been at his home the night he died. Miss Garvey looked at these before you knocked, but she hasn't had a chance to tell me what she thinks."

Andrew picked up both pieces of paper and laid them on the table, smoothing the creases and perusing the words. He glanced at Margaret, then at the sheriff, his eyebrows raised. "Where did you get these, and what do they have to do with Miss Garvey?"

"They were found in Martin Jenkins' home the same day they—" he dropped his voice near a whisper—"found his body."

"I still fail to see the connection or why you're here." Andrew placed his forearms on the table, his eyes not straying from the sheriff's face.

Bryant stepped close to the table and squatted on his haunches, keeping his voice low. "I think it has something to do with those two." He nodded toward Sammie and Joel. "From what I can gather, these aren't the only notes found. Several people had food disappear, and notes were left. The handwriting is the same. Other than the one about the book, that is." He plucked up the poorly written missive and gave it a slight shake.

Margaret looked over the sheriff's shoulder at Sammie and Joel. Both heads were bent over the open book, and the girl carefully pronounced the words in a firm but quiet voice. Joel's intent gaze studied the pages, as though he were trying to picture each scene as his sister opened a new world to his imagination. Margaret knew Sammie had left notes while hunting for food, but it never occurred to her they might have stumbled into the Jenkins' home near the time of his death.

There was no way Joel could be involved, although she had little doubt he'd penned the second note. The boy was big for his age, and if provoked, might defend his sister—but she didn't believe he would harm anyone. She'd doubted he'd even think of such a thing, much less know how to carry out an attack on a grown man. But what did the note about the book mean, and what had he taken?

Sheriff Bryant stirred beside her, and she turned back to him. He rocked on his heels and studied her face, then looked back at the two heads huddled over the book in the corner. "You know I'm right, don't you, Miss Garvey? You recognize the handwriting?"

Margaret shook her head and met his eyes. "I've never seen Samantha's handwriting, so no, I don't *know* you're right." She wanted to jump from the table, grab Sammie's and Joel's hands, and dash out the door—away from this man with the piercing eyes and probing mind, this man who could destroy the children's lives.

"But you know something about what's going on, and I have to insist you tell me."

Andrew cleared his throat but kept his voice low. "She doesn't have to talk to you, Sheriff. If she doesn't recognize the handwriting, you need to leave it at that."

The sheriff glanced from Margaret to Andrew, his face still and intent. "Just because she doesn't know the handwriting doesn't mean there isn't more she does know. I'd like to hear how the children came to be with you, Miss Garvey, and how long they were in town prior to their arrival at your home. Exactly what do you know about their past and their family?"

* * *

Wallace Stedman stomped up the stairs of his mother's house and pushed open the door, banging it behind him. He made a beeline for the most comfortable piece of furniture in the house, her over-stuffed sofa, and slouched full length on it, propping his shoes up on the arm. Sweet bliss, getting off his sore feet and onto something soft. He closed his eyes and settled down for a much-deserved rest. His mother mightn't be happy with the news he'd brought, but she couldn't blame *him*. All he could do was try, and he'd done that, for sure and for certain. Peace settled over the room, and oblivion crept over his mind.

Heavy footsteps thudded across the wood floor of the adjoining kitchen, then stopped. Wallace let out a sigh. Ma was fixing dinner. The footsteps started up again, but this time they headed toward the small parlor where he lay. He opened one eye a slit, anticipating a call to dinner, although he'd yet to smell any tantalizing odors drifting from the kitchen.

Ma walked into the room and screeched. For a woman of her substance she moved amazingly fast. Within seconds, she was looming over him. "What are yer filthy shoes doin' on my sofa?!"

He sat up, then bolted to a standing position. He ought to have known better. Ma was protective of her furniture. But before he could even open his mouth to apologize, she leaned closer and squinted at him.

"What you home for, anyhow? You better a'brung those kids back."

"Now, Ma, I did my best." He plastered on what he hoped was his best smile. "You got any of that stew you're famous for? I sure am hungry for some of yer good cooking."

Her mouth tightened further. "Don't you be changin' the subject. Speak up now, and be quick about it."

Wallace rocked on his heels and frowned. His feet screamed to be loosed from the too-tight shoes, and his stomach reminded him that he'd not eaten for hours. Ma could be so difficult. He scratched his chin. Worse, she was gonna be plumb irate when she heard his news. Maybe he could hold her off for now and get dinner first. "My feet hurt, Ma. Can I have something to eat and sit for a spell first? My

BRIDAL VEIL 1902 ORE.

stomach's done ate a hole in itself, I swear. I ain't had nothing to eat since yesterday."

She took a step back. "I suppose you can eat a bowl of stew and talk at the same time."

A jerk of her head toward the door sent him racing for the kitchen. No way was he waiting around and giving Ma a chance to change her mind. No sir.

A couple minutes later he sat at the wobbly table pushed into the corner of the dimly lit kitchen. A candle burned near his plate, dripping wax onto the marred wooden surface. Wallace gulped the stew and swiped a chunk of bread into the savory depths, bringing the dripping morsel to his mouth and inhaling the bite. Ma sat across from him, watching every spoonful enter his mouth until he'd cleaned the bottom of the bowl and held it out for more.

She shook her head and withdrew the bowl. "Talk, boy."

He plunked back against the spindles of the chair and sighed. When Ma got in one of her moods, there was no help for it. He'd best be telling what he knew. He'd almost stopped at another orphanage on the way back home and asked if they'd give him another brat but couldn't decide if Ma would want a boy or a girl, so he let it go. 'Sides, he didn't care to tackle the paperwork they'd expect him to sign, and his stomach was howling for vittles.

"I didn't find 'em." He cringed, wondering where those blunt words had sprung from.

"Where'd you look? You go to the places I told you?"

"Yes, Ma. I went back to where them kids come from, just like you said, and I talked to the neighbors. No one's seen them since the orphanage people took them away after their parents died."

"Where else did ya go?"

"I talked to the people at the orphanage where you got them, tole 'em they ran away, and that we wondered if they'd made their way back to 'em."

"You what?" Ma sat back in her chair, her mouth hanging open. "Now they'll think I ain't fit to have no more kids, if I can't keep the ones they give me. Why'd you tell 'em somethin' like that?"

He scratched his head, not comprehending the logic. "I thought you'd want me to talk to them people. It's the only other home those kids knew besides the one with their ma and pa, so it seemed natural they'd go back there."

"You didn't think, that's yer problem." Ma shook her head and sighed. "Never mind, don't matter now. Where else you look?"

"Please, Ma? I'm still starving."

She grabbed his bowl, clomped over to the pot simmering on the blackened stove, and slopped a dipperful into the dish. "Now finish talkin'."

"I will." Wallace dipped in his spoon and gulped a large bite, then started to talk. "I went to the police in Portland, but they didn't care. Said runaways ain't their problem. Told me more'n likely they're long gone by now. Wanted to know if they'd committed a crime. I said no, just run away is all."

Ma rolled her eyes and groaned. "Why didn't ya make somethin' up? If they thought they'd done wrong, they'd be more apt to look for 'em. Don't you got a brain in your head, boy?"

Wallace's back stiffened, and anger surged through him. His stomach was full now, but his feet still hurt and he'd been tramping around the country for days, with no thanks from his mother. He pushed back his chair and stood. "I'm tired, and I'm sick of you talking down to me. I did what you asked, and nothing makes you happy. Go find 'em yerself, if'n you think you can do better." He jutted out his chin. "I'm going to get some sleep." He belched again, just because it would rile her, and left the room.

Ma had been testy for weeks, and he'd had about as much as he could take. She needed to start appreciating him, that's what. Those two brats were orphans, and he was her own flesh-and-blood. Time she started remembering that and quit nagging at him so much. He dropped onto the sofa, kicked off his shoes, and leaned against the soft back. She couldn't say nothing about his shoes on her precious furniture now. He let out a grunt and turned on his side. Blamed kids. Ma could hunt for them next time. He'd had enough.

Chapter Twenty-six

. . . .

Nathaniel stooped over and plucked a chunk of dried mud from the edge of the braided rug in the front room of his home. He stalked to the door, yanked it open, and pitched the mud as hard as he could, hoping to find a sense of release from the pent-up emotion he'd been stifling since Margaret walked away an hour or so ago. Why hadn't he insisted he walk her back to her cabin? What kind of man was he, letting her go home alone while he retreated like a whipped pup with its tail between its legs?

Had she secretly wished he'd followed and wondered at his absence?

It was past suppertime, and he supposed he should fix something to eat. He shut the front door with more force than necessary, grabbed a cast-iron skillet from a peg on the wall, and dropped it onto the stove. He glared at the pan, then snatched it from the grate and hung it back on its peg. Food didn't appeal—not much did, except finding a way to wipe the distress from Margaret's face when she'd heard the news about her father. He muttered a quiet curse, then lifted his voice and shouted the words again.

What he wouldn't give to take back telling Margaret about the box. But then, she'd never have known he hadn't intentionally left her in Bridal Veil. He groaned deeply, leaned his hands on the table, and dropped his head. He'd wanted her to know he hadn't deserted her, but it had never occurred to him how she'd react. Would she calm down and see he'd not intentionally abandoned her, after she'd had time to think about it? Fix it. He had to fix it.

Where was his hat? A quick look in the kitchen didn't reveal the gray felt, and he strode into the front room. Not there either. Where was the blasted thing? He lifted his hand to run his fingers through his hair and stopped, shut his eyes, and shook his head, then tugged the brim of the hat perched on his head down closer to his eyes. He stalked out the door. Margaret might not want to see him right now, but he had to see her. Somehow he must make her understand he hadn't intended to hurt her. Somehow he had to make it right.

* * *

Margaret stared at the sheriff and felt the muscles of her face tighten. How much should she tell this man? Would answering his questions put Joel and Samantha in danger? Her stomach twisted, and a burning sensation rose in her throat. Mama and Papa had drummed honesty into her mind, and she knew God hated lying as well. The need to protect the children drove her almost to the point of fabricating a half truth, but her innate honesty and desire to please God held that thought in check. "I'm afraid I don't know much." She gripped her hands together in her lap. "I think they'd been in town for at least several days before Mr. Gibbs brought them to my home."

Sheriff Bryant rose and took a step closer. "Gibbs brought them? Where did he find them, and what made him bring them to you?"

"He came home early one day and found Joel sitting in his yard petting Buck, his dog. Sammie was terrified and wouldn't come inside the fence until Mr. Gibbs held Buck's collar."

"Why were the children there?"

Margaret lowered her voice. "Joel let it slip that they were hungry." She glanced across the room. Sammie had paused in her reading and lifted her head but wasn't looking their way. *Please God, don't let her be aware of what's going on.* She couldn't stand it if Sammie took Joel and tried to run again. They might not be so lucky, and she might not be so blessed to find them easily the next time. What if Sammie spooked badly enough to take her brother and hop a train again? They could end up in Portland, living on the streets, and who knew what would happen to them there. "We need to keep our voices down." Sammie bent her head over the book, and Margaret could hear her soft voice. She turned her attention back to the sheriff. "I presume they may have come to find food."

The sheriff spun his hat in his hands, drawing the brim through his fingers. "So do you believe they'd been taking food and possibly leaving notes?"

She hesitated, hating the thought of agreeing but knowing she didn't have a choice. Andrew's face showed strong sympathy for her dilemma, and his slight nod urged her to continue. "Yes, I do. But I can't believe anyone as honest as Sammie would do something bad and not own up to it, either."

"Ah-huh." Sheriff Bryant leaned against the nearby cupboard for a moment, as if contemplating her words. The silence was broken only by the hum of Sammie's low voice reading the words and the turning of a page in the book.

Andrew cleared his throat. "Are you thinking they might be involved in some way in Jenkins' death?"

Bryant raised his head and met Andrew's eyes, then shrugged one shoulder. "Not sure yet. The boy's big enough to hit a man on the head with a skillet. Might be they came planning on finding food and got surprised. Might not have meant to hurt anyone."

Margaret loosened her hands and laid her palms flat on the table. "What now? Are you"—she dropped her voice and hissed through her teeth—"considering taking Joel into custody?"

"No. I'll ask them some questions, but I have other possibilities, as well. Someone saw hobos walking the tracks around the same time, and I hear there was bad blood between Jenkins and one of the log skidders—a Dan Meadows."

Andrew nodded. "I talked to him on the job several days ago. I'm felling trees back of the Palmer mill for the rest of the summer, and Meadows is working up there. Jenkins was his boss—Meadows said he wasn't sorry Jenkins was dead, or something to that effect. I don't remember his exact words, but his tone said a lot."

"Ah-huh." The sheriff placed his hat on his head and took a step back. "Maybe I'll wait on talkin' to these youngsters. You happen to know if Meadows stays up at Palmer on the weekends?"

Andrew shook his head. "Not sure. He has a cabin at the logging site, but he's a drinking man. Some of the men take the back road from Palmer and head to Corbett or Troutdale over a weekend."

"I'll see if I can track him down. I've also sent word to Seattle and Vancouver to be on the lookout for two men riding the rails coming from this direction. Not much we can do to find someone when we don't know what they look like, but from what you said, they might be wanted."

Margaret released her breath and leaned forward. "That's wonderful. I was afraid those men were being completely overlooked."

The sheriff opened his mouth, but a sharp rap at the door snapped it shut again. "I'll not impose on you again, Miss Garvey. It's your home."

"Thank you, although I can't imagine who'd be calling." She cast another look at the children. Sammie had quit reading and stared at the door, then turned with a worried expression toward the sheriff and over to Margaret. How much had the girl heard? A stab of fear bit at Margaret's heart. *Please, God, help.* She rose from her chair and stepped toward the door. *Please let it be good news.* They'd had enough pain, fear, and trouble to fill a year, and didn't need any more. She swung the door wide and stared into the stormy eyes of Nathaniel Cooper.

Chapter Twenty-seven
....

Margaret bit back a groan, wanting nothing more than to shut the door in Nathaniel's face. She hadn't even had time to consider the meaning of his revelation, and now with this added complication, it didn't look like she could deal with her questions anytime soon. "May I help you, Mr. Cooper?"

She felt rather than saw someone step up behind her, and a moment later, the sheriff's voice spoke close to her ear. "Ask him in, if you please."

"What?" Her back stiffened. Sheriff Bryant had promised not to impose again, and now he was making demands? "Why?"

"Mr. Cooper is the one who found the notes. Please ask him in."

She hesitated. If she suggested the sheriff step outside to talk, it would be rude—and she'd not find out what Nathaniel wanted or what he told the sheriff. She swung the door wide. "All right."

The sheriff stepped up and hooked his thumbs in his belt. "Cooper. You were my next stop. Looks like Providence brought this group together tonight."

Margaret frowned. "I doubt Providence had anything to do with this."

Nathaniel stepped across the threshold. "I didn't expect to find you here, Sheriff. You were heading to my place? May I ask why?"

"If you'll come in and sit down, I'd be happy to explain."

Nathaniel walked in and stopped, staring at Andrew. "Looks like you're having a regular get-together." He swung his gaze from Margaret to Andrew, then around the room at the silent children.

Andrew stood and shoved his hands into his back pockets. "Mr. Cooper."

Nathaniel didn't thrust out his hand but took off his hat and tucked it under his arm, giving Andrew a bare nod. "Browning. I didn't expect to see you here."

"I'm staying at my home in Bridal Veil on the weekends. I'll head back up the mountain on Sunday afternoon."

Joel tapped Margaret's shoulder. "I need to go to the privy again, Miss Margaret. Can Sammie go with me?"

"Sure, Joel." Margaret turned to the quiet girl who was watching the group of adults with wide, frightened eyes. "You can play outside when Joel is done, but please stay near the cabin where I can see that you're safe, all right?"

Sammie nodded and gripped Joel's arm. "Yes, ma'am. Come on, Joel." She steered her brother around Nathaniel and cast him a dour look before heading out the door.

Margaret stepped over to the kitchen window and pushed it up a couple of inches. With this many bodies in the small house, it wouldn't hurt to have some fresh air—besides, being able to keep an ear turned toward the children would be a good idea, as well. She turned to the men seated across the room. "Gentlemen, I realize we're a ways from the window, but I don't want Sammie and Joel to hear. I hope you'll keep your voices down if we're speaking about anything"—she glanced out the open window toward the woods—"sensitive in nature?"

Nathaniel frowned after the girl, then swung back to Margaret. "I don't understand why those two are still in your home, Margaret."

She lifted her chin and crossed her arms. "You don't need to understand, Nathaniel, as it's not your business."

His face blanched, and he drew back a half step. "As you will." He turned to Bryant. "Sheriff?"

"You brought two notes that you found in Martin Jenkins' home. I showed those to Miss Garvey, and she believes it's possible they were written by Sammie and Joel. I understand from talking to people who were at Jenkins' cabin that you"—he nodded at Andrew—"had a run-in with a young man who accused you and Miss Garvey of being in the Jenkins' home the day before."

Nathaniel lifted a hand. "I must protest, Sheriff…"

"I can speak for myself, Cooper." Andrew cut across Nathaniel's words. "And I can speak for Miss Garvey, as well, since I was at the cabin when she arrived in the clearing."

Margaret laid a hand on Andrew's forearm, then dropped her arm to her side. "Andrew, it's all right. No one is accusing me of anything." She looked from Nathaniel to Sheriff Bryant. "Are you?"

The sheriff shook his head and smiled. "No, ma'am, I'm not. Just trying to get a feel for what happened, and when. Why don't we all take a seat?" He motioned toward the sofa and drew a couple of chairs across the floor from the table. "Miss Garvey?"

She hesitated, then sank into one of the hardback chairs, leaving the men to decide who'd have to sit next to each other on the cozy sofa. Nathaniel gripped the back of the one remaining chair and spun it around, then sat, while the sheriff and Andrew each took a corner of the cushions.

Margaret laced her fingers in her lap and met the sheriff's eyes. "I was there twice, actually. But I didn't enter the house either time." She paused, but no one spoke. Andrew sat on the edge of the sofa, forearms propped on his knees, while Nathaniel leaned back, arms crossed.

Sheriff Bryant laid his hat on his knees. "Why did you stop by the cabin?"

"Jenny Jenkins is one of my dearest friends, and I'd gotten a letter that day, expressing concern over her father. She worried he might not be eating properly. I took over a dish of stew but didn't find anyone at home." She hesitated, looking from one face to the other, then shook her head.

"What is it, Miss Garvey? I'd like to know anything you observed, even if you think it's not important."

"Well…" She took a deep breath, then expelled it. "It was no doubt my imagination, but I was certain I heard something in the woods after I knocked on the door. I called out, but no one answered." She uttered a small laugh. "An owl hooted and flew out of a tree, so I probably was mistaken."

The sheriff's eyes narrowed. "What kind of sound did you hear?"

Margaret thought for a moment, trying to recall exactly what had alerted her. Was it simply a feeling, or had there been something tangible that made the hair stand up on the backs of her arms? "At first, it sounded like someone may have stepped on a dry branch, and it snapped. I called out, asking if anyone was there, but no one answered. I waited a moment, then decided to return home when I heard"—she shivered as the memory surfaced—"what sounded like loud breathing not far from the porch."

Andrew gripped the sofa arm and leaned toward Margaret. "Someone was watching you?" A groan escaped his lips. "This town has always been safe for women to walk the trails at night, but I don't like the sound of that. Did you see anyone?"

She met his worried eyes. "No. I wasn't sure what to do—try to get inside the house and bolt the door, or run for home. Then I heard an owl hooting nearby, and he flew out of a tree only a few feet from the porch. I decided I'd been imagining things and hurried back home."

Nathaniel had sat quietly through her recitation, but now he turned a worried face toward the sheriff. "The morning we found Jenkins, Donnie Williams was at the house. He mentioned seeing Margaret knocking on the door Friday evening, as well as seeing her talking to Browning on Saturday morning." He nodded at Andrew.

Sheriff Bryant leaned against the high back. "Miss Garvey, would this Williams character have a reason to be following you around?"

She shook her head and frowned. "Not that I know of. I don't really know him, other than…" A thought made her pause. "I'd forgotten about that."

"What?" the sheriff asked.

"Donnie carried my order from the company store home for me awhile back, and asked me to the ice-cream social. I turned him down and explained that Andrew"—she blushed—"Mr. Browning was escorting me. Donnie grabbed my hand and held it and told me that he knew I liked him." She shook her head and brushed a tendril of hair from her eyes. "I jerked my hand away and told him I didn't, not in that way, and asked him to leave."

"How did he respond?"

"He got agitated and said that I'd soon find out that he was a better man than Mr. Browning, and stalked down the path toward the store. I didn't see him again until that Saturday morning at the Jenkins' home."

Andrew pushed to his feet and faced the sheriff. "It must have been Donnie Williams spying on Margaret outside the house that night, and it's possible he killed Martin Jenkins before she arrived. He's been trying to place the blame on everyone else and accused Margaret and me. I hope you'll at least take a serious look at the man."

Margaret wrapped her arms around herself and rubbed her upper arms. "He could be right. Donnie's been acting odd lately, and it's hard to say what he might be capable of. Either way, I certainly think this should remove any suspicion from Joel."

Nathaniel raised his brows and looked from Margaret to the sheriff. "Suspicion from Joel? What's that all about?" He stood and faced the sheriff. "You think the boy that's staying here might be the killer?"

Sheriff Bryant rose to his feet and tucked his hat under his arm. "No sir, I didn't say that. I'm looking into all possibilities and just asking questions at this point. No accusations are being made against anyone, yet. I'll want to talk to the boy, of course, as well as this Williams person and Dan Meadows, and I'm trying to track down the hobos who've been seen in the area. We're not ruling anything out." He took three long strides toward the kitchen area and peered out the open window over the sink. "You think you could call Samantha and Joel in now, Miss Garvey? I might as well talk to the pair of them before I head over to see Donnie Williams."

Margaret placed her hand over her heart and inhaled sharply. She'd forgotten to check on the children. She pulled open the door and nearly bolted outside. "Sammie? Joel? It's time to come in." A quick step brought her to the edge of the porch. "Sammie! I need to speak to you for a moment."

She waited, listening, barely aware of the three men standing in the open doorway behind her. A chipmunk chattered from a branch in a maple tree, and a small flock of finches fluttered from a nearby willow tree, but she didn't see either of the children playing outside.

Andrew stepped to her side and lowered his voice to a whisper. "You think they overheard?" He nodded toward the open window.

She hugged herself. "Maybe. I wouldn't put it past Sammie to take Joel and run again. I was afraid she was acting too calm earlier. She must have been listening the entire time she was reading."

Sheriff Bryant cleared his throat and moved forward. "Miss Garvey? Any idea where the children might head?"

She turned and stared into his eyes, noting the spark of compassion in their gray blue depths. "No, sir. I don't. And I'll admit I'm worried." A glance at the sky showed the sun heading toward the horizon. "They ran away one other time and we found them huddled in a shallow cave in a wash, not far from Bridal Veil Falls. They may have gone back there again, I don't know."

"We'd best check before it gets dark." Sheriff Bryant tugged on his hat brim. "I'm sure there aren't too many places a young girl would feel safe hiding on a dark night."

Margaret frowned. "You don't know Sammie. That girl has spunk—lots of it. And if she thinks she's protecting Joel, she'd go to the ends of the earth."

Chapter Twenty-eight

....

Sheriff Bryant headed toward Donnie Williams' home with the assurance that he'd check back with Margaret on behalf of Sammie
and Joel. Margaret, flanked by Andrew and Nathaniel, rushed across
town and into the grove of trees where they'd found the two children
hiding last time. Margaret tried to calm her breathing and willed
her heart to quit pounding so hard, but nothing she told herself
seemed to help. She'd prayed all the way from her cabin to the patch
of woods but couldn't seem to find any peace. A hard knot gripped
her stomach, and it was all she could do to hold down her supper.

Andrew moved ahead when they neared the spot and got down
on his knees and crawled through the brush toward the hollow in
the hillside. Even before he reached it, Margaret knew what he'd find.
She'd known in her heart that Sammie wouldn't return to the place
she'd hidden before. The girl was too quick-witted and wary to choose
the same hiding spot twice. If only they'd discovered where they'd
hidden when they first came to town. But would Sammie choose to
return there? Probably not.

"Nothing here and no sign they've been there tonight." Andrew
backed out of the brush on all fours, then stood and brushed the bits
of twigs, dirt, and leaves off his trousers. "Think we should talk to Art
and see if he'd use his dog again?"

Nathaniel pushed forward and peered into the surrounding
brush. "What makes you think they'd come here?"

Margaret met his eyes and didn't flinch. "Sammie got spooked the first time you and the sheriff came, and after you left, she took Joel and ran. She figured the sheriff came to take them back to the home they ran away from. We found them here." She pointed at the brush. "But I didn't really think she'd come back." She swiveled her gaze to Andrew. "Yes. Let's head to Art's house and see if Buck can help."

Margaret saw Nathaniel start to speak, then clamp his mouth shut. A good thing, because she didn't have the time or patience to deal with whatever he was thinking right now.

Andrew struck off down the path, with Margaret close on his heels, and Nathaniel brought up the rear. Silence fell over the group as they wove through the trees. The path they trod was cast in deep shadows as the weak rays of the setting sun were gobbled up by the swaying boughs. The wind had kicked up, and threatening clouds piled in towering black billows against the darkening sky. Margaret shuddered and squeezed her eyes shut for a second, then stared at the clouds. It looked like a thunderstorm might be building. Another thought stilled her breathing for a moment, and her heart rate picked up speed. Were Sammie or Joel afraid of lightning storms, and would they find a safe shelter out of the storm? *Please, God. Take care of them. You brought them back safely last time and protected Sammie when the two men followed her. Hold them in the hollow of Your hand again.*

The trio approached the fence surrounding the small house where Art Gibbs lived, and Andrew paused at the gate. Nathaniel reached over the top and grabbed the latch, but Andrew laid a hand on his arm. "You might want to wait."

Nathaniel drew his hand back and scowled. "What for? Don't we need to hurry before it gets dark?"

Margaret nodded and moved up beside him. "We do, but Mr. Gibbs' dog doesn't care for strangers. If he's loose, you're apt to get bitten."

Andrew stepped close to the fence and cupped his hand around his mouth. "Ho, the house. Art Gibbs—you in there?"

No answer came from the small wood-sided house, and no patter of feet or barking dog came racing around the corner. No lights lit the windows facing the road running past the house. Andrew tried again. "Gibbs. You home?" He lifted the latch on the gate and pushed it open, then held up his hand to the others. "Why don't you wait here, just in case?" He gave a wry smile. "No sense all of us getting bitten, in case the dog suddenly wakes up and bolts around the house." He pushed the gate closed and walked across the short space to the house. After rapping on the door, he waited a minute, then rapped again. Quiet continued to reign, and no lights sprang to life.

Margaret called across the yard. "It appears he's not at home, Andrew. What should we do now?"

Andrew made his way back to the gate, a worried look on his face. "I'm not sure. I guess we need to find the sheriff and start looking."

"It's going to be dark in another hour. We need to hurry." Margaret opened the gate and shut it behind Andrew.

Nathaniel stepped up beside her and extended his hand. "Don't worry, Margaret. You said they were on their own before you took them in. I'm sure they'll be all right. If we don't find them tonight, we can keep looking tomorrow."

"We have to find them tonight." Margaret moved away from Nathaniel's hand and tried not to let her voice rise. "What if whoever killed Mr. Jenkins is still around and goes after the children?"

Andrew nodded. "I have to agree. Let's head over to Donnie's house and see if we can find the sheriff. There's no time to lose." Thunder pealed and lightning flashed in the east as gusts of wind bent the tops of the trees. The clouds building in the Gorge grew darker, and a scattering of drops started to fall.

* * *

Three hours later Margaret stood on the edge of her porch, staring at the small group of people gathered in the lantern light. The east wind had picked up over the past two hours, and occasional lightning flashes showed whitecaps churning on the river. Sheriff Bryant had brought some volunteers together, but the children hadn't been found. Word had spread through Bridal Veil and neighbors turned out, offering to search again in the morning.

The sheriff waved his lantern to quiet the murmuring crowd. "I think we'll have to call it a night, folks. Not much sense trying to hunt during this storm, and we don't want someone getting hurt. Why don't you head back to your homes, and let's gather in front of the schoolhouse first thing in the morning."

A man standing just back of the circle of light cast by the lantern called out, "Hey, Sheriff, is it true these two young'uns are the ones leavin' the notes in people's homes sayin' they'll pay for the food they took?"

"We think so, Hiram, but we're not certain yet." Sheriff Bryant held his lantern higher and peered out into the crowd. "They've been stayin' at Miss Garvey's for the past couple of weeks, and she vouches for them."

"I heard you were asking questions about that big boy. You worried he might a'had something to do with Jenkins' death?" Another voice spoke from the other side of the small group.

"I don't think so, no. I'm checking into a number of possibilities right now. We're just concerned that two children are missing."

The wind whistled through the tops of the trees and swayed the limbs, sending fircones and needles flying across the clearing. Thunder rumbled in the distance, and a sprinkling of rain plopped on the dust in front of the cabin. But the clouds were scuttling by at such a dizzying pace that it didn't appear they'd get any substantial rain, despite the dry woods and their need of moisture.

Vernon Myers lifted his hand and grabbed at his hat. "He didn't look like no child to me. He appears to be at least sixteen or seventeen. That isn't no child."

Margaret stepped to the edge of the porch. "Samantha is only thirteen, and her brother is fourteen, but yes, he's big for his age. Joel is a sweet boy. He's a little simpleminded, but he wouldn't harm anyone."

Vernon kept his hand on his hat and shook his head. "Maybe not. All I know is, someone came into my house and took food right off'n our table."

"They were hungry and scared," Margaret said. "They didn't know who they could trust when they came to town, but they're just children."

Hiram scratched his head. "Where'd they come from? Don't they have parents, or someone to watch over them?"

"I wish I knew, Hiram. I think they ran away from someone who hurt them. Sammie told me their parents are dead, and they're searching for relatives, but that's all I know for sure."

Sheriff Bryant cleared his throat and held the swinging lantern. "Thank you all for your help. Any of you who can make it, meet us at six in the morning." He turned to Margaret as the knot of people dispersed. "Too bad your friend Mr. Gibbs isn't around with his dog this evening. He'd probably find those two mighty quick."

"One of the men said he'd headed to Portland for the weekend to see Glenna, his fiancée, at her parents' house. He's supposed to be back on Sunday evening. Hopefully we'll have found them before then, and we won't have need of Buck."

He wagged his head and stepped down off the porch. "Well, good night, Miss Garvey. Try not to worry too much." He turned to Andrew standing silent beside him. "Walk with me, Mr. Browning? I'd like to talk with you for a bit."

Andrew shot a look at Margaret, then nodded. "Good night, Margaret. I'll be praying for the children. I'll start looking for them first thing."

She lifted her hand and attempted a smile, although the muscles in her face protested at the effort. "Thank you, Andrew."

Nathaniel Cooper stood off to the side, then moved forward as the sheriff and Andrew tugged their hats low over their eyes and trudged off down the path. "May I speak with you, Margaret?"

She tucked a strand of hair behind her ear and leaned a hand against the wood post on the front corner of the porch. "It's late, and I'm tired. Can it wait?"

He hesitated, then shook his head. "I suppose it could, but I promise I won't keep you long."

"All right. We can sit on the porch." She led the way to one of the two chairs set back from the edge and sank onto the hard surface. "I'm glad the wind's died—at least for now."

"Knowing the Gorge, I doubt it'll be calm for long. Probably going to blow hard tonight." Nathaniel gripped his hat and sat on a nearby chair. Thunder continued to roll and lightning lit up the sky on the Washington side of the river. "It's quite a sight, the sky all lit up like that."

"Yes, it's such a testament to God's power. Lightning has never frightened me, but it does remind me how insignificant we are."

"I don't agree. Man is the most powerful force on this earth. I believe one day we'll even harness the lightning storms."

Margaret folded her hands in her lap and shook her head. "That may be, but man isn't the most powerful force—God is."

Nathaniel shrugged. "I won't argue with you about it. God is all-powerful, but I meant that man's intelligence outweighs all else." He leaned forward, his face and eyes intent on Margaret's. "I need to know if you'll forgive me for leaving you here. I didn't know you'd answered me." She started to speak but he held up his hand. "Please. Give me a moment?" She settled back against her chair and he continued. "I shouldn't have assumed you didn't care, but I guess my pride got in the way. I know now that I should have found you, talked to you, made sure of what you were feeling, but I didn't. I'm sorry. I'll always regret my decision, and I hope you can find it in your heart"— he dropped his head, then slowly lifted it—"to forgive me and let me have another chance."

* * *

Margaret paced the cabin, too keyed up to sleep. She'd changed into her nightgown and wrapper but hadn't been able to stay under the covers. Her mind struggled to take in all that had happened in the past twenty-four hours and make some kind of sense of it. Nathaniel arriving with news about the box, the sheriff bringing the notes, Sammie and Joel running away, her feelings about her father—it was too much. Now all she could focus on were the young brother and sister alone in the night. If only they'd been more careful and kept their voices down, or she'd checked on the youngsters sooner.

The window facing the river rattled with the force of the wind, and she could hear what sounded like small branches hitting the roof. The thunder and lightning had abated for the last hour but picked up in earnest now. A peal of thunder rang through the cabin, and close on its heels, lightning lit the room, creating dancing fingers of light and shadow on the walls. *That was close.* If only God would send rain, or the woods could be in serious trouble—but what if the children didn't have good shelter? She didn't want them soaked and shivering, hiding under a tree trying to stay warm.

Another thought struck her, and her knees went weak. What if the hobos never left town and found Sammie and Joel before the searchers could? *O God, you've got to keep them safe!* Margaret sank into her mother's rocker. If it weren't for Sammie and Joel being out in this storm, she'd almost enjoy it. Thunder brought a sense of awe, and the jagged flashes of light were a source of delight when she was a child.

Sammie must be so frightened, and Joel—she couldn't begin to imagine the terror the boy would feel, trapped in his simple mind, unable to understand what was happening. She prayed that, somewhere in their past, their mother had found a way to turn what could be a fearful situation into one of wonder. How it chafed at her to sit here, waiting for daylight. Common sense told her that Sammie had found shelter for at least two weeks before coming to live with her, and she'd do so again—but that didn't make it easier to wait out the night. The men would have kept hunting if not for this storm. *Please, God, let it stop soon. Take care of the children, wherever they are.*

A sudden awareness of her father's care struck her, and her hands started to shake. Papa often worried about her when she was Sammie's age and she stayed out after dark. Now she was responding the same way to her two young charges. She'd so often resented her father's watchful eye, thinking him controlling and overly anxious. Now she wondered. Had she been unfair to judge him the way she'd done over the years? If her fears for Sammie and Joel were any indication, the answer could be yes. She pushed out of her chair and paced over to the window, staring out at the stormy night. She'd have to think this through, and maybe even pray about it, as well. Yes, it might be a good idea to ask God to lead her in this one small thing: helping her to understand her father.

Nathaniel's words earlier that evening rang in her mind. He wanted another chance. Why wasn't her heart singing with the joy she'd expected? Isn't that what she'd wished for all these years? At least, at first, before anger and hurt had pushed those feelings to the back of her heart and stomped them down. Now she wasn't so sure what she wanted. Part of her longed to return to the days of her youth, when she'd been head-over-heels in love with Nathaniel. But what about Andrew? She'd thought her liking for him was only respect at first, but now she wasn't so sure. Admiration and respect became mixed somewhere along the way with genuine caring and attraction, but dare she allow her heart to get more deeply involved? She groaned and sank back down into the rocker. If only she could let go of her fear and trust God with her entire life—Andrew, Nathaniel, the children. All of it.

If she gave Nathaniel the chance he asked for, she'd have to be open and honest with Andrew. Tell him about her past and let him know she wasn't sure what—or who—she wanted in her future. She couldn't blame him if he decided she wasn't worth the effort, or the wait. Did she want to take the chance of losing him, like she'd lost Nathaniel? But would she ever really be content with Andrew, or any other man, if she didn't find out for sure if she still had feelings for Nathaniel?

A mighty clap of thunder rattled the windows, and she clutched the arms of the rocker. That felt close. Too close. The lightning that followed struck mere seconds later, bringing everything in the room into stark relief. An ear-splitting crash shook the cabin to the foundation, and she jumped from the chair. What in the world? She whirled around and covered her head as the ceiling creaked, groaned, and then split wide open.

BRIDAL VEIL
1902
ORE⌣

Chapter Twenty-nine

Samantha crouched beside Joel and held his hand as he cowered behind the hay stacked in the loft of a barn almost a mile west of town. It wasn't the same one they'd stayed in when they first came to Bridal Veil—that would be too dangerous. She couldn't take the chance they'd track her to the old barn they'd used before. This one housed dairy cows that munched contentedly in the stalls below, seemingly unaware of the storm raging around them. Sammie patted Joel's arm, hoping to calm his fears as the lightning sliced across the sky and thunder shook the wood floor. "Shh, it's all right, Joel. God is with us, remember? He sent the lightning so it wouldn't be so dark."

"But I don't like the noise. It's too loud. It sounds like the lightning is tearing the sky apart." Joel clapped his hands over his ears as another volley rang through the loft.

"Come on, sit closer to me. Do you remember what Mama used to tell us about the thunder and lightning when we were little?"

Joel shook his head and shivered. "No." He hitched himself across the loose hay and leaned against a pile in the corner. "What?"

She looped her arm through his and squeezed. "She said the thunder was the angels beating on drums and making a mighty praise to the Lord. When it gets loud, we're to think about the angels, and not be afraid."

He nodded slowly, thoughtfully. "I remember. But I wish they didn't have to play so loud."

"It's all right. The drums won't hurt you."

His body relaxed, and he let out a long breath. "Just angels playing their drums and praising God."

"Ah-huh. Pretty soon they'll get tired of playing and put their drums away, and the night will grow quiet again." She held up her hand. "Listen. The thunder is getting farther away, and it's not as windy now, either."

"When the angels stop playing, can we go back to Miss Margaret's house? I didn't get supper." He wriggled around and stared at his sister.

Sammie bit her lip and hesitated, hating that she'd dragged her brother out of the warmth and comfort of Miss Margaret's home. But from what she'd overheard the sheriff say, she knew it was no longer a safe place to stay. He wanted to question them about that man's death, and no way would she let anyone haul her brother to jail. Over her dead body, that's for sure. "I know, and I'll try to find us something to eat in the morning. Do you think that if I make us a nice soft bed in this hay, you could go to sleep?"

He twisted his mouth to the side and furrowed his brows, then shrugged. "Guess so, but my tummy's complaining. It don't like being empty."

She reached up and kissed his cheek. "I know. You're a good boy, Joel. A real good boy. And I'm proud of you." She jumped to her feet and gathered armfuls of the sweet-smelling hay out of the large stack, spreading it in a deep mound close by. "We'll pretend we're camping out again, and the cows down below are our pets watching over us while we sleep."

Joel perked up and smiled. "Like Buck. He's Mr. Gibbs' pet, and he'd watch out for us if he was here."

"Yes, like Buck."

"I miss Buck. I thought we were going to get to play with him tomorrow, and Mr. Andrew was going to take us for a walk. Maybe even a picnic." He heaved a sigh and rubbed a hand across his eyes. "I'm tired, Sammie. Is the bed ready yet?"

"Yes, come lie down." She patted the pile of hay and rubbed her tickling nose, trying to hold back a sneeze. "And don't you worry. Everything will be fine when we wake up tomorrow."

"You promise, Sammie?"

She hesitated and turned her eyes away. "I'm praying it will. God loves us, Joel, and He'll take care of us." A thought niggled at the corner of her mind, and she tried to push it away. If she really believed that, why had she run this time? Hadn't God watched over her when those men tried to catch her in the woods? Hadn't Miss Margaret been kind to them ever since they'd arrived at her house? Sure. But that didn't mean she shouldn't use common sense and do everything she could to watch out for her brother. God didn't want His children to lie down and quit doing anything for themselves, did He? She'd trust Him to keep the sheriff from finding them, but she'd do her part to make sure they kept out of sight, as well.

* * *

Margaret raced to the kitchen and huddled in the corner, her heart racing and ears ringing with the crashing noise. Total darkness covered the room, but she felt small bits of wood and—what? fir needles?—cascading over her head. She covered her mouth and choked back a gasp that turned into a sob. Maybe it wasn't so terrible that Sammie and Joel had run away. They could've been seriously hurt if they'd been sleeping in their normal place in the corner. The fir tree standing twenty feet behind her cabin must have been struck by lightning. Another bolt raced across the sky and gave her several seconds of light. The trunk of the once-mighty Douglas fir lay cross-wise over the exposed beams of what used to be her ceiling, and the branches of the tree reached almost to her floor.

She lit a lantern and stared at the hole in her roof, then around at the broken bits of branches and shattered wood from her ceiling. What a mess. Thank the Lord it hadn't rained, but the tree branches continued to cast needles onto her braid rug and table in the far corner of the room. There was no possibility of sleep now. She shook her head and kicked a fircone back under the branches and out of her sight. At least it hadn't brought the entire ceiling down. She could be thankful for that much.

She headed to her room and plucked a quilt off her bed. Morning would be here soon, and at least the temperature rarely dropped below sixty or sixty-five degrees this time of year. She slung the quilt over her shoulders and snuggled into the sofa, ten feet from the branches and the gaping hole in her roof. Some of the men would arrive at first light to start hunting, and she'd wait and see what could be done about repairs then. No sense in trying to roust out anyone tonight, not with the lightning still streaking across the sky.

She drew the quilt up to her chin and curled her legs under herself, thankful the rolling thunder seemed to be lessening. Her heart kept repeating a prayer over and over. *Watch over the children. Please, God, watch over the children.* Even as her mind drifted toward Nathaniel's request again, her heart continued to sing the same pleading song, lifting the refrain toward heaven.

Nathaniel. She leaned her head against the arm of the sofa. Was this God's hand bringing Nathaniel back into her life? She'd believed God had promised a perfect mate for her, and she'd been so sure it was Nathaniel. When he'd disappeared from her life, she'd had to work at not being angry at God. He could have stopped Nathaniel from leaving. Maybe, though, it was better this way. She'd been so young and still had much to learn about life. She smiled and sank further into her warm nest. What was she thinking? She still had a lot to learn, and her journey toward wisdom wouldn't stop until the day she passed on.

What to do? Her heart yearned to understand and take the right path. She'd made no promise to either man, and Andrew had never spoken openly about his intentions. A gust of cool air shot down through the hole in the roof, scattering needles across the room. The fragrance of fresh-cut fir boughs filled the air. In spite of the damage to her home, she inhaled deeply. It smelled like Christmas, her favorite time of year. But her smile faded as pain shot through her heart. Papa wouldn't be with her to celebrate this Christmas. It would be her first one without either parent.

O God, show me what to do! She thought of Andrew—his kindness, strength, and protective nature. The last thing she wanted to do was hurt him, but would it be fair to allow him to court her, if she didn't first search out her feelings for Nathaniel? No. Maybe she wasn't still in love with Nathaniel. He'd irritated her more than once since returning, and she didn't know for sure where he stood in his relationship with the Lord. But part of her would always wonder what might have happened if she didn't give Nathaniel the chance he asked for.

BRIDAL VEIL
1902
ORE

Chapter Thirty

....

A loud knocking and a man's voice shouting her name jerked Margaret from the restless slumber she'd fallen into sometime before daylight. "Just a minute." She flung off the quilt and pushed to her feet, running her hands through her disheveled hair. She still wore her wrapper over her nightdress, and she tugged on the belt. A couple of steps brought her to the front door, and she opened it mere inches and peered outside. "Andrew?"

He stood on the porch, his face looking as she'd felt when the children ran away. "Thank God you're safe. When did the tree come down?"

"Sometime after midnight. I assume it was struck by lightning, but as hard as the wind was blowing, you never know." She opened the door another inch. "Give me a moment to dress? I fell asleep on my sofa and just woke up."

"I'll walk around back and take a look at the damage." He cast her another worried look, then swung on his heel and strode off the porch, disappearing around the corner of her cabin.

Margaret hurried through her morning routine, loosening her braid, brushing out her hair and rebraiding it, then washing her face and changing into the dark green dress that she saved for house-cleaning. Today would be a long day—no sense in ruining a good gown.

She walked outside and breathed in the clean, fragrant air, doused by sunbeams and the scent of nearby honeysuckle. "Andrew?" She shielded her eyes against the glare of the rising sun but failed to find him.

"I'm up here."

Margaret squinted toward the peak of her cabin. Andrew perched on the trunk of the fallen tree resting on the roof. Her hand flew to her chest. "That looks dangerous!"

He laughed and shook his head. "Don't worry. It's secure against the cross timbers, which is why the tree didn't crash through to your floor."

"I'm sure you've climbed higher while felling trees, but it makes me nervous, just the same. I've never been fond of heights."

"I've seen what I need to." He gripped a large limb and clambered down the trunk a couple of steps, then walked the rest of the way without mishap and jumped to the ground. "It's not as bad as it looks. It ruined a section of roof, but the timbers appear to be intact, so the repairs should be fairly easy. I'll get a crew out here right away. Do you have somewhere you can stay until tomorrow? I'm afraid your cabin will be a mess and will need a thorough cleaning before you move back in."

"I'm sure I can stay with Clara if need be. You're right about the mess. It rained needles and cones for a while last night, and bits of the wood ceiling are scattered around the room."

"Don't worry. I'll make sure it's cleaned up before you come back."

She shook her head and folded her arms. "It's my home, and as much as I appreciate the offer, I'll not put it off on someone else."

He grinned, dimples showing at the corners of his mouth. "As much as you do for everyone else, I thought it was worth a try. But I didn't expect you to say yes."

She laughed, then suddenly sobered. "Sammie and Joel. How could I have forgotten?"

He straightened from where he'd been leaning against the trunk. "Some of the men should be here soon. We'll break into teams. A couple of men can stay and help with the repairs, and the rest can fan out and search. Too bad Gibbs is still out of town."

"Do you know when he'll be back?"

"Someone told me they think by late this afternoon, but he sometimes stays over till after church on Sunday." He shook his head and frowned. "I'm guessing we'll find Sammie and Joel before then, and it won't be a concern."

"I surely hope so."

Silence fell between them, and Margaret's mind raced. This would be a good time to speak to Andrew.

"Margaret…"

"Andrew…" She stopped and bit her lip, wondering what he'd started to say. She waved her hand. "You go first."

"No, I insist. Please." He nodded and smiled. "I'm sure whatever you have to say is more important."

She laughed nervously. "I'm sorry. What I have to say isn't funny. It's just that, well…"

Andrew gently touched her arm. "Take your time, whatever it is."

She held her breath a second, then slowly exhaled. "Thank you. I don't quite know how to say this. You've been so wonderful these past few weeks."

His eyebrows shot up, and he stared at her but kept his peace.

"Please. Would you come around to the porch and sit for a moment? We probably don't have much time before the others start arriving." She led the way to the front porch and gestured to the chair snugged against the outer wall.

He sank into the chair, worry tugging at his normally sunny countenance. "What is it, Margaret? Is something besides the children worrying you?"

"Yes. I mean—oh, it's all so confusing." She clasped her hands together on her lap and met his eyes. "I'm not even sure how to say this, since you haven't declared yourself in any way, but—"

He sat bolt upright and then leaned forward. "Declared myself? As in do I care for you? Is that what you're needing to know? If so, I can easily answer that." A happy smile lit his face, and his eyes shone with a warm light. "I care—"

"Wait." She held up her hand and spoke the word sharply. "Please. Don't say anything more." Her hand started to tremble, and she lowered it back to her lap. "I'm so sorry, Andrew. This is so unfair to you."

His brows furrowed. "What's unfair to me?"

Her breath released in a whoosh. "It's Nathaniel Cooper."

"What about him? Has he bothered you in some way?" He started to rise, but she stilled him with a raised hand.

"No. Nothing like that. Do you remember that he mentioned at the ice-cream social that we knew one another before?"

He settled back in his chair, watching her intently. "Yes."

She wished she could read his thoughts, but the quiet stillness that had crept into his eyes gave nothing away. Why did it have to be so difficult? She knew why, if she were honest with herself. Something more than fondness had been growing in her heart for Andrew recently. But she couldn't ignore Nathaniel's request out of hand, either.

Margaret looked down at her skirt and smoothed imaginary wrinkles out of the fabric, hating to raise her eyes and see the disappointment in Andrew's eyes that would surely follow. "I was in love with him once and wanted to marry him."

Andrew sucked in his breath, but no words followed. Margaret raised her eyes and met his questioning ones. He opened his mouth, closed it, and tried again. "Why didn't you, then?"

She bit her bottom lip and hesitated, then decided to say it straight out. Andrew deserved that much. "We had a misunderstanding. Nathaniel left a note for me, asking that I travel with him to Portland and marry, then go on to the job that awaited him in Salem. I left one in return, saying I would, and left it in our trysting place." She paused, a lump rising in her throat and threatening to choke her. "But he didn't find it, and he thought I'd changed my mind. He"—she twisted her hands—"left without me."

Andrew leaned forward. "You said you left the note? Why, then, didn't he find it?"

She plucked at a fir needle resting on her sleeve and flicked it away. "Nathaniel came to see me recently and brought something with him that I've not seen in four years. The note that he'd left for me, with my answer."

"He took it and left town without you? The cad!" Andrew clenched his right fist and slapped it into the open palm of his left hand.

Margaret stared, not realizing he'd think that. She shook her head, making her long braid swish back and forth. "No. Oh, no, Andrew, he never found it the night that I left it."

"Then what? Why?"

"A week ago he decided to do some work in our old yard. The Company assigned him our house, you know."

"I didn't, but I've not paid much attention to Mr. Cooper's personal business." He crossed his arms over his chest and gave a short nod. "Go on."

"He dug up a dead rosebush, and his spade hit something. Another spadeful of dirt and the item came up—it was the box we'd once used for leaving notes."

Andrew raised his brows, and his head gave a slight backward start. "Ah-huh."

"My father thought me too young to marry and wasn't happy about my relationship with Nathaniel." She felt a warm blush rise from her neck to her cheeks and raised her hand to touch her skin. "I was wrong, I know that now, to continue seeing him when Papa didn't approve. But I was young and believed I was in love, and Nathaniel wanted to marry me."

"Did he know how your father felt?"

The blush intensified, and she dropped her head. "Yes."

Andrew muttered something she couldn't discern, then fell silent.

Margaret raised her head and met his eyes. "I believe he loved me. I turned seventeen a month after he left town. Papa married Mama when she was that age. He had no right to interfere."

"He had every right, Margaret. He was your father." The words were spoken softly, without malice or censure. "He loved you and felt he knew what was best. I imagine he thought he was saving you from making a mistake."

She shook her head, frustration and doubt warring inside. "I'd prayed about it for weeks, and I believe God told me it was all right."

Andrew stared into her eyes for a long moment. "God wouldn't tell you to sneak off against your father's wishes. He tells us to honor our parents. You were still living under his roof—under his protection. God doesn't go against His Word."

She closed her eyes, wanting to be done with this conversation. Andrew didn't understand. He couldn't. He'd not lived through the hurt and pain of finding Nathaniel gone. "It doesn't matter now. I thought God told me He was taking care of it, and it would all be all right, but He didn't, and it wasn't. I've shied away from trying to hear His voice because I don't trust that I'll hear correctly. But that isn't why I wanted to talk to you. I need you to know..." She paused and gripped her hands in her lap. "That Nathaniel has asked for another chance, and I feel I must give him one."

Andrew jerked back as though he'd been struck, and his eyes grew wide. "Another chance? What does that mean, exactly?"

She worried the edge of her bottom lip with her teeth. "To see if there's still anything between us. To court, I suppose. I haven't really asked him what he meant, but that was my understanding."

He stood and pushed his chair back, bumping it against the wall. "You're sure that's what you want to do? Even though the man left when he didn't find your note?"

"His train was leaving a short time later. He didn't have time to wait and talk to me again, and he assumed I'd changed my mind."

"I'd have stayed another week and lost the job, rather than assuming something and leaving you behind." Andrew ground out the words between clenched teeth. His head swung away from her. "I hear voices on the trail." He stepped off the porch, then turned back to face her. "I'll step aside, Margaret. I don't cotton to a man who'd go against your father's wishes, but you've made it clear that it's not my business. I care for you, and I'd hoped to court you proper. But more than anything, I want your happiness. If you can find it with Cooper, then I'll wish you the best and step out of your life." A sad smile touched the corner of his mouth.

A man with a long stride entered the clearing in front of the cabin and raised his hand. "Margaret." Then, seeing the cabin roof, he broke into a run. "Oh, my dear, are you all right?"

Nathaniel Cooper had arrived.

Chapter Thirty-one

The sheriff arrived on Nathaniel's heels, along with Hiram, Grant Cowling, Julius, and three other men who'd been friends of Margaret's father. Andrew eyed them as they entered the clearing, trying his best to keep his turbulent emotions from warring on his face. Margaret had almost married Nathaniel Cooper, and now she planned on letting him court her again? Andrew gave a loud snort, and Julius clapped him on the back.

"My sentiments, exactly. Looks like that there tree did quite a number on Miss Margaret's roof, don't it?"

Andrew plastered on a smile and looked in the direction Julius pointed. "Yes. I climbed up to take a look. The damage isn't bad, but it needs to get fixed before dark, if possible."

Nathaniel stepped to Margaret's side and grasped her hand, whispering something Andrew was unable to hear. He turned away, his stomach roiling. "Sheriff, we need to organize a search party for those children, but a couple of men should stay and see to Miss Garvey's roof."

Nathaniel stepped forward. "I'll stay. Margaret says those two have run away before. It's more important that we take care of the house and ensure she has a warm, safe place to stay." He stepped back and gestured toward the tree lodged on top of the cabin. "If a couple of men can bring some crosscut saws, wedges, and whatever other tools you think you'll need, we'll start on the removal and repairs."

Andrew grunted and clapped his hat on his head. "Suits me. I'll take Julius, and we'll start searching for Sammie and Joel. He's met them, and they're more apt to trust someone they know. Sure wish Gibbs was back."

Hiram moved forward, scratching his morning stubble that he hadn't taken time to shave. "Got word he's comin' back t'day."

"Good. That dog of his can find them, sure as the world." Andrew turned to the sheriff, his eyebrows raised. "Sheriff, you going to help us hunt, or work on the roof?"

"I think I'm better suited to helping you hunt, but I'm guessing the young lady might get skittish if she sees me." He looked around the small clearing at the faces of the men. "How about you, Hiram, Grant, and Julius split up in pairs and head different directions? Any others that show up, I'll send them along to cover a different area. I'll stay in case they come back on their own, and be available for any newcomers who stop by to help."

Andrew nodded and clapped Julius on the back. "How about you and me team up, old-timer?"

Julius grinned but shook his head. "Sure would like to, Andrew, but what you said made sense. Them youngsters need to see at least one familiar face, and I don't reckon they know Hiram, or Grant, neither one. Am I right?" He turned his attention to the two in question and waited.

Hiram scratched his head and frowned. "Cain't say I ever laid eyes on 'em, myself. How 'bout you, Cowling?"

Grant wagged his head. "No, sir, not to speak to, anyway. Guess one of us best go with Julius, and one with Andrew."

Julius beckoned to Hiram and headed off down the trail. "We'll take the area between here and the mill. They's not a lot of places to hide, but best we look, just the same. When we're done there, we'll cover from the mill to the Company store." He jerked a thumb at Andrew. "You want to start at the west end of town and go on past the waterfall? There's houses and shacks out there where them two might a'decided to hunker down."

Andrew nodded. "Sounds good. Let's meet back here at noon and report in if we've not found them. Sheriff, we'll count on you to give us some type of signal if they're found."

Sheriff Bryant drew his gun from his belt and nodded. "I'll shoot three times in the air, if anyone brings me word. You find them, high-tail it back here in a hurry. Godspeed, all of you."

Andrew strode up the path with Grant Cowling's long stride close behind. They traveled in silence from Margaret's cabin past the now quiet mill yard, and through the brush and trees to the stream at the base of Bridal Veil Falls. Grant quickened his steps and swung along beside Andrew. "You seem mighty worried, Andrew. You pretty close to those children, are you?"

"I guess I am." Andrew slowed his pace. "They're good youngsters, and I can't blame them for running. Sammie's protective toward her brother, and if she figured the sheriff thought him involved in Martin's death, I can see why she spooked."

Grant's bushy eyebrows rose nearly to his drooping hair. "The sheriff's interested in her brother? He the type that could a'done somethin' like that?"

Andrew shook his head decisively. "No. I don't believe so, and nei-ther does Margaret—Miss Garvey. They've been with her for a while now, and we've gotten to know them as well as we could, given the circumstances."

"Which are?" Grant drew to a stop and crossed his arms. "Might be good if you'd give me an idea what we're up against."

Andrew wiped his sleeve across his brow. "Sammie is thirteen and sharp as a tack. Joel is fourteen, and he's a mite slow. She watches out for him—makes sure he takes care of himself, and mothers him. But she doesn't tolerate anyone talking down to the boy, if you get my gist."

Grant nodded and smiled. "Yes, sir, that I do. Keep talkin', but let's mosey along and keep our eyes peeled."

"Sure." They jumped the stream at a narrow spot and struck off up the path, staying close to the edge of the placid Columbia River. What a difference from the white-capped waves pounding the shore last night. You'd never know the wind had howled and the storm raged by the look of the sunshine and calm waters today. "Margaret—uh, Miss Garvey and I—"

Grant grabbed Andrew's arm and pulled him to a stop. "Cut that, boy. I know how you feel about Missy, and there's no need for you to hide it. Fact is, I'd like to know why you hightailed it out of there and left that other fella to take care of her?"

Andrew felt the muscles in his face freeze, and he took a deep breath. "Noticed that, did you?"

"Ah-huh. Also noticed he's the same man her pappy wasn't too keen on some years back. Knew he'd come back to work at the Palmer mill but didn't realize Missy was still interested." He released his grip on Andrew's arm. "You intend to fight for that gal?"

Andrew shook his head and gazed into the older man's eyes. "She knows how I feel, but I'll not interfere." He'd let her father down, he knew that now, and not helped his own cause, either. Why hadn't he found a way to protect Margaret from the man her father had disdained? Guilt dragged at his heart and sank its claws into his mind. "Margaret has to find her own way in this."

Grant snorted. "Pshaw. Not with someone else leading her, she won't."

"You think Cooper isn't honorable?"

"I'm not sayin' that. He seems like a decent sort. Just doesn't set right in my craw that Margaret's papa didn't approve of their union, that's all. I know she's a grown woman, but that don't mean you have to stand back and do nothin'."

Andrew met Grant's stern gaze and didn't flinch. "I'll not compete with a memory. If we're to have a life together, I want her to be certain. Margaret has to decide what she wants, and I'll accept her decision." He turned and headed up the path toward a farm in the distance. "We'd best get going. We been jawing long enough."

Grant mumbled something too low for Andrew to hear, then the older man laughed and clapped his hands. "Guess I plumb forgot for a minute that God's in charge. I'll just commit to prayin' about you and Missy."

Andrew tossed a grin over his shoulder, his heart suddenly lighter. "Thanks, Grant. And while we're at it, let's say a prayer for Sammie and Joel."

"Yes, sir. Good idea."

They fell into silence as they strode side by side across a field and toward a house sitting several hundred yards back from the river.

Andrew's heart turned toward the One who knew all things and heard all prayers. Please God that they found the children, and that God granted Margaret clear vision and wisdom in the days ahead. His future, as well as hers, depended on it.

* * *

Margaret stood on the edge of the clearing, her arm linked with Clara's, watching the men at work. The two women had spent the first hour inside, hauling items away from the debris and covering her furniture with the large canvas tarpaulin one of the men brought. She'd put some of her things in boxes and stacked them on the porch, hoping to avoid the dust and needles sifting down through the hole. "I wonder if any of the men have found Sammie and Joel. It makes me feel sick, thinking of them alone again."

Clara squeezed her arm. "It's a small community, and someone's apt to see them. As long as they don't try to hop a train, they'll be found."

"That's what worries me. Sammie's a smart girl, and not afraid of much—other than being sent back to wherever they ran from. They arrived by train, and I wouldn't put it past her to take that way out."

"I'm guessing your influence might keep her from running too far. She seemed to stick pretty close to your side, the couple of times I saw her."

Margaret nodded as she continued to watch the men tossing the last of the branches and cut wood down from her roof. "I thought she was starting to trust me—maybe even like me—then this happened. Not that I blame her for running. I'm just praying they're not hurt."

Clara gripped Margaret's arm and turned her around to face her. "There now, hush. You've got to trust God, and quit worrying so." She angled her head toward the area where Nathaniel was working, his shirt-sleeves rolled up above his elbows. "Are you finding yourself interested in Mr. Cooper again?"

Margaret glanced at the serene face beside her, not sensing or hearing any rebuke. "I'm not sure. I think so, and he's asked me to give him a chance." She shrugged.

"How about Andrew? It seemed to me that he was warming up to you."

"I know. I'm still trying to sort out my feelings. It's confusing, and I'm not entirely certain how I feel." She heaved a large sigh and walked over to a stump and perched on it. "I care about Andrew, and before Nathaniel came back, I thought I could have more than just friendly feelings for him. Now? Well, I guess I need to know if it's just old feelings being stirred up after all these years, or if there's something still there that I need to investigate with Nathaniel. I just know I can't walk away from him without finding out." She bit her lip and glanced down at her lap. "I talked to Andrew first thing this morning and explained about Nathaniel."

"How'd he take it?" Clara sank down on a patch of green grass not far from Margaret's resting place.

One of the men gave a shout and waved his arm.

Two men appeared just up the path from the girls, hoisting boxes over their shoulders. "Morning, ladies," one of them said. "We brought the new shakes for your roof. Looks like we may have it finished before nightfall." He dipped his head in farewell and strode on.

"Oh, good. I won't have to trouble your mother for a place to sleep tonight, if they finish before dark."

"I insist you at least come to dinner, if nothing else."

"I'd love to, thank you, but only if they find the children." Margaret brushed some dust from her skirt and looked back up at Clara. "You asked about Andrew. He went a bit white when I told him and didn't say much at first. I know he was hurt, and I hate that. But he told me that he cared about me and wanted my happiness above all."

The memory of Andrew's words shot a pang of regret through her heart. His words had made her feel loved—something she'd longed for and hadn't expected to feel again. She almost wanted to take back her words to Andrew, but the pull toward discovering where her heart lay was too strong.

Clara's eyes widened. "It takes a big man to say that." Her brow puckered. "You said you believed your father hid the box with the note in the rose garden. Have you had time to think about that?"

"You mean, how am I feeling about what Papa did?"

Clara gave her friend a sweet smile. "Yes. I imagine it came as a shock."

Margaret propped her feet on a nearby rock and wrapped her arms around her knees. "I haven't had time to really think it through. Part of me understands his need to watch out for me, but the other part feels betrayed. He was concerned about how young I was when I was seeing Nathaniel, but I never dreamed he'd interfere." She swiped at a tear that threatened to spill over onto her cheek. "I found out he asked Andrew to take care of me if anything happened to him. I don't even know for sure how Andrew feels about me, or what I feel about him, or Nathaniel. I wish it wasn't such a mess."

Clara leaned over and patted Margaret's hand. "I'm so sorry. But I don't think your father tried to hurt you. I'm sure he did what he thought was best—and was trying to protect you."

"I know. He told me the day he died that he was sorry, but I didn't know why. How could he dislike Nathaniel so much?"

"I don't know. Maybe it was just the thought of losing his only child so soon after your mother's passing, and being left alone. But you need to forgive him."

Margaret sniffed. "I know. I need to pray about it." She gave Clara a lopsided smile.

"Exactly." She turned and rose to her knees. "Someone's coming up the trail. It looks like Julius and Hiram. Maybe they've found the children!"

BRIDAL VEIL
1902
OREG

Chapter Thirty-two
....

Sammie brushed bits of hay off her clothes and ran her fingers through her hair, feeling dirty and unkempt. She had to admit it felt nice living with Miss Margaret and getting to take a bath and wear clean clothes. Too bad that sheriff had to come along and ruin it all.

"Joel." She gently shook his shoulder and smoothed the hair off his face. Drool ran down the side of his cheek, and she withdrew a hanky from her pocket and dabbed at it. She loved her big brother with all of her heart.

He rubbed a hand over his face and squinted up at her. "Time to get up?" He pushed to an elbow and stared around the barn. "What we doin' here, Sammie? Why aren't we at Miss Margaret's?"

Sammie knelt beside him and patted his arm. "Remember the storm last night, Joel? The angels playing their drums? We went to sleep in this barn."

He sat all the way up and kicked the hay off his legs. "Oh, yeah. I remember. Can we eat now?"

Sammie sighed, suddenly feeling so much older than her thirteen years. She was tired—so very tired of being responsible for everything. Right now she longed to stretch out in a bed with a full stomach and sleep. Or better yet, dress up a real doll in fancy clothes and pretend that she was little again. Mama would be in the other room singing while she fixed breakfast, and Papa would be teasing her and making her laugh. Joel would be playing with his train set in the parlor and begging Papa for a puppy.

Joel tugged at her arm. "I'm hungry. What we gonna eat?"

Sammie stood and shook out the folds of her skirt, then reached for Joel's hand and helped him to his feet. "I'm not sure, but we'll find something. Come on, we need to get out of here before the owner comes." She led him from the far corner of the loft to the ladder leading down to the back of the barn.

They tiptoed across the loft, and she beckoned for Joel to go down the ladder first, holding her finger to her lips. As soon as he was halfway down she started her descent. She'd hit the midway point when Joel reached the bottom, and she saw him jump from the second to last step onto the floor below. "Oww!" Joel rolled onto his back and clutched his ankle, moaning and rocking from side to side. "I hurt my leg. Owww…"

Sammie scrambled down the rest of the way, fear gripping her stomach and making her legs shake. Joel couldn't be hurt. *Please, God, don't let anything be broken.*

She knelt beside him and touched his ankle, but he whimpered and pulled it away. "Don't touch it." His cry rose to a shriek, and the tears rolled down his pale cheeks.

"Shh, it's all right, Joel. Don't cry. Just rest for a minute and see if it gets better." She brushed her fingers across his cheeks, trying to still the flow of tears. "Lie there and don't move."

"What's goin' on here?" a voice boomed behind Sammie, and she jerked her head around. A large man dressed in overalls and holding a pitchfork towered over them, a grim frown creasing his narrow face. He moved a step closer. "You two tryin' to steal from me? I won't have it, I tell you!"

BRIDAL VEIL 1902 OREG

Chapter Thirty-three

....

The noon whistle sounded at the mill, and Margaret's heart skipped a beat. Julius and Hiram had returned after an unsuccessful search, and there'd been no word from Andrew and Grant yet. The thought of Sammie and Joel going hungry for yet another meal pushed aside any desire she'd had to eat. The men had taken a break from working on her roof, and most of them had headed home for dinner, but Nathaniel had stayed. He climbed down now from the ladder propped against the front of her house and wiped his stained hands on his jeans. She mustered a smile. He'd been working so hard to help remove the fallen tree and all the debris.

"Would you care for a sandwich? I have bread I baked yesterday and some slices of cured ham."

"That would be nice, thanks. I'll get washed up first, then join you, if that's all right?" He stepped up onto the porch where she'd left a washbasin and earthenware pitcher of water, along with a bar of lye soap.

As Margaret gathered the supplies she'd need for the meal in the kitchen, the splashing of water in the basin outside came clearly through the open door. There was a funny fluttering in her stomach. What would she say to Nathaniel now that she was alone with him? She raised her eyes to the ceiling. *Please, God, help me make wise decisions in my life from now on.*

The clomping of boots headed for the front door alerted Margaret, and she slipped the sandwich onto a plate, setting it on the table. Nathaniel hesitated after crossing the threshold. "I washed—but I'm not too clean otherwise. Afraid my clothes might have pitch on them from climbing up that tree. Want me to sit outside and eat?"

"The chairs are wood, and the pitch will wipe off easily, so no need to worry." She drew the chair away from the table and beckoned him to sit. "Would you care for milk or coffee? I have a fresh gallon from the dairy outside of town, and the coffee is hot."

"Coffee is fine, thanks." He slid into the chair and picked up one of the sandwiches, lifting it to his mouth and taking a large bite. After chewing and swallowing, he raised his brows. "How about you? Aren't you going to have something to eat?"

Margaret set a mug of coffee next to his plate, then slipped into the chair across from him holding her own. "I'm not especially hungry." She shrugged. "I'm sure my appetite will return after Sammie and Joel come home."

Nathaniel's eyes widened. "Home? You're going to continue to allow them to live here after the trouble they've caused?"

Margaret clutched the mug tighter. What was wrong with Nathaniel? Anytime the subject of the children came up, he seemed antagonistic. Not wanting to get into an argument with him, she chose her words carefully. "They're simply frightened children, Nathaniel. They haven't intentionally caused trouble, and they've not done anything wrong. Besides, they don't have anywhere else to go right now."

He cocked his head toward her. "You always were a soft touch whenever someone had a need."

BRIDAL VEIL
1902
ORE.

"Maybe so, but I can't just abandon them. Julius is asking around amongst some of the out-of-town teamsters to see if anyone's heard anything about two runaway children. I'm not sure what else to do."

"Why not turn them over to the sheriff? That seems like the sensible thing to do. He can figure out where they ran away from and take them back." Nathaniel chomped down on another big bite of his sandwich and chewed.

Margaret stiffened, not bothering to hide her growing frustration this time. "I wouldn't think of doing that, Nathaniel, and I can't believe you'd suggest it."

He looked up as if startled at her rebuke.

She went on. "Sammie's made it clear she ran away because they were frightened of the person they lived with. Why do you think she took Joel and ran again this time?"

He shrugged and frowned, then took a sip of coffee. "Haven't really thought about it much. Guess I figured they were just being kids and took off without thinking."

"No. They ran because she thinks the sheriff wants to question Joel about Martin Jenkins' death, and they'll lock him up, or send him back where he came from." She leaned back in her chair and crossed her arms.

Nathaniel hesitated, then softened his tone. "Well, what if he did have something to do with it? You could be harboring a murderer, Margaret. Have you thought of that? Of your own safety?"

"You don't understand, and obviously you don't care about either of them." Margaret bit off the words.

She pushed her chair back and grabbed her mug, whirling to dump the remaining contents into the sink and pumping the handle to rinse the grounds out of the bottom. Nathaniel's chair legs scraped the floor, making a screeching sound that resounded inside Margaret—the same type of noise she felt like making right now out of frustration at this unyielding man sitting in her kitchen.

He walked up behind her and placed his hands on her shoulders, gently turning her around to face him. "Margaret?"

She kept her eyes down, battling against the warring emotions evoked by the touch of his hand and the words he'd just spoken. His finger touched her chin lightly, and she raised her face. "What?" Her body began to tremble, and she took a step back, bumping into the sink. "Please don't touch me, Nathaniel." Her mind flashed back to when she was sixteen and she could think of nothing but him.

He drew back a step and shook his head. "I'm sorry," he said softly. "About everything. Your cabin being damaged, the children running away, my upsetting you." He caught her gaze again, though, and she saw the steel in his eyes. "But I truly do believe you need to let the sheriff take charge. Maybe your heart is overriding your common sense. That boy could be dangerous. I don't want you hurt next."

Margaret didn't care to hear more. She brushed past him and headed toward the front door. "Thank you for your concern, Nathaniel," she called back, "but Joel isn't the least bit dangerous. I'm going to stay outside so I can watch for them, if you don't mind."

She opened the door and walked out into the fresh air and sunshine, working to push down her irritation. Nathaniel meant well, she was sure, but he wouldn't listen. She knew Joel wasn't a threat to anyone, and sending those two back to where they'd come from would be a huge mistake. Sammie would find a way to run away again, and this time she might not find a place as hospitable to hide.

Margaret wrapped her arms around her sides and shivered, remembering the hobos following the girl into the woods.

A shout from the trail jerked her head up. It sounded like Julius. Hiram had stayed to help with the roof, but Julius had headed to Art's house to see if he was back. Seven figures came into sight, with Julius in the lead. Art Gibbs had returned, and trailing behind him was Joel, limping along with Buck leaping at his side. Sammie, head cast down and face sullen, came just behind. Margaret couldn't quite make out who the next man was, but Andrew and Grant brought up the rear.

Joy exploded inside. Margaret grasped her skirt and lifted it, jumping off the porch and dashing up the path to meet the group. "Sammie, Joel!" She opened her arms and Sammie flew into them, stifling a sob. Joel stood with a happy grin, his hand still patting Buck's head. "I was so worried about you. Are you both all right?"

Sammie raised tear-swollen eyes and hiccupped. "Joel twisted his ankle, but we're all right." She swiped the back of her hand across her cheeks. "They're going to take Joel away, aren't they, Miss Margaret? The sheriff, I mean? I heard him saying he wanted to talk to Joel, and I can't let anything happen to him. I just can't!" Her eyes filled with fresh tears and she started to cry in earnest, her slender shoulders shaking with her sobs.

Andrew stepped up beside her and squatted down, putting his arm around her shoulder and pulling her close. "We talked about this, remember, honey? We'll do everything we can to help you and your brother. None of us believe Joel would hurt anyone, and we'll tell the sheriff that, but you can't keep running away. You scared Miss Margaret, and both of you could have been hurt. We don't want some hobo trying to run off with you again, do we?"

She shook her head and sniffled. "I didn't think. I just got scared, and we left in a hurry. I didn't take any food or a blanket or anything. Joel got hungry, and we had to huddle under the hay to sleep."

Margaret leaned over and ran a finger down the young girl's cheek, wiping away some of the moisture. "Let's get you inside and find you something to eat. You both must be starving."

Andrew stood and held up his hand. "No, Fritz here"—he nodded at the silent man standing back from the group—"fed them at his place."

Margaret nodded at the man. "Mr. Luscher, it's good to see you. You took the children in?"

"Ya, they slept in my barn last night, and I found 'em this mornin'. Thought they come to steal milk and eggs, but then I realized they were just hungry." He hefted a burlap sack over his shoulder and set it on the ground, then hitched at his trousers held up by heavy suspenders. "Brought you some things since you've got extra mouths to feed." He nodded at Joel and grinned. "This one likes his vittles, that he does. Methinks you could use extra milk, and the missus sent some smoked and fresh salmon, as well."

"How generous of you—please thank Anna for me. Won't all of you come in?" Margaret turned toward the cabin and beckoned them forward.

Julius lifted his hat and scratched his head. "No, ma'am, I reckon not. Now that the young'uns be safe, I got to take care o' my mules. The girls get downright cranky this time of day if they aren't brushed proper and fed their grain. Don't want them feelin' neglected, no sir."

Andrew clapped the slender man on the shoulder. "Thanks for all your help today, Julius. You're a true friend."

"No trouble a'tall. Anytime you folks needs anythin', just holler." He plopped his hat back on his thinning hair and grinned. "You kids take care now, and don't be causin' Miss Margaret no more worry." He ruffled Joel's hair and grinned at Samantha. "You're both right good young'uns, and I hope you'll come see me and my mules sometime."

Joel tore his attention away from the dog and lifted eager eyes to Julius. "Could I ride one? Would they let me?"

"Sorry, son, I'm afraid not. They don't cotton to ridin', just pullin' things. But you can come pet them and feed them carrots if you'd like."

"Oh, boy! Thank you, Mr. Jules."

Sammie mustered her first smile. "It's Mr. Julius, Joel." She nodded and held out her hand. "Thank you for helping us, and we'd like to come pet your mules someday."

Julius's smile-wreathed face grew serious, and he gripped the small hand with his large one, holding it for a moment. "I'll look forward to that, little missy. You take care, now." He turned to Andrew. "I'll be back later and help finish up that roof, once I check on my girls."

Art Gibbs knelt down beside Joel and stroked Buck's head. "I need to take this fella home and feed him, Joel. How about I come over and check on you later?"

Joel's anxious look brightened at the final words. "You'll bring Buck with you, Mr. Art?"

"I will, if Miss Margaret doesn't mind if we stop by." He lifted his eyebrows at Margaret and smiled.

"Of course not. You're always welcome."

Art nodded, then grasped the dog's collar and headed up the trail toward home, Julius striding along beside them, whistling as he disappeared around the bend.

Andrew reached out a hand toward Sammie and Joel. "Let's head to the house and get cleaned up, shall we?" He gave a small nod toward Fritz. "I'll leave you to chat with Miss Margaret for a moment. Thank you again, Fritz."

Mr. Luscher hefted the bag onto his shoulder and nodded toward the cabin. "I'll take this inside for you, Miss Garvey, and on my way I'll be. Still got my own chores to do, and milking later this evenin'."

Margaret laid a hand on his arm and dropped her voice. "Thank you, Mr. Luscher. You have no idea how grateful I am that you cared for the children."

"I think they been stayin' in my barn loft, from the look of things. Poor mites, I scared them plumb bad when I came around the corner of a stall with my pitchfork. Thought I was goin' to hurt 'em, they did, but I'd never lay a hand on a child." He shook his head and smiled. "That little girl, a tiger she is. When she saw me with my fork, she jumped in front of her big brother and out flew her arms. I knew right then they weren't up to mischief. Sorry I am that I scared them."

"Sammie's very protective of Joel. I'm thankful you found them when you did."

He hiked the bag a little higher on his shoulder and moved toward the cabin. "I think they was headin' out when I found 'em. They'd just come down the ladder and close to the back door they were. Reckon another few minutes and a'missed 'em, I would. Guess the good Lord must a'been watchin' out for 'em."

Margaret nodded as she strode along beside him. "I think He has been since they arrived here, and I'm guessing He'll continue if I can just keep trusting Him."

"Ah, I think He'll keep on even if you struggle to trust Him. God's pretty big, you know, and He don't need our permission to care for those we love."

She hung her head, suddenly ashamed of the way she'd sounded. How right Mr. Luscher was—God didn't need her trust to do what He knew was right. What a fool she'd been. God had been watching out for the children all along—on the train, when the hobos chased Sammie, when they ran the first time, and now. Even in bringing them to Art Gibbs' house, and then on to hers.

God knew what He was doing, and all her fear and worry didn't change what His plans were for Sammie and Joel. Sure, she needed to trust Him and not allow worry to pull her down, but God was bigger than all the anxiety she could muster. She lifted her head and smiled. "Thank you, Mr. Luscher—for the food and for bringing the children home, but mostly for the reminder that God is in control."

"Ya, you're welcome, Miss Garvey. Glad I am to help on all accounts." He hefted the bag onto the porch.

Sammie and Joel had already darted inside, but Andrew still stood out in front of the porch. Margaret smiled at him.

Then her smile faltered. Nathaniel leaned against the doorjamb, arms crossed, staring at Andrew's smiling gaze locked on hers. A frown drew down the corners of Nathaniel's mouth as he swung his attention to her.

BRIDAL VEIL
1902
OREG

Chapter Thirty-four

Matilda Stedman wiped her floury hands on her already grubby apron and scowled. She hated cleaning the kitchen even worse than she hated cooking. Why hadn't Wallace tried harder to find those kids, instead of hightailing it home when his feet started hurting? The boy had never been much for sticking to anything, so guess there was no reason to expect him to do it this time, either. Grabbing a dirty cast-iron skillet, she gave it a couple of half-hearted swipes, then set it aside. Good enough.

She jerked off her apron and threw it onto a chair. Maybe she'd try to find Sammie herself. The girl had a sassy streak that tied Matilda's tail in a knot, but Sammie could cook and clean better'n most women she knew. That dead mama of hers must a'been a good teacher, she'd give her that.

Footsteps sounded on the porch and she turned around, recognizing the tread. "Wallace. Where you been?"

Wallace slouched through the door, his eyes bleary and tinged with red. A flush coated his cheeks. "Jist out to the privy." He tugged at the top button of his flannel shirt and popped it open, heaving a sigh. "Got me a bit of a scratchy throat and a cough. I just took a couple swigs of that stuff I got off that medicine man who came through with his wagon last week. Remember, he said it would cure anything that ailed you?"

Her irritation with him faded as she realized what he'd said. "You feelin' poorly? Sure hope it's not serious. I heard some folks in the next county got hit hard with whooping cough. Maybe we'd best get Doc Samson out to take a look at you, just in case."

He put the back of his hand over his mouth and coughed, then shuffled over the threshold and into the house. "Don't think it's nothing. I'll be better tomorrow, but I wouldn't mind resting for a bit, if you don't mind? Maybe have me a cup of tea if you got the pot boiling?"

She gripped his arm and led him over to the sofa. "Just sit yourself down, and I'll see to it." A couple of tugs at his shoes and she'd removed them from his feet and tossed them into a corner. "Yer shiverin'. You cold?"

"Naw, I'm a mite warm, but the house ain't cooled off much yet. Sure am glad August is almost over. I hate this heat." He lifted his head and allowed his mother to push a pillow underneath, then burrowed in with a sigh. "Thanks, Ma."

Matilda straightened and thought back to her time in the kitchen, struggling to remember what she'd been irritated at before Wallace had come home. She'd finished washing the supper dishes and tossed her apron on the chair. Oh, yes. Sammie. She dropped into a chair close by the sofa and grunted. "I decided I'd go lookin' for those brats myself come mornin'."

She shook her head and fingered a small tear in her cotton skirt. Another thing she disliked—the mending. How had she gotten along without that girl all these weeks? If she didn't turn up soon, she'd have to see about getting another girl from the orphanage, much as she hated the thought of breaking in a new one. Sammie knew what she liked and how to do it, and she'd rather have Sammie back than anyone else.

Wallace pushed himself up on his elbow and started to cough, then sank back onto his pillow without covering his mouth. "You go ahead. I'll be fine here whilst you're gone."

Matilda jumped from her seat, all thought of Sammie pushed from her thoughts. "I'll get that tea. Don't you worry, we'll fix you up." She bustled from the room, worry gnawing at her heart. Wallace had his faults and oftentimes made her mad, but he was her own blood kin, and all she had left in the world. She'd be lonely without him around. If the cough didn't die down by morning, she'd get Doc Samson out here, even if it took all of her egg money to pay him.

BRIDAL VEIL
1902
ORES

Chapter Thirty-five

....

Sheriff Bryant stooped down to Sammie's level and smiled, but Sammie couldn't tell if the smile was real, or if he was trying to make her feel better just so she'd talk to him. Lots of adults did that. She'd seen it plenty of times. Mrs. Stedman didn't smile often, but when she did, you could be sure it wasn't for a good reason. Miss Margaret, Mr. Art, and Mr. Andrew had helped her get past some of her fear and distrust of adults, but this sheriff gave her goose bumps all the way down to the tips of her fingers. No sir, she wouldn't trust anyone wearing a badge who could send her and Joel back to that mean woman, even if his smile did light up his eyes.

"Sammie, I'd like to talk to you and your brother, if it's all right with you?"

Sammie squinted her eyes and frowned, then shook her head. "Don't want to talk to you and don't want Joel to, either."

Miss Margaret stooped over and placed a gentle arm around Sammie's shoulders. "Honey, the sheriff just wants to ask you some questions about the note you left in Mr. Jenkins' house, that's all." She dropped her voice and spoke close to Sammie's ear. "You know, when you went in his kitchen to get some food." A squeeze of her shoulders and Margaret dropped her arm to her side and took a step back.

Sammie looked at her brother sitting on the floor of the cabin talking to Buck. The dog licked the boy's hands and panted, obviously enjoying the ongoing attention. If only Joel could have his own dog. If only they could both have their own home. Better yet, that Mama and

Papa were still alive and she and Joel had never been sent to that awful orphanage and then to Mrs. Stedman's house in the first place.

Not that she wasn't grateful to Miss Margaret, and to God, for bringing them here and keeping them safe—she was. But sometimes she got so lonely for a family of their own, where they could really belong.

Mr. Art had come back with Buck after he'd had something to eat, and now he and Andrew stood near the door talking together, while that other man—Mr. Cooper—hung around Miss Margaret. She scowled and bit her bottom lip. How come Miss Margaret let him come around her house so much? Of course, he was a lot nicer than Wallace Stedman, and he'd never done anything mean to her, but she could tell he didn't like her or Joel overly much.

Miss Margaret touched her arm again. "Sammie? Will you talk to the sheriff?"

Sammie walked over to Joel and sat on the floor next to him. "I guess, as long as he's polite to Joel."

Sheriff Bryant placed his hat carefully on a nearby sideboard and squatted down on his haunches nearby. Buck immediately took a stand between the man and the boy and emitted a low growl.

Mr. Art swung around from his place near the door. "Buck. That's enough. Lay down now." He pointed to the floor and waited until the dog sank down on his belly and put his head down on his paws, but his eyes never left the sheriff.

Miss Margaret took a seat on the sofa a couple of yards from where Sammie and Joel sat, and Mr. Cooper sat down on the other end.

Sheriff Bryant cleared his throat. "This won't take long. Is it all right if I call you Sammie, or would you prefer Samantha?"

She lifted her head in wonder. No one had ever asked her that, and she wasn't sure how to respond. A shrug would have to suffice for now, but she'd need to ponder that for a while. Mama and Joel mostly called her Sammie, but Papa called her Samantha. He loved that name, and it used to belong to his mama. She'd never minded being called Sammie, but the older she got, the more she thought it might be nice to become Samantha for good. But she wasn't going to spill her guts out to this stranger, and for sure not with Mr. Cooper looking and listening. Maybe she'd tell Miss Margaret after the rest left—of course, Mr. Art and Mr. Andrew could know as well, and she'd let Joel call her Sammie for as long as he pleased.

"Well then, young lady, I think I'll call you Samantha. It's a very pretty name for *a nearly grown-up girl.*"

Sammie gritted her teeth. If this man was a mind reader she'd best be careful of her thoughts.

But a small part of her heart experienced a shaft of pleasure at the words. A nearly grown-up girl—what a fine thought. Sometimes she longed to be a little girl again, with no cares beyond what was for dinner or which rag doll to play with that day. But those days were gone forever, so best to move ahead and become a grown-up quick. "Thank you." She whispered the words but lifted her head and met his eyes. "I'm beholden to you for the kind words."

He nodded, and another smile lit his eyes. "I have a note here that I'd like you to look at, if you don't mind?" He fished in the breast pocket of his light brown flannel shirt and plucked out a folded paper. "Can you tell me if this is something you wrote?" He held out his hand with the note extended and waited for her to take it.

She tried to keep her hand from shaking as she unfolded the paper and stared at the familiar words—the same ones she'd left at nearly every house, assuring the owners they'd do their best to pay them back for the food they'd taken. She stared at the paper for several long moments. "Yes. I wrote it."

"Ah-huh. Thank you." He reached into his other front pocket and withdrew another paper and handed it over. "Do you recognize this one, as well?"

The words printed so carefully on the scrap in front of her blurred as her eyes lingered over them. She'd taught Joel his letters and tried to help him sound out words and put short ones to paper. It wasn't easy for him, but if he concentrated, he could write short sentences that were readable, and this was clearly one of his. Sheer terror raced through her mind, and she tried to take in the meaning of the words. What book had he taken, and why hadn't she seen it? She couldn't let the sheriff know, but she hated to lie. Somehow she had to believe the Lord would understand and forgive her if she chose to protect Joel over telling the truth. She met the man's eyes. "No."

He rocked back on his heels and cocked his head to one side. "No?" His eyes seemed to shoot an arrow right into her soul. "Are you sure that you don't know anything about someone taking a book, Samantha?"

She didn't answer and, instead, reached down to pat the now quiet dog. Joel had been listening to the exchange of words with a puzzled look on his face. "I took the book and a nice pen to write with. The man wasn't using it. He was sleeping on the floor."

Sammie gasped in horror, then covered her face with her hands. Now they were in for it. They'd take her brother and lock him up, and maybe her as well. She dropped her hands and straightened her back. If they took him, they'd better take her as well. No way would she let Joel go to jail alone.

Chapter Thirty-six

....

Nathaniel gaped at the words that seemed to fall so easily from the big boy's lips. He'd taken a book and pen and seen Jenkins "sleeping" on the floor? Had the boy hit him when Jenkins tried to stop him from stealing from him, and Joel thought he was sleeping? Was the boy really as simple as he appeared, or was he simply sly and hiding behind a mask to keep from being caught? What did Margaret, or any of them for that matter, know about these two, other than what they'd chosen to share? He didn't like it one bit, and the sooner he convinced Margaret to get them out of her house, the happier he'd be.

He'd felt Margaret stiffen beside him and heard the sharp intake of breath from Andrew Browning. Both of them must surely see now how wrong they'd been to encourage these children to stay here.

Sheriff Bryant stood and walked over to Joel, then knelt down beside the boy, who still had his hand resting on the dog's head. Buck's eyes followed the man's every move, but no more growls emanated from his throat. "Joel, can you tell me more about the book and the pen? Was Mr. Jenkins sleeping when you got there, and did you try to wake him up?"

The boy raised wide eyes and shook his head. "No, sir. He was sleeping when I came in the room. Sammie told me not to bother nothin', and I didn't figure I oughta bother someone who's sleeping. Wallace Stedman, he used to holler and smack me if I woke him when he was sleeping on his ma's sofa."

Sammie whirled on Joel. "You never told me he smacked you, Joel. Why didn't you tell me?"

The boy shrugged. "Don't know. He never hurted me bad, Sammie, don't worry."

He smiled at the sheriff. "Want to see the pen?"

Sheriff Bryant raised his brows. "Yes, I would, young man. And the book, too, if you've still got it."

Joel lumbered to his feet and walked to the corner where they'd stowed their things in a box. He dug through the small stack and found the jacket with the short sleeves that he'd been wearing when they'd first arrived. Slipping his hand into a pocket, he took out an ornate fountain pen and walked back to the sheriff. "See? Ain't it pretty? I was just borrowing it. I told the man in the note I'd pay him for the book, but I needed somethin' to write with and didn't think he'd care if I borrowed the pen."

The sheriff accepted the proffered pen. "Thank you, it's very pretty, and I'm glad you took good care of it." He let it rest on his open palm and smiled up at the boy. "Do you have the book, Joel?"

The boy shook his head and lowered his brows. "Nope."

Nathaniel leaned back and crossed his arms, irritated at the answer. He'd bet the boy remembered where he'd hid it and didn't want to tell.

Sammie leaned over and touched his arm. "Joel, why didn't you tell me about the pen and the book?"

"Forgot to. I was gonna have you read it to me. The words weren't like the ones in the storybooks you read, they were all squiggly. I tried, but I couldn't make out none of 'em, and it didn't have no pictures at all. Figured it weren't worth much, and I don't remember what happened to it."

Sheriff Bryant turned to the small group hovering on and near the sofa. "Some of the ladies in town got rid of the worthless items in the cabin and packed up the rest. They were sent by train to Mr. Jenkins' daughter, Jenny, who sent me a letter. She said her father had always kept a journal and was surprised it wasn't in any of the boxes. She asked if I could check with the people who'd cleaned the cabin, as she'd like to have it. I did, and none of them remember seeing it. One of the men mentioned a pen that Mr. Jenkins was quite proud of—it had been a gift from his daughter—and wondered at its absence, as well."

Nathaniel was unable to keep quiet much longer. "Sheriff, what do you plan on doing about this? Are you taking this young man back to Troutdale with you, or holding him here in town?"

There was a stunned silence, then Andrew said angrily to Nathaniel, "What are you thinking, man? That boy wouldn't kill a spider, much less hurt a person. He's about as gentle and sweet as God made anyone, and he'd have no reason to hurt Jenkins." He turned toward the sheriff and raised his brows. "Sheriff? What's your opinion?"

The sheriff picked up his hat and dusted off the rim, then swung it around on his finger. "Don't rightly know yet. Got me some thinking to do, and it seems to me we might want to find that journal. No telling what the man wrote before he died. It might shed some light on the situation. 'Course, if it was just a hobo or someone up to mischief and things went awry, there probably won't be nothing at all, but it's worth knowing." He turned toward Margaret. "I know it would cause some serious upset if we try to separate these two. You got any suggestions?"

Andrew stepped forward. "I do, Sheriff."

"Spill it, then. Time's a'wastin.'"

"I'll bring my bedroll and sleep on the front porch. If there are any problems, Miss Margaret will have a man close by, and Sammie won't be separated from her brother. That is"—he leveled a hard look at the sheriff—"unless you're seriously considering following Cooper's advice and taking them with you to Troutdale?"

"No, sir. I think that's a bit premature, and besides, I like your suggestion—that is, if Miss Garvey is willing to allow you to sleep outside on her porch."

Nathaniel cut in before Margaret had a chance to speak. "Over my dead body. Browning will not be sleeping on Miss Garvey's porch if I have anything to say about it."

* * *

Margaret stared in shocked disbelief at Nathaniel. Over his dead body? Who did he think he was, making decisions for her? Just because she'd decided to forgive him and see if they might still have a chance at a relationship didn't give him the right to dictate who could, or couldn't, sleep on her porch. She turned to Andrew and mustered the sweetest smile possible, given the circumstances. "Thank you, Andrew, I'd appreciate that."

She glared at Nathaniel, thoughts racing through her mind faster than she could comprehend them. This would give her a chance to speak to Andrew about the request her father had made and let Nathaniel know he couldn't boss her around. This nonsense needed to end, and she planned on seeing that it did—sooner rather than later.

Nathaniel stifled a retort and swung on his heel, stalking from the house. Margaret stared after him as he leapt down the three steps to the hard-packed ground and hit the path at a quick pace. Fine. Let him go if that's the kind of attitude he wanted to take.

* * *

Nathaniel strode up the path leading away from Margaret's cabin, his lips pressed in a tight line to keep the cuss words from spilling over into the air. They weren't words he often used, but right now it would feel mighty fine to let loose with a few, even though his granny would be grieved if she'd lived to hear him. He kicked a fircone lying in his path, but that did nothing to relieve the stress building inside.

The amazement on Margaret's face had turned to swift irritation only moments after the words had left his mouth. Then he'd known he'd stepped into a kettle of hot oil. But why hadn't Margaret told Browning he couldn't stay, and why had the sheriff pushed the idea? He struck his hand against his fist and kept moving up the path toward his home, intent on getting away from the cozy group at the cabin. He'd asked Margaret to give him another chance, but since then, there'd been nothing but friction between them.

Deepening frustration pressed on his chest when he thought about that girl and her brother. It would've been better for Margaret if they'd not been found. Did she plan on keeping them forever and raising them as her own? He shook his head. Surely not. But Margaret had always loved children, no matter the age, and she wasn't one to go with normal conventions.

If she did, how would that affect any relationship he might have with her? Did he want to help raise two nearly grown siblings, especially with one that might never leave home?

He frowned and stuck his hands in his jeans pockets and slowed his pace. He had nothing against either of them, but the idea of taking on someone else's children at this stage of his life wasn't attractive. Of course, someday he figured he'd probably have a child or two of his own, but they'd start out as babies. Besides, that girl didn't like him, and he couldn't see her willingly putting herself under his leadership.

An idea dropped into his mind, and he smiled. Margaret was a teacher here in Bridal Veil—he'd almost forgotten that, since he'd returned after school let out for the summer. He couldn't imagine the schoolboard being pleased with a boy living under their roof who was being investigated for murder. A quick stop at Robert Ludlow's house might just do the trick.

BRIDAL VEIL 1902 ORE

Chapter Thirty-seven
....

Sammie broke the uneasy silence that had settled over the room. "I'm tired. Did the men get the roof done so we can sleep here tonight, or do we have to go somewhere else?"

Margaret suddenly realized that Sammie and Joel must be exhausted after hiding out in Mr. Luscher's barn. They'd had a meal at his house and snacks again an hour or so ago, but they both drooped on their feet and looked about ready to collapse. "Yes, honey, the men finished the roof enough for us to be safe. They have more shingles to put on tomorrow, but it's all right, even if it rains."

Sammie smiled and leaned against Margaret's arm. "I'm glad Mr. Andrew's going to stay, and that other man is gone. I don't like him."

Margaret didn't respond and kept her eyes averted from Andrew's. What a mess this had all become. Somehow she had to find time and quiet to sort through the questions, before the quagmire got any thicker and sucked the energy and life right out of her body.

How she longed to turn this over to God and let Him figure it all out, but niggling doubt remained. She'd prayed about so many things these past months, and nothing in her life seemed to be working. Nathaniel had come back, but she'd found herself irritated at him more often than not. Maybe she wasn't being fair to him or to God, but right now she was too tired and perplexed to try to unravel the threads.

A half hour later the sheriff and Art had taken their leave, and Andrew had returned with his bedroll and pillow. Margaret had laid out a tarp and a couple of folded winter quilts on the wooden floor of the porch, in hopes it might help soften his sleep. She heard him clomping around outside, washing up and readying for the night. Offering him a cup of coffee might be nice and could give her the chance to broach the subject of her father's letter.

She glanced in the corner at Sammie and Joel curled up on their pallet of blankets, fast asleep. Why anyone thought she needed protection from Joel, she couldn't understand.

A light rap at the door drew her across the room, and she swung wide the door. "How about a cup of coffee, Andrew?" she asked softly.

He twisted his hat in his hands but met her eyes. "No, thank you." He cleared his throat. "I'm sorry about today, Margaret."

She wrinkled her brow. "You mean the children running away, or my cabin roof falling in?"

Andrew scratched his head, then shook it. "I mean Mr. Cooper storming off like a hive of bees had busted open and were chasing him. I didn't mean for that to happen when I offered to stay."

Margaret stifled a giggle as the image he'd portrayed flickered across her mind. She must be more tired than she'd realized to even consider laughing at Nathaniel—he'd been upset at someone other than himself staying to protect her. Of course, that wouldn't have been appropriate, after he'd asked to start courting her again.

Then an image of his expression as he'd insisted Andrew couldn't stay washed over her mind. Her smile faded. "I appreciate that, but I'm sure he'll be fine." She lifted her chin. Even Nathaniel had tried to make choices for her and didn't seem able to trust her.

"But you told me you cared for him, and I'm sure he's not happy about my sleeping on your porch."

She stepped over the threshold and onto the porch, gently shutting the door behind her. No need to continue talking in the house while the children slept. She sank down into the chair and waited until Andrew took the other one. "I said I used to care for him and need to find out where my heart is in the matter. I'm considering giving him a chance, but that didn't give him the right to be angry. He has no claim on me yet and may never do so." She paused. "I need to ask you a question."

"Sure. Anything."

"I discovered something about Papa that affects me."

Andrew's body tensed. "What about your father?"

She clenched her hands in her lap. "I found a letter he left me."

Andrew didn't reply, just nodded.

"I need to understand something he said." She continued with a rush. "Papa wrote that he'd asked you to care for me and implied"— she felt a flush of warmth move up her neck and into her cheeks and was thankful the night would hide her discomfort—"that he'd asked you to marry me."

Her fingers hurt with the intensity of her grip, so she tried to relax. "I don't hold you to any promises you made out of respect for my father." She lifted her chin and straightened her shoulders. "I don't care to have any man interested in me due to a promise he made, no matter how solemn. That's one of the reasons I might give Nathaniel another chance: I don't care to have you, Papa, or anyone else deciding my future."

Andrew's mouth opened, but he didn't utter any words. He closed it and opened it again, with the same result. At last he cleared his throat. "I'm sorry I didn't tell you, Margaret. I can see how it must look, but it's not true."

"You're saying Papa didn't ask you to take care of me?" She leaned back and crossed her arms over her chest.

He shook his head. "No. Yes. I mean—" He sighed and scowled into the darkness. "He asked if I'd watch out for you in the event that anything happened to him, but he didn't ask me to marry you. I didn't take his request too seriously at the time, as he seemed to be in good health. Then when he died, I remembered what he'd asked me."

"And you felt obligated to continue seeing me." She started to rise. "Just as I thought."

Andrew reached out to touch her arm, but she drew it away. "Please, Margaret. Hear me out."

She wavered, wanting nothing more than to rush into her bedroom and never look at his handsome face again. She was so tired of being hurt—so sick of being betrayed. Why listen to anything he said after he'd acknowledged that Papa's letter was true? Finally, unable to resist his pleading look, she sank back into her chair. Andrew had never lied to her in the past, at least not that she'd ever been aware of, and he deserved the time to explain. "Go ahead. But I expect you to be completely honest. No more secrets."

The muscles in his neck moved as he swallowed. "That's fair." He sat forward and clasped his hands between his knees. "When I first saw you, I was interested in you, although I didn't fancy myself falling in love. When your father made his request, I took it with a grain of salt, and all but forgot it until after his death. Did I feel a sense of obligation to keep my word? Of course."

Margaret started to speak, but Andrew held up his hand. "Wait. Please." She leaned back in her seat, and he nodded. "I felt a sense of duty for only a short time. The day I helped unload your wagon, that changed. Knowing your sadness but watching the effort you made to rise above it, hearing your laughter and seeing your determination to make a home for yourself in spite of your circumstances—I realized what an amazing woman you are. I'd come planning on asking you to the ice-cream social as a friend—to help you pass the time, and so you'd not be alone. I came away from your cabin with my heart pounding and the knowledge that you'd brought great joy to my life when you said yes."

Margaret held her breath as the impact of his words hit her heart so hard she could barely breathe. Her thoughts flew to Nathaniel and how she'd felt recently when with him—the joy and uncertainty, not knowing if he were the man she remembered or someone she no longer knew. Now the same dilemma confronted her with Andrew. "You're saying you really care about me? Not just because of Papa, but on my own account?"

Andrew nodded, a quiet joy shining from his eyes. "Yes. I care more than…" Just then his body stiffened and he raised his head. "Shh, I hear something."

Margaret sat without moving, straining to listen for anything un-usual but failing to hear more than the normal night sounds. A group of crickets chirped not far from the foundation stones to the side of the porch, and a chorus of bullfrogs sounded down at the river's edge. The lonesome cry of a coyote yipping for its mate echoed from the nearby hillside, but nothing else disturbed the night air. "Andrew? What is it?"

He shook his head. "I'm not sure. Probably nothing. Could have been a deer moving through the brush." He pushed himself from his chair, walked over to his bedroll, and reached under the pillow. A Colt revolver was clutched in his hand when he stood and faced her.

"You think someone's out there?" Margaret gripped her hands in her lap and stared at the gun. Most of the men had handguns or rifles for keeping varmints away or bringing in venison for the winter. Papa had owned a fine shotgun he kept for pheasants and grouse, and he'd taught her to shoot. "It could be a coyote, I suppose, but they never come close to the house."

Andrew stood on the edge of the porch. "Could be, but I heard there's been bear sighted around here, and I'd rather not take any chances. Not that a handgun would do much good against a full-grown bear, but it might scare one away."

Another loud crack in the distance drew her attention toward the east. What in the world was out there, and why couldn't they see it?

* * *

Nathaniel tossed and turned in his bed, unable to sleep even after his satisfactory talk with Robert Ludlow earlier this evening. The head of the schoolboard had been shocked that Margaret would consider allowing Joel to stay in the cabin while under investigation by the sheriff for a possible murder and agreed to speak with her the next day. So why couldn't he get to sleep?

The look in Margaret's eyes when he'd left her porch still haunted him and kept him punching his pillow in frustration. She'd been saddened by his lack of acceptance of those orphans. Part of him longed to stand by her side and assure her of his support, but he pushed that aside. Impatience at his weakness at even considering giving in to her desire to keep the children made him kick off the lightweight covering and roll off the mattress. If he wasn't going to sleep, he might as well be up. From the angle of the moon it must be well after midnight. Maybe if he sat up for a while he'd be ready to go back to sleep before daybreak lit the eastern sky.

He padded barefoot into the kitchen and reached for the coffee pot, then shoved three more sticks onto the glowing embers in the firebox of the stove. Good thing he'd fixed dinner late and coals still remained; it wouldn't take long to heat the pot.

Had it been a mistake to return to Bridal Veil after all these years? Was he chasing a dream where Margaret was concerned? It appeared she still held to her strong faith and desire to attend church weekly. He could live with that. But this issue of the children was another matter entirely. He bristled at the thought of that big boy living in her small cabin. It was unseemly and possibly dangerous, but he doubted from the obstinate set of her chin when he'd left that she'd listen to anything more on the subject.

Then there was Andrew Browning. Nathaniel ground his teeth in frustration and set the pot down on the grate a mite too hard, slopping coffee over the top. The crackle and sizzle of the droplets hitting the hot grate assured him there'd be nothing left to clean.

Browning kept popping up like a cork on the end of a fishing line. Maybe he needed to have a talk with the man and inform him of his intentions toward Margaret. He couldn't imagine she'd be smitten with Browning, anyway. The man didn't appear to have much, and his job as a faller didn't promise a prosperous future. Of course, he'd probably get shifted back to the lower mill once the need for him on the logging crew ended. At least he'd been able to remove his competition for the balance of the summer and keep Margaret from seeing him so often.

He grunted and grabbed the handle of the pot, then flinched and jerked his hand away. Hot. A dishrag lay close by, so he lifted the pot with the rag and poured the mug to the brim. Yes, that had been a smart move asking to have Browning transferred up the mountain, but now he was sleeping outside the door of the woman he planned to court. There was no justice in the way some things worked out.

He settled into a chair in the front room and propped his feet on a low stool, his mug clutched in his hands. A shout in the distance roused him, and he stepped to the front window. Dim light from swinging lanterns moved between the trees. A group of men separated, seeming to head toward different homes, and he heard continued shouts. He grabbed his socks and boots and headed for the door. Something had to be wrong at the mill. He yanked open the door and stepped onto the porch. "What's going on?"

A tall, slender form moved up the path and held up his lantern. It was Julius, the teamster who delivered goods to Palmer.

"Something wrong at the mill?" Nathaniel called out.

"Yessir, by jing. Fire! It's burned two houses and looks to be headed right for Palmer!"

Chapter Thirty-eight

....

Margaret jumped out of bed and raced for the porch. Men's voices and swinging lanterns had roused her from an uneasy dream where coyotes charged at the children in the shadowland somewhere between waking and sleep. She'd fallen into a fitful doze after Andrew had patrolled the cabin, finding nothing amiss. He'd urged her to get some rest and assured her he'd keep watch well into the night.

She wrapped a robe around her waist and cinched the belt, pushing the hair out of her eyes and peering out into the darkness. "Andrew? Who's here?"

Andrew stood with his gun drawn, obviously unsure what the commotion might be. Margaret prayed that some of Jenkins' friends hadn't heard about the sheriff questioning Joel and headed over in the night for their own brand of justice. Then an instant later she shook her head, feeling foolish at the thought. The citizens of Bridal Veil were fair, open-hearted people who cared for their friends and neighbors and tried to do what was right. They'd never hurt a child, no matter the circumstances. She shivered, the image of the coyotes nipping at Joel's heels in her dream coming back to haunt her. It had been a dream, nothing more.

Andrew held up his lantern with his left hand. "Who's there?" Then relief crossed his face, and he slipped the pistol into his waistband. "It's Hiram and Grant." He called over his shoulder and stepped to the edge of the porch. "What is it, men?"

Grant moved into the circle of light. "Fire! It started somewhere to the east and climbed up the mountain to Angel's Rest. Looks to be headed toward Palmer. The Trickey family got word to Palmer and sent a rider down to Bridal Veil."

Margaret stepped up alongside Andrew and clutched his arm, fear for the people living on the mountain making her breath catch in her throat. "How can we help?"

"We're asking any able-bodied men to help fight the fire. The east wind is blowin' a bit, but not bad yet. Pray it don't pick up any, or more homes could be in danger. Lots of canyons up there, so doubtful it'll jump 'em all."

"Best not to take chances, though." Andrew placed his hat on his head and turned to Margaret. "I'll stay here if you're concerned about Joel."

"No. You need to go help." She looked into his eyes and felt a stab of alarm. "Be careful, Andrew."

"I'll be fine." He gave her hand a quick squeeze. "I'll come check on you as soon as we get it under control. If it's already moved up the mountain, you and the children should be all right, but keep an eye out, just in case."

"I will. Come back safe." She reached out to him, but he'd already turned and bolted off the porch, disappearing into the night behind the bobbing lanterns.

Margaret shivered and stared off into the night to the east. Was that the popping, cracking sound they'd heard earlier, the fire causing dry trees to explode as it moved through the tops? Fire was every timberman's nightmare. *Please, God, keep all the men safe, but especially Andrew and Nathaniel.* A flash of guilt made her cringe.

So many men had families and people who cared for them, but she couldn't help singling out the two who meant the most to her. She'd not yet decided where her heart lay concerning Nathaniel, but hearing Andrew's words and looking into his eyes before he'd left, she'd felt a deep yearning and connection to him. Andrew's strength of character, as well as his masculine strength, stirred her heart in a way Nathaniel had never done. Andrew had been so kind about the children, so supportive of her wants and desires, and he had a genuine love for the Lord.

Had the love she thought she'd felt for Nathaniel been based only on the physical attraction she'd felt at the time? Had it ever possessed the depth needed for a lasting relationship? She'd thought so at the time, but since his return, what she'd thought was love felt shallow and tinny.

Maybe Papa's idea of Andrew watching out for her wasn't such a bad one, after all. Recently she'd felt so safe and protected in Andrew's presence—was that what Papa had hoped for? A deeper understanding of her father caused the petals of restoration to open a bit more, seeming only to need the rays of forgiveness to shine in and complete its work. She tucked the thought to the back of her mind, determined to think on it later.

Nathaniel, on the other hand, didn't appear to have changed much in that regard. She'd hoped and prayed that as he matured he'd see his need for God, but if the comments he'd made were an indication, that hadn't happened. Could she join herself to a man who didn't share the same godly values? At sixteen years old she'd not thought that mattered, but now she knew better. If Nathaniel truly hadn't changed, she couldn't see a future with him.

She raised her eyes toward the starlit heavens. "Lord, give me wisdom and help me to make wise choices. I've tried to trust You in the past, and I keep making mistakes and not listening to Your gentle voice. Open my ears, and help me to hear this time." She turned to go back inside, then paused. "And Lord, please protect the lives of the people who call this area their home, and bring Andrew and Nathaniel back home."

Chapter Thirty-nine
....

Andrew, Julius, Grant, and Nathaniel climbed into Julius's wagon, loaded with shovels and burlap bags they could soak with water to help fight the fire moving toward Palmer. Other men were heading out on horseback or on foot, and lanterns bobbed in the air like fireflies dancing in the night. The warning had gone out to Palmer for the residents to leave the town and head west to the outlying farms. Some of the men would stay behind to protect the buildings and mill.

Andrew prayed that the homes and residents of Palmer would remain safe and that the fire could be contained or die out in one of the deep canyons before reaching the town. Thank the Lord the Trickey family had sounded the alarm, but they'd been driven from their home by the flames, along with at least one other family on Angel's Rest.

Silence lay over the wagon like a wet woolen blanket. Each man seemed wrapped in his own reflections, and even the normally loquacious Julius kept a still tongue as he guided his mules up the hillside in the gloom. A pale moon had peeped out and hovered above the horizon, casting a paltry light that further muted the atmosphere.

How he hated leaving Margaret alone at her cabin. Not that he worried about Sammie and Joel—not for a moment. But the winds were fickle here in the Gorge, and all it would take was a shift in direction to send the flames roaring toward Bridal Veil. It had taken all of Andrew's control not to kiss Margaret before he left. He'd promised himself he'd not press his suit after learning of her interest in Nathaniel Cooper, but he'd been hard-pressed to keep to that promise. If the man won her heart, Andrew prayed he'd deserve her.

Was Grant right that he shouldn't give up without a fight? It was something to consider. Not that Margaret wasn't worth fighting for, but he wanted to be loved because she chose to love him, not because he wheedled her to. She'd not been happy about the letter her father left, or the request he'd made, and Andrew couldn't blame her. He'd tried to convey his feelings, but she didn't appear to have heard—and the fear over the fire had overshadowed everything since. He'd have to trust that God would lead her decision where he and Cooper were concerned.

Andrew peered ahead as the mules pulled the wagon and men over the last rise. The sawmill and outlying buildings were lit by men running from one place to the next with lanterns in hand. Smoke hung heavy on the air, and each gust of wind increased the acrid smell.

The blast of a train whistle split the air as Andrew and the rest of the men jumped to the ground. Andrew grasped the arm of a worker hurrying past. "What are they doing with the locomotives?"

"The engineers are moving them back into the hills to be safe. The company can't afford to lose Peggy and Jumbo." The man shifted the box he carried on his shoulder and scurried away.

A lantern bobbed nearby and Dan Meadows, the burly bull-whacker, stepped closer. "Glad you fellas made it. Unload your shovels and dig a ditch on the east side of the mill buildings."

Nathaniel grabbed a shovel from the back of the wagon. "You've got plenty of water in the millpond. Can you pump it out?"

"That's the plan." He jerked a thumb over his shoulder. "Let's get busy. We got men rigging hoses to the pump carts."

The four men spread out, shovels over their shoulders. Other strong hands grasped the hoses and dragged them across an open space. Men rushed around, some digging a fire break in front of the main mill building, while others steadied the hose that shot water onto several of the outlying buildings closest to the stand of trees to the east.

An hour passed and Andrew gauged the time to be nearly two in the morning. He frowned at the eastern sky, worry clouding his thoughts. A red glow backlit the night, and the smell of smoke intensified. The explosion of another tree in the fiery inferno to the east was a reminder that the fire was increasing in intensity—and that, with each new explosion, it drew closer.

Andrew plodded on, tossing dirt with his spade and widening the ditch now spanning a length of over one hundred feet. Would it be enough to save the mill and keep the fire from jumping into the cluster of homes beyond? The shouts of men and cries of children came clearly to his ears as families packed what they could and abandoned the rest.

A man's booming cry echoed across the clearing. "It's coming!"

Andrew raised his head. Orange tongues of fire licked the treetops on the crest of the ridge and hungrily made their way into the timber below. The hair on the back of his neck rose. "Faster, men, faster!" Andrew bawled at the top of his lungs and dug his spade in yet another time.

He heard Nathaniel bellow to the men holding the hose, "Point it onto the east side of the mill building. Dose her good, and keep the water coming!"

In what felt like a matter of minutes, the sheet of fire consumed the entire hillside, creating a spectacle the like of which Andrew knew he'd never forget, if he got out of this place alive. Fear twisted his gut as flames ripped through one tree after another, dancing from treetop to treetop in amber balls of light. Had it not been so sinister and destructive, it might have been beautiful.

A shudder tore through Andrew's body. His thoughts flew to Margaret, Sammie, and Joel. *Please, God, let Bridal Veil be spared.* He couldn't stand the thought of anything happening to the people he loved. He renewed his efforts on behalf of this town, but futility pressed hard on his spirit. The fire was moving closer, and it didn't seem possible that ten times as many men could possibly save this mill or the town that lay beyond.

Suddenly a tree on the edge of the woods closest to the frenzied crew fell, exploding as it hit the ground, and sent a gigantic shower of sparks across the clearing. Men ran from the onslaught, slapping burning embers from their clothes. Andrew watched in horror as flames ignited the cedar shakes on the building nearby. The heat of the raging inferno must have dried the water they'd sprayed not long ago onto the roof, leaving the buildings once again at the mercy of the fire. Men stood back, gaping, as the flames took hold and grew in size, quickly engulfing the roof and working their way out toward the walls.

Cries of fear and disbelief rose from the group as the blaze jumped from one rooftop to the next. "Pump harder, men—we need to get the water up there!" someone holding the hose shouted into the night.

"No use!" The men manning the pumps raced from the area where they'd been working as sparks and flames cascaded around them. "The pumps are useless; the heat is melting the hoses. There's nothing

more we can do. Save yourselves! Leave the town! Leave the town!"
Men scrambled to get out of the way, dashing across the nearby bridge
toward the homes on the west side of the mill.

Frantic, the remaining men, women, and children raced past
their now doomed homes and headed up a road toward farms to the
west. Flames roared against the night sky, shedding light on the path
out of town. The frightened cries from some of the children pulled
at Andrew's heart, and he continued to utter prayers for safety with
each step he took.

A half mile up the road they came across a clearing in the woods,
and the ground leveled out into pasture. A farmhouse stood on the
far edge, and a man, woman, and several children stood huddled on
the porch. The husband lifted a lantern and peered at the group of
stragglers approaching his home. "Has the fire reached Palmer?"

A man's voice came from the back of the small band. "Yes, sir. The
town's on fire and it's not far behind us. Don't think it's safe to stay
here. You'd best take what you can carry and come with us."

The man shook his head. "Don't want to leave my farm. I turned
my animals out already, just in case, but I'll stay and fight the fire if
she comes."

A mighty roar filled the night air, with another close on its heels.
Grant's face twisted in horror, and he turned toward the farmer. "That
was two of the boilers explodin' at the mill. I'm guessin' the other six
will follow. It's an inferno back there, mister, and you'd best not stay.
It's not safe for you or your family."

The woman on the porch tugged at her husband's arm. "We need
to listen, Sam. If the good Lord wants to save our farm, He can, but
we need to think of the children."

Another explosion seemed to rip a hole in the sky, sucking the air and energy right out of the clearing. Andrew drew in a deep breath. "Your wife's right. You need to leave. Now."

The woman raced into the house and came out with a box in her arms, shoving it at her husband. She scooped up a toddler and bounded down the steps. "Let's go, Sam. There isn't anything we own that's worth dying for."

Sam hefted the box to his shoulder and handed his lantern to one of the nearby men. "All right, Martha." He nodded to his wife. "Come on, kids, let's go."

The rest of the group followed their lead as the rumble of the remaining boilers' demise shook the ground beneath their feet.

* * *

Matilda Stedman stood by the wagon and looked up at her son. His cough had finally cleared with her nursing, but now she'd caught whatever he'd had. Wallace had grudgingly agreed to hunt for Sammie and Joel one last time. She'd promised to ask the orphanage for another girl if nothing came of this hunt, but she was loath to give up a trained girl like Sammie. "You got to promise me you'll talk to everyone on my list afore you come back, ya hear?"

Wallace picked up the reins and scowled. "I hear, Ma. You said it at least a dozen times already, and I'm getting tired of jawing about it. Let me get out of here so's I can get back, will ya?"

Matilda stepped away from the wagon seat, torn between letting her son go and boxing his ears. "Don't sass me, boy." Letting him go seemed the wisest choice if Sammie were to be found. "Remember, I don't care if you bring the boy back or not. Someone wants him, you give him away. I just want the girl."

Wallace rolled his eyes and nodded. "Yes, Ma." He grabbed the reins with both hands and slapped the horses' rumps. "Yaw! Git up there." The wagon jerked forward with a squeak of the wheels and rumbled across the open space in front of the barn, raising a cloud of dust that sent Matilda into a fit of coughing.

She waved her arms in the air, but it did little good. She retreated to the porch and climbed to the top step. A deep groan of the wood beneath her feet gave her only a split second of warning before the board broke in half and her ankle plummeted to the hard ground beneath. "Oww!" she shrieked as the sharp board gouged the tender flesh beneath her stocking.

"Wallace, come back, son, I need your help!" she yelled.

But the wagon didn't return.

She stood for a moment, one foot still on the broken step, the other plunged a foot below. "Blame it all!" She jerked her leg up. "Yeow!" Pain shot through her ankle, but her foot came free and she staggered onto the porch. "Dad-gum steps. Worthless son," she muttered as she pushed open the door to the house and limped toward the kitchen.

Wallace had best bring that girl back and then get to work fixing stuff around this place. She'd had it with just about everything and wasn't going to tolerate much more.

* * *

Andrew brought up the rear of the group he'd found himself with. Some of the others had headed down a road they were sure would lead to safety, and the rest had continued on toward the small town of Latourelle, about three miles below Bridal Veil. They had at least one canyon to cross, and the fire still raged not far behind.

Martha, Sam, and their children had remained with his group, as had Nathaniel and another man named Silas, whom he didn't know. Sam still lugged the heavy box of belongings on his shoulder, and Martha trudged behind him, carrying a toddler in her arms. Andrew could see by the droop of her shoulders that her strength must be failing. He picked up his pace and drew abreast of her. "Here, ma'am, how about letting me carry the boy? You need to rest your arms."

She glanced at him and started to shake her head, then stopped and heaved a sigh. "All right. Thank ye." She lifted the dozing child burrowed against her chest and handed him to Andrew, then reached out a hand to the next youngest child trudging beside her.

Her husband turned his head and grunted. "That goes for me, too, mister. I was about to toss this box and carry my boy."

Martha peered over her shoulder, and a shudder shook her slender frame. "You think the fire got our house?"

Andrew followed her gaze, regret and sympathy tugging at his heart. "I don't know. It's possible it could have skirted the clearing. I'm praying for God's protection."

She nodded and resumed walking, quickening her pace to catch up with the men forging ahead. "Guess that's all any of us can do, and I thank ye for praying. Hope we'll find shelter soon so these babes can rest."

Thirty minutes later the tired band waded across a stream at the bottom of the steep-sided canyon. Andrew set the little boy gently on a bed of moss and stooped to cup water in his hands, then tossed it over his head and neck. "The air's cleaner down here. Shouldn't take long to get to Latourelle once we're out of the canyon, but I hate to start up the other side and get back into that dense smoke."

Nathaniel nodded. "Yeah, but we don't have much choice. Got to keep moving."

Sam lifted his head and sniffed at the air. "You think we've left the fire behind? Doesn't seem to be anywhere nearby, from what I can tell."

Nathaniel sat on a rock and pulled off his shoe, shaking it until something small tumbled from inside. "Doubtful. The wind is still blowing out of the east, and there's been nothing to stop it from spreading. If our luck holds, we'll find a farm and hitch a ride back to Bridal Veil soon."

Andrew leaned over and picked up Martha's boy from where he rested. "Luck has nothing to do with it. God's leading us out of this forest, and He's the one who will take us on through safely."

Nathaniel scowled. "Think what you want to, Browning, but I don't buy it. God could have kept the fire from starting, but He didn't, so I'm not putting too much hope in Him getting us out of this fix. No, sir—we'll have to do that on our own hook."

"Sorry you feel that way, Cooper." Andrew hefted the dozing boy against his shoulder and nodded toward the hillside before them. "We'd best get at it."

They spent the next hour trudging through brush, slipping on fir needles, and struggling to see their way by the dim lantern Nathaniel held aloft. Martha gripped the hands of her middle and oldest children, a girl of about nine and a boy of eleven, while Sam stayed close to his family, balancing the box of belongings on his shoulder. When they finally crested the top of the hill, gasps were heard from Martha and her son, and the young girl whimpered. "The fire's close!" Martha pointed off to the right. "It can't be more than a quarter mile from the path."

Sam grabbed his daughter's other hand and tugged. "Come on, we've got to hurry."

They quickened their pace and covered at least another mile, with the crackling of flames surrounding them on three sides. The path took a sharp bend, and they rushed to round it.

Sam's voice pierced the night just ahead of Andrew. "Lord, get us through this. It doesn't look good, men."

Andrew stopped abreast of the now quiet group and stared at the sight ahead of them. They stood on the edge of a clearing with a stand of trees on the far side. A lone tree had ignited, and the flames raced up through the dry branches and into the top. Sparks leapt from the crown of the tree and into its neighbor. They watched as a gust of wind blew across the clearing and acted like a bellows, chasing the tongues of fire from treetop to treetop.

Nathaniel turned and lowered the lantern, no longer needed to light their way. "We've got to go back the way we came before the fire closes off the path. Hurry!"

Chapter Forty
....

Margaret stood on the steps of the Company store, praying for news of the men who'd gone up the mountain. No word had arrived from Andrew or Nathaniel. For the last two days stragglers had made their way into town on foot and by wagon, coming from the west where they'd escaped the firestorm that ravaged the town of Palmer. Reports had filtered down a day after the fire was spotted that the Trickey farm had burned, along with several others, and Palmer had been completely consumed.

During each hour that dragged by, Margaret struggled to hold on to her faith. So many times in the past she'd begged God to answer her prayers, and the heavens seemed to be brass. What if God chose not to answer this time, as well, and took the man she loved? She placed her hand over her heart. Where had that thought come from?

"Margaret!" Clara's voice rang out from just up the path, and Margaret spun around. "I stopped by your cabin." Her friend walked rapidly the rest of the way to the store, her breath coming in quick little gasps.

"I'm so thankful you've come. I've been beside myself with worry." Margaret pressed her cheek to Clara's hair and returned the warm hug, then stepped back. "I can't stand the waiting much longer, and no one seems to know anything new. Sammie and Joel are playing at Art Gibbs' home, so I have a little time. Would you walk with me to the waterfall?"

Clara slipped her arm through Margaret's. "Of course. I've been praying for the men that haven't returned."

The two women struck out on the path that led west from the front steps of the store and walked the several hundred yards to Bridal Veil Falls. The sound of the mighty falls had increased in volume over the past two days, now that the mill at Palmer was no longer diverting water down the flume and into the mill. The two women climbed up the path that bordered the stream. Margaret paused beside a large, moss-covered boulder and sat down in front of it. Clara sank down beside her and leaned against the rock.

Margaret stared at the tumbling water striking the pool at the base and kicking up a delicious-looking froth. If only they'd had this abundance of water to put out the fire. But no, lack of water hadn't been the problem; rather, the heat and flames were what had destroyed the pumps, making the hoses useless. "Have you heard anything more?" She turned toward Clara.

"Just that a few people got trapped in Palmer and had to stay almost submerged in the millpond while the fire passed over. Thank God the pond was there, or they'd never have made it."

Margaret nodded. "I heard about that, but not much about the surrounding farms, other than the Trickey family. It's a miracle no lives were lost."

"You didn't hear about the Hamilton boys?"

"Cecil and Gerald?" Margaret sat forward, her heart pounding faster. The brothers were about ten and twelve years old. "What about them?"

Clara laid a gentle hand on her knee. "I'm sorry. I assumed you'd heard. They—they perished in the fire."

Margaret gasped and leaned back hard against the rock, not caring about the small protrusion that poked her shoulder. "What happened?"

Clara took a deep breath and let it out slowly. "Their father woke them and told them to dress quickly and get out of the house. He sent the boys on ahead while he got the baby. Apparently Cecil and Gerald hadn't put on their shoes before leaving, and the burning embers were singeing their feet. They scooted into a nearby shed and sat to put their shoes on." She stopped, and a sob rose in her throat.

Margaret gripped Clara's hand, not wanting to hear the rest of the tale but knowing she must. "Go on."

The blood had drained from Clara's face, and her voice shook. "A burning tree fell across the opening of the shed and shut them in. Their father"—she covered her face with her hands—"wasn't able to get them out."

"How awful." Margaret tried to shut out the image the words had painted. How could the parents survive the grief and loss of their boys? The fire was mostly out now, but how many other lives would they discover had been lost? Her mind flew to Andrew and Nathaniel, and she wrapped her arms around herself and rocked with the pain. She couldn't stand the thought of losing either one of them, but especially—

Clara gripped her arm. "We should pray for the others who haven't returned."

"Yes." The two women bowed their heads, and Clara offered a simple but heartfelt petition for the safety of those remaining on the mountain. She raised her head and looked into Margaret's eyes. "I know they'll come back. Somehow, I just know it."

"I've had a sick feeling in the pit of my stomach all day and can't seem to shake it—it's felt like a premonition of sorts." Margaret shook her head. "And now with the news of the Hamilton boys—"

"I know. The waiting is hard." Clara offered a sympathetic smile. "But we've got to trust the Lord, Margaret."

"I've done that so many times in the past, and I keep getting disappointed," Margaret said, hating the tone—the near whine—of her voice and knowing she had no right to complain after the tremendous losses of the families around her. "I'm sorry. That was uncalled-for."

"No, it's all right to say how you feel. But you've got to realize that God doesn't always give us what we want. Sometimes He says no, and sometimes He makes us wait, but we still need to trust Him."

Margaret shifted her position against the rock, then leaned forward and pushed to her feet. "Come on; let's walk back to the store. I can't sit here any longer." She offered her hand to Clara and helped her to her feet. "I know you're right. I'm beginning to see God's hand in all of this, clear back to the time Papa hid the box with my note to Nathaniel, and even him asking Andrew to look out for me."

Clara tucked her hand into Margaret's arm and they began to meander down the path. "How do you mean?"

Margaret drew in a deep breath, thankful most of the smoke had cleared from the air and she could breathe without choking. Birds sang in nearby trees, and no breeze stirred the leaves of the willow trees as they passed by. The men attributed Bridal Veil being spared to the wind dying down when the sun rose the morning after the fire started.

"I'm beginning to wonder if the Lord used Papa as an instrument of His will for my life. I haven't worked it all out in my heart yet, but

I think I'm getting there." She squeezed Clara's hand. "When I do, I'll explain it to you, I promise. Right now I'd best get back. Mr. Gibbs has been kind to allow Sammie and Joel to stay so long, but I'm sure they're hungry. I'm meeting them at the store soon."

A piercing train whistle heralded the arrival of a locomotive pulling a number of freight cars. The girls covered their ears and hurried the final hundred yards to the store. The train slowed near the depot manned by a Bridal Veil Lumbering Company employee.

"Miss Margaret!" Joel's voice, wavering between the high-pitched tone of a boy and the deeper timbre of a man, met her ears and caused her to smile. "Sammie and I got a peppermint stick!" The boy stood on the porch, waving a red-and-white-striped candy in the air, then plopped it back into his mouth.

Margaret smiled at the boy. "That was very nice of Mr. Art."

Joel shook his head. "Nope. Not Mr. Art. Mr. Cowling gave me and Sammie one. He said we're both well behaved and he's plumb happy to have us visit his store." The boy patted himself on the chest. "I'm well behaved, just like he said."

Sammie came up beside him and patted his shoulder. "You sure are, Joel, and you thanked Mr. Cowling right and proper. I'm proud of you."

Just then the smile on Joel's face drooped and fear replaced the smile. He lifted his hand and pointed toward the train depot and the dust-covered man who'd stepped off the train. "I'm scared, Sammie. What's Mr. Wallace doing in Bridal Veil?"

BRIDAL VEIL 1902 ORE

Chapter Forty-one
....

Margaret stared for one long moment at the man in the distance saun-
tering away from the train depot, then scurried up the stairs toward
the children. "Get back in the store. Quickly now."

Sammie didn't hesitate. She grabbed Joel's arm and dragged him
across the threshold, closing the door behind them. Margaret stood on
the covered porch, unsure what to do. It was obvious from Sammie's
pale face that this Mr. Wallace was someone she feared.

A shout penetrated her thoughts, and she raised her chin. Was that
Andrew's voice? She looked wildly around. A small group of men—
stooped over, dirty, and walking slowly—had just emerged from one
of the freight cars.

Andrew raised his hand and started to move toward her. "Margaret!"

Nathaniel stood nearby with a woman who was holding a small
child, along with two other children and a couple of men, both strangers to her. Nathaniel's head turned, and his face broke into a smile. He
too stepped away from the group and headed her way.

Margaret picked up her skirts and flew toward them. They were safe!
God had answered her prayers. Tears brimmed in her eyes, and warm drops
cascaded down her cheeks. A happy laugh burbled out, and she nearly
danced the remaining distance. "Andrew! Thank God you're alive!"

He opened his arms and stopped, allowing her to run the last several paces and throw herself into his embrace. Dust flew as she wrapped
her arms around his neck and buried her wet face on his shoulder.

"It's so good to see you," his husky voice whispered in her ear.

The smell of smoke and dirt clung to his hair and clothing, but it conveyed life and restoration to Margaret. She'd never smell smoke again without remembering this day. She raised her face and took a half step back but still kept her hands on his forearms. "Are you all right?" Margaret appraised him from head to foot, worry tugging at her heart.

"I'm fine. Hungry, tired, filthy, but not hurt." A dimple showed at the corner of his mouth as he turned a radiant smile on her. He beckoned toward the small group standing nearby. "We came through it together. I'll tell you about it later, but I think I need to get home and wash up before I do anything else."

She continued to clutch his arm, loath to let him go, even though she knew he must be tired and longing for a bath.

Then, suddenly, Nathaniel cleared his throat, and Margaret swung toward him, horrified that she'd nearly forgotten his presence. "Nathaniel." She took a step toward him and held out her hand. "I'm so happy you're all right, as well."

He didn't raise his hand but met her eyes squarely. "Thank you. I see you've made your decision." It wasn't a question but a flat statement, as his eyes took in the two of them. He swung around and headed for his house.

Margaret felt a wave of heat rush to her cheeks, and she dropped her eyes. Nothing about this meeting had been planned. She'd not even been completely sure of her own heart until she'd heard Andrew's voice and seen his face. She turned toward Andrew and squeezed his arm. "I'll be right back." She picked up the hem of her skirt and dashed down the path. "Nathaniel?"

He slowed his pace and turned to look over his shoulder. "Margaret." He swung to face her and crossed his arms over his chest but remained silent.

"I'm sorry, Nathaniel. I didn't plan for things to happen this way."

"I asked you to give me a chance, and I thought you'd at least do that much."

She shook her head, and a deep sadness welled up inside. They'd shared something in the past, but the feelings she thought she remembered hadn't returned. "So much has happened the past few days. I didn't have a chance to talk to you again, but I've been thinking about what you asked. It's been too many years, and we've both—changed."

He shook his head. "No. You've just grown up." A smile flitted across his face, then disappeared. "Browning is a good man. I learned that this past couple of days. I'm sorry you and I won't share a future, but I'm happy for you." Sadness lingered in the corners of his mouth. "I don't share your faith, Margaret, although I have to admit this fire has come close to making a believer out of me—but Browning does, and I know that's important to you. I'm going to get cleaned up."

Margaret touched his hand. "Thank you. I pray that someday you'll go beyond coming close to believing, Nathaniel. God is real, and if it weren't for Him, none of us might be standing here today."

Nathaniel gave a quick shrug. "Maybe. It's something I'll think on." He lifted his hand in a salute and turned away.

Margaret's heart twisted with sympathy for Nathaniel and what might have been, but she'd made the right choice. Andrew was all she'd ever wanted or needed in a man—loving, thoughtful, hard-working, and above all else, he loved the Lord with all of his heart. Of course, they'd only started seeing each other not long before Nathaniel came to town, so nothing was settled. But she knew Andrew cared for her. At this point, that was all that mattered, and God would take care of the rest. She turned and walked back toward the area where Andrew waited in front of the store.

"Everything all right?" Andrew held out his hand, his brows raised.

She nodded and returned his smile, then realization hit her. She gripped Andrew's arm and looked toward the man who stood talking to a mill worker not far from the Company store. "Andrew, I need your help."

He turned, and his eyes lit with warm caring. "Can it wait until after I get cleaned up?"

She shook her head. "I'm afraid not. You see that man?" She nodded toward the man Joel had called Mr. Wallace. "He means trouble for Sammie and Joel. He came on the train at the same time that you did, and the children recognized him. I sent them back into the store, but I can't get them to my house without their being seen."

Andrew took a long look at the man and straightened his drooping shoulders. "You stay here. I'll see what he's up to." He gave her hand a squeeze and strode toward the man.

Margaret watched, her heart beating double-time, wishing she could hear their conversation. She walked closer to the store and stole a look at the window. Sammie's face peeked out from the lowest pane of glass. Margaret caught her eye and shook her head, and the girl immediately disappeared. Good. No sense taking chances. She'd prayed for the children's safety and future, but she hadn't planned on having to deal with someone from their past showing up—especially not someone they feared.

A dim shadow passed over her spirit as doubts started to flood in once again. Why was it so hard to lay everything at God's feet and leave it there? She wanted to trust Him, but it seemed as though her world kept turning upside down. *Please, God, keep Sammie and Joel out of this man's clutches and bring good into their lives. Forgive me for allowing my heart to race toward fear with each new problem. I keep stumbling and doubting whenever hard things come, and I want to walk in faith.*

Andrew walked toward her with the rumpled man in tow, his gray felt hat dusty and black pants wrinkled from too much sitting. "Margaret, this is Wallace Stedman."

They stopped, and the stranger tipped his hat. "Ma'am."

She nodded but didn't trust herself to speak. Something about this man gave her the shivers, and she instantly empathized with Sammie's fear.

"Mr. Stedman is looking for two children whom he claims ran away from his mother's care. He believes he's tracked them from Salem to Bridal Veil."

Margaret crossed her arms. "What are the children's names, Mr. Stedman, and how old are they?"

Wallace Stedman cleared his throat, then covered his mouth and coughed. "I say, you got a saloon in these parts, or someplace a man can get a pint of whiskey? It was a long, dry trip riding that wagon to Portland, and they didn't serve nothing on the train."

Andrew raised his brows. "No, we don't. Bridal Veil is a company-owned town and doesn't care to have their men liquored up. A sawmill is a dangerous place to work if you aren't sober."

Wallace wiped his mouth with the back of his hand. "Anyone you know have something to drink they might part with, then?" His voice took on a whining tone and dropped to a lower pitch. "I can pay."

"I'm sorry, no. I'm sure Mr. Cowling would offer you a cup of coffee or cold water at the store," Andrew said.

Margaret bit her lip to keep from crying out. Andrew had forgotten the children were hiding in the store. What if this odious man entered and found them there? It was all she could do not to dash inside and push them out a back window to escape.

"Naw. Guess I'll make it." He turned toward Margaret and pasted on an ingratiating smile. "You asked about them kids. Names are Sammie and Joel, but I don't know how old they are. The boy's big and the girl's a skinny little thing, but real cute—know what I mean?" He turned leering eyes toward Andrew and smacked his lips.

"No, I don't." Andrew took a step closer to the man and glowered. "Nor do I think that's an appropriate thing for a man to comment on."

Wallace took a half step back and winced. "Didn't mean nothing by it, just talking, that's all. So you seen 'em around here?"

Andrew looked at Margaret but didn't reply. She gave a tiny shake of her head and tried with all her might to send him a warning.

Stedman narrowed his eyes. "I already contacted the sheriff over to Troutdale, and he tole me them two kids are in town. I'm here to take 'em back to my ma, so you'd best be leading me to them, if you don't want to answer to the sheriff."

Margaret stifled a low groan. The sheriff was involved? But why would he allow this man to take them, when he was still investigating Martin Jenkins' death? She didn't believe it. "What's the sheriff's name, Mr. Stedman?"

A brief confusion flashed across Wallace's face, then he folded his arms over his chest. "Don't matter what his name is. Those kids belong to my ma, and I aim to take them back with me, sheriff or no."

Andrew drew a step closer and stared into the man's eyes. "I don't think so, Mr. Stedman. You won't be taking those children anywhere. You don't have a legal claim on them, and we don't know that your mother does. She'll have to come to Bridal Veil and bring papers proving she's their guardian, or they won't be leaving." He leaned to within a foot of the man's face. "You understand what *I'm* saying?"

Wallace scurried backward. "Ma's not going to like it, no sir. She tole me to bring those kids home, and she'll be plumb mad if she has to tote 'em back herself."

"That's her problem, not ours. You tell your mother to do her own dirty work and bring proof she has the right to those children, or she'll be wasting a trip." Andrew pointed at the train sitting a hundred yards down the siding. "I suggest you climb back on that train and return to wherever you came from, before you get stuck here with nothing to drink."

Wallace glared at Andrew, then glanced at the train. He jerked on the hem of his dusty jacket and swiveled on his heel. "Fine." He shot the word back over his shoulder. "But Ma will be coming with those papers, and the lot of you will be sorry you didn't make it easy on yourselves this time around."

Chapter Forty-two

....

Margaret clutched Andrew's arm as her legs nearly gave out beneath her. "What do we do now?" Her mind raced, trying to take in all that had just happened. Mrs. Stedman would be returning to claim the children and take them away. If her son was any indication, she was no fit guardian for Samantha and Joel.

Andrew bent his head down and smiled into her eyes. "She may not even return after her son tells her what happened. It's not cheap to travel this far, and I'm guessing they aren't people of means."

"But if she does?"

He shook his head. "I guess we'll have to wait and see. Sheriff Bryant will be back in town soon, and he may not allow Joel to leave. He's still hoping the boy will remember where he left Martin's journal."

The train whistle blew again, and the wheels began to turn. Margaret peered over Andrew's shoulder just in time to see the detestable Wallace Stedman clambering onto the freight car. "Good, he's leaving." She straightened her shoulders and raised her chin, new strength flowing into her body at the man's departure. "And he'll have to ride clear to The Dalles before he can catch a train back."

She stifled a chuckle. How silly she'd been giving in to her emotions because that man threatened them with his mother's return. God was bigger than Mr. Stedman or his mother, and she'd do well to remember that.

A sudden thought turned her away from the departing train. "We need to let Sammie and Joel know he's gone." She dashed for the steps and bounded up and across the front porch, throwing open the front door. "Sammie? Joel?"

Grant Cowling stood chatting with Dan Meadows, the bullwhacker from Palmer, but turned at the sound of her voice and nodded toward the back corner of the store. "Donnie's workin' stocking shelves, and the children are somewhere in the same area. They're fine."

Margaret's shoulders tensed. Donnie had tried to create trouble, and she didn't want Sammie and Joel near him. The door opened again and she stifled a groan. *Andrew.* She'd raced off without him and must have shut the door in his face. She turned. "I'm sorry—"

Sheriff Bryant stood in the doorway with Andrew beside him.

"Oh, my." Her hands flew to her face. "I didn't realize you were in town!"

The sheriff's eyes crinkled at the corners. "Had me a little unfinished business and took the steamboat down. I needed to talk to some folks out east of town, so brought my horse and stopped at their place." He took off his hat and tucked it under his arm, then looked over at Andrew. "Glad to find both of you here at the same time." He glanced across the short distance to the counter and nodded. "Cowling, Meadows, good to see you, as well."

Dan Meadows emitted a grunt that passed as a greeting, and Grant Cowling raised his hand.

Andrew turned to the sheriff. "What can we help you with this time?"

"Now that the town's safe from the fire, I'm hopin' Joel can give me a mite more information." He turned his head and scanned the interior of the store. "He here with you?"

Andrew cleared his throat. "Sheriff, I just got back from tramping over the hills and canyons for the past two days, trying to stay ahead of the fire. I need to head home and get cleaned up and grab a bite to eat. Do you suppose you can give Miss Garvey and me some time before you talk to Joel?"

The sheriff turned his hat in calloused hands. "Don't see any reason why not. I've got other business I can attend to."

The door opened again, and Margaret turned, fear gripping her at the realization that Wallace Stedman might have seen the sheriff arrive in town and decided to stay. Instead, Robert Ludlow stepped over the threshold, a bag gripped in his hand. "I say, Cowling, did I miss the train? There's no one at the depot office."

Grant Cowling sauntered over, wiping his hands on the front of his apron. "'Fraid you did, Ludlow. Won't be another one till tomorrow morning. Sorry 'bout that."

Robert Ludlow mumbled a low curse, then jerked his head up and met Margaret's eyes. "Pardon me, Miss Garvey. That was uncalled for."

"Certainly," she said graciously, then gestured toward his bag. "School starts shortly, and I expect you'll want to be here for the opening day. Are you taking a short trip?"

He set his bag on the floor and took a handkerchief from his pocket, mopping his forehead. "It's unseasonably warm today, is it not?"

Andrew stared at the man. He started to speak but then checked himself.

Samantha and Joel peeked around a corner of a nearby aisle, and Sammie's low voice called out, "Miss Margaret? Is it all right to come out?"

Margaret walked over and put her arm around the girl's slim shoulders, relieved that the children were still in the store and hadn't slipped out. "Yes, honey. I'm sorry. I should've told you right away. We're heading home now."

Sammie peered around the front of the store, then stood on her tiptoes and looked out the window toward the tracks. "Is he gone?"

"Yes, he's gone." Margaret hugged her, then released her grip and turned to Joel. "I'll bet you're getting hungry, aren't you?"

His eyes brightened. "Yes, ma'am, my tummy is grumbling somethin' fierce. I asked Sammie for one of them big pickles in the barrel, but she said I'd have to wait."

Sheriff Bryant strode over to the barrel Joel pointed at and cocked his head toward Grant Cowling. "Charge this to me, Grant." He turned to Joel and grinned. "Pick out the biggest one you can, son. You, too, young lady, if you care for pickles."

Both children raced to the barrel and jabbed at a pickle with the long-handled fork lying on a shelf nearby. "Thank you, sir," they chorused.

"You're welcome. Now, I have a favor to ask." The sheriff took a step closer to Joel and placed his hand on his shoulder. "Remember you told me that you took a journal from Mr. Jenkins' house?"

"A journal?" Joel wrinkled his nose and twisted his mouth. "No. I took a book and a pen; don't know nothin' about a journal."

The sheriff smiled and nodded. "That's right, a book. It's very important to me that I find that book. When you go home with Miss Garvey to have lunch, could you think on it for a while, and see if maybe you can remember where you left it?"

The room grew still as each set of eyes rested on Joel. No one moved, and even Robert Ludlow and Dan Meadows seemed to understand the importance of the moment as they stared at the boy, each one holding his breath as he awaited the answer.

Joel popped the end of the large dill pickle into his mouth and sucked on it, then took a bite and munched for a moment before swallowing. "Yep. I'll think on it."

"So you don't remember yet where it could be?" Sheriff Bryant asked.

Joel shook his head, then shrugged. "Might. It was a nice book, and I wanted Sammie to read it to me."

Andrew stepped closer and touched the boy's shoulder. "Joel, it belongs to someone else. The man who died has a daughter, and she'd like to have his things to help her remember her papa. Do you have anything to help you remember your mama?"

Joel twisted his mouth to the side and scrunched his brow, then nodded. "Ah-huh. Mama give me a top when I was little. Papa carved it for me, and Mama painted it all pretty. Sammie keeps it in our bag for special times, huh, Sammie?" He turned an excited face toward his sister. "Can we play with it when we get back to the house?"

Sammie smiled. "Yes, but you need to help them find the book first, Joel. The man's daughter would like to have it, just like you have Papa's top. Will you tell me where you left it?"

He shrugged. "Maybe after we get home and have dinner, I'll remember."

Margaret drew in a deep breath and let it out slowly, trying to quiet her pounding heart. If Joel could produce the journal, it might remove any lingering suspicion. But it would also free him to leave town, if his rightful guardian came to claim them. Part of her hoped he'd never remember, but she knew that wasn't right. God would want the truth to come out and the murderer to be found. Besides, it was His job to protect the children. "Then let's go home and eat, so you can help the sheriff find the book when we're finished." She reached out a hand to Sammie and another to Joel, and they both grasped her hands eagerly.

Andrew gave Margaret a dimpled smile. "I'll see you after I get cleaned up and grab a bite to eat." He turned toward Sheriff Bryant. "Want to meet me at Miss Garvey's in about an hour? I'd like to fill you in on something that happened before you arrived."

"Sure."

Dan Meadows pushed forward, a question clouding his face. "What's this you're saying about some journal of Jenkins'? He leave some kind of record that might tell you who killed him?"

Sheriff Bryant motioned Margaret toward the door. "Why don't you take Sammie and Joel on home now, and I'll stick around and answer these fellers' questions?"

"Thanks." Margaret tugged on Joel's hand as the boy paused, his face seemingly intent on the sheriff's words. "Let's go, Joel."

He hung back for a moment. "But I remember, Miss Margaret. It must a'been the pickle 'cause my tummy's not grumbling anymore, and I remember! I left the book in the—"

"Wait!" Sheriff Bryant held up his hand and clutched Joel's shoulder. "You can tell me later. Let's keep it a secret for now, all right, Joel?"

The tension in the room slowly dissipated. Donnie Williams had come from the back of the store and stood off to the side, his arms filled with boxes and his mouth gaping. Robert Ludlow's frozen stance near the door didn't change even after the sheriff's last words, and Dan Meadows and Grant Cowling appeared caught up in the moment and barely breathed.

"A secret?" The boy clapped his hands and grinned. "Goody! I love secrets!" His big smile slowly changed to a frown. "But I thought you wanted to know where I put the book?"

The sheriff glanced around the room, then leaned over and lowered his voice. "I want you to tell me, but this room isn't good for telling secrets. Do you think you can still remember if we wait until I come over to Miss Garvey's house, after you eat?"

Joel nodded and the grin came back again. "Ah-huh! I won't forget again, no sir."

"Good, then I'll see you after dinner."

Chapter Forty-three

The man skulked behind Margaret Garvey's cabin, taking care to stay in the shadows behind a clump of brush and trees. He mumbled a low curse, wanting to lash out and hit someone. Jenkins had kept a journal. Why hadn't he thought to stay and scour the man's house for anything that could incriminate him, instead of running away so fast?

He'd slipped out of the store and drifted down the path toward Miss Garvey's cabin, hoping no one would suspect what he had in mind. The sheriff had entered the woman's door moments earlier, and the man outside had relaxed just a little. He'd thought the sheriff would have headed this way earlier, but he'd obviously been mistaken. Strange that he came without Browning, though. Maybe the man had fallen asleep after his long ordeal of running from the fire. He shrugged. Guess it didn't matter.

A window sash rose at the back of the house. Smoke still lingered in the air after the big fire, and a lot of folks were leaving their windows open during the day, hoping to air things out. He moved around the stand of brush and stepped carefully, watching the ground for anything that would give away his presence.

Voices drifted out into the still, late summer air as he eased a little closer. Margaret Garvey's clear, feminine voice was easily distinguishable from the rest. "So now that we know where Joel left the journal, what's next?"

"After I finish this fine cup of coffee, I think I'll mosey over to the other side of town and take a look-see in that abandoned barn at the Jorgensens.'"

A rattle that sounded like a cup on a saucer made the man standing near the window hold his breath and take a step back. Had someone stood up and headed toward the window?

He sidestepped around a pile of firewood and darted back into the trees, careful to crouch low and watch his step. Time to get moving. The sheriff didn't appear to be a lazy man or one who'd sit nursing a cup of coffee long, now that he knew evidence lay a half-mile away. He should have time to get across town and grab that journal before anyone showed up at the old Jorgensen place. There may not be anything written there that mattered, but he couldn't take the chance.

* * *

Andrew Browning squatted behind a musty pile of hay in the old barn and waited, happy that he'd been able to help the sheriff lure the man who'd killed Jenkins. Too bad they still didn't know who it was, but the sheriff seemed convinced that one of the men in the store was the culprit.

He shook his head and stifled a sneeze. Too much dust in this place and the hay must be several years old. Hopefully no mice or rats had found the journal and destroyed it.

When the sheriff had come to Andrew's home shortly after he'd left the store, Andrew had been intrigued at the man's plan. Bryant would slip out to Margaret's home, get the location of the journal from Joel, and meet Andrew right after that to fill him in. He'd asked Andrew to put off his bath and meal until they nabbed the murderer. Of course, that assumed whoever it was would follow Bryant to Margaret's house in hopes of discovering what Joel knew, then try to give them the slip by getting here first. Andrew grinned, knowing the sheriff would sit near an open window and talk plenty loud.

He wouldn't have considered the plan if the sheriff hadn't agreed to leave a guard at Margaret's home. Not that she should be in any danger, but you never knew what a desperate man might try. Knowing the sheriff would follow close on the man's heels and be here to help apprehend the murderer set his mind further at ease. He'd not thought to bring his revolver when he left his house but knew the sheriff would come armed.

Andrew's thoughts drifted to Margaret, and joy surged through his heart. He still had a hard time believing she'd run to him, not Cooper, when they'd stepped off that train. The last thing he'd known, she'd decided to give Cooper a chance. Of course, a hug of relief at seeing him alive didn't mean she was in love with him, but it was definitely a great start. Once this mess with the journal was finished, he meant to get cleaned up and court Margaret Garvey good and proper.

His mind settled on the other problem yet to be resolved, and he frowned. What about Sammie and Joel, and that scum who called himself Wallace Stedman? Would Stedman go through with his threat and bring his mother back for the children? They'd need to question the children more closely and see what could be done to stop Mrs. Stedman from taking them.

He'd hoped Margaret might be able to keep them indefinitely and maybe—

Heat rose at the back of his neck. It might be too early to think about the future, but after the way Margaret greeted him, there was a good chance she returned his feelings. If that were to happen, he'd be happy to take Sammie and Joel and help raise them as his own, if they wanted to stay.

The rusty hinges on the side door of the barn squealed in protest after so many years of disuse. Then the noise stopped, and all was quiet. Had a gust of wind propelled the door? He waited, holding his breath. Thirty seconds went by, then a full minute, and he started to relax. The squeak came again as though the door had opened another couple of inches. This time soft footfalls followed the sound as someone moved from the door to the cow stalls.

Muttered words that Andrew couldn't discern met his ears as the man stumbled in the dusky interior. Stall doors opened, and the sound of rummaging drifted over to Andrew. Where was the sheriff? Fear shot through him when he realized the intruder could find the journal and bolt from the barn before he had a chance to see him.

If only the sheriff had been able to hunt for the journal before anyone arrived. Andrew shifted his body to the left and peered around the stack of hay, hoping to get a glimpse of the man. Nothing. It appeared he'd have to vacate his position and come out in the open to get a good look. Better wait awhile and give Sheriff Bryant a chance to arrive.

More mumbling and an occasional curse drifted across the barn, along with the continued sound of searching. At least the intruder hadn't found the book yet.

"Ahh, got you!" A familiar voice grunted the words, and the movement ceased.

The hair stood up on the back of Andrew's neck and he straightened his spine, ready to rush from his hiding place and tackle the intruder. He pushed to his feet slowly and rubbed his hands down the legs of his grimy trousers. He eased from behind the pile and took a step toward the man who stood with his back toward Andrew.

"Glad you found what you were looking for, Ludlow." Sheriff Bryant's calm words broke the charged interior of the barn, and Andrew took a step closer, keeping his eyes fixed on Robert Ludlow's back.

Ludlow snarled a curse, shoved the journal into the front of his shirt, and spun on his heel. He leapt forward, running for the big front door that stood open just a crack, not seeming to notice Andrew standing in the shadows a couple of yards to the side. Andrew gave a mighty lunge and landed on the man's back, bringing him hard to the ground. Ludlow grunted and struggled, but Andrew pinned his arms to the floor.

Boots sounded on the wood floor, and little puffs of dusty hay rose near Andrew's face. "You can get up, son. I've got him covered," Sheriff Bryant said.

Andrew looked up into the business end of a Colt revolver. He rolled to one side, pushed to his feet, and stood next to the sheriff. "Glad you got here when you did. I figured he was ready to bolt, and I'd have to hold him till you arrived."

"You did a good job, son. I'm beholden." The sheriff leaned over and prodded the prone man with his foot. "Roll over and hand me that journal."

Ludlow didn't move.

The sheriff grabbed the back of his jacket and hauled him over onto his side, then reached inside the front of his coat and yanked out the journal. "It'll be interesting to see what's in this book."

Ludlow pushed to his knees and lifted glaring eyes. "You got nothing on me. I happened to come in this barn and stumbled across that book, that's all."

"Ah-huh, we'll see." Sheriff Bryant trained the gun on the man without wavering. "Browning, how about you take a look at this, while I keep our guest covered." He handed the journal off without moving his gaze. "Just skim through it, and see if you catch any mentions of this gent."

Andrew flipped the book open at the front and noted the date was almost a year ago. Figuring any entries about Ludlow might be more recent, he turned to the center and started thumbing through each page quickly, hunting for Ludlow's name. "Ah, here we go." He lifted his eyes and met the sheriff's stern gaze.

"Read it aloud."

Andrew returned to the place he'd marked with his finger and let his eyes travel over the words for a moment, then cleared his throat.

"I don't trust Robert Ludlow, not one whit. He's been flirting with my Jenny, and him a married man. She don't give him no encouragement. Ludlow keeps up his vile ways, and I'll have me a talk with the man."

Robert Ludlow grunted and spewed a curse, then spit on the dusty floor. "Just because I gave the man's daughter a compliment a time or two doesn't mean a thing. It's certainly not a crime and nothing I'd kill him over."

The sheriff stared at the man on the floor. "Might not be too comfortable for you if Jenkins threatened to tell your wife. Could be you'd lose your standing in the community and maybe even your job." He turned his head just an inch but kept his gaze fixed on Ludlow. "Anything more, Browning?"

Andrew flipped through several more useless pages, frustration mounting in his chest. Early afternoon sunlight filtered through large cracks in the walls as the sun broke through the clouds that had blown in an hour or two before. A light breeze wafted through the open door, stirring the dirt on the floor and causing Ludlow to sneeze. "Can't you let me up off this filthy floor?"

"You're fine right there." Sheriff Bryant waved the gun muzzle. "Just you lie back down and quit squirming. You're making me nervous."

Ludlow sank back prostrate on the floor, his arms out at his sides. "Fine. But you're not going to find anything else, and you can't hold me for something as trivial as flirting with the man's daughter."

Andrew quit turning the pages of the journal and raised his head. "Found something more, Sheriff. Want me to read it?"

"Go on."

"This is dated just a week before Martin's death." Andrew's firm voice echoed in the empty barn as he read:

"Ludlow's worse scum than I thought. I got proof now that he's stealing money from the school fund. I been checking around amongst some of the other board members without raising a ruckus and found out how much ought to be there. Guess Ludlow's in charge of the money, but my Jenny works at the railroad depot where they keep it. She ain't supposed to tell me these things, but she's been worried of late, after she got aholt

of some papers Ludlow filed with the depot man. The figures don't add up, and it's clear the rat has been skimming money."

Andrew looked over the next paragraphs and saw nothing more about Ludlow. He flipped another couple of pages of commonplace records.

Ah—one more page. "Here's the last entry. Jenkins says this:

"I'm going to confront Ludlow. I came home early today and found Jenny crying. She had to fight Ludlow off and barely escaped with her virtue. Her blouse was near torn off and her hair down around her face. I'm sending her to her aunt's in Portland, and then I'm tracking that scoundrel down. I've already sent him word that I intend to run him out of town if he don't come clean about the money, but now he's gone too far. I plan to turn him over to the sheriff."

Andrew looked up and met Bryant's eyes. "The entries end two days prior to Jenkins' death."

Sheriff Bryant reached down and grabbed Ludlow by the back of his collar, jerking him up to a kneeling position. "I've heard enough. Between this journal and Jenny's testimony, you're headed to jail. Let's go."

Chapter Forty-four

....

Three days later Margaret walked hand in hand with Andrew on a trail through the woods, relishing the cooler weather and enjoying the smell of air freshly washed after a rain shower. They'd left Sammie and Joel at Art Gibbs' home after Joel begged to stay and play with Buck. Margaret's heart swelled with joy at the chance to be alone with Andrew—this was the first chance they'd had to talk privately since Andrew had returned and Robert Ludlow was arrested. Margaret smiled and lifted her face toward Andrew. "I'm glad you thought of this. I've been hoping we'd have time to talk."

Andrew nodded and squeezed her hand. "Me too." He gestured toward the majestic trees clinging to the sides of the nearby hill. "I'm thankful the fire didn't make it down here last week. It's bad enough that it wiped out Palmer and they have to start over."

"So they're going to rebuild, then?"

"Yes. They've already started. Several of the families are working together to remove the burned rubble, and Mr. Palmer is allowing employees who owned their homes on outlying farms to buy lumber at cost. Of course, the Company will rebuild the new mill up above, as well as the workers' cabins."

"I heard the schoolhouse burned. Do you think they'll replace it?"

He sidestepped a large root growing across the path, then guided her around it. "Yes. It's doubtful school will start anytime before the first of next year, but they plan on rebuilding. It looks like they'll push everything back at least a mile or so from its old location, though—closer to the logging site and away from the burned area."

"Good." She walked for a while in silence, her thoughts and prayers going to the families who'd been hit by the tragedy. "I never heard what happened after you left the upper mill and had to flee the fire."

"It was tough." He drew his free hand across his brow. "A group of us fought the fire for as long as we could, until the cry went up to abandon the town. We traveled a short piece up the road where Sam and Martha Jenson lived and we heard the boilers start to explode, one after another. We tramped for hours through the woods and along dirt roads trying to outrun the fire. Sometimes we thought we'd put it behind us, then we'd come face-to-face with it again. We were trying to get to Latourelle and had just climbed to the rim of a canyon when we were faced with a wall of fire on three sides and were forced to run for our lives back the way we'd come."

Margaret gripped Andrew's hand, her heart pounding at the image his words conveyed. "Thank God you weren't hurt!"

He nodded. "I'd been praying the entire way, as I think most of the men must have been, and God intervened. A man driving a wagon with several people aboard came around the bend a short way down the road, and he knew a way out. The women and children climbed on, and the rest of us had to run behind the wagon for several miles. We took turns spelling each other, as the wagon had room for only one more man. It took a number of hours, but we made it to a farm that hadn't been touched by the fire—at least while we were there. I pray they escaped any damage later."

"So you stayed there?"

"They fed us, and we collapsed on their floor and in the barn, while one person stood watch for the fire. We were thankful to be alive and safe for the time being." Andrew led Margaret off the side of the trail and over to a fallen log. He took off his jacket and laid it across the bark, then sat down beside her. "We spent the night there, then made our way to the tracks and flagged down the freight train."

Margaret rubbed her hands along her upper arms and shivered. "What a horrible ordeal."

"It was." He reached for her hand again and cradled it in his own. "All I could think about while I was running was whether or not you were safe. We had no way of knowing if the fire had shifted or made its way down the mountainside and spread to the town. I wanted nothing more than to get back and take you and the children to safety."

Margaret smiled. "I spent the entire time praying for your safety." Warmth rose to her cheeks. "I think that's when I started to understand my own heart, when I realized you might never come back to me." She lifted a hand to her face.

Andrew leaned closer and slipped his arm around her shoulders. "I've been hoping you felt the same as I for a long time. I care deeply for you, Margaret, but hesitated to tell you when I believed you still had feelings for Cooper."

Margaret leaned her cheek against his chest, releasing a small sigh. "I thought I did, but I came to understand it was only a childish memory that had no substance. I think I first started to realize that when I saw the difference between him and you spiritually and in the way you treated the children, among other things. His lack of faith didn't matter to me as much when he first came back here, since I was still fighting my own spiritual battles." She raised her head and looked into his eyes, seeing her own deep caring reflected there. "I guess I never saw how demanding Nathaniel could be. In so many ways, you've shown how much you care about me."

Andrew gently touched her hair, smoothing a wayward curl back into place behind her ear. His hand brushing against her cheek sent a warm wave of longing over Margaret, and she leaned in to his touch. She held her breath for a moment, wondering if he might kiss her. His face hovered close as he held her with his gaze, but he didn't bend his head to hers.

Then he cleared his throat and drew back a couple of inches, dropping his hand into his lap. "You said you've been fighting your own battles. Did that include being upset with me for agreeing to look out for you?"

She didn't realize she'd been holding her breath, waiting to see what would happen. A slow hiss of air now escaped through her slightly parted lips as she released it. "I've been frustrated with the Lord for months—maybe even for years—thinking He let me down when Nathaniel left town. I was so sure God had sent him into my life and that He'd promised He'd take care of the relationship. When Nathaniel disappeared, I thought God had misled me, or that I couldn't trust Him anymore. Finding out Papa buried the note I left for Nathaniel shook me at an even deeper level. I was positive that both God and Papa had betrayed me." She looked down at her lap and fiddled with a bit of lace on her skirt. "And yes, I was upset with Papa for asking you. I was so afraid you didn't really see me as a person—that your interest was out of a sense of duty to my father."

Andrew turned his shoulder to face her, and his other hand moved to cover hers already held gently in his own. "What do you think now?"

"That God knew and understood what I needed from the beginning." She dropped her head and bit her lip, guilt and relief warring within. "I can't believe I didn't see it earlier, and that I've been blind for so long. It's been hard for me to accept that people love me for who I am, not for what I bring to their lives. I guess that was my biggest fear where you were concerned."

"I'm sorry you felt that way," he murmured. "I've always admired you. I think you're an amazing woman."

Margaret's eyes met his earnest ones. "I'm glad. God was in control even when I didn't trust Him to be. I've asked the Lord to forgive me and to help me to trust Him from now on. I have to admit something, though."

His dimples peeked out from their hiding places again. "What's that?"

"I'm still battling with completely trusting."

"You mean about your future?" He lifted her hand and pressed a kiss on her palm. "I think that God has your life in His hands." Then a small pucker of worry crept into his expression. "Unless you're still not sure? I care deeply for you, Margaret, and I'd never do anything to hurt you."

She laid gentle fingers over his lips. "I know. I was speaking about the children, not myself this time. I'm struggling with worry about their future, now that we know Mrs. Stedman could return."

Andrew nodded. "I understand. I've been entertaining the same worry and trying to give it to the Lord. I spoke to the sheriff about it, but I'm afraid he didn't offer much help. He said if the woman returns with papers showing legal guardianship, there's little he can do."

Margaret groaned and slumped against Andrew's shoulder. "That's what I'm afraid of." She pushed to her feet and held out her hand. "Let's head back to town. I hate leaving them any longer than we have to, even though it's been wonderful having this time alone."

He stood and took a small step closer to her, once again brushing the hair from her face and allowing his hand to linger against her cheek. His hand slid down, and he cupped her chin, lifting it just an inch or two, and looked into her eyes. "Margaret—" His dark eyes held hers, leaving her breathless. His mouth moved closer, hesitating a hair's breadth above hers, then dropping the last little bit to claim her own.

Sweet satisfaction poured through her, sending incredible joy and a deep longing pulsing through her body. Margaret raised her fingertips and stroked the side of his face, then slipped both hands around his neck as the kiss deepened and drew her into dizzy oblivion. Sometime later Andrew raised his head and drew back a fraction, then planted tender kisses on her closed eyelids, her forehead, and finally the tip of her nose. "I love you, Margaret Garvey, with all of my heart, soul, and mind. I was terrified when I thought I might lose you, and I'll thank God to my dying day that you saw fit to choose me."

Her mouth felt dry and her voice came out husky, but she kept her arms clasped around his neck, never wanting to let go. "I can't believe it took me so long to realize I loved you. Thank you for being patient with me." She stood on her tiptoes and kissed him lightly, then drew back. "As much as I'd like to continue, I think we'd best get back." She let her arms slip from around his neck and stepped back a foot.

"All right." Andrew rubbed his hand over his face, then gave her a brilliant smile, both dimples turning his countenance into a bit of a rogue's. "But I have something else to say to you when we have time, and if you'll allow me."

Margaret touched her finger to his cheek. "Oh, I'll allow you, never you fear."

Chapter Forty-five
....

Margaret and Andrew held hands until they reached the edge of town, and then they walked side by side without touching the rest of the way to Art's house. They neared the front yard to find Buck and Joel rolling in the grass, the boy's arms wrapped around the dog's neck and Buck licking Joel's cheek. Happy chortles danced on the air. What a blessing that boy could have these moments of joy after so much sorrow, Margaret couldn't help but think. She lifted a hand and waved at Sammie sitting on the grass nearby. "Having a good time?"

Joel let out a squeal and Sammie grinned. "Yep. Mr. Art gave us cookies and milk, and he gave Buck a cookie, too."

Margaret was delighted to see the pleasure on Sammie's face. "Where's Mr. Art now?" She paused outside the gate to let the dog notice her presence, then carefully pushed it open.

"He went back in the house to write a letter to his intended." Sammie pushed a wisp of straw-colored hair out of her eyes. "What's an 'intended'?"

Andrew chuckled, and Margaret stifled a smile. She sat down on a low stool close to where Sammie lay on the grass. "Glenna is Mr. Art's intended—that means he intends to marry her. She's his fiancée."

"Why doesn't she live in Bridal Veil, then, if they're gonna get married?"

Margaret plucked a fir needle from her skirt and tossed it aside. "Her parents live in Portland, and she won't move here until she

345

and Mr. Art marry next spring, but Mr. Art goes to visit her whenever he can."

"Oh." She narrowed her eyes, but a sparkle still penetrated between the hooded lids. "It's nice you don't live in Portland."

Andrew's grin turned to a genuine laugh. "You're right about that, Sammie."

Sammie raised her chin, and a solemn look smoothed the laugh from her cheeks. "Could you start calling me Samantha now? I don't think I want to be Sammie anymore." She turned toward her brother, who'd moved close, and tweaked his nose. "Except to Joel. He can call me whatever he wants to."

Margaret put her arm around the girl's shoulder and squeezed. "Samantha it is. I think that name suits the young lady you're becoming."

Andrew grinned again. "I agree. Miss Samantha McGavin it will be from now on."

Margaret lifted her chin. "Want to go thank Mr. Art for letting you come? I need to stop by the store, then we'll head home and start supper."

"All right." Samantha jumped to her feet and grabbed Joel's hand. "Come on, Joel. We need to thank Mr. Art for the cookies."

Joel lumbered to his feet. "Those were yummy cookies. Do you think he'd let me take some home?"

Samantha frowned. "It's not polite to ask, Joel. We need to be grateful for what he gave us and not ask for more." Joel hung his head at the mild rebuke, and she patted his arm. "Don't worry. Maybe Miss Margaret will let me bake some more when we get home."

The grin returned to his face as he bounced to the front door and disappeared inside after his sister. Minutes later they returned, Joel clutching a cookie. He held it up where Margaret and Andrew could see it. "I didn't ask for it. He just gived it to me."

When Margaret and Andrew finally convinced Joel to leave Buck behind, the four of them headed toward the store. As they neared the building, Grant Cowling stepped to the open door. "You hear the news?" he asked, wiping his hands down the front of his apron.

Margaret stepped past him into the store. "What news?" After a scan of the interior, she was relieved to see they were the only patrons at the moment. She still had a dread that the Stedman woman might return, but she couldn't imagine Grant being so cheerful if she had.

He glanced at the two children standing by her side. "You kids can go get a pickle from the barrel, if it's all right with Miss Margaret." He nodded toward the oak barrel ringed with metal bands standing in the corner.

After a nod from Margaret they scurried happily away.

Andrew stepped up beside Margaret. "Something happen?"

Grant dropped his voice and kept an eye on the corner. "Yep. Sheriff Bryant says he thinks they'll get a conviction on the murder charge brung against Robert Ludlow."

Andrew nodded solemnly. "That's good news, all right." He slipped an arm through Margaret's and sent her a long, tender look. "Besides, now the sheriff won't have cause to question Joel anymore." He turned and scanned the store. "What about Donnie? I've been worried about him, ever since he tried to put the blame on me for Jenkins' murder and tried to draw Margaret into that mess."

Grant heaved a sigh. "Donnie's a good lad, but he's not always too bright. I had me a talk with him and explained you and Missy looked to be workin' out an agreement. He admitted he was a mite jealous and that's why he tried to stir things up. He was hopin' he'd get Margaret to forget about you and choose him."

Margaret sighed. "Poor Donnie. Do you think he'll be all right now? I'd hate to think he'd try to cause any more trouble for me, or for the children."

Grant shook his head. "He won't if he wants to keep his job. I think he's settled down now. He's not workin' today, and I think he might be sparkin' Sally Mae Kent." He turned to look at Samantha and Joel. "Those are good kids you got there, Margaret. They goin' to start school next week? I'm guessin'—"

His words were disrupted by the rumble of a train entering town and the piercing shriek of its whistle.

The afternoon train was the only one that occasionally towed along a passenger car and typically created interest in town whenever it approached. The three adults walked to the open door and the window beside it, peering outside at the nearby depot where the train slowed. Sure enough, Margaret noticed a passenger car trailing along near the end, just before the caboose. "I wonder if it's bringing visitors."

Whispers of fear tickled her mind. What if Wallace Stedman's mother made good on her son's threat to return with papers claiming the children? Why was it so hard to trust God where Samantha and Joel were concerned? She'd almost worked through her feelings concerning her father and was putting those issues to rest. Now, if only she could give her fear over the children to God, as well.

They stepped outside onto the porch, leaving Samantha and Joel still hunkered over the pickle barrel. The churning wheels of the steam engine drew to a halt, and the conductor leapt down from the caboose and trotted toward the passenger car. He pulled down a set of steps and waited.

The door opened, and a woman appeared. She stood without moving, staring at the small depot, then allowed her gaze to travel to the front porch of the store. Her white blouse looked dingy and worn, and her hair was askew. Margaret watched as she stared at the conductor's extended hand, then turned up her nose and stepped down without his assistance.

The woman took a quick step, then paused and looked back at the car, her strident voice carrying across the open space. "You comin', Sheriff? I won't put up with any guff from the people in this town. Them kids belong to me, and I aim to take 'em home. That's my right under the law." She waved a paper in the air and lifted her voice, glaring toward the store. "I got the proof with me, and ain't nobody sendin' me packin' the way they did my son."

Sheriff Bryant climbed down from the car and stopped beside the irate woman. "Now calm yourself, Mrs. Stedman. There's no need to get worked up over something that hasn't happened." The sheriff offered her his arm, but she huffed and turned away.

"I ain't no softy needin' to lean on a man." She jerked her head toward the store. "That redhead looks like the gal my son described." She raised her voice again. "You got my charges here?"

Margaret gaped at the woman's outrageous behavior. Did she have no manners at all? But what had she expected, after meeting the son? This woman could not be allowed to take Samantha and Joel back to her home. Obviously, she'd not be a fit guardian for a donkey. She turned to Andrew and gripped his arm. "What can we do? We can't let her take them!"

Andrew frowned at the woman stalking toward the store. "I'm not sure we can do anything. If she has legal papers, the sheriff will back her claim." He turned tortured eyes on Margaret. "I hate this, but short of knocking her out cold, hog-tying her, and putting her back on the train, I don't see what we can do."

Grant Cowling moved to the edge of the porch and stood shoulder-to-shoulder with Andrew. "That sounds like a right fine idea. If the sheriff weren't here, I'd help you ship her back where she came from."

Margaret peered over her shoulder and exhaled in relief. Grant had closed the door behind him, and she didn't see any eyes peeking out the window. She shot up a prayer for help. An instant later, confident peace washed over her spirit, and she lifted her chin. God loved those children even more than she did, and that was a lot. He'd find a way to save them. "God's got a plan." She whispered the words to Andrew, assurance putting a lilt in her voice.

He blinked a couple of times, then smiled. "I'm glad you're praying, as well."

Margaret noticed the conductor still standing at attention beside the open door and allowed her gaze to flick back there for a moment. A tall, well-dressed man wearing a dark blue suit stepped to the ground and turned to hold out his hand. A petite blond woman who appeared to be in her midthirties reached out and allowed him to assist her from the car. A warm smile creased her attractive face, and the gentleman tucked her hand into the crook of his arm. Who could that be, Margaret wondered, and what would have brought a couple dressed in such fine clothes to Bridal Veil?

A snort from Mrs. Stedman brought her attention back to where the woman had stopped at the foot of the stairs. "You the woman who's been hidin' my kids?" She crossed her arms across her bosom and glared.

Margaret started to speak, but Andrew squeezed her hand and took a step forward. "Sheriff Bryant, may I have a word with you, please?"

"I reckon that would be fine, Mr. Browning." The sheriff removed his hat and nodded at Margaret, then turned back to Andrew. "Would you like to step over to the side for a moment?"

Mrs. Stedman stared at the sheriff and opened her mouth, but Sheriff Bryant held up his hand. "Not now, ma'am. I'm going to have a word with this gentleman, then I'll see to your needs."

He walked a short distance away, and Andrew followed. The two men put their heads close together and talked for a couple of minutes, then Andrew drew back with a frown.

Margaret couldn't help but overhear as the sheriff said, "I'm sorry, Browning. There's nothing I can do." He turned away and trudged back to the woman standing nearby, tapping her booted toe in the dust.

"Miss Garvey?" The sheriff turned a troubled gaze her way. "I'm sorry to ask you this, but could you please bring the children outside?" He took off his hat and ran his hand over his hair.

"Do I have to, Sheriff?" Margaret gripped a post that held up one corner of the roof.

"I'm afraid so. I hate this part of my job, ma'am, but I don't have much choice. This woman brought the papers from the orphanage that proves her guardianship."

Margaret drew in a quick breath. "You mean she hasn't adopted them?"

"No. Not yet, but I understand she intends to as soon as she returns, to strengthen her claim." He put his hat back on his head. "Are they in the store?"

Margaret's shoulders slumped, and she felt the energy drain from her. *Please, God, do something. Please don't let Samantha and Joel be dragged off by this hideous woman.*

A movement at the corner of her eye caught her attention. The neatly dressed man and his female companion had stopped a yard or two to the side and behind Mrs. Stedman, curious expressions on their faces. Did they want to enter the store, but felt impeded by the activity outside? It didn't matter now, Margaret thought. Nothing mattered but saving Samantha and Joel.

"Miss Garvey, please bring out the children." Sheriff Bryant's tone grew firmer with his last words.

Margaret could feel the tension in both Andrew and Grant as they stared at the offensive woman standing at the bottom of the steps.

"Yeah. Hurry it up, too, will ya?" Mrs. Stedman's strident voice grated on Margaret's nerves, and she turned and hurried inside the store.

Samantha and Joel were nowhere to be seen. Margaret stood for a moment, praying they'd found a way to escape. This was one time she'd not help in hunting for them. She took a step forward and peered down the aisle laden with lanterns, pots and pans, and various household goods. "Samantha? Joel?"

No whisper or sound met her ears, but she waited, not sure how to pray. If only that evil woman would disappear—just get on the train and go back to wherever she'd crawled out from. No child should have to live with such a creature.

"Samantha? Honey, I need to talk to you. Will you come out, please?"

What could she say to the girl that would make it better? It was obvious she'd seen Mrs. Stedman out of the window and was probably trembling in some dark corner trying to protect her brother. Tears welled in Margaret's eyes—tears of rage and frustration, as well as fear and pain. She wouldn't let them go without a fight.

A rustling at the far end of the aisle drew her attention. Margaret walked quickly to the empty space where the shelving ended and the light barely penetrated. She allowed her eyes to adjust for a moment, then peered into the shadows. "Samantha."

A small cry tore from the girl's throat and was almost Margaret's undoing. She held out her arms, and Samantha rushed into them, sobbing against her blouse. Tears spotted the front of the pale blue material, but Margaret didn't care. She smoothed back the hair from Samantha's forehead, too choked to speak. Finally, she cleared her throat. "Joel? Come on out, honey."

The boy stepped forward, and she saw genuine fear in his eyes. "Don't want to go back to live with that old woman, Miss Margaret. Please don't make us."

Margaret's hands started to tremble, and she feared she'd be sick to her stomach. The bell on the front door tinkled as someone pushed it open. Andrew appeared at the end of the aisle, silhouetted against the sun coming through a nearby window. "Margaret? Are you all right?" He didn't wait for a reply but strode to the back of the store.

Joel gave a yelp and launched himself into Andrew's arms, nearly knocking them both to the ground. Andrew staggered backward but retained his footing and wrapped his arms around the boy. "Shh, it's going to be all right. God's going to bring good out of this somehow, you'll see."

He reached an arm out toward Margaret and she rushed forward, bringing Samantha along with her. The four of them wrapped each other in a long embrace, then turned toward the door.

"Do we have to go outside, Miss Margaret?" Sammie's words were choked and breathless.

Margaret stared mutely at Andrew. He nodded once and tried to smile. "Yes, I'm afraid we have to, Samantha. But Miss Margaret and I will be right beside you." He kept one arm around Joel and held out the other to Samantha, and she scrambled to fit herself close to his heart.

All four went to the front door, holding tight to each other until they walked over the threshold. Margaret lifted her chin and went out first, leaving Andrew to follow with Samantha and Joel. She met Mrs. Stedman's gaze with a firm one of her own.

The two children burrowed their faces in Andrew's shirt and didn't budge. He kept his arms around their shoulders and turned his face toward the sheriff.

Mrs. Stedman gave a loud grunt and held out her hand. "All right, you two. Git yerself down here." Neither child moved. "Sammie! Joel! I said, git down here this instant, or you'll wish you had."

The children's heads lifted, and Margaret saw fear shining from both faces.

Just then the woman who'd arrived on the same train took a step forward and gasped. "Samantha? Joel? Is that you?" She took another step, then stumbled and almost fell.

The man at her side gripped her arm with one hand and slipped his other arm around her waist. "Come on now, Lydia, it's all right."

"Mama?" Samantha's whisper barely reached Margaret's ears. "Mama!" The shriek tore from her throat, and the girl flew down the steps and into the woman's arms.

Joel stood for a second, staring at the two huddled together, both sobbing and talking at the same time. Suddenly the boy reared back his head and let out a full-throated whoop. "Mama's come back to life! Mama's come back to life! God raised her just like He did with Jesus!" He bounded from the porch and would have launched himself at the sobbing woman, had the man not stepped in his way.

Gentle hands landed on the boy's shoulders. "Whoa there, son. You don't want to hurt your mother now, do you? Just take it slow, so you don't knock her over."

Lydia McGavin wiped her eyes and turned a radiant smile on the waiting boy. "Joel!" She held out her arms and the boy glanced at the man, then stepped into her embrace, leaning over her small form to lay his head on her shoulder. "Mama. Oh, Mama. I missed you so much."

The cluster of people witnessing the scene suddenly came to life. Mrs. Stedman screeched, and Sheriff Bryant rushed to her side, grasping her arm when she raised it to strike Joel on the back. "No, ma'am, you won't touch that boy." He hauled the woman backward and placed his arm in front of her.

Mrs. Stedman waved her papers in the air. "I got my rights. Them kids belong to me!" She started to move forward again, but Andrew leapt off the porch and grasped her other arm.

Margaret came out of the stupor she'd been mired in and raced down the stairs. She slowed her pace as she approached the small family huddled nearby and addressed the petite woman. "You're Samantha and Joel's mother?"

Lydia McGavin raised shining, tear-filled eyes. "That I am. Lydia Miles is my name now." Both of her hands were gripped by that of her children, so she simply nodded.

"But how—why—the children thought—" Margaret stumbled over her words, confusion continuing to blanket her thoughts.

"That I was dead. And I nearly was, for a time." She turned toward the man standing silently nearby and smiled. "My husband was killed in the buggy wreck, and I was taken to the hospital, presumed all but dead. This wonderful man was my doctor, and he worked for months to keep me alive." Her smile widened and her tears of joy spilled over. "Dr. Miles is now my husband, and he's been helping me hunt for the children ever since I came out of my coma."

Mrs. Stedman quit struggling, and her mouth fell open. "You was in a coma? That's why you never claimed these brats?" Her chin quivered. "You abandoned 'em, and I took 'em in, so they're still rightfully mine." A hard jerk released her arm from Andrew's grasp. "'Course, I can always get me more kids from the orphanage, but I got Sammie trained real good, and I want her back. You kin keep the boy."

Sheriff Bryant moved a little closer. "I'll be speaking to the folks at the orphanage, Mrs. Stedman, and advising them against putting any more children into your care. I'd suggest you get on the train and head home. Your business here is finished."

She glared at each person in turn, then snorted. "I ain't givin' up so easy. You say you're their ma, but I fed and cared for 'em for two years. I want that girl, or I want my money back, and I aim to fight for it. You ain't heard the last of me." A flounce of her skirt marked her exodus as she stormed her way back to the waiting car.

Dr. Miles took a stride toward the woman, and Lydia gripped his arm, tugging him toward her. "Let her go, dear."

He turned, a worried look furrowing his face. "I don't want that woman causing trouble; you've been through enough already."

"We'll deal with whatever comes, just as we've done for the past two years. God will see us through. Besides, it sounds as though money is her main concern."

Her husband relaxed from his tense stance and shrugged one shoulder. "All right. I'll get in touch with our county authorities and see what can be done."

Samantha looked up into her mother's face. "I can't believe you're here. All this time, we thought you'd died." Samantha's smile illuminated her face as she turned toward Margaret and Andrew. "Miss Margaret saved us, Mama. She and God kept us safe after we ran way from Mrs. Stedman." A shudder shook the young girl's slender frame.

Joel nodded fast and hard. "Buck and Mr. Art saved us too, and Mr. Andrew, when we ran away and hid."

Lydia stroked the girl's hair and leaned over to kiss her cheek, then patted Joel's arm. "I'm sorry, dear ones—so very sorry for what you've both been through. I was in the hospital for a long time, and then they moved me to a sanatorium for several more months. By the time I was released, you and Joel were gone, and the orphanage had changed hands. The new people running it claimed they had no records about an adoption. If it hadn't been for Matthew coming to my rescue and helping me search, I doubt I'd have found you."

She turned to him and smiled. "He made people listen when they wouldn't answer my questions."

She reached out a hand toward Margaret. "Thank you," she whispered, then lifted her voice as new strength seemed to flow into her. "Thank you so very much for all you've done for my babies." Fresh tears welled in her eyes. "I'll never be able to repay you."

Margaret shook her head and wiped moisture from the corner of her eye. "They're wonderful children, and I was blessed that God allowed me to help them. But how did you find them, tucked back here in Bridal Veil?"

Matthew Miles smiled and stepped forward, putting his hand on Joel's shoulder. "We heard about a freighter from Bridal Veil named Julius, who was asking about two children named Sammie and Joel. He was in Portland a couple of days ago, talking to Charlie, the man who hauls vegetables to our local market. Charlie's a likable man and loves to talk, but he didn't know Julius, so he kept what he knew to himself and came to us. We took the first train bringing passengers this way, praying we'd find Samantha and Joel here in Bridal Veil." He beamed at his wife. "And glory be to God, here they are."

"Yes." Margaret raised her eyes to the heavens. "All glory and praise be to God, for indeed He has done wonderful things."

BRIDAL VEIL 1902 ORE.

Epilogue

....

Christmas, 1902

Margaret looked out over the rail of the steamboat and gathered the collar of her heavy coat closer around her neck. Andrew wrapped his arm around her shoulder and pulled her against his side. "Are you sure you want to stand out here in the cold, dear?"

Margaret smiled up into his face and nodded. "I'd love to see the falls as we pass. It's been a wonderful honeymoon, but I am anxious to get home to Bridal Veil."

He nestled his face against her hair. "I know what you mean about coming home, but I think it would've been nice to stretch our time away to two months instead of just ten days."

She reached up and stroked his cheek. "You've got to get back to work, and I have my students to see to after the Christmas holidays are past."

"Yes." He straightened but kept his arm firmly around her shoulders. "It was nice seeing Samantha, Joel, and their folks when we stopped in Portland."

Margaret nodded eagerly. "I'm thrilled that Dr. Miles and Lydia promised to allow the children to stay with us a couple of weeks next summer, and that they've allowed Joel to get a puppy."

The blast of the steamboat whistle split the air and covered any response Andrew might have made. The snow-covered town of

Bridal Veil lay only a couple of hundred yards away, and Margaret raised her eyes, searching for the falls she'd loved since childhood. "There it is. Look, Andrew! The sun is shining on the water. There's a rainbow across the top!" She drew in her breath and held it, awestruck at something she'd never seen before.

He leaned over and placed a gentle kiss on her forehead, then tipped up her face and lowered his lips to hers, leaving them there for a long moment. "Beautiful." He looked into her eyes and breathed the word softly.

Margaret giggled and blushed. "Andrew, did you even look at the rainbow?"

A shrug and a grin met her rebuke. "I've seen rainbows before, but they can't compare to what I'm holding in my arms."

She snuggled her head against his shoulder and his arm tightened, drawing her close. "I'm so thankful now for the choices Papa made."

"You mean discouraging you in your relationship with Cooper?"

"Yes. I understand now why he did it—even his decision to bury our note. I was so young, and ready to marry someone because I felt excitement whenever he was around. But I didn't really know Nathaniel's heart, and I didn't think about the things that mattered: how his lack of faith would impact my life, or those of any children we might one day have. Papa realized all of that and wanted to keep me safe."

Andrew drew back a bit and looked into her eyes. "So you've forgiven him?"

Margaret nodded and a deep well of joy bubbled in her spirit. "Yes, I've forgiven him, and I'm blessing him for his wisdom when I had none of my own. I used to think he was always trying to change me—never accepting me for the woman I was becoming—but now I understand he simply loved me and wanted God's best for my life." She reached up and kissed her husband. "I'll be forever grateful that Papa listened to the Lord when I wasn't able to hear. If it wasn't for Papa's choices, I wouldn't have my future with you."

Author's Note
....

While this story is mostly fiction, it does contain certain elements and people who were real. At the turn of the century the Bridal Veil and Palmer sawmills were owned and operated by the Bridal Veil Lumbering Company, founded and run by Mr. Loring C. Palmer. The homes, school, and store were owned by the Company, not the workers, and all supplies were brought into the one store by freight train or the sternwheeler from nearby Portland, Oregon. Latourelle was the closest small town to the west, with Corbett lying just beyond. Latourelle, which is not in existence today, boasted a steamboat landing and was a popular spot for city partygoers. Multnomah Falls, now a draw for thousands of tourists each year (as is the entire Columbia River Gorge), lies two miles to the east. Troutdale, the town between Corbett and Portland where Sheriff Bryant (a fictitious character) traveled from, was a booming small town at the time.

The fire that took place in September 1902 is believed to have been started by sparks from train wheels igniting dry brush approximately two miles east of Bridal Veil and was blown by an east wind up the mountain into the Trickey farm, then on to Palmer. Cecil and Gerald, the two young brothers, actually were killed when they stopped to put on their shoes in a nearby shed. Several people stayed nearly submerged in the millpond when unable to escape, waiting all night in the water for the fire to pass while the boilers exploded at the mill. Palmer was rebuilt on a new site, with millworkers starting to build almost immediately after the fire.

Mr. Luscher, the dairy farmer, did own a successful dairy for many years, located on a large plot of land near current-day Rooster Rock. The dairy was in business until sometime in the 1960s.

Art Gibbs was my great-grandfather on my mother's side. He moved to Bridal Veil two years after the book takes place, which is why he's not depicted fighting the fire. All events referring to Art are fictitious, except for two. He owned a team of horses and skidded logs for Bridal Veil Lumbering Company. His team was touted as being one of the best in the country. He and his wife, Glenna, lived in Bridal Veil for several years, and he went on to use his team to help build a section of the original Columbia River highway. He did have a dog that was fiercely protective, although we don't have a record of the dog's name. Buck was named after a dog my son had when he was young. Art and Glenna had a son named Rex (my grandfather), who married Maude (my grandmother).

Men called "walking visitors" would come through the town looking for work, singly or in small groups of two or three, following the tracks and sometimes riding the rails. Most were good, honest men, but the idea for the hobos in the story came from the possibility of men of bad intent who could also hop a train. The experience Samantha had with the two men hunting for her was taken from an episode in Jami's life (a friend from our church) when she was twelve, as two men hunted her in the woods and God spoke to her, showing her where to hide.

Sand Island, just to the west of the town, kept the steamboats from docking there, and also provided a source of ice for the townspeople in the summer. The schoolhouse in Bridal Veil was a two-story structure and boasted two teachers covering grades 1–12. There was a railroad depot building in Bridal Veil, the Company store, a church, a boardinghouse, and a community hall, along with a number of small homes scattered through the trees and on the hillside on the eighty acres between the mountainside to the south and the river and mill to the north.

The fog and wind in the Columbia River Gorge are accurately depicted and can roll or blow in and last for hours or days. In fact, the Gorge is considered to be the windsurfing capital of the world.

Today, Bridal Veil is nearly a ghost town, with the mill closed for over forty years and the workers moved away. The eighty-acre plot of land was recently sold to the U.S. Forest Service by a preservation group who tore down most of the historic buildings, including the mill, homes, store, and depot, during the 1990s and returned the land to its original state. There is currently a small church and a scattering of homes that lay outside of the parcel of land once owned by the lumbering company, as well as the nation's second-smallest operating post office. Bridal Veil Post Office is manned by a postmistress who offers a unique service. She personally hand-stamps wedding invitations with a special Bridal Veil cancellation mark. Invitations are sent by the boxful from places all over the U.S. to be hand-cancelled and mailed.

I was raised in the beautiful Columbia Gorge, in the town of Lyle, Washington, where Rex and Maude Gibbs eventually settled. My parents were both teachers there, and I went on to marry and currently live in the heart of windsurfing country, a short distance from Bridal Veil. The entire Mid-Columbia area has a rich heritage of logging, with several sawmills still in existence along the corridor. My husband, Allen, and I owned and operated a small sawmill for over fourteen years a few miles north of White Salmon, where I worked pulling edgings and boards from the head rig and planer and helped in other capacities. We moved the mill to Glenwood, where our partner still runs it today.

Want a peek into local American life—past and present?
The *Love Finds You*™ series published by Summerside Press
features real towns and combines travel, romance,
and faith in one irresistible package!

The novels in the series—uniquely titled after American towns with unusual but intriguing names—inspire romance and fun. Each fictional story draws on the compelling history or the unique character of a real place. Stories center on romances kindled in small towns, old loves lost and found again on the high plains, and new loves discovered at exciting vacation getaways. Summerside Press plans to publish at least one novel set in each of the 50 states. Be sure to catch them all!

Now Available in Stores

Love Finds You in Miracle, Kentucky by Andrea Boeshaar
ISBN: 978-1-934770-37-5

Love Finds You in Snowball, Arkansas by Sandra D. Bricker
ISBN: 978-1-934770-45-0

Love Finds You in Romeo, Colorado by Gwen Ford Faulkenberry
ISBN: 978-1-934770-46-7

Love Finds You in Valentine, Nebraska by Irene Brand
ISBN: 978-1-934770-38-2

Love Finds You in Humble, Texas by Anita Higman
ISBN: 978-1-934770-61-0

Love Finds You in Last Chance, California by Miralee Ferrell
ISBN: 978-1-934770-39-9

Love Finds You in Maiden, North Carolina by Tamela Hancock Murray
ISBN: 978-1-934770-65-8

Love Finds You in Paradise, Pennsylvania by Loree Lough
ISBN: 978-1-934770-66-5

Love Finds You in Treasure Island, Florida by Debby Mayne
ISBN: 978-1-934770-80-1

Love Finds You in Liberty, Indiana, by Melanie Dobson
ISBN: 978-1-934770-74-0

Love Finds You in Revenge, Ohio by Lisa Harris
ISBN: 978-1-934770-81-8

Love Finds You in Poetry, Texas by Janice Hanna
ISBN: 978-1-935416-16-6

Love Finds You in Sisters, Oregon by Melody Carlson
ISBN: 978-1-935416-18-0

Love Finds You in Charm, Ohio by Annalisa Daughety
ISBN: 978-1-935416-17-3

Love Finds You in Bethlehem, New Hampshire by Lauralee Bliss
ISBN: 978-1-935416-20-3

Love Finds You in North Pole, Alaska by Loree Lough
ISBN: 978-1-935416-19-7

Love Finds You in Holiday, Florida by Sandra D. Bricker
ISBN: 978-1-935416-25-8

Love Finds You in Lonesome Prairie, Montana
by Tricia Goyer and Ocieanna Fleiss
ISBN: 978-1-935416-29-6

Love Finds You in Hershey, Pennsylvania by Cerella D. Sechrist
ISBN: 978-1-935416-64-7

Coming Soon

Love Finds You in Homestead, Iowa by Melanie Dobson
ISBN: 978-1-935416-66-1

Love Finds You in Pendleton, Oregon by Melody Carlson
ISBN: 978-1-935416-84-5

summerside
PRESS

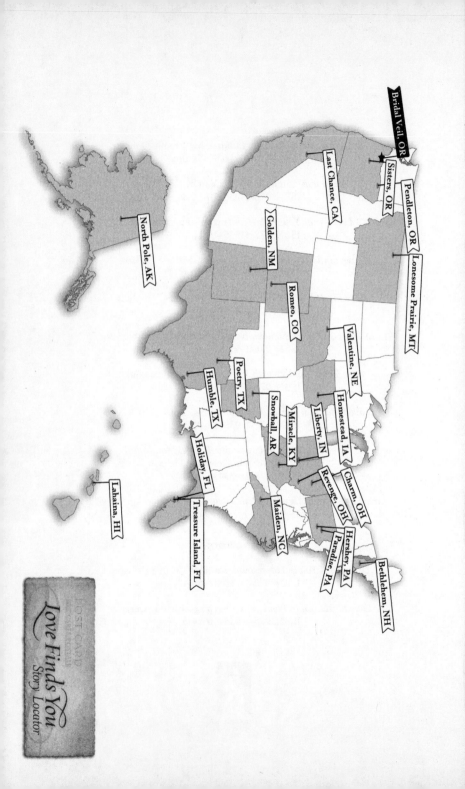

Bridal Veil, OR

Last Chance, CA

Sisters, OR

Pendleton, OR

North Pole, AK

Golden, NM

Lonesome Prairie, MT

Romeo, CO

Valentine, NE

Poetry, TX

Humble, TX

Snowball, AR

Liberty, IN

Homestead, IA

Miracle, KY

Holiday, FL

Lahaina, HI

Treasure Island, FL

Maiden, NC

Revenge, OH

Charm, OH

Hershey, PA

Paradise, PA

Bethlehem, NH

POST CARD

Love Finds You

Story Locator